ONE THOUSAND EYES

ONE THOUSAND EYES

BARBARA LALLA

The University of the West Indies Press
Jamaica • Barbados • Trinidad and Tobago

The University of the West Indies Press
7A Gibraltar Hall Road, Mona
Kingston 7, Jamaica
www.uwipress.com

A catalogue record of this book is available from the
National Library of Jamaica.

Cover photograph: Ondřej Prosický, mangrove in Caroni Swamp, Trinidad
and Tobago. ID 127002564 © Ondřej Prosický | Dreamstime.com
Cover and book design by Robert Harris - email: roberth@cwjamaica.com
Set in Bembo 12/15 x 27

ISBN: 978-976-640-820-6 (paper)
978-976-640-821-3 (Kindle)
978-976-640-822-0 (ePub)

Printed in the United States of America

FOR ELI, LIAM, CHLOE AND ANNA
. . . in good time

i woke one morning and the Caribbean was gone.

—Kendel Hippolyte, "Avocado", *So Many Islands*

CONTENTS

THE CHARACTERS

CHILDREN OF THE TRUST

Myche
Brand (Myche's younger brother)
Pwessus and Tweetums (twins)
Telma
Darati (Telma's younger sister)
Nat
Janice
Josiahmarshall (Janice's younger brother)
Tiffney (Janice's baby sister)
Indira
Shant
Marilyn
Wikki (Marilyn's younger brother)
Five Cent
Zef
Colin
Ananda
Chunks
Bry
Kyle
Robber Boy

THOSE WHO HAVE GONE

Shine (older brother of Myche and Brand)
Sonson
Daughts
Celie

Mitch
Ash (died)

BAANYA

Ena (the birdwoman)
Pawi (a chantwell)
Cora (a healer)
Didi
Babu
Casey (an engineer)
Bois
Ferne (niece of Didi and Cora)

Isaiah (the singerman)
Suraj
Lu Marie (Isaiah's daughter)
Bunji
Ouiji

Nkomi St Juste
Nastasia St Juste
Roget St Juste
Celeste St Juste
Nurse Flo
Sir Hector Ramnarine
Dean Ivan Blake
Dr Chesterfield
Mr Justice Gerard Cuffee
Francisico Marquez
Elizabeth St Juste (sister-in-law to Nkomi)
Naomi Ali (a doctor)

Kiskidee

SHARDS

KISKIDEE

ONLY MY GRANDMOTHER CALLED ME KISKIDEE, and that was because our
real names were the same.

She never spoke of the part she played in the end – only of those
earlier blasts that had shattered the place to begin with. She had heard
about things *Before* – before the flash, the thunder and breaking apart,
the floating cinders of paper as shelves and even whole libraries gushed
flame then shrivelled and curled away into ash. *Before*, she said, people
seemed to have lived together without seeing each other at all.

"Why they couldn't see?" I grappled with it. "People were small-
small? Like a ants?"

"An ant?" She stroked my cheek. No, no, she said. Normal size,
but they only saw differences – between temples and hair and bank
accounts. "As if they lived in separate worlds," she said. And when
the country came falling apart around them very few cared whether
the rest lived or died. They never even noticed those around – just
looked right through them.

I shivered. "Like ghosts?" I whispered. Sometimes these slivers of
information were sharp-edged.

"Right." She nodded. "So, they arrived at this uncomfortable
thought: perhaps they were all – all of them – spectres."

What happened next was not to be found in any official record,
for who was there to write it down and what was there to write on?
Versions of the story passed down mainly from mouth to mouth.
But, mostly, it was just as if those who survived had never existed at
all, *Before*.

Still, all around, the tortured countryside itself testified that fire did
tear open the night sky and smoke blotted out the sun. People groped
around, disoriented by ruins everywhere, before taking up various

haunts, coming and going as they found convenient, and making up accounts of how they had got to where they were – which was nowhere. And then the cruiters came, slashing their way through the bush and whoever stood up to them, and snatching up whom they pleased. There was nothing left to do but hide.

As for the flotsam – those other children – no one paid them any mind, for they never lasted long.

PART I

THE DON'T TRUST

1

THE TRUST

MYCHE

THE TWINS HAD TRAPPED HER AGAIN, backed up tight with the dull green pads of a prickly pear that bristled with vicious spines inches from one side of her face and a soft fuzz of shorter prickles a breath away from the other cheek. She screamed for Shine.

They had closed in as Myche raced back to the Trust. The twins had grown heavier on whatever they ate out there in the bush, and she would have no chance of fighting her way out once their grubby paws clenched on her. She held her breath as they pressed forward, unwashed as ever, faces too smeared for her to recognise which was which, clothes hanging in filthy shreds and, now they were older, attended by some rank odour she could not place.

The last time they cornered her, she had tricked them with the old ploy of signalling to someone behind them, but that could not work again. She faked a dodge to the right almost onto the long sharp cactus spines and steeled herself. Then when the boy nearest to her shot out a hand she squeezed one eye tight and lunged left, scooping up a cheekful of fine hairlike prickles, and clutched at a low branch. She swung from that onto a sturdier limb, screaming again for Shine, as the other twin grabbed for the first branch.

A rending sound brought a grin to her aching face as the branch beneath broke under his weight and his body thudded to the ground.

"Jabmolassi," she yelled. All the children had adopted Five Cent's name for the twins. "Shine going give you *one* cut-tail."

The twins had always been too clumsy to scramble up a tree. Now they could only pound the trunk and hurl abuse. But when they stopped, the one who had fallen stepped back and grinned. And who was he to call anyone crapaud-face? From her perch way above his upturned face he seemed to be only that gaping lipless grin.

"Is so?" he shouted between hands cupped around his mouth. "Keep on bawling for Shine. They come for he and he ent cutting nobody tail no more. A good. Quail up in you tree. See how it feel to be mines from now on. Shine gone for good."

That, more than tuft after tuft of needles in her cheek, put an end to any inclination to smile even as the two older boys lumbered away.

· · · · · · · · ·

"How you mean – gone? You story." Brand stared at her almost on eye level when she got back to the Trust.

He was tall for his eight years and Myche short for ten. (Nearly eleven perhaps, it occurred to her.) They knew their ages at least roughly because Shine had seen to that, but more urgent things like the meanings of words could be slippery.

Myche was not sure herself what *gone* meant now, only that she had had an older brother for as long as she could remember but they had not seen him for two nights. At first she had closed that out. She refused to contend with it even though his vanishing should have surprised no one. Shine was tall and broad for fourteen – or more? – bigger than Mitch, although Mitch was older. Shine was too quick and powerful for anything else to have happened to him.

The last time they had spoken, he warned Myche to keep hidden in the Trust, now more than ever. Hurriedly, he had whispered things he wanted her to know, signs she must look out for. Daughts had known, he said.

Myche struggled to remember Daughts, an older girl who had disappeared several years before. As for Shine's warnings, Myche had been too busy puzzling over a frantic look on his face she had never seen before, and she had hardly taken in what he said. Now, try as she might, she could not connect the instructions he had thrown out while gripping her shoulder and shaking it to keep her attention. All very well him urging her to remember stuff after years of ordering her to forget.

Once she had thrown off the twins she searched the Trust with Brand, and they called as loudly as they dared from the branches beyond the entrance. But she knew better than to venture any distance outside so soon again, especially when there might be a cruiting underway.

The emptiness that yawned before her now seemed to engulf all that had been solid in her life. Without Shine, who would order things? And then – no one to watch over Brand but herself. The idea turned her knees to water. Brand was younger but stronger than she was. He probably thought faster than she did too, yet so differently it was often hard to follow him. Her thoughts whirled and she shut her eyes, deliberately braced her back to the wall of the vortex. Charybdis. The name came back from one of the stories Shine had told them about the wandering man after that battle and the fire he had left behind. Then she opened her eyes again and forced herself to gaze directly at this hole in the centre of her life.

Myche was sturdy, though not nearly as nimble as Brand, and her mind was agile. Yet she could sit still for long stretches, listening, watching, rapidly working and reworking things through in her head to account for whatever was going on. Brand never waited and rarely listened. He ran headlong at things. Rash, Shine had said with a groan. Not that kind, he added, grinning, as her eyes flashed anxiously over Brand's skin.

Now Myche groaned too, her face flaming with pain. She realized the fine fluff of prickles was deceptive. She had watched Mitch years before, picking them, tuft by tuft, from Shine's arm. Now – to pluck them from her own face. She tore a strip of old cloth, worn thin by years of use and washing, and she measured it over the area as she had seen

Mitch do. Then she pasted on the mixture she had rubbed smooth in a bowl, hoping she had got it right, and slapped it on over the beastly fur on her cheek. She waited as it thickened before plastering on the cloth. The challenge would be peeling it off her face when it dried.

She spun through her few options for help, someone who would yank it off with brutal speed, and she came up with Telma. Some prickles would stay fast (they had little barbs, Mitch had said), but she supposed after a while they would go.

"The good thing is, two of them caught in my eyelash," she said.

"How that can be good?" Brand demanded.

"Not on my eyeball." She was glad to see that he glanced up, horrified. Then she returned to the most pressing problem. "I guess we could ask the others if they saw Shine."

He shot a surprised glance. "Ent we not supposed to ask?"

Never about someone else's loss, it was true, but surely one could enquire about one's own? "Shine would've asked after us," she mumbled.

But she knew. Not as if *he* could have just drifted off and lost himself like some smallie recently stumbled in from the shore.

Shine had been certain of every step. He slipped among roots and branches leaving the moss unbruised and leaves unturned, hardly interrupting birdsong. Even if the ocelots laid back their ears when he passed, they did not show their teeth.

Now a large female, draped along a low limb, let Myche and Brand pass too, but as the children swung up onto a branch near to the tree where she stretched out watching for prey, she deepened her breathing to something more like a snore interrupted by breathy coughs. Still, it was the best way into the Trust. Mitch and Celie had insisted that branches offered a route that left no tracks or scent of human feet around the fence. Only the newest children to wash up were allowed to back in through the overgrown entrance, led by whichever older ones they had wandered into.

Always backways, Mitch had said. Then any prints they left would lead away from the Trust and not towards it. In any case, what had been the entrance was wildly overgrown, and it was better not to disturb the tangle more than necessary.

Inside, around the lake, wound paths whose paved surfaces had been eaten up over time but could still be made out, shaded by cassia and hibiscus that hung over the water so their blooms reflected between the lotus pads. On the other side of the lake grew bushes with pigeon peas, huge heart-shaped dasheen leaves and, further back, fruit trees – mango, orange, and the deep red pomerac that Telma called apples, for she had a different name for everything.

However strange the other children found the names she gave common things, no one was about to correct Telma, who was thin but tall, surprisingly strong and grumpy. She could work tirelessly, dragging palm boughs to strip, plaiting their thongs, tearing down the brown mesh that clung to the stems of some palms, under the boughs. Even when the water blisters studded her hands she threaded vines along the edges of the mesh to draw it into baskets, working with a grim tightness around the mouth that made the others keep off. And if she called the brown sapodillas *naseberries*, no one contradicted her.

Between the taller fruit trees grew lower ones with hard yellow plums and those bright red cherries that had seeds you chewed on till they were ragged. So then you spat them out, and they swirled and sank near the edge of the lake. Fish might dart up or the ducks waggle away in alarm across the water, and sometimes there would be a rare glimpse of a crusty grey-green back before a caiman submerged again.

Only a film of tension held the water surface intact, and nothing kept anyone back from tumbling through this thin shining skin into its depths. Familiar as it was, the lake was circled by superstitious dread. It rose and fell in rainy and dry seasons under eyes that were watchful not only because the children lived in terror of flood – of rains scouring, rivers breaking banks, sea crashing in – but also because even still water could be deadly. Green or murky water dealt death by belly pain, Shine had warned, emptying bowels and heaving your insides in wave after sickening wave till you were too faint to lift your head. Even to live near still water without swallowing any could be fatal: raging fever, shattering joint pains, tormenting rashes. The children who remembered bush remedies used leaves from the noni and from man-better-man bush, but these did not always work. Or perhaps one child or the other had not remembered, from the time Before, which leaf Tan Tan had held up. So many plants looked exactly alike. Then the sickness lingered, and in the end came the long cold stillness.

But at the near end of the lake the water lapped clean and busy with fish, and some of the path around the edge remained firm with bits of the thing Mitch called *asphalt*. Beyond that, a provision ground Telma had started was holding its own. The children allowed odd bushes and weeds to carry on in between, and Telma instructed them to scatter in other plants randomly – tomato, peppers, beans. "So if anybody pass by chance dem wouldn' notice how much we plant, and say is here we live."

Above the gathering of children, the samaan spread its limbs wide and wafted down fluffy pink blossoms everyone ignored or brushed aside. In its shade Brand cast around at the group, and it was obvious that he too had seen how many others were missing – the oldest, as usual. Except for the twins. They prowled in the wilderness outside the Trust but never seemed to vanish permanently.

Nor Nat either, Myche saw with relief. Not loud or burly like the twins (how could he be with whatever it was that had happened to him?), Nat was lean, and quiet-spoken when he spoke at all. When the smallest ones raged and threw green mangoes at each other, Nat said, "Taima!" Or now, more usually, he said, "Done iit," in his usual good-natured tone, and the quarrelling muted or dissolved into sniffs. But he was only a year or so older than Myche, and it might be two years more before he would look anything like Shine or Mitch. Well, he never would, because the limp and slight twist of his body held him back from most activities that built hard muscle. Perhaps the cruiters never would take Nat.

She scanned the group again. Instead of these bigger boys and Celie (no sign of her either), there were new faces as one might expect. One was a girl about Myche's age, there with a younger boy. Sand clung to their wet clothes, and their soft feet and legs were bruised and blistered. Nothing surprising there. What was odd was that the girl gripped some sort of bundle that must have been hard to manage when she was struggling for the shore, especially with a smallie to look after. Perhaps the water had been unusually calm, or they were strong swimmers like Nat. Yet what could be so important to clutch through all that heaving blue death?

Only, then Myche saw it was not just a package but something moving, whimpering. When she went over to look more closely, the girl pulled away, eyeing her fiercely.

"We can't keep it," someone else said, not unkindly – Telma as it turned out. "Is what it going eat?"

"She's not *it*," the girl snapped. She said *not* in a funny way, with an odd sort of hiccup at the end. "She name Tiphanie."

"And oi'm Josiah Marshall," the smallie put in belligerently, but no one even glanced at him.

"*Tiffney?* What sort of name dat?"

"Is a raakhas." One of the twins spat out the word no one else knew. The rest hadn't even seen him slide from behind the samaan. "Watch. Like a rat, only no teeth don't grow yet. You have to mash that with a rock."

"Stupidness," Telma shouted, even as the new girl clutched the thing tighter, staring around uncertainly, her eyes wide with terror. She might not have understood the words Pwessus uttered, but no one could miss the venom in his tone.

"Choro," Nat muttered, then shouted, "Get 'way from here."

Myche massaged her nose, which had stuffed up the way it always did in the dry, and she craned for a better look. Something echoed in her brain: she remembered Brand as she had seen him first. A voice that had dropped from memory for years came back to her: *Your own brand-new little brother.*

Myche stared. A baby.

. . . .

So it began – pictures fluttering back into her brain.

Big people. Big. They ran this way and that stuffing things in bags. She stooped, snatching up book after book, the ones that were mostly words and not just pictures.

A woman's face pressed close to hers with a whisper: "Only what we can carry. No book and thing. And quiet, Popo. Quiet!" No one else would call her Popo.

The trek to the boat went on and on. Shine had lifted Brand, but Myche had to walk, almost running to keep up with the long legs striding beside her.

From the boat, the trees on shore had shrunk smaller and smaller. Water, water. The sea slapped the side of the boat and churned against the oars. *Slap-slap churrrn. Slap-slap churrrn.* Myche must have fallen asleep by the time it was light, for she opened her eyes to the long shadow of a bigger boat, a ship. Men leaned over the side, towering above her, and shouted. Brand slept on somehow across Shine's lap. A heavy form crashed down, boots just missing her head, and the boat tipped wildly. Then, a hand gripping thick black hair yanked up the woman's chin while his other flashed steel, and Shine grabbed Myche and clamped his hand over her eyes. He never made a sound, but his body heaved with sobs.

The rope they let down from the tall ship chewed into her as they hauled her up. Shine again, his arms clamped around Brand and Myche. He whispered that they must be quiet or the men would hurt them.

"Nah." One of them laughed. "We go throw she in the hold with the rats." On cue a big one whisked by, paused and looked back furtively. The huge grey sat up and quivered its nose at her above a show of incisors, then leapt away from the seaman's boot with a pale whip of long bare tail.

"You want see more?" The man grinned at her. "Come, I go take you down wih me."

As the man turned away laughing again, Shine's grip tightened on her almost cruelly. "Never go down there," he whispered. "Not with anybody."

"Rats?" Her voice was thin and raspy.

"Thousands of rats," he answered after a moment, "all sorts."

She stayed on deck, even when it rolled and sloshed as if she must be swept overboard. She remembered water all around the ship, limp forms bobbing in it and the red stains darkening, then rushing away.

Days emptied from her brain even before they saw the shoreline: rough sand and stone all the way to a dark wall of trees.

After the chill when she slammed into the water, the sucking, crushing, battering strength of it that wrung her to a limp rag grating in over sharp pebbles, it was too hot to stay on the shore. Shine walked Myche and Brand towards the shade, gripping each painfully by the hand. "We have to find the rest, like they said. Whoever they are." When he could bear their crying no longer, he ordered them to just forget everything that had happened, because now they must begin again. Learn from the others.

What others?

"Anyone we find here. The men said there were others like us."

They ran to the forbidding line of dark green, because the gravel was scorching their bare feet.

Their feet were still soft, then.

. . . .

The big ones told the new ones and especially the smallies how it was, bit by bit.

"This island is all it have for now," Celie had said. "Is that why they say is we land. But is not the one place in the world. Mitch say, that way – cross the sea – it have a place so big we could lost WeLand in it. But is no use to us. They don't want hear nothing bout we. He say what we must remember is it have other islands like this one even though they not beknown to us."

"H-how he know?" someone was sure to ask.

"Mitch older than the whole of us. They never push he off no boat. When he see them pelting children off the deck is then he jump off and swim."

"Ent Mitch say it have a ch–chain of island?"

"Is true."

Then Celie had begun one of her stories.

"Longtime, the first people come over the bridge, from one island then the next. They came following the stars. Then, they hear like thunder, and it was rocks breaking and tumbling in the sea, the bridge between the islands mashing up and falling down behind them. And is that why they did build boats – if in case they ever need to go back."

Telma had steupsed, small as she was then, and interrupted a good-good story. "Not like now when boat dump you over the side and you sink down or keep up for youself and find you way." Telma grumbled.

"Shh!" Celia was kind-hearted, but she could get really tired of Telma. "Talk something good."

At night, if it rained hard, they slept in the long room that had a sign on the door saying *Museum*. All around it a platform of wooden planks had gone rotten in parts. Vines had crept up the supports and twisted their way together to cover the entire building. There were windows in the outer walls of the museum, but they looked out on nothing but the narrow walkway the vines had left around the platform, and the view was only branching stems that grew thicker year by year, enmeshing the museum more tightly.

One window had had a shutter that banged in the wind, but over time the greenery had sealed that down. Other windows had broken and let in air. The heavy grille door had squealed on its hinges when they swung back and forth on it, until Mitch rubbed in a few drops of precious oil. But after a while it seized up with rust and fell silent, forever ajar. From outside, though, all that could be seen now was a mound of vegetation.

Inside was dry and dim, usually cool. When the heat and humidity made it unbearable – well that was what the shelters outside were for. "And don't bring nothing inside here but water," Shine had said. Clay pots, metal, plastic – any containers were to be found and tightly sealed. The museum was a hiding place only, lined with shelves of crumbling books, wood-backed glass cases with stuffed caimans, faded scarlet ibises and other barely recognisable objects. It held no clues about the lives of those who had visited it Before. The children had only what lay before their eyes or had remained scattered in their heads.

In a dry corner of one shelf Myche had stored the few books Shine had found and brought in – *The Gruffalo, The Tempest, Huckleberry Finn*

and *Summer Lightning*. There were loose pages with poetry she mostly
hadn't understood, until he read them with her the way he had read
The Tempest. If he found a few sheets of paper, she hid them there as
well, until he was able to lay hands on a pencil.

Once, before any of the children who were still there had washed
up, there was a bigger boy who had disappeared. Before he did, he
made a poem. Some of them found it hard to understand, but they
liked the sort of music it had and the pictures it flashed into their
heads. Mitch had written it down and given it to Shine, and, at times
like these when they were trying to understand things, Shine used to
read it for them. Myche remembered how the boy they never knew
had sent his voice forward through Mitch and then through Shine.
And it had got into her head as well, for now and then it came back.

Now it comes back,
the thunder growling overhead. Hearing
the shout of splitting brick and screech of metal tearing.
Gushes yellow, red, lit up the sky at night.
Sparks fountained in the distance. Fireworks, we squealed out in
delight.
But – blackening to clouds of billowing ash and cinders floating.
Choking.
And nearer, the thunder and the roaring. Louder.

Silence. Then, a quiet afternoon.

Over, we thought. By then the clouds had cleared.
And just as dusk rushed on the last light flared
upon the gleaming belly far above us
of a monster that belched flame. A swarm shrieked overhead –
their breath: fire and death.
So it comes back – that time we gave a name
then blotted out,
The night the dragons came.

So, that was another story again, lodged in Myche's head with the rest.

And now, in the clearing, here was the new girl who said her name was Janice, clutching the baby tight against her, rocking from side to side and keeping time with clicking sounds she made with her tongue; and she darted ferocious glances at the bigger children in the circle that closed round.

"Don't touch her."

There it was again, the funny hiccup thing at the end of *don't*. She didn't sound – or look – like any of the rest, for there was that long, flying hair, not straight like the two littlest smallies. The same pale yellow like the hair Colin and Zef had, but frizzy. Well, it would have to go. Janice might not like that, though.

Janice was heavy-set, a bit awkward and continuously looking over her shoulder. It was the sort of thing that irritated Telma. So many things irritated Telma, but the fact that Janice was obviously suspicious of everyone there provoked Telma so much she turned her back and walked off. But it was all very well for Telma to take offence just because *she* wouldn't dream of hurting anyone. After all, the twins were part of Janice's first introduction to the group, and that kind of bad-mind was enough to unnerve anyone.

When Telma shrugged and was marching off with Darati tagging after her silently, Myche glanced around to confirm that neither of the twins were to be seen, and refocused on her own emergency before everyone scattered.

"Anyone see Shine?" she demanded, louder than necessary. Just in case they might shush her, she scowled and balled her hand into a fist. They fell silent, and Nat shifted his eyes from her – which was answer enough. There were things not to be spoken, Nat's suddenly wooden expression declared. Better not to know.

It infuriated Myche: once more, what she most wanted to find out was shrouded in silence.

Of course, there were the stories that older ones like Daughts and Sonson had passed around before they went, but these were mainly tales to keep the smallies from wandering deep into the bush or losing

themselves through hillside crevices. Or perhaps they might fall into
the hands of jinns, wanderers imperfectly formed from smoke when
the last fires burnt out.

The children could not see jinns but knew they were there, slipping in and out among the trees – and of course *they* could see the
children. After a shaving the children would collect all that hair and
burn it to keep the jinns away. At first, thinking she might be a baby
jinn, most of the children had even shied away from a wisp of a girl,
about four years old now, whom Mitch had brought in two years ago
coated in ash. He had stumbled over her in the bush while hunting.
There she lay, sleeping on a wide flat stone, hugging a little brown and
white dog.

The dog refused to follow through the wall of ocelot spray, and the
child cried for a while, but then she calmed down and, when asked,
gave her name as Ananda. She made a pet of anything, an injured bird,
a frog, a wood slave slithering along the rotting beam outside of the
museum, a lost duckling. But she would never, under any circumstances, stay beneath a proper shelter. At the suggestion of entering the
museum, Ananda had crumpled screaming on the ground and wrapped
her arms around her head. The shelter of a few branches propping up
fronds of fan palm was the most she would tolerate.

Then, only months ago, Shine had found another tiny child alone
in a ruin. They could not make out what she said, except for *wi* and
non. They called her Chunks, not knowing what else to do. Mitch
had asked her about her Mamam, but she stared at him blankly, and
when he tried to question her further, she screamed, "Kite m 'pou
kont li" over and over, until he backed away and let her be. There
was no clue of how long she had been there or what she could have
found to eat. Water – well, the place was flooded, Mitch said. Not
clean. Deepish in places.

Keeping the smallies out of deep water was not a problem, though.
Just about everyone had escaped drowning to have arrived at all, and
none had the slightest inclination to set foot in water more than an ankle
deep. But tales of rocks that clenched fangs on children who strayed
into holes in the mountainside, or of trees that looped strangling vines

then dangled a small form as a warning – those stories, whispered on dark nights, lodged splinters of ice along the spine.

So then there had to be ways of comforting them. "Watch," Mitch said, and he ran two fingers to circle his eyes, then theirs, with black ash. Then he painted dark lines from the inner corners of their eyes up to the hairline and marked two black bands across each cheek. Soon they started daubing other parts of their faces and their shoulders with yellow-brown silt, and smeared those spots to patches.

"Look at Shine," Brand shouted, for Shine began filling the first two circles into patches of ash to make the great black rings around his eyes.

"What name sky?" Celie intoned, raising up her palms, and the ritual chorus came back from the smallies.

"Sky is a giant ocelot watching down. Them mark on she fur is eyes too. Night-time, she eyes open and that is the stars."

The big boys painted their faces before raiding a litter. Celie had never gone, but Telma said she would one day. It was a mark of fitness for the bush, to rob a nest of one ocelot cub, because the mothers were fierce. Only three or so feet long and little more than a foot high, but thirty to forty pounds of enraged cat could bring down a small child. Shine had worn the slash marks on his cheek as a badge of honour.

The kit he brought his own smallies was so dark-furred that Myche and Brand had named him Night. Someone had remembered hearing that a cat could seem pure black if the dark patches on its fur clustered tightly enough. No one had seen such a cat grown to adulthood, but Myche named the black kit Night, just in case. After a while, though, the dark markings spread until it grew to be tawny, with rather more spots and streaks than the rest.

The kits that grew up in the Trust interbred with those outside, and a sort of understanding had come about between the children and the ocelots. Before, Mitch said, the cats may have led solitary lives. Then they began to cluster farther south, on that western side of the island, whatever it was that had driven them there.

The dragons, said Celie, with a delicious shiver that showed she didn't think that for a moment and was only trying to keep the smallies' eyes on her.

"Whatever," Mitch said tiredly. Something had blasted the wasteland across the centre of their usual hunting grounds, he said. That must have destroyed the cats' corridors in another part of the island and brought them here.

What with leftover food the children flung into the bush, the ocelots prowled close, snarling at anything unusual that approached the clearing. Few creatures did: the smell of urine marking the surrounding trees was stunning. But the odour made no difference to the children. They lived quietly behind thick foliage where the cats let them come and go, especially as the children's feet picked up the musk that was just another wall in the way of more dangerous predators. Recently the cats had begun to snarl and rake the air at the sight of Pwessus and Tweetums. Which just showed.

Ocelots were a force to emulate. *Emulate*, Shine said, meant learn from and copy. He must have read that in one of those books he was always searching out. There were so few books to be found.

"Why aren't there more?" Myche had asked him.

"Used to be plenty, but so many spoilt."

"What makes books spoil?"

"Fire. Damp. And insects. Silverfish eat paper."

Eventually books fell apart, even in the museum, and that distressed Shine at first. Then he said they would have rotted away in some ruin anyhow without him getting to read them or pass to Myche. That he could do this, find and then *give* books, awed her. Myche was more eager to emulate Shine than any stinky old cat.

But she did love Night, and there was a great deal to learn from the cats. The children grew alert even as they imitated the silent prowling and the ability to disappear by lying motionless. By still watchfulness Telma and even Brand – restless, impatient Brand – found out eggs in well-hidden nests. Wikki held back patiently until the fish had manoeuvred themselves deep enough into the traps he had pushed out into the lake with a bamboo rod. There the trap stayed, untouched till it began to jolt at the end of its line. Or when a wild chicken bustled up to the edge of the clearing, Myche could freeze, barely drawing one shallow breath spaced from the next, her eyes unmoving, unblinking, until the fowl had wandered almost into her hands. They all watched the ocelots for secrets of survival, and most of all Myche studied the cats for the balance they maintained between taut and tranquil.

"Hraaghnaarrrawghn," Brand snarled as he practised tightening himself to the sort of tension a cat needed to walk along the underside of branches, and loosened up to rest comfortably on narrow spaces with limbs dangling carelessly. It did not come naturally to Brand, but at last he had grown adept. He could lie on another branch of the same tree as an ocelot while he and the cat studied each other dispassionately before resting their heads comfortably on the rough bark and drifting into a near sleep that did not dull the senses. All that remained to make him one of them was the long slow tongue for languid, endless grooming.

2

PASSING OF NIGHT

TELMA

Telma worked out it was four years now that Marilyn and Wikki had been living in the Trust. They had come about the same time as Myche and Brand. Only Marilyn and Wikki were closer in age.

They came from a fire island. Telma strained for the right name, but it was gone. "Me no know," she had said, when Myche was trying to work out where everyone came from. "Is either Marilyn forget or she fraid to talk. She fraid everything."

Telma recalled her surprise when Marilyn welcomed Hyyy without a sign of fear. Shine had got the kit for the two of them when they were too small to wrestle one for themselves. It was so they could get to feel part of the bush: they would never have done that otherwise. Even now Marilyn was a bag of nerves, and perhaps that same jumpiness might make her a good watcher. But she could never be a finder like Shine or even Nat: Marilyn shied away from anything new, anywhere strange. Besides, she was too heavy to venture far out of the Trust. She couldn't run fast.

It bothered Telma that this Marilyn just ate and ate all the time. She didn't look like she enjoyed food; she seemed to eat just because it was there. Her eyes strayed nervously over the children, the shelters and kits, the wall of bush. Her shoulders cringed at swooping birds, and her body jerked at a clap of thunder. And all the time she ate. Telma felt the girl had no idea what she was putting in her mouth: like it never matter.

Just as well that Wikki cooked. Telma had watched him stretch up to pick limes, carefully so pika wouldn' juk him, and he washed fish. When Telma showed him where cassava ran wild under the ground, he dug it up and cut green seasoning he had stuck in the soft earth behind the museum. And when he cooked *that*. Laad. Nobody else coulda do it so. Eventually Celie and Shine would hand over to Wikki every bag of salt they found in their scroungings outside the Trust, and he hid it away lest those worthless twins came to waste it out on green mango. Anywhere Wikki walked he was watching out for a pepper bush or fine thyme, or he was gathering stones for the slingshot he used to bring down pigeons.

So everybody was glad about the kit Shine brought for Wikki and Marilyn. Of course, the first thing it did was to hiss and scratch up their arms. But somehow that didn't worry Marilyn. She named it Hyyy and seemed glad for it to follow her around. Everybody came to accept that when Wikki trapped fish, some was for Hyyy.

When Myche and Brand lost their own kit, Marilyn fully expected Shine to come down on her and Wikki, and to take Hyyy back. But he laughed off the idea.

"I go just raid another litter," he said.

Only, now Shine was gone.

As usual Myche betrayed nothing. But anyone could see Marilyn was mashed up. Wikki put on a better face, but Telma knew Shine had been like a god to him. After a time Marilyn came straight to the point. "Myche, gyul," she said, "make we just join up the two shelter and the four of we go live together and share Hyyy. We go do good together," Marilyn promised, kissing her palm in that way she had and adding, "Faith!" by way of further confirmation.

Telma knew that was the last thing that was going to happen. Myche had enough to do keeping track of Brand, without adding two extra pickney. Well, the boys were hardly smallies anymore. Wikki could take care of himself better than some of the older ones, and Brand – well, Brand was force-ripe, but he was what Mitch had called *capable*. The real point was – who would want Marilyn living in the same shelter, eating in that harum-scarum way and rocking back and forth holding her head and gasping for breath if so much as a mango thumped down on the thatch above?

Anyway, Hyyy couldn't make up for Night. And Myche had made it plain from the outset that she knew very well Night had not just *died*.

The older ones had ruled that whatever any of the children remembered from Before they should try to wrap up tight in the brightest and softest thoughts there were to be found. And if something that came back to mind was truly terrible, then that was to be rolled over and over in soft dark fur and pushed back, back to the furthest dimmest corner in one's head, so it could never get out. After a while, Celie had said, it would be gone, like the pains some of the older girls had, making them rock back and forth for a while before the cramps passed – only those came back. Besides, there was no medicine for the memories that hurt, and the big girls could at least drink the tea Telma drew from the bellyache bush, tea she had seen her grandmother make, Before. Telma's mother had said it was cerasee Gran Gran used to make the tea, but here cerasee grew long and thick on the vine, and Mitch said some people ate it. Not Telma. Even when Wikki cooked the thing he called karaile, its taste made her shiver.

So yes, Telma remembered stuff like cerasee from Before. But the rule was not to harp on Before, so she did not. Myche had a way of picking and choosing which rule she was going to keep and which she wouldn't bother about. Telma reflected that everyone knew, inside themselves, that Night didn't just die; but it had to be Myche to blurt it out loud.

And of course it was the twins and their beastness at the bottom of the whole thing.

And talking about twins – that heap of pika in Myche's face must be feel like somebody set fire to her skin. Telma had torn plenty out when she ripped off the cloth, but it couldn't be all. Some must leave back. Myche pretended the pain was gone, because Telma had said only her sewing needle could root them out one-one. "But make her stay," Telma said to Darati (even though Darati no longer answered). "Give her likkle chance – if I don't see it heal up good I know what fi say. I going tell her – if she leave it to turn bad, rat will come fi it. And she wi beg me use me needle so fast." Then Darati had gone out to collect and cut aloes. Wordlessly, she peeled and sliced thin juicy filaments for the poultice.

But, yes. Them twins.

There was this girl who vanished years ago. So long that her name . . . her name was gone too. Aah. A big girl they called Daughts. Daughts came with two brothers, young-young, before Telma and Darati reached the Trust. These twins had been tiny when they washed up with Daughts, so Mitch said. It must have been when Sonson was still here, and Telma had never known Sonson, only heard about him. But what Mitch said was that Daughts never taught the babies anything. She washed them by the lake and chewed their meat for them and picked up mango skins after them, and they would sleep all day and roll about playfighting and screaming and waking up the other smallies in the night. Daughts only babied them and let them have their own way.

Then one morning everybody woke up to find Daughts and some others gone. The rest of the children kept on calling the twins Pwessus and Tweetums, because no one had ever heard them called anything else.

And what could anybody really do for the two little leave-back boy pickney, except throw food and put out clean water? Celie would say, "Nobody can't tell them nothing because nobody ever teach them to listen." Daughts was gone, so they brought themselves up. They grabbed what they could.

Sonson had said, "Them two going grow into two little jabmolassi, you see them there." And that was long before Five Cent turned up and pounced on this word he said he knew but had forgotten. Anyway, the twins turn demon fi true. And they grew. They crouched down and waited for whichever smallie was carrying a Jew plum or a gourd with water. Or meat. Don't talk bout meat. And the two of them lied to whoever was bigger than they were. Like, about what stuff did disappear from whose shelter, or anything else gone wrong in the night.

According to Telma's calculation Pwessus and Tweetums had to be at least two or three years older than Myche, and a couple years back they set this trap for Night, carried him off and tied him behind the disgusting little lean-to they called their shelter. When Shine descended on them and demanded they give back the ocelot, they turned, meek and mild, round to the back of their shelter. In a little while they came back and said, "Oh-oh! Like the cat gone and dead." But Shine knew. Everybody knew. Only Myche screamed it out, "You kill him for nothing. For nothing!" (Myche did never fraid anything – except rat.) It was from then Darati start to loosen that grip on Telma, like Darati saw this Myche now like another one who could hold her up.

So Darati and Telma went with Myche and the rest up to the cliff over the place where the river rushed out to sea. Six children went along taking turns, two by two, because the cat had not even finished growing yet, until they reached the place and let him go. Well, seven, counting Nat who couldn't lift for long but walked behind them the whole way. That girl, Indira, sang a song no one understood (as usual), and Shine read some poem that sounded right, though Telma couldn't have told anyone afterwards what it said. But Myche was too angry to say anything. She just stood as if she had grown out of the jutting rockstone they were standing on, and after that she became a hiding place for Darati.

Marilyn and Wikki still talked about Night, especially when stroking Hyyy. Telma, Myche and the rest couldn't always make out what they said. Marilyn and Wikki had come from somewhere with different words mixed in among those the other children knew. Some children remembered stuff, like Telma, though others, like Myche self, had no idea where they were from. But Shine? Shine must have known, because he was older and read books, but he never said. The older ones agreed everyone would get on better if they forgot about Before, because now they were all from the one place that mattered. They were even beginning to sound alike.

"If you listen," Shine had said, "you going to understand each other."

Anyway, however strangely Marilyn and Wikki talked, they were easier to understand than Colin and Zef.

Shine worked it out that those two had come to the Trust from a nearer place than anyone else, yet their real home must be farthest away. Their parents had visited the island nearest by, on holiday, and got separated from their children. Then these two strange pale things washed up, so white (especially Zef) they were almost transparent on the sand. They were so young that even four months later they couldn't say how this kit they named Sarpie had managed to wander into the shelter Mitch and Celie had made for them. But Sarpie took them on, sleeping in between them, bawling for food and tearing them with his claws when they tried to lift him. Somehow the three survived together.

In truth, this Colin and Zef washed up so young they couldn't have told anybody what had happened. Lids, they said, or something like it, when Mitch asked them who they were. It was only that miserable boy Shant – he said his name was Justin, but Telma self renamed him Shant, because *shan't* seemed to be his favourite word. When Mitch said this boy and the twins had come in together and he must take care of them, he added, "I shan't be doing nothing for them. What them have to do with me? I don't know nothing bout them." But he did know a little, Telma remembered. He had said Colin and Zef had parents, tourists that got caught up in the troubles and died, leaving them behind.

"Tourist again," Telma had said. "Tourist can be good smaddy, but they can't take care of you, because they don't have nowhere that belong to them to take care of you *in*. Sometimes dem can't take care of demself – much less. How you think me and Darati land up here?"

Telma remembered and probably Darati did as well, even though she didn't talk about it. Well. Darati didn't talk at all anymore.

Telma and Darati came from a larger island, farther north. They had lived in town. It was a tight, loud place with heat radiating off the sheets of metal that were walls and roof. Zinc, Telma called it, though now she said *galvanize* so the others would understand. When their stepfather put them out, they walked and walked till they came to a wide-open paved space on the waterfront. Telma and Darati had found their way there a year before and learnt to dive for coins white people threw from ships and shoot back up to the surface with a money or two in their fists. But now they looked about for food. So one day they were searching a bin where people threw leftover food and stuff cleaners swept up from street, as well as the fish guts dumped by the couple of fishermen who had cast a net from the dock because their boat had been stolen from them long before. That was when a woman called out to ask the two little girl children rifling through the garbage whether they wanted a thing called plantain tart.

Want plantain tart? Any pickney woulda kill fi plantain tart. The woman said somebody bought it for her to try, but she didn't fancy it. She had thought the thing would have meat.

The tourisslady watched them closely while they were nyaming down the pastry, and she decided to buy them chicken. She told them her name, but it wasn't anything they could pronounce, and since it made no sense to them they now remembered her only as Tourisslady.

Anyway, now they were friends with this tourisslady who had come off a cruise ship and was getting ready to board again. And just as she was saying that she wished she could take them along, what had become a crowd thickened, tightening around them – desperate people shouting and cursing on the waterfront, demanding to get on the cruise ship. The people in charge of the ship hustled their passengers onto the launches and up the narrow steps on the side of the ship. Then the ship pulled away as fast as it could go, because people on the shore were pushing off in any little thing that could float, and some just threw themselves into the water and swam frantically for the ship.

But somehow in this fracas, Tourisslady manage to smuggle the two little girls (born and grow in ghetto) onto the ship. One big shiny ship, with brass rail and glass cut in pretty shapes tinkling around the lights overhead. In no time she had them bathed and dressed in two of her T-shirts, which fitted them like dresses, and she said she would grease some palms to keep the children with her. Whatever that meant. It sounded to Telma like some type of dirty work.

Only, in no time, it came down to the same-same story.

They were barely out to sea when another boat drew up with man and woman cursing and slashing, ordering some people into cabins and locking them in. When some of the crew on the cruise ship agreed to join up with them ruffian – that was that. The people who had taken charge separated the adults into groups, deciding who they could get money for, and locked those up. They threw the rest overboard (some they shot first, some they didn't) and one of them was Tourisslady. The children scrambled away into any crevice they could find, behind stacks of beach chairs, under lifeboats, every nook. But that was no escape.

The cruiters sailed that cruise ship with they own boat close behind till they reached whatever point suited them; then they told these children that the water near the shore was rough that day, and they must do the best they could to reach land and stay alive till they were big enough to be useful. And they throw these children in the water. Plenty pickney, as Telma recalled – might be thirty or so. But most couldn't swim at all, let alone in rough sea, or not so far. In the end just five or six washed up that time.

Every year, those people the children called *cruiters* came back for whosoever they wanted. But the rule was not to talk about that.

· · · · · · · · ·

Ananda, now, she talked nonstop. Words just tumbled out of her. She had turned up before she was big enough to have a kit, and Shine found her a half-bald baby chick fallen from some nest and stumbling about in the bush, and it grew into what looked like some sort of parrot, but bigger, with bright blue wings and a long streaming tail. So Qwa took up residence in the tree Ananda had accepted as her shelter, because she couldn't bear anything like a roof, only low limbs matted with some sort of thick vine. Up near the top where the branches waved so light and thin that no ocelot could reach him, Qwa set up house.

Although Telma had tried to question her, Ananda couldn't say where she came from, so she made up stories about Qwa – what brought his parents to the Trust and what made them fly off when he had barely hatched. Most of the children preferred to tell other people's stories they had picked up, some overheard on board or half-remembered from Before. When one of the big children was a smallie, she had strayed out and lost herself. It may have been Celie. Weeks after, she wandered back babbling what she claimed to have heard in the Don't Trust. Whispers out there in the bush, she said. But who whispered? She couldn't tell.

Still, the stories passed back and forth, and grew. Some of the bigger children could read, or Shine had read to them, but others, especially the younger ones, could not. So the bigger ones told stories. Everyone liked to hear about ocelots. How their eyes lit up the night, and how the rings on their fur were eyes too. How a bigger, heavier, fiercer ocelot with a thousand glimmering eyes lay sprawled above them, waiting to lunge down from the sky and devour whoever came to harm a child.

Good thing if he came down for Pwessus or Tweetums. Preferably both.

The twins were almost identical in build, flesh stacked on by nyam-ing down all the food they had bullied from the smallies. They had lost some teeth and smelt like they had never bathed in their lives. And who had there been to make them? When they ate they left trails of banana peel behind them for a pickney to slide on or fish bones to juk bare feet. Then it was Darati's job to prise the bone from the bawling struggling child, because it had to come out before the little wound turned hard and hot, circled in angry red or purple. Someone had to hold that smallie down while Darati tried to grip the end of the bone before it worked its way deeper in the foot-bottom. After a while Telma said, "It come like is just easier to clean up after them beas'."

Now the children in the Trust had to keep watch over the perimeters, so it was just as well the new girl, Janice, was good for that at least.

This Janice was jumpy like Marilyn, but a good watcher when she could take her eye off the two pickney she had got to shore. But she was spoiling them: anything they wanted she gave them, and what

Josiahmarshall wanted was attention nonstop. He was forever making stupid jokes that only Janice laughed at, while the baby – Tiffney,
they called her – refused to unclench her arms from Janice's neck and
screamed if anyone else touched her. When she finally started creeping, that was when the twins decided to drop in again for a couple
days, and Pwessus kicked Tiffney aside to grab up a set of good deep
red pomerac Brand had just brought down.

Well, Brand lowered his head and drove it at Pwessus full force,
right in his belly. Myche snatched up the pickney and handed her to
Janice, then turned with the rest on the two brothers, with branches,
ropey vines, anything they could grab up, and they lashed Pwessus
and Tweetums till they scrambled back over the fence.

So that was how they drove out those two brutes for good. Telma
always thought back to it as a good day's work. She and Myche, Brand,
Wikki and a couple others chased the twins into the bush. She and
Wikki screamed they would tie them up leave them fe corbeau, or
throw them for caiman, or nail dem down pon ants nest. At last even
Brand was satisfied to head back.

After that, the twins mostly stayed away. Sometimes they came
sneaking near the fence. Only that coulda get dem ocelot rile up so.
The twins had had the habit of stoning the cats whenever they could,
so the children would hear hissing and growling at night, and heavy
bodies plunging through bush with dry leaves under foot. Whether
the twins eventually went off on they own or the cruiters took them
would have been good news either way, as Darati had liked saying a
couple years back. She did talk then.

But two years ago, Darati lost Spat. Spat was older than most kits
were when a litter was robbed, and even after a year with Darati and
Telma, when Spat knew them well, they didn't leave him free outside
the Trust in case he ran away. "Not tame-tame," Telma said. "Is that
what make us tie out Spat in the bush when Darati and me and the
rest take him gone out the Trust looking fi egg. We say him wouldn't
able jump up inna tree like the rest of the puss-dem and get lost. And
is then the men come down on us."

Huge fierce men with bright head-ties, swiping the bush with machetes. The children screamed and scattered. Only Darati crouch down beside Spat and refuse to leave him, so Telma one crawl back to see.

"Nah. We not taking you yet," one of the men told Darati. He gave a grin so friendly that Telma could feel it crawl along her skin. "You wi worth more later."

Then he wrenched Spat away with one hand and swiped down the blade with the other. And in no time Spat skin rip off and everything supposed to be inside the puss skin on the ground and they kick it 'way. Then the same man throw the skin over his shoulder and grin at Darati again. He say, "How you fat and nice – I go come back for your skin too. Next year or so."

It was after that happened that Mitch, Celia and Shine started to insist the younger ones stay in the Trust all the time. Darati had never spoken since.

3

SCATTERINGS AND BINDINGS

MYCHE

BEFORE WAS THE THING TO LEAVE BEHIND, and *now* the puzzle to unravel. Everything outside the Trust had come to them in driblets from the older ones like Shine. Myche had read everything Shine brought in, but books that had survived were few and far between, and in scrounging for overlooked caches of oil, cloth, sugar, Vicks, knives, ointments or garden tools, he said there was little space to stuff in the odd volume he might find. When he did, it was the rarest of all treasures, transporting her to places that she could not distinguish between as real or made up. Either way, none of it told them anything about where they were or why they had come there.

"What else is there?" They had asked Shine before he left. Brand and Myche had been lying on their backs looking up at the sky, but she added, "Not up there. Down here."

And Brand insisted, "What else?"

"The whole world," Shine said. The world had five big parts, and the nearest was a huge place where different countries or parts of countries had united. Homeland was one of the names it had for itself, and it was a powerful influence on other places.

Shine had been in school, Before. When the trouble started, he had had to stay home, reading all he could on his own.

"I don't know much," he said, "but some countries got together so as not to get taken over by others and made this agreement they call a Treaty. Homeland was part of the Treaty, Before. But I guess a set of tiny countries can't join up, as how they scatter in the sea." The island where the children lived in the Trust hung close together with others, like in a necklace, but only here were there children living on their own. Normally the islands had helped each other if a hurricane hit or a volcano blew up, or sometimes Homeland lent a hand. At least, it used to be that way.

Myche cracked her knuckles as Shine traced a map in the dust to show them what the world was like. Homeland had remained strong while some other countries had come through wars or disasters like earthquakes and tidal waves. A few still stuck up for each other, others were in turmoil, and the necklace of islands Shine had told them about got left more and more to itself. It was no point Brand asking him why, because he did not know.

Myche remembered Shine's grin when he said that, for at least Brand asked questions.

Shine and Mitch had still been at the Trust when the boy they called Five Cent washed up, and the first thing Shine noticed was that the child never asked questions. He hardly paid attention to what went on and rejected anything new.

"That boy harden," Shine groaned.

Nothing Mitch said could interest the child in hunting, in building a shelter or even accepting an ocelot kit. In fact, after he had been several weeks in the Trust, Five Cent had nothing of his own.

"That child more trouble to keep alive than all the rest," Mitch would say. "And is because he feel he know everything."

"Is here I from," Five Cent said, "not like most of all-you." And he kept on and on about stuff he should not have put in words (like about those who should have got back ashore with him but went down into the water). After a while, though, he shut up about that, but he could not get out of his mind some huge snake that had been the last of his catastrophes. It came to him in the night too, in his dreams, and when he cried out and woke the others, he seemed to be wrestling with it, thrashing and squirming.

Then, after the first days in the Trust when everyone had shared food and shelter long enough, the stupid little boy nearly starved to death because he still could not catch on to the idea of hunting out food for himself. What he had done was to hold out a small, flat, shiny, useless thing to the others in a bid for them to find him food, and when he explained what that was about they named him Five Cent.

Five Cent survived only because Mitch, who was more patient than Shine, had sat the troublesome child down and told him stories. When all else failed, it was always the stories that brought some glimmer of understanding.

It came as no surprise to Shine that Five Cent had his own stories, about soucouyants flying around in flocks, for one. His father had told him, so it had to be true, Five Cent insisted, and nothing would convince him otherwise.

"If soucouyants exist at all," Shine said, at the end of his patience, "they travel alone: they certainly don't flock." Shine lost his temper, but Mitch eventually made the annoying little pest shut up and listen.

"You think soucouyant is la belle?" he jeered.

When the boy stared at him in bewilderment, Shine steupsed and explained, "Candle-fly."

"It have nothing else that fly with a light," Mitch said. "The only flock that matters here is us," he added, "and if we we don't fly together, we going dead."

So Mitch taught Five Cent to live in the Trust, then Mitch was gone.

But by now even the hard-ears boy they called Five Cent had learnt to respect the bush, from the tales of Papa Bois. He had grown convinced about staying close to the other children, after all he had heard about douen. The douen were those children who had not made it, yet who had not fallen sick and gone to the Place of Return. They had merely faded into the forest and become a part of it, like leaves rustling around the feet of Papa Bois. Five Cent learnt, as the others had, not to follow signs of beings from outside the Trust and never to stray out beyond the borders of the bush they knew. Even if it had not been for the cruiters, stories of the baanya taught them that.

Celie had told her stories mostly to Marilyn, to quiet her down at night. Then Marilyn had recited them to Josiahmarshall and Ananda. The ones smaller than them were too young to care.

According to the old tales, the baanya were ancient ones with knowledge of what came Before on the island. They alone understood what the places of fallen stone meant or what the rusting metal towers had been used for. The baanya were those wise enough to claim nothing, even if it had first been theirs. It was safest to think of them as gone now, extinct. They were not part of the bush, or likely, on occasion, to flash out across the open spaces like iguanas.

These and other tales Celie had told the smallies as dark came on – how the ancestors of the baanya had first walked to the island across a landbridge and stopped short of the last narrow neck of rock because of billowing smoke and flame ahead. There they lived for months, fishing from the one canoe they carried for the purpose.

Then, one day, pausing on a high flat area of the ridge, they noticed a section of the rocks behind them had fallen, and there was no way back to the place they had left. Well ahead was the large firm island, but there was still smoke and fire rising from it. As the flames subsided, it seemed best to wait on their ridge, although it was lower now, nearer sea level. All around they found supplies of food and fresh water. Cool breezes fanned the ridge.

When the path between them and the island ahead sank, they worried. Still, they knew they could always use the canoe to ferry across in small groups; and now that the fire was gone and the smoke appeared to be clearing, they knew it would be safe to cross over in a couple days.

But the next morning they woke to find water swirling around their legs. The bridge behind them had disappeared, and a widening swathe of mud churned between them and the island ahead. The ground they were on had become an island itself, and even that was giving way, sinking as they scrambled for the canoe, and by the time they had crammed the littlest ones aboard, there was no more space.

There was no time for directions, only shouts to keep paddling towards the smoke and not look back.

So that smaller island sank, and every decade or so rose again to stand sad and empty, as even the memories of those children who had sailed from it faded and were lost. It came to be known as Jumbie Island, and after a while only a few people actually believed in it.

Those first children who had paddled to the big island – children with skin the colour of honey like Indira, sapodilla like Brand, or mahogany like Mitch and Five Cent – had grown wide and muscular. "Is them self build a set of huge stone place to live near to each other," Celie had said. Eventually their children harnessed the black goo that oozed from the earth and could be set ablaze, and they ground cane stalks to make sweet crystals. But in the end, all of it fell in the explosions. So the baanya came and left in smoke, unless there was any truth to the story that they had taken to the bush to avoid looters who swarmed ashore after the fires.

"Looters and cruiters is same thing?' Indira asked, but neither Mitch nor anyone else could say for sure.

Yet Mitch knew a lot. He had run away from home to join the cruiters just when stories of them began circulating. He was twelve when he saw what they really were, but by then he had no way of leaving the ship. Only, one day when they handed him a baby to toss overboard, he jumped.

Mitch had told Shine that the cruiters were only interested in sea traffic. They sank or seized all boats, gathered anyone strong enough to be of use and dumped the adults they didn't need. They dropped children near the island, and, periodically, they came back to collect any survivors who had grown enough to be worthwhile.

It was Shine who discovered that the cruiters had other interests. "Whatever they find, they carting it off to sell somewhere else," he said.

Somewhe' else? Five Cent insisted that there was only one real place: the island where they lived and where, he said, he was born. When his father had tried to run away elsewhere, it hadn't worked. So there *was* nowhere else.

Shine had tried to help him work through it logically. "If children keep coming in, they have to be coming from somewhere," Shine said. "Besides, if the cruiters selling stuff to places far away from here then those places must be more than story." Then he grew serious. "The most important question is whether it have any limit to what those people willing to buy and sell." Then he looked around at the older ones and concluded, "Don't ever take you eye off them smallies."

Not everyone thought like Shine. Shant had been eight or nine years old when he arrived about two years ago, along with two tiny boys. He argued loudly that they were not his brothers, just two little frog throw off the boat at the same time. Shant said the boys' parents . . . well, it had three adults with the children, and he didn't know who was whose parent. But they'd been visitors who hadn't managed to get off the island and go home when they should, and they were all in the same small boat together when the ship bore down on them and they got hauled up on board for sorting. When the men threw Shant overboard, it was a calm clear day, and he knew he could swim to land. He was almost on shore when he noticed the two children, practically babies, wiggling along like white tadpoles behind him through the water – as if born to it.

He was surprised but took no further notice at first, because they had nothing to do with him. But they followed him across the beach and through the bush, and when Nat found them and brought them in, everyone insisted Shant and the smallies had come in together and he would have to look after them.

Shant was miserable and quarrelsome, "because they ent have nothing to do with me," he said. "And what make it fair to saddle me with two little pest who name I don't even know?"

When Indira asked them, they said they were Colin and Zefwi. At least that was what Indira could make out. They could have been about two or three at the time.

"Brothers? C-cousins?" she asked. "Lids" was all the explanation they had – which got nobody any further. Colin was possibly older. They did not look much alike except for having very fair skin.

Now they seemed to be around four. Colin's hair was turning light brown, and Zef's stayed pale yellow, almost white. Their eyes and ears were different too. Even now, Shant took no interest in them, and when Nat, Telma and a couple others clustered round the plum tree near the lake to gather fruit for sharing out, Shant just picked himself a few and set off for his shelter, munching as he went.

· · · · · · · · · ·

Big ones like Sonson, Daughts and Mitch had passed on what they knew. Celie and Shine had taught the next lot, Myche, Telma and Nat – even Shant when he was willing to listen. One essential lesson was to hide, for as long as possible, signs of their bodies changing. Among the plunder the older ones discovered outside the Trust, cloth was most valuable. With long strips of it the older girls bound their bodies ruthlessly tight from chest to thigh, under whatever else they wore. As their makeshift clothes wore out, they patched in new bits of cloth or broad leaves threaded together with vines. Life in the bush kept them thin, and if there was no way to avoid growing taller, they could at least try to keep lean. Waiflike.

They also trimmed their hair close to the scalp and, when need arose, shaved other parts of their bodies. Janice objected at first, then gave in. "Anything for nobody not to notice me, yes." She told Myche and Marilyn she had heard the cruiters arguing about how much they might get for her, a short time before they tossed her overboard with Josiahmarshall and the baby. They had said she wouldn't bring enough yet to make up for the cost of keeping a child on board alive.

All that was in Janice's head, disorienting her along with the shock of impact and the plunge deep under the surface, yet she managed to fight her way up to a small form bobbing above her and another, tinier, drifting down in its mass of sodden blanket. She clutched the baby and kicked up towards the light and away from the huge ship slanting above. She kicked again violently in one vast breath-stopping rejection of the vessel, its crew . . . the beastliness. Even the swell of water was better than the boat, and when she looked frantically over her shoulder, a glimpse of Josiahmarshall striking out filled her with the strength to keep paddling one-sidedly, till finally they found themselves scraping up on rough sand.

No, Janice was not the scaredy-cat Telma took her for, Myche decided, because it was never herself Janice was afraid for.

. . . .

Shine heard about Janice's arrival even though it happened after he left, because one night he came back.

That night, when Myche and Brand got back to their shelter, Shine was waiting for them. He stepped out of the shadows with his fingers to his lips and said, "Shh! I'm supposed to be recruiting, and I going have to say I get lost. I can't stay."

It was unreal, his appearing from nowhere. Brand shrank back to take it in, then grinned broadly and threw himself at his brother. From the shadow came a hoarse snoring, interrupted by rasping breaths, and Shine tugged forward something on a lead.

"I have this one's sister on board. Pure black. I named her Night."

The ocelot he led forward seemed as big as any adult Myche had seen. Yet it looked young, ears larger than expected and a little fluffy. It butted its nose against Shine playfully. Kittenlike. He had caught the two when the crew stopped on the mainland to the south, Shine said, and he convinced the captain to let him raise them. Probably the crew wanted the cats to grow as big as possible so they could take their skins, but meanwhile he got to keep them. "The other's black-black. True. I going tell them this one got away and jumped ship. Keep it safe and train it fast – it's different from anything you know."

"How?"

Playful for such a big ocelot, for one thing. It threw itself on its back like a baby and pawed the air. There was nothing for it but to rub its belly. Gold eyes closed in ecstasy. It was the sort of encounter – Shine's coming – that seemed unreal even while it was happening. As if they were dreaming him up out of their desperate need and longing. Myche ran her hands tenderly along the raised scars on his cheeks, two on one side, three on the other, as they showered Shine with news of all that had happened since he left and with questions about what he was doing.

"It's all different to what I thought." He sat turning it over in his head for a while. "I'm in it now, and it's . . . much worse than I . . . than any of us could have . . ."

"How it got like that?" Myche asked.

"Years before we washed up, a country nearby fell apart, so even people who had been rich became desperate, and the poorest of the poor turned to anything that could keep them alive from one day to the next. Fishermen who could not sell fish took their boats out to raid other vessels, and soon bands of them were attacking luxury yachts. They killed whoever they found on board," he said. "They used knives or just dumped them over the side. Children and all. Attacks like that spread, and soon the raiders were heavily armed and bolder than ever, taking over huge vessels." He got to his feet and took a few restless turns around the little shelter before sitting down again. "The one I'm on is a cruiser and they've armed it. They have to show they're vicious – so everyone will know to be afraid."

"And you work with them?" Myche whispered it.

"I've never killed anyone. I don't know how long I can keep on this way. If I don't show I'm one of them, they'll put me below."

"What's below?" Brand demanded.

"Cargo. Stuff to sell."

Myche stared out into the night, into the impossibility of the thing. "So you can't run away?"

"How? Where to? What about you two?"

"But we never can be safe, can we?" Myche could hear the bitterness in her own voice.

"Listen."

But she pulled away from the two of them, wrapped her arms around herself and rocked forward and back, forward and back. "We can never be safe."

"Pay attention," Shine said briskly. He had no time to be of comfort. "Myche, they coming for you next time. They'll come to the Trust. See, eventually they going to catch the twins."

She stared at him intently.

"The two of them will talk to save themselves, and that will lead the whole lot of them on your trail." He had actually been protecting Pwessus and Tweetums, he said – to Brand's disgust. "Only to make sure they don't get carried off onto the ship," Shine said, "because the twins know everything about the Trust – not just where it is but how many of you there are, what you look like, which of you are growing up. You won't be able to stay here long," he warned. Then he glanced outside as if remembering.

"Hold on. I'm here too long. Before I go I want to make sure you know something about yourselves, however small. It's dangerous to know too much." He glanced at Myche and added as if it were being torn from him, "But do you even know your name?"

She stared at him, shocked. "Myche," she said in a small voice, suddenly uncertain.

"Short for *Mychelle*. I was there in the church. They christened you Mychelle Shabina." He shot another look over his shoulder. "I have to get back, or . . ." He was already ducking back out towards the shadows around the entrance. "The trade is . . . Look. Get out of here before the next dry and find your way deep into the bush."

Myche and Brand were still besieging him with questions when they realized there was no one there. They might have thought they had imagined his coming, if it weren't for the cat.

"So what we calling it?" Brand had been rolling on the ground with it, and he stank and was covered with scratches.

"One Thousand Eyes." Myche hadn't even stopped to think.

Brand's lips moved silently as if he were trying it out on his tongue. "Yeh," he said.

She sat rocking, her eyes on Brand. For how was she to hide as Shine commanded? She had Brand to keep safe.

4

WAIFS AND STRAYS

MYCHE

MYCHE PAID NO ATTENTION TO THE other children's outcries when they
saw what had strayed into the Trust in the night and heard what she
had taken it into her head to name it. Indira threw up her hands in
horror at what an adult-size baby might mean.

"What you mean, *mean*?" Brand taunted her. "You think is a jinn
or what?"

"Is too big to train," Marilyn argued. "Is no baby. Wait till it start
to bite us up."

"And stink up the place," Telma added with a wry grin.

Darati studied it with her head to one side, and then drifted away.
Only Five Cent showed any real curiosity and seemed to find the idea
vaguely comforting although he kept his distance. He was quite pleased
when he found out that Wikki was feeding the cat all the eel-like fish
that invariably came up in his contraption of wiry stalks and grasses.
Sometimes the nasty, coiling things worked their way up in the mud
around the lake and hunted frogs there for a while, so over the years
the children had argued over whether they were eels or some other
type of fish, or water snakes. But no one would eat them, so Wikki
had always thrown them back. Now he collected them for the new cat,

and after a while One Thousand Eyes would plunge in to search out whatever he could find for himself. Five Cent approved of anything that reduced the population of snakelike things.

Still, even Five Cent gave the huge cub a wide berth – which was easy. At first the cat slept with Myche and Brand; then, after a while, One Thousand Eyes dozed on the branch overhanging the entrance to their shelter.

No one but Darati seemed wholly unafraid. She said nothing, of course, but they had grown accustomed to that. She turned up the glossy curve of her cheek and tilt of her nose, and something like a smile twitched the corner of her mouth, plump lips the colour of caimet, and she walked unconcerned under the branch where the big cat lay dangling a peculiarly heavy leg above her head. Almost as if she had known him for a long time.

And perhaps she had, some of the children whispered. After the thing had happened to Darati's ocelot, its duppy had come in the night to torment her – it must have been that, because they had heard, in between her strangled screams, the grunting, hissing noises of the ocelot. At least that was one theory that came up when they tried to work it out. Another explanation was that she had nightmares about the cruiters. Or maybe Spat visited her between those nightmares and comforted her. They were talking, Darati and Spat – that was it. Perhaps the only talk she had left was ocelot talk. Anyway, Darati was not afraid of One Thousand Eyes.

Curiously, although neither Myche nor Brand told anyone about Shine's visit, several of the other children associated the cat with him. Months later, Indira and Marilyn were saying Shine hadn't gone but had merely changed shape. Josiahmarshall said he had seen Shine under the samaan and that Shine had shortened and sunk onto all fours, mottling into an ocelot that sprang at once onto a low branch. Myche had no time to argue with the craziness Josiahmarshall dreamt up. But Brand was frankly pleased with the idea. If Shine was a lagahoo, Five Cent added, that would explain all he knew about the bush, and how he had disappeared, come back and reshaped into an ocelot. He could be any of the cats out there. Anywhere. Anytime. But Five Cent betrayed himself, watching the effect of this speech, by a twinkle in his eye and crinkle at the corner of his mouth, and Myche decided the boy wasn't the fool Telma said: he just liked messing with people's minds – as Shine would have put it.

At any rate, a few of the children remained convinced that Shine had stayed on, concealed from the cruiters and from anyone like Pwessus or Tweetums, and this was why the new ocelot kept growing, so as to accommodate the volume of a big boy, almost a man. It became the thing to say: Shine was still around, disguised as One Thousand Eyes.

........·

Myche quickly concluded that she had no right to depend on Wikki to find food for the cat, and she began studying the wild chickens near the Trust more carefully. No chicken with any sense would stray near to the ocelots in the first place, but not far from the Trust a wide wire enclosure showed openings that a chicken could shuffle through. The top was meshed as well as overgrown with vines, so chickens had found safe shelter and multiplied, popping out through holes at the side only to find food.

Myche sat perfectly still, watching them walk about nervously, their heads bobbing strangely – as if they were dizzy, she thought, for every time the chicken jerked its head it blinked. But the blink happened too fast for her to grab the bird. She would have to wait for one to walk further from the enclosure and to come right up to her.

Not happening.

It was a few days before she decided that something in all that bobbing and blinking must be helping the chicken to see, rather than distracting it or making it dizzy, perhaps to keep a steady view of everything around it and pick up anything that moved.

She found herself thinking of Darati, who could sit still nearby for quite a while, so if a chicken fluttered out of Myche's way, the other girl might grab it. Besides, Darati wouldn't jump or cry out if One Thousand Eyes suddenly appeared. When he did follow them out, he started catching his own chickens, and that seemed better for everyone. In fact, it worked so well that Telma intervened.

"Unnu! Dem fowl mustn't eat faster than they have chick. Or this time nex year we nah have none. Then you going bawl bout 'fowl done!'"

· ·········

A year after Shine's disappearance, the cat was too heavy for that branch he had first chosen, and he began sleeping on a thick limb nearer to the trunk. He was different from any ocelot Myche had ever seen. His broad head and short thick neck showed no streaks, just the same dark spots, circles really, on the thicker part of his body, flowerlike as if black petals clustered into round markings on the yellow fur. Wait. Circles with a central spot like the pupil of an eye. The eyes were closed dark spots on his head and lower limbs but opened across the back and shoulders and flanks. And his face was watchful too. Playful, but a twitchy type of playful, more tense than Night had been. And less peaceful.

Gradually the other children paid less and less attention, because he stayed aloof, stalked round the perimeter of the Trust at night and uttered grunts that grew deeper as the months passed. He passed the day sprawled in the fork of a tree, apparently inattentive to their movements, flicking a haughty glance in the direction of sounds from beyond the fence. A leg dangled negligently, its whiter fur and smaller spots all but invisible against the pale trunk.

Myche was bigger too – still shorter than Nat and (of course) Shant, but sturdy. She had determined that no one was going to tell her what to do, but that there were ways of getting the others to do what she wanted without actually ordering them about. So she was quieter, calculating the next step. She had reread everything Shine had ever brought her, several times, and Marilyn said that was why Myche went on as if she knew better than anyone else. Nat said it was not that at all. True, she would have her way in the end; but meanwhile she would listen and try to pick up everything she could.

The fact was there was need for her to think hard, because she was eleven now (had probably been for a while, she thought) and filling out more than was safe. All very well for Brand to shoot up, or even Telma. Telma remained thin, and flat as a board. She continued grim in protecting Darati or lacing together scraps to cover the smallies. Darati, on the other hand, had put on weight, but she was still shapeless, and seemed mostly lost in her own silent world. Yet she had begun to reach out of it sometimes, to bind Wikki's ankle that twisted when he fell out of a tree while trying to grab a pigeon, or to wash the smallies' scratches. They were always snatching at ocelots or tumbling on stones or asphalt while running away from the old drake that ruled the eastern corner of the lake. In particular, a new child called Kyle liked to swing from low branches he could reach and inevitably lost grip and landed screaming.

Otherwise the rest of the children were much the same but for being one year older. Five Cent was just as own-way and know-it-all, although, as it turned out, softhearted to the youngest ones. Indira, who had been there for three years, still ate nothing that had ever been alive, or could be (no eggs), and routinely set out flowers and pieces of food in small bowls before saying prayers. The prayers were in a language no one understood, and Myche believed it was not a language at all but a sort of memory of one or a wish for one. Yet Indira said she had learnt the prayers from her uncle, the sadhu, and they were real, real prayers. Indira's chanting was high-pitched and nasal, rising and falling monotonously. She had arrived three years ago crying for someone who seemed to be called Fish, though she pronounced it "Vish", and now and then her prayers would include his name.

Which raised the question in Myche's mind of whether she too should be saying prayers. She felt she should, but did not know any – or perhaps she once had but no longer remembered.

She had wondered about that when Ash died. Ash had arrived twelve weeks ago with two smallies, Bry and Kyle; but Ash had a terrible wound. "Bullet," Telma pronounced. "I see bullet hole before." So Ash died, and the biggest ones covered him on the grid of branches they used for drawing him away to the Place of Return. Telma had gone along, though it meant leaving Darati for the whole day, and even Shant had been willing to help draw the litter over the rocky part of the uphill trail. Telma had said a prayer, and Marilyn and Wikki had joined in, but Myche couldn't recall any of it except the *amen* at the end. She wondered whether any of the others did, like Five Cent, who had stayed behind with the smallies. But it was the sort of thing you didn't ask.

Of late, Five Cent had taken over Kyle and Bry, Kyle wailing as he often did for no reason, and Bry, as usual, refusing to keep on clothes of any sort. "And what it matter whether he keep on clothes or not," Five Cent demanded, and for once everyone agreed with him.

Nat and Telma ventured forth on raids to surrounding areas, and sometimes they took Janice if Indira or Wikki would agree to watch Tiffney. Janice could look at anyone and tell them brass-face that she wasn't trusting them with the baby. They moved with greater care than ever, because Nat was not as fast and sure of foot as Shine had been. But they came and went about their business, much as Shine and Mitch had done, hauling in increasingly rare finds of yellow oil, salt, matches, the odd bucket or other container, or the occasional machete. They foraged further and further afield, but even Telma reported that there was no cloth to be found again. "Nowhere. Like claat done."

In the past Sonson, and later Daughts and then Mitch, had noted landmarks along the different paths, and Shine had drawn these together with his own discoveries into a sort of map. It was not on paper, just sketched by word of mouth into their minds, but it made things easier, for they knew which paths led nowhere or into open fields where they could easily be rounded up. Myche, like most of the others, rarely left the Trust. They stayed behind to fork up the ground for provision like cassava, or clean around plantain trees or bushes bearing pigeon peas.

Myche knew why they preferred her to stay behind, so she hoed and weeded too, though it was not to her liking.

One morning when she held the garden fork raised before slamming it back into the ground, her wrists bounced against soft flesh, and she realized how right they were in wanting her to stay hidden. She didn't think she was twelve yet, but she would have to band her chest more tightly to keep it flat, and it was getting harder to do that without hurting herself. Things Shine had said fluttered vaguely back to mind, and when a few of the others got together under the samaan tree, she brought the talk around to the cruiters.

The night before, lying awake and wishing Shine would appear again, she had realized that since his visit she had done nothing about his warnings to leave the Trust. She went cold at the thought of living alone in the bush far from the rest. Then something else came back to her, something Shine had said – something about the cruiters making people talk. Anyone left behind could give away the rest. She could not tell them Shine had come, but she could use what he'd said.

"Suppose Pwessus and Tweetums are working with the cruiters," she said. "We haven't seen those two for ages."

Brand nodded thoughtfully. "And why they would leave us in peace?"

She cast a grateful look his way. "The twins can bring them here," she urged. "They can easily show the way to the Trust."

A knowledgeable glance passed among Myche, Nat, Telma and Janice. Time must have circled round again for a cruiting.

So how should these older children escape, and what would happen to the rest? A buzz of argument broke out. Marilyn suggested that if the baanya still existed, they must have a system. Otherwise, how had *they* escaped? And if they were no longer there – how had they left? What about the landbridge?

Five Cent steupsed.

"Landbridge," Marilyn repeated. "Same one like in the story."

"It don't have no story like that," Five Cent objected.

"Oh yes," Marilyn pronounced, "the same landbridge."

"Well, I never hear bout no landbridge and where it come from and where it go," Five Cent said mulishly.

Josiahmarshall said it couldn't go nowhere, and his sister, Janice, muttered that it must be only to the places people were running away from. Wikki suggested it might go to the place where the cruiters lived. Five Cent said, yet again, that this island was the one place.

But there had to be another place – even Shant joined in to interrupt him, although he'd heard nothing of Shine's account of Homeland or anywhere else, and what could Shant know anyway?

If it had nowhere else, Wikki chimed in, where he and Marilyn had come from? And how had the baanya got here in the first place?

"Then, ent it sink?"

They all stopped to stare at Brand. Even if the old story of the landbridge had anything in it, Brand concluded, there was no bridge left. "Because, then, why anyone would stay?"

So it had to be like Janice said, Josiahmarshall insisted. If the landbridge existed, it went to the places everyone was running away from.

"Why people were running?" Brand didn't have even those confused memories that haunted Myche, and he was too rebellious to care whether he was carrying the conversation into forbidden zones.

Wikki remembered more than anyone could have expected. He said a mountain had blown up, only that was not what he remembered; what he remembered was hearing about that. It had happened even before *Before*. As the others caught their breath at his rash talk of the forbidden past, Marilyn gathered the nerve to rush in and say that their father had told them.

And so, as if a spell had broken, the two plunged on with their story.

They remembered living amid mounds of black lava and playing in the ashes. On the slopes above them, steam rose through cracks, and the earth rumbled as if it had not spent its anger completely and would open hungry mouths anywhere, randomly, to roar again and spit fire, to spew molten rock. Their father used to sit on a black rock and sing songs of green days before the mountain top blew off, but there was less and less food to go around, and when some aid that was promised did not come, they got on the boat.

For a while they talked in hushed voices about boats, and about the charred land, and soon there were other voices and other fragments about hordes of looters tugging and making off with stuff on their heads, injured dogs howling, choking smoke and blooms of flame in the sky – but not all from exploding mountains. It was hard to recapture: a myriad of unexplained things clung in odd bits to the mind of one child or another. Then, for no reason anyone could see, Ananda started counting in a loud voice, and Chunks and Kyle followed tonelessly.

·········

"There must be a school," Shine had once insisted, and he had tried to get each child to teach what they knew to the rest in the evenings before going to sleep. It got mixed up in stories and argument and, often, if the bickering became painful or any distressing topic dragged on too long, Ananda's counting broke it up. At first her counting was broken too, after twelve, with gaps and disordered numbers and a few letters in between. Now it was loud as if to drown the rest out. But that evening's foray into the subject of Before continued on in the evenings that followed, with here and there something new among stints of repetition. The tales might be true or made up. The children liked supposing – about the far reaches of the island, and about how the baanya still made their homes in the forests or highlands. Or, perhaps, in some deep ravine or murky lake.

"It have snakes in the lake?" Five Cent had maintained his horror of snakes and enquired for them in every setting.

He had told them repeatedly about the snake he had met when he washed up – in fact, on the way to shore. He had been paddling in with an older sister who did not swim well, and he saw a thick tree limb bobbing on the waves. Just when he thought she would sink, it drifted barely within his reach, and he shoved it towards her. She reached out and snatched at it, and a thick body that had seemed part of the limb uncoiled almost under her hands. She opened her mouth to scream, and the water swirled in and over her, and in the turbulence from her struggle the limb bobbed away with its passenger, leaving only heaving water where she had been. The boy repeatedly tried to gulp air and poke his head under water to look for her before coming up and paddling furiously again, but he could not keep it up. It was all he could do to keep afloat until the waves tumbled him up onto the sand.

But Five Cent was no coward. He was even ready to risk searching for the landbridge he did not believe in, once no snakes were involved. Still, the idea that there was somewhere else to go brought a scowl of disbelief to his face.

"It have only water," he protested, "all round."

"Almost everybody here come by boat," Nat argued.

"So-so water all round WeLand," Telma agreed, "but they have other places, eejit. Is that why people make boats."

Wikki added, "We just tell you we came from another island. Is a line of them one-one."

"Necklace," Brand said.

"Right." Myche grabbed up a stick and began ploughing it through the sand to make a rough map as close as she could to what Shine had described to them months ago. "Everyone knows there are other places," she said. "Anyway, some of us have to find somewhere else besides the Trust."

Still, it wasn't clear to her either. Shine had said the islands were alike just by being islands, but after all that had happened some were in confusion and could be dangerous, and a few might even be empty. Even the weather had made it worse. None of the children had ever experienced a real storm, and hurricanes were fables to them, like dragons. But Shine had said one or two huge storms had made life on two of the islands impossible. Myche felt sure Nat knew more of what lay beyond their shore than the others, but he was quieter than ever.

It was the following day when it occurred to her that he might be worried about slowing them down. Suppose he was the one to get caught and be forced to give the others away. All he would say was that they must all go or all stay, together. Myche grew more edgy. There was no urgency for the younger ones and so no keeping them on the subject. Time was frittering away. And one couldn't walk off and leave them. Right now she wanted to do just that, and if Ananda started to count or Marilyn to whine she would just slap them up, she thought. She squeezed her eyes shut to get a hold on herself.

"If you think it have a landbridge, we better find it before the cruiters come again," Nat declared, and Josiahmarshall laughed because Nat still said *it* like *eat*, but Myche shushed him. "Yes." She pounced on Nat's suggestion, although she felt sure he didn't believe in the landbridge any more than she did. "How we'll find it?"

"Walk round the island," Five Cent said. "It ent have no bridge, but we might find somewhere else to live."

"Whole way?" Marilyn stared at him.

"Whole way."

Brand jumped up, ready to swing over the border of the Trust and set off at once.

Myche was not surprised. Shine had told her he believed one of the three of them was *chosen*, and she had naturally assumed it was Shine, until he disappeared. Afterwards she had realized that it must be Brand. He was strong and fearless.

The problem was that he was reckless too. He talked as if saying a thing made it true. He had no idea where actions might lead, because he had no memory of what had brought him to where he was. Myche had the odd clue, although her memories were cloudy. She recalled arms tight around her and an ear close above her forehead.

"Leave the man," an old woman said, leaning over them. "You and you children going run and hide with him forever? Or hide from him? *Pwan douvan, avan douvan pwan ou.*" But what did that mean?

Myche thought again of the baanya. The stories said everything the baanya had laboured to build over years (ages, perhaps) had been taken away. Everything they had created was wiped out without trace, except in areas no one could reclaim. It seemed it was in the nature of life to empty of value every so often. She told herself severely that there was no point clinging to the Trust or anywhere else. Yet Myche was equally certain that they needed to gather their wits before leaving, if only to decide what they should take.

But no one knew exactly what to be afraid of, so there was no clear idea of how to prepare – short of getting together what cloth and light tools they could carry, packing up any food that could keep fresh for a while and filling what they could with water. Then they froze for a few more days before the enormity of it – of heading out into the Don't Trust.

One morning Nat and Telma began waking those a little younger than themselves, and Myche joined in thankfully. Janice, Marilyn and Wikki pushed the others, and soon they were all gathered under the samaan, fidgeting and trying not to meet each other's eyes. Then they started walking, straight for the entrance where the sign still dangled with *The* on the left side, a dark patch in the middle, and *Trust* on the right. They were terrified about what they were about to do.

Between the children and other living things there had once shimmered a wall that had grown thinner and more transparent with each passing month on the island, and in a while it had faded altogether, so that they were all simply creatures of the wild, together yet apart. In a while the ocelots' predatory instincts, which the children had absorbed unknowingly, along with the nervousness of birds and lizards, the evasiveness of agouti, had all come together in a way of walking, waiting and seeing. There was a fearful sense, too, growing with each day, that somewhere beyond the children's knowledge might be other humans, bigger than themselves and growing increasingly more savage. Their thoughts turned to Pwessus and Tweetums, produced in their very midst yet transforming themselves into predators and the children they had lived with into prey.

Those boys had been so mean to the ocelots that of late the cats had turned on them when they tried to get back into the Trust. Although no one had seen either of them clearly for a while, Telma had recently reported sudden frantic hissing and tense stalking back and forth before she glimpsed one of the twins withdrawing, creeping awkwardly backwards along a thick branch that reached over one border of the Trust. At least she said it had looked like one of them, but more hairy.

"Then suppose Pwessus and Tweetums outside w-waiting for we?" Indira's voice quavered, as they stalled just beyond the entrance.

And how come the cruiters hadn't taken *them*, Marilyn wanted to know.

"P'raps they're more use to the cruiters here," Myche said.

A minute's silence passed in gathering alarm.

Janice's eyes widened. "You mean – Pwessus and Tweetums working for them? Here?"

"Would be just like them," Brand said.

Now it was actually worded, that idea spawned countless possibilities.

"They'd help the cruiters round us up?"

"But the ocelots . . ."

"The men'll kill them." Brand had cut back in. "Easy. They want the skins anyway. We better get far away from where they'd expect to find us."

And that, at last, launched the whole of them out of the Trust.

When they stepped through the entrance, it occurred to Myche, now she thought about being hunted, that leaving the Trust would not be enough. They needed to vanish in a way that accounted for them vanishing. She held up her palm, and the little group stopped and gathered round. She told them things would have to look as if they had been dragged away, violently.

"By what?" Janice asked anxiously.

"Don't matter. If we set the cruiters against each other, and the twins – all the better."

They went back and stamped and rolled in the mud around the lake, then tore off bits and pieces of clothes and scattered these with other stuff anyone would think was valuable to them. They held each other and tugged to leave drag marks.

Brand paused at a bush on the way out, and Myche shouted to him, "Over here."

"Doesn't matter where I pee," he grumbled. "We're leaving anyway."

"But pee over here. Right here." She pointed to the clues of a scuffle they had mocked up.

He stared, and then his face cleared. "Right." He grinned. "They going think we frighten till it get 'way."

Only then did they actually walk out of the Trust, glancing behind to see if their cats were following. It was one of the things that had delayed the march. Time after time they had agreed to set out, but it was impossible to round up Hyyy and the others. Now, a couple of the children were crying bitterly and pleading to turn back. The ocelots refused to follow them out of their regular habitat, and it was only the thought of cruiters swooping in with machetes to round up cats and children alike, slitting and skinning mercilessly, that forced the band from the Trust away into the bush, the bigger ones pushing the smallies forward.

Not far beyond the gate, in a patch of bush that was still familiar to most of them, they almost collided with the oddest boy. Boy? He looked so much older, but thin as a reed, in a wild collection of clothes that included an oversize shirt with shiny spikes sewn all over it and a hat with a crown so tall and a brim so wide you would have thought it would swallow him up, but it sat firmly enough on his head. Yet nothing was as strange as the rubbish that poured out of his mouth when he started to talk in the most foolish rhymes while flourishing his hands extravagantly, about how he had got there. He pointed two fingers on each hand like guns and twirled them around, babbling about his marvellous parentage, his journey with all its dangers and triumphs along the way.

It just flowed on incessantly until Telma said, "Nah! This eejit going send we mad. We cyan't take this with us pon road."

But there was nothing for it. He had seen them and could report on them, Nat reminded the group. So the mamarracho had to go along.

"But shut up, for God's sake," Nat added. Then his eyes narrowed. "What you name?" he demanded inconsistently.

"The Man."

"Stupidness! We nah call you no *The* anything," said Telma.

"Robber Boy," Five Cent exclaimed. "Is that self."

"Robber Boy would be more polite," agreed the new addition to the group.

"Robot Boy?" Shant asked.

"Nah! Is Rabba Bwoy im say." And Telma emitted a long slow sour suck-teet.

So Robber Boy went along, swirling his big open shirt like a cape, gesturing with the hat and talking nonstop in a motley of nonsense rhymes and words that were strange to most of them.

"You understand he?" Brand asked Myche — quietly so as not to encourage him. "You think he making up them words too?"

"No," she said. "I don't know all, but is real words. I want to ask him where he get so much, but then he might never done talk."

"He not planning to done anway," Nat grumbled.

"To dung?" Josiahmarshall jeered at Nat's pronunciation, and Brand remarked that it had people around more annoying than Robber Boy.

Myche looked away, distracted by a swift movement nearby. One Thousand Eyes had tracked them through the trees and shrubs. Sometimes the cat disappeared, then crept to an overhanging branch up ahead, and after they passed underneath, jumped down behind them and slipped out of sight again.

Weird sort of ocelot.

5

MAS

AFTER A WHILE, HAVING NAMED THE newest member of the group, Five Cent seemed to feel some sort of duty to find out more and asked, "But where you really come from in all this bush? How you get here and you clothes not even wet? You walking long?"

The strange youth replied, "I'll tell you. Flew." He heaved an extravagant sigh. "If you only knew!" He swung around and walked backways a few steps before pausing, bringing them all to a halt. "First saw Pa on TV, and you'll agree he's big 'n bad, too busy for the likes of you and me. Dire. My ma, she flew out breathing fire, left me free to be me but instead – I'm *he*. Left me at large. I've studied Pa – the walk, the talk. In charge."

Janice scowled. "You can't be your own father."

"And too besides that don't help, because we don't know he anyway," Five Cent added triumphantly.

Robber Boy drew himself up so he was taller than all the rest and capped that by donning the hat with a flourish before announcing, "I fill spaces, break places, drag faces into grimaces of fear. No time for kings – unfair how they raise themselves up over the rest. I raze em down, faze em out. 'Cause I'm the craze – the blaze in which a new and greater Homeland flashes into being, foes fleeing before my face, the faithful unfolding in my grace. I am commander-in-chief, to be brief. If you oppose me, I am grief."

PART 2

JUMBIE ISLANDS

6

BURNOUT

MYCHE

Telma let off one prolonged suck-teet so close behind Myche that she jumped. "Is what that?" Telma demanded. "One young boy could chat so much old rubbish?"

And not that young either, Myche decided. Tall and thin with clear reddish skin and frizzy ginger hair, running his mouth about all kind of thing he do and who he know and where he come from. His mother was a model, he said – whatever that was – and she met his father on some trip. She grew up the little boy in a hotel room *in front a screen* (so he said, and who knew what that meant?). Then, when she tried to squeeze help from the father, he *de part . . . port . . .* anyway he put her out the country and must have sent the boy with her too.

Well, good for Robber Boy. In fact, big mouth Telma had to say it right out: "Plenty pickney find themself leave back, or else is them get drive out." Then she said she'd have thrown the little maaga beast out herself, but Nat insisted the boy had to come along with them.

Myche could only agree. She knew Telma was being extra miserable simply because she was afraid of leaving the Trust. Who wasn't? Janice had gone on and on about having to take Tiffney into bush. Even Josiahmarshall was too skittish, Janice protested, and Myche knew she

61

was right. It would be just like him to run off and lose himself. But that was just it: the first rule was to stay together. Besides the cruiters, there were Pwessus and Tweetums to consider, out there, with all the secrets of the Trust. They even knew about the museum huddled under its greenery. Even those who were usually willing to bend the rules could see that this time *no one* could be left behind.

....

Hours after they had added Robber Boy to the group and lost sight of their own lake, they came to another. Nat, the only one among them who was fearless in water, talked of wading in it to confuse anyone who might follow, but the rest were too afraid. Besides, Thelma reminded him that getting out of the water meant leaving deep tracks in the edge, just as they might when getting in. He bit his under-lip in embarrassment about having to be told something so obvious, but Telma added quickly that his plan would work when they got to a lake or river with rocks they could walk on.

"How come you don't mind water?" Brand asked Nat.

"I took lessons once, to strengthen my legs. And make my arms and legs move the way I want them to go. Together." After a while he added, "In the water I'm not like I am on land."

Together Telma and Nat led the rest south, along what they believed might be the safest way to the sea. Striking off west could take them to the shore where most of them had washed up, and for all they knew that might bring them in the way of the cruiters. Those who would have been sure of the way south were gone, and although Nat was the age at which Shine, Mitch and Celie had begun wandering far outside the Trust, those older ones had not wanted to drag him along on rough hikes. But now, as the day wore on, the children followed him without question.

Telma and Nat had made them use the trees when they could. Brand had showed what he figured out for confusing anyone who tracked them, by stepping from one bit of hard ground to the next, doubling back, zigzagging, and from time to time even walking backwards.

One thing they learnt from Robber Boy was the value of a hat, and they began to search out the broadest leaves and to lace withes through them to tie under their chins and keep off the sun. Now and then there were wide trees along the bank of the lake they were circling, and the smallies dipped behind the trunks to jump out, squealing, at the others. Josiahmarshall inevitably fell and once almost rolled into the water.

Once Myche looked back anxiously for One Thousand Eyes, wondering whether they had lost him, and a terrified flock of long-legged birds flapping off drew her eyes to him, where he basked in this new lake among the water hyacinths nearest the edge, almost invisible. He never seemed to behave normally.

He was solitary and self-contained. He looked lazy but was only pretending, eyes half closed, legs sprawled. But by now they all knew he was eternally alert, padding along silently or diving off the track when least expected to. Or he lay motionless, like now, in the water among the broad, thick glossy leaves and dreamy purple-blue blooms. He was too big to get tangled in the roots. In the Trust, Indira had tried to fish out one of the flowers for her prayers and given up in disgust at the trailing mess of feathery purple black. Long enough to tie up Tiffney, she had wailed. Indira's usual drama.

Not the cat, though. It would take a lot more than some stupid plant to trip him, even under water. He could drop – from the sky, it seemed – to fell an agouti, stunning it with his body weight before his fangs effortlessly pierced the skull. Then, when he had eaten, he seemed lazy and inattentive again, apparently unconcerned about the children's comings and goings.

The others kept looking back over their shoulders, searching the bush for their ocelots, but without a glimpse of them. Marilyn and Wikki still grieved along the way, for Hyyy, and Kyle bawled because that was what Kyle did.

The distance grew between the band of children and the Trust, but they were not yet in sight of the sea. Still, they had come further than most had ever been since washing up. Under their feet the ground smoothed sporadically to asphalt carpeted with yellow flowers that showered from high thick trees. A few fat drops of rain fell intermittently on a couple of the children who straggled apart. The others felt nothing and cried out that it must be bird poop Five Cent and Marilyn had felt, but soon enough a drizzle intensified to rain slanting on a light wind. They ducked under a spreading poinciana that had little foliage to protect them, and as the rain beat harder and more urgently, pounding, soaking, drenching and gathering force with a growl, they ran to look for shelter.

Now Myche felt asphalt underfoot most of the time, broken in places with grass shooting through, and, along the way on one side or the other, slanted tall metal poles with wires drooping in between. A few were straight, but most leaned, and some lay flat in the grass that bordered the asphalt.

The downpour drummed around them with a deepening base, and the sky darkened, driving them harder, until they found themselves right up against a blackened wall. They crept to a space with a fallen gate and moved cautiously inside. Myche remembered Shine telling her there were many of these places of fallen brick and twisted metal, scorched and empty. Long ago after Sonson and Daughts disappeared, he had searched those that looked safe with Mitch and Celie and found the odd treasure. More recently they had reported that there was hardly anywhere else to search that they could risk entering.

From under piles of rubble these bigger ones had occasionally dug up tins or packages of food. When Telma started to go with them to the nearer places, Shine had said there were other buildings further away, where the fire had not been as thorough. From one of these he had come back with as much cloth as he could carry.

At first he had always set off with Mitch and Celie. Later he took Nat or Telma on shorter runs, but he made them wait for him beyond the broken fence that enclosed the buildings. Telma grumbled, but Nat always said, "Chamo knows what he's doing." They had returned safely to the Trust with bowls, sheets of clear stuff that kept off rain, bottles of sweet dark drink, a tube of cream Shine said they could use on cuts or burns. He had found it in a box with instructions, but once he had read them he threw away everything but the tube so as to have space for carrying more.

A year or so after they washed up, Shine had dug out a couple books Telma had no interest in, and he reminded Myche she had once been able to read quite well. He said they must teach Brand what they could, for with each passing year, fewer and fewer of the younger children could read. Now she eyed with interest the blackened walls that had come into sight. *Books*? she wondered.

But these burnt places were unsteady. Nat said they could collapse without warning, which was why Shine had never taken him inside, let alone Myche, Brand or any of the younger ones – not inside nor even up close. Near as it was to the Trust, this place was unfamiliar to them all. Yet Myche decided it was good in some ways – dry, to begin with. And some of the walls had bricks that looked strong.

"Is only the wooden parts burn out," Telma said.

"Of course." Five Cent threw a withering glance that made them want to hit him. "Stone doesn' burn. You ent know that?"

. . . .

In the end, they spent weeks drifting among the ruins, sleeping deep inside the sturdy ones away from the rain, and tiptoeing into others to turn over the rubble for odd finds Shine or Mitch had missed in bygone raids. Here, Myche noticed that Five Cent developed an instinct for uncovering hidden treasure. Dragging a sack behind him, he would ease himself out from under a sagging entrance with a tin of biscuits, cans of some sort of meat, and even of something else that those like Brand and others who had come to the Trust when they were very young could not remember.

"Cheese," Myche breathed, taking the tin but warning him not to go back in.

She turned back to the sack to search intently through a tangle of mysterious implements and pounced on an odd gadget she recalled as something for opening tins, though she could not at first see how. When she got the hang of it, she cut up the cheese – which was orange. Odd. She cracked her knuckles and eyed it questioningly, because she felt sure she remembered cheese being yellow. But anyway. She shared out small squares for them to pack and carry along, although before night it was all gone.

One place had a cupboard, far behind a pile of rubble where the roof was falling in, and when Myche took her eyes off Brand, he dived in and grabbed an armful of stuff then rolled out again through the unsteady entrance as a shower of plaster and concrete rained down. He raced back to them through the outer door and flung his finds down triumphantly. Huge rectangles of cloth in different colours, hemmed around the edges.

"Sheets," Myche sang out, as more pictures of the past flashed back. And pillowcases too.

That was when Telma brought forth a medium-sized box with a handle and said she had found it days ago and kept it, although she'd seen no use for it at the time. Now she opened it up to reveal reels of thread, needles, pins and scissors.

"It was no point telling any of unnu," she muttered, to no one in particular. "You woulda just say leave it because it heavy."

But once they took everything out of the box and rolled its contents in some of the cloth, the parcels were light. They divided up the sheets, stuffing a few in pillowcases, and took them along – except for one pillowcase that Telma kept back. She slashed out holes for neck and arms from one of the cases and hauled it over the head of the scrawniest of the smallies who had been naked for the past few weeks.

"No point bawling," she snapped. "Watch, Bry. You whole back chew up with mosquito bite."

Bry dried up as a huge green gourd landed at his feet and split open, pitching out mush all over his toes. He ran to the tree and grabbed another calabash to hurl at his brother, Kyle, but then Wikki shouted, "Wait. We can't always find them ting."

That was true. Telma insisted they each cut and clean out one gourd
and made everyone set them to dry before taking up the pelting game
again. By the next day the whole area stank, and they moved to the
ruins on another road, carrying their gourds.

One of the smaller buildings revealed a box with long-necked
bottles. It stood there in full sight, but no one would have bothered to
lug that back to the Trust. When they opened one, Indira leapt back,
wrinkling her nose and mouth. But Telma reached for it thoughtfully.

"Rum good fe medicine," she said, passing it to Darati.

Darati tightened back the top and wadded it carefully with the cloth.

They sprang away as a building nearby rumbled and caved in with
a resounding crunch of concrete and clatter of wood and galvanized
roofing.

"I was just going in there," Brand exclaimed with a grin that appalled
and infuriated Myche. "May as well now, it's down already. Watch.
Part of it wide open. Nothing left to drop." And when the dust settled,
in he went, the others trailing after.

The open area was covered with shattered tile that they swept aside
to uncover a host of knives – long and short, pointed and curved,
razor edged and jagged. Almost everything else around here was
broken, though even more had been burnt. Thelma began turning
everything over roughly, pitching aside what she did not want. The
others dumped the forks and other worthless stuff, though Wikki said
to keep spoons. Darati held up a brutal-looking thing Nat said was
an ice pick. From under another pile, Darati drew a large round pot.

"Nah!" Telma exclaimed.

"Too heavy," Myche agreed.

Something caught Thelma's eye, and she scrabbled through the rubbish, filling one of her pillowcases till it bulged with small spiky stuff
that punctured it in places and smeared it over with dirt. The rest went
on quarrelling about the pot until Brand – who had wandered away,
as he often did during an argument – returned dragging something
on wheels. It was a complete mystery to all of them, a round, wheeled
frame with a cracked-up plastic bin of dirt and dried plant. But then
Marilyn came alive and insisted that if Brand managed to rip out the

plastic rubbish he was wrestling with, it would leave the metal frame with its wheels. That done, Brand snatched up Wikki's pot and fitted it in the circle, and Wikki threw in his knives and spoons.

"While we walk, ent they going jiggle bout and fall out?" Ananda piped up, but Marilyn said they could tie them down with vines or wad them with cloth, and Wikki added they could take turns lifting it over the rough parts. At that a howl went up from the smallies, but he scowled ferociously and they shut up.

Then, to everyone's surprise, Thelma put in, "Watch! Is one set a match me a find."

Quiet spread as it sank in that they had acquired not only a pot and spoons but matches. In the speculative silence, Chunks whispered that she had seen wild chicken in the bush.

"Bare neck, though," she added, "but don't that can still eat?"

"Peel-neck fowl is fowl," Telma pronounced. "Eat it, yes."

They went back outside the ruin to have a look, and a flapping of wings nearby seemed to confirm Chunks's report. Then a rasping cry made Ananda jump and clap her hands. Qua had caught up. The rest were happy for her, but Marilyn and Wikki exchanged glances of longing, still half hoping that Hyyy might follow.

Outside, the rain poured on, hammering leaves, tender shoots, drilling into the soil and gouging it away from roots, battering stones and scouring away crevices into channels and then spilling over those into widening streams. The sodden earth could hold no more and the water, refusing to be absorbed or contained, forced its way forward aggressively, trickles converging into pools. Gush by gush, churning, tumbling along the ground until an angry rush of water swept between snapped stalks and pulverized the yellow flowers that had been beaten off the tall trees in the last shower and gradually faded to brown. Then the mud itself started to flow, sucking at their toes as if jeering at them: *You are small and soft and light, just as easy to upend and sweep along.* And one by one, Zef, Colin, Kyle, Bry and the other smallies backed into the nearest ruin, so the older ones had to follow, and they hid there until the rain subsided and the water began seeping away.

Here, digging around in the rubble near the entrance, Wikki came upon a plastic bag with a leather case inside. It held papers, pencils and, safe in the centre, folded up, large sheets of paper with lines of print, a few larger and darker than the rest.

"Newspaper, ent?"

"*Guardian* paper," Five Cent announced importantly.

"Nah. *Gleaner*," Telma corrected.

The paper was clean and dry, the pages supple. Telma wanted it for wrapping another bottle or two of rum, but Myche said, "No. I want to see what it says." And she ignored Telma's long, disgusted steups.

Nat settled it by saying he would carry the rum, wrapped up, and Myche could take off the paper when she wanted to read it. But she should wrap it round the bottles again afterwards.

When she got the chance to read it, she had to go over and over trying to work it out. It was like a riddle. A set of riddles locked together. Something about air space closed. A whole lot about entry permits withdrawn and passengers turned back. *Further devaluation*, announced another set of large, dark print. *Fight in market over rice*, said another.

If Shine were here, he would have explained it. But the further they got from the Trust, the less likely they were ever to see him again. Foreboding set in heavy above her eyes, pressing down as night came on, hardening to pain.

Nat said, in his offhand way without a glance at her, "Once Chamo can get to shore he'll track us."

·········

After weeks in the shadow of the ruins, though, the notion crept up on them: Pwessus and Tweetums might lurk in such a place if they came upon it. The idea galvanized the children into gathering up all they could carry and burying as many signs of their stay as possible. But then they realized it was hopeless hiding the fact they had been there. They thought of the smashed calabash all over one of the roads, the charred patches where Wikki had boiled soup and all the signs they could never find again, let alone erase. And that spurred them to pack up quickly.

"Nah!" Shant turned away from the pillowcase Telma had stuffed with sheets and was handing over for him to carry. "I not toting no load. I look like bison to you?"

Robber Boy had already tied on his sack, and now he hoisted the one Telma held out, so as to fix it onto Shant's back. "If I can bear, you share."

"And who you?" Shant said, then caught himself. "*Don't* answer that." But he was too late.

The hat came off and swept the air expressively.

"Your worst fear: a new world peer. Rode into power not through property and breeding but through money and bleeding – your blood not mine. (I'm fine.) I am bender and breaker, shredder and shaker. I batter facts, tatter oaths, scatter friends, shatter foundations with a toss of my hair, strike of my pen. My voice is thunder – no stars shone to show me blunder into being."

"Is he voice I can't take," Janice moaned.

"How nobady ever strengle him?" Telma demanded. "And the set of lies dem. Samfie man. Must be rabba in truth."

Robber Boy acknowledged her interest in him with a bow. "I am the voice you heard before I arrived, the one for whom the mini-series was derived to loom out of the screen, knot this bad dream tight around you head, this bad dream until you scream, and stuff it (with you inside) into the TV – so you can't get out the box, undo the locks, sever the noise that annoys, but must writhe in there forever. I am the loud voice of the mad king on screen howling *off with his head*; and I'm the hand on the axe."

Mini-series? TV? Myche felt around cautiously in her mind. Then she allowed herself to ask him: "Where you get all them words, man? Book?"

"Look! Don't talk bout book. I dreamt dreams of life on screen, and screens I had of every sort, brought all the talk, hounded down words, rounded them up in herds . . ."

"Right," Myche said hurriedly, "got it." And she moved off.

"True?" Brand whispered, scurrying after her. "What are screens?"

"Just let it go," she said.

· · · · · · · · · ·

In the end it took hours for them to get themselves ready, and they had no choice but to spend another night, but by the next daybreak they were scuttling out of the Burnout, making their way downhill, where they expected to find a shore.

Nat watched the sun so they would keep south, and this time they avoided each maze of blackened wall and charred wood. Behind one of these ruins, though, they came across bushes flourishing with pigeon peas, and they picked off all the dark-speckled pods they could, stuffing them in the pillowcases on their backs. Telma had punctured each gourd under the rim and run a vine through, so they could tie them round their waists and keep their hands free.

"Full it up with the gungo," she told them.

Once they had left those bushes behind, they began reaching back into their sacks for pods and popping them open to squeeze the peas out into the gourds.

When the smallies began complaining about the hot sun, and stones under their feet, Five Cent snatched up a few peas and shook them in his fist.

"How many men on board?" he asked Kyle.

They gathered round laughing and guessing, and whoever got it right won the extra peas, until Five Cent said, "Okay. Game over. Or I wouldn' have no peas leave to eat."

But Nat scooped out half of his and handed them over without a word, and the game continued, so the smallies trudged along the scorching road without a whimper.

Around the next lake lay bare wet earth where the water had shrunk since the last rains and not yet risen back. They could do nothing about their prints but hope that rain would soon pound down heavy enough to fill and wash those away. They forced themselves to walk right into the water and make their way through the shallows along the edge till they came to a flat rock over which they could scramble back onto another asphalt path.

There was not a track to be seen, and Nat grinned at Telma, who said, "Is that same thing I was telling you."

This way was broad and open: it felt too unsheltered to walk along, and now the sun was so high it was hard to work out which way was south. Edging parallel to the path through the thin regrowth of bush, they came to a place where they could take almost any direction, and they began to argue. Brand swung up onto the branch of a soaring chennette tree and climbed on up and up till he disappeared. It was a while before he returned from his perch and pointed the way. But he looked odd, disoriented.

After an outcry from Telma, Wikki, Colin and Ananda about him having brought no chennette down with him, Brand steupsed and demanded whether they wanted to eat green chennette to tie up they belly. This shut them up. He explained that although the road they were to take would soon climb uphill again, it would dive steeply after the crest of that hill and run along the shore. Before that first slope there was a Julie mango tree weighed down with pink fruit. But at the same time, he fanned with one hand as if dismissing all of it. Myche had never seen him so agitated.

"What is it?" she demanded. "What else you see?"

But he would only say, "This way. You going find out for yourself."

After a while there was less and less cover, more scorched stone and twisted metal, clumps of melted stuff in which bits and pieces no one could identify fused untidily. Sometimes along with what was left of the asphalt lay piles of tortured metal and shattered glass, with a mess of burnt rubber showing from beneath. It seemed to them that a whole half of the island must have been burnt away. There were few mature trees left, and even the bush was thinned –

They halted and stared.

A vista opened up of enormous tanks and towers of blackened metal, twisted pipe. Nearby lay fallen trees that might have been uprooted and hurled aside by a force they could not imagine. Others, perhaps torched where they stood before toppling, lay by torn, collapsing fences of rusted mesh overgrown by vines. A vast blackened crater yawned in the earth itself.

What had done this? The question hung in their caught breath.

No answer came to them, and after a time they edged away, and then hurried on, stunned into silence.

7

SHIFTING GROUND

BRAND

THEY HAD TO HAVE WALKED MILES over the past four hours, and Brand's feet plodded forward automatically, even after the hard dark surface came to an end and they got onto short grass here and there between skimpy bush. After a while he saw the asphalt had cropped up again, and it was just as well, because the bush jutted forward in thick clumps. Sharp stems here and there between the grass pushed into his feet. The sun blazed down, but a few trees threw their shade over the warm yielding road surface. The others had fallen quiet, watching where they put their feet when they were outside the shadow of the trees, because the pitch was hot in places.

When the children had picked up mangoes from the ground and eaten those parts that were still firm, a couple of them felt like talking again. No one quite wanted to sift the mystery of the Burnout, because there seemed no natural explanation. And what other could there be? Brand could hear Myche, Nat and Telma agonizing over what might lie ahead.

At first Brand paid no attention, his mind darting between the different images of ruin behind them, but then the chatter dragged him in.

Indira's mournful voice always seemed to make every statement into a lament. "They say it have a b-black lake," she said, "with the asphalt self instead of water, and the cruiters does come and d-dig it up."

"They who?"

But nobody bothered to answer Josiahmarshall.

"For what?" Ananda piped up. "What use it have for a hard lake?"

"For the ships," Nat explained. "To stop holes. Keep seawater out."

"Hold on," Shant said, pointing at a hefty bunch of green fig, and Telma unwrapped her machete from its padding of leaves.

"Look —" Brand broke in. "I told you." A glimpse of grey blue water tipped with white.

The sides of the path and the overhang of branches crowded nearer, so they were making their way slowly, glad for the trees growing close by the road that followed the stony edge of the sea. After a nervous run to the shore, they drew back under the trees, and Wikki boiled the green fig in salt water. Five Cent said his mother used to cook chip-chip, little shellfish they gathered on the beach, but no one wanted to linger in the open.

"You bring your chip-chip, I cook it," Wikki said. "I ain' gathering nutten out there. Next ting something gather *me*."

After eating the fig, they went on along the edge of the bush, but sometimes the land turned them uphill, following an overhanging ledge. When the rocky surface widened again, Josiahmarshall broke away and ran ahead. Then he shrank back from the cliff edge and pointed over and down to what they had expected to be calm water in the centre of the bay.

What they saw was water churning, disturbed in two places. No, not disturbed, for it remained clear though no longer blue green. Wavering circles of pale grey, dark at centre gazed up at them — not like lids opening from slit to oval but like black points that widened at different speeds, to different extents, and turned as if they were not in sync. Each eye was ringed like an ocelot's, but with dark grey-brown against pale grey-white, and the eyes themselves were the blackest black of bottomless holes. Brand sank to the ground with the other children, squatting and staring at the sea, hypnotized by the eyes that wandered weirdly independent of each other.

"Food," Telma pronounced at last. "We have fe eat food before we fall down."

They tore themselves away and unpacked the green fig Wikki had saved. Then they had to wait – the smallies whining and the bigger ones growing contentious – as Wikki worked on the fig some more with another sprinkle of salt and a clove or two of garlic.

Wikki was frying up the boiled fig with the garlic and a few pimento peppers, when Indira passed him a couple okras she had yanked down along the path and Nat pulled an onion from his pocket.

"Piece of fish woulda nice," Telma said, "but it can eat just so."

It was afterwards Brand discovered the narrow stream hidden by giant leaves. Marilyn and Wikki had carried between them an extra bunch of green fig, so when Chunks pointed out crayfish under the rocky ledges in the stream, the children threw up a frail shelter nearby and settled in.

The next day they surprised a blue crab six inches across the back, with purple and blue orange-tipped claws.

"Why you didn't come out when it had fig?" Five Cent demanded angrily, and they tried to corner it, but it slipped away into a crevice.

· · · · · · · · · ·

Days later it occurred to them to get back nearer to the shore and see whether anything else had happened in the bay.

By now the grey rim of each eye had bulged and begun to grow up from the depths. Brand could see them clearly, even though the eyes were still beneath the surface of the water. Then a spray of foam hissed up, and below, a muddy swirl bubbled and was still. Then nothing more. The sea seemed quiet, until they noticed a brown current churning, lengthening and then widening to a swathe of muddy turbulence.

It was Marilyn who complained that the full blaze of the sun was on them and insisted on retreating to what shade the bush could offer. The rest followed unwillingly, stayed for a while but broke away every now and then to run back and study the sea, fixated on this drama. Meanwhile they ate anything they laid hands on without caring what was in their mouths, so it was mainly fruit, and they kept on needing to run and crouch in the bush.

"And now my bambam hurting," Kyle bawled.

Five Cent hushed him and got him to sleep.

Eventually Wikki agreed to keep watch while the others settled in, so at last they dropped into a fitful rest. Brand was aware of Myche close by, clinging to his foot, and though he had a feeling that should annoy him, it was strangely comforting. Just before falling asleep, he caught a glimpse of Wikki sagging against his tree and knew he was out too.

It was dawn when Five Cent's yelling woke them, and they sprang up, choking on fumes misting up over the ledge, stunned by the roaring of the sea – or of whatever was breaking from under the dark water. Before their eyes, a black-crusted shape like a broad snout bulged up, then withdrew again, hissing, under the water. Paralysed, they watched a hump of rock push up and belch smoke or gas into the air, then vomit gouts of mud that spattered down even as more gurgled up. A black plume of the gas billowed, towered amid the roaring and withdrew in a hiss of spray.

Unnerved, they leapt back under the trees, tumbling into the foliage. There they cowered until later that morning when the gurgling and splattering had abated. They stole out again and stared down at the water. Turbulent, muddy water sucked at the edges of a flat wet island where a few days before there had been clear sea.

Telma whispered she had heard of a lake, where she came from, that formed then disappeared then formed again. Sometimes it reappeared so many years after the time before that no one remembered, except for old people – but who listened to them? Then one eejit after the next would build a big house there again, only for the lake to rise and flood years later and cover their floors and furniture and sometimes their roofs with water.

She knew about this because Tourisslady had told them. Before meeting Telma and Darati on her way back to the cruise ship, Tourisslady had travelled across the island on a tour. In the little time she had with the children on board, she had talked of how the bus had turned off the main road to show visitors the lake with houses standing under the water, and others nearer the edge of the lake partly submerged, row boats plying between the upper floors of different buildings to salvage what could be found.

Telma said, if there was a landbridge perhaps it was made up of parts that came and went too.

The children camped near the cliff for days, afraid to climb down to the shore, had they even been able to find a path. They foraged for food, hacking plantains from a tree along the way and cleaning a couple fish Brand dragged from a pool by way of the latest trap Wikki had rigged up out of vines. They used Wikki's knives to scrape the fish, lighting dry bush with one or two of Telma's precious matches.

"Here," Telma said one day, handing Robber Boy a knife and pushing some plantains towards him. "You and Shant better set up house together, because except for unnu big mouth the two of you is one and the same: you fraid work. What you ever do apart from talk?"

He eyed her haughtily. "I have mined gold oil blood diamonds uranium, thrown up mansions of pink marble, black skyscrapers, torn down neighbourhoods and livelihoods (and I've elevated hoods) to spawn resorts with exorbitant fixtures and contentious mixtures of metallic glint, gilt mouldings and mouldy financing and carvings on their carvings. I am pure intelligence, a spawner of grand schemes, a deluder colluder intruder, ruder than the most extravagantly vulgar performer voyeur, the one who triggers a cancerous growth of money, devotion and defection of a playboy bunny. Behold my wealth, my ever-burgeoning health, my forthright stealth."

He handed over the plantains peeled and cut up, and Telma said grudgingly, "You really not as wutless as Shant, if you could only keep you mout' shut."

That night and for a few nights afterwards, they lay watching the sky, tracing patterns in the pinpoints of light from dancing candle-flies and pointing to where the great ocelot kept watch over them with its myriad of bright-bright eyes.

·········

Then came a cool clear morning when they felt able to go on.

First they crept back to the cliff edge and looked out. The new island had grown to a massive table raised above the sea – almost as big as the Trust, Marilyn said. It was very still but for puffs of smelly gas from the crater that had been the smaller of those two fierce eyes. Beyond, subsurface but clearly visible through the still water, was the larger eye. They could make out the centre of a huge peak just below the surface.

"Deeper than it looks," Myche insisted, "because – watch: no waves breaking on it." She wanted to believe, like the others, that this was the landbridge they were waiting on, forming just in time. But how would they ever get to it? And why would that further one rise and join up, as Marilyn was now insisting it would, to allow them passage to some other place? Why mightn't both sink again into the waves? Like that lake Telma spoke of.

Myche pointed to the edges of the island before them that kept on scouring away and reforming. "Is not even staying the same shape. How we know it won't disappear when we get there?"

"Or what about the sea?" Shant grumbled. "Next thing it break in and tear us out."

"Or what about if it only looks solid and . . . and is only mud." Wikki eyed it suspiciously. "What about sinking down and down into mud?"

"Well, this is no place to stop. We going on." Myche as usual, telling everyone what to do. "Not one of us setting foot on *that*."

Brand felt sure she was right, but he wasn't going to say so and encourage her in her bossiness. It was Nat, of course, who nodded and pointed the way west.

"And why we don't go the other way?" Shant asked.

Nat shook his head. "That way, it have partly nothing left, Shine told me. There were houses like in the Burnout and tanks and stuff, but it's all mashed up and whatever roads there were – all gone. Would be hard to pass, and we mightn't find food."

"Is true," Telma confirmed. "Shine say even the shore tear up."

They turned away from the sea keeping west into a dry, area with stunted bush, and in the hours that followed they found the ground more and more strewn with black shapeless lumps. As the sun rose in the sky, the ground blackened more and softened beneath them, and as noon approached, the asphalt grew hot under bare feet, so they made little runs from one patch of scraggy grass to the next.

Somewhat forlornly they concluded that this had to be the black lake, an expanse of asphalt interrupted by rock and occasional bush. Soon, though, they came across pools of water, of varying lengths and depths. Some they avoided, but mostly they tramped along the shallow edges so as to cool scorched feet.

Wikki reminded them that the leftover plantains would not last forever, and they agreed to split up into groups of two or three to see what else they could find and then make for a ragged stand of palms he pointed to in the distance. Nat and the others turned away, leaving Myche and Brand leaning over a pool – in which, by the most unlikely luck, small fish darted fearfully about in a shrinking prison. The murky mirror of the pool gave back the ragged bush nearby, a passing cloud, and their own forms, short and squat under a high sun, until a larger form blotted theirs out, and they whirled around to see a tall broad man in the carelessly bright colours of a seafarer rising up from the mound of rock and pitch and thorny grass directly behind them.

"I've been following you for days," he said.

Even in their terror they knew Shine's voice, although it seemed deeper than they remembered. They stared at him, taking in the rest.

"I've been waiting to catch you alone and to head you off from the asphalt. You can't go on." He gestured at a ridge of rock and clay. "The rest of us are just beyond, mining it."

Us?

"You have to turn back."

He crouched and hustled them along in front of him to a clump of thorn bush. From there he drove them from one cover to the next, rocks, tall reeds, a towering pile of asphalt, until they reached larger trees.

They ran along eagerly, expecting him to stay when they got to whatever safer spot he intended for them. He would stop and tell them all that had happened to him, explain stuff they needed to know, listen to the idea about finding the landbridge and advise them.

Instead he pushed them back to the trees almost roughly. "Get away from here," he said. "Get into the bush and stay there."

"Tell us . . ." Brand pushed forward.

"I said get back." Shine shoved them away, back under cover of the bush, and just as abruptly he was gone.

The disappointment crushed them. Myche too – Brand could see that. The relief of glimpsing Shine, the flood of hope – that he would tell them what to do, but mostly just the sight of him, alive – all-all trickled away. Brand scowled.

"Who cares? If he want to run off and lime with them cruiters, make him."

Only, the answer screamed in his head: *They did.* Whether Shine cared for them again or not. They needed him with every breath they drew. Each step without him was a risk, every night a quaking in the dark, and every morning – new questions that no one else could answer. Shine's had been the arms around Brand in a rocking boat with huge men shouting and slashing around them. Shine's shoulder to bury his face in, Shine's hand leading them through the bush, putting food in his mouth. (*Swallow this. There's nothing else.*) Shine painting Brand's face with silt and ash.

"Who need he?" Brand could barely get the words out in the strain of keeping that tremor from his voice. "I hate him. He get so thick with them now – he go hand us over to them next time. You think he have we to study?"

"Shut up," Myche said. Her voice was unsteady too. She was just as stricken. Then she said, "No. He wouldn't. He was just hurrying to make sure they wouldn't come looking for him and . . . find us."

Brand knew she said it just to make him feel better, but once she had said it, they stared at each other, realizing it was true. They squatted there, drained of hope, and in a couple hours, sick with hunger.

Shine found them like that, huddled in the shadows that lengthened

around them and mud-spattered by a downpour of rain. He gave them
the couple slices of bread and meat he had in his pack while he told
them about the ship he was on. Then he showed them the way back to
the others, talking softly and quickly along the way. He didn't know
where they should go, he admitted, but they were right to have left
the Trust and must keep out of sight whatever happened. When he
left them, Brand knew Shine was returning to the ship because he
could think of no other way to keep them safe.

They also knew that their journey over all these miles had brought
them almost in a circle. Continuing as they were going, they would
simply return to the Trust – if the cruiters didn't pick them off, for
they were now hugging the western side of the island. If the other
children found out, there would be an outcry to return to the Trust
and stay there. So Myche told Brand she would insist on turning
well inland and trekking north again before heading back to the
western shore.

By the time Myche and Brand caught up with the rest, the littlest
ones were whining from hunger. The older children shut up about
it, because they had learnt that complaining only made things worse,
but their insides growled louder than ever in protest. Everything was
too wet to start a fire, so they passed banana trees and looked away
because of the belly pains they had each experienced at some time or
other after eating the green fruit uncooked. The breadfruit were too
high, and Telma pointed out that even if they could have got at them,
they were as useless as the green bananas (which was what she called
green fig), because there was no way to cook.

As for coconuts, even if one dropped (and who would be waiting
underneath for that), how would they get inside it? Brand knew that
even Telma couldn't manage the machete accurately enough for that.
All around was food somehow out of reach or unmanageable, and
nothing could be done but to steups and turn one's eyes away. Myche
and Brand kept a prudent silence regarding the meagre meal they had
had from Shine. They were hungry again, in any case.

As it rained on, soaking their clothes and hair, running down their
faces, there was no need to wipe the tears, for no one could tell who

was crying and who was not. Which at least was something, Brand thought. He knew it was all Myche could do to stop herself from taking them back in search of the Trust, where they could shelter in the museum and dig up cassava behind it. Then his mind got busy with Nat. For he must know, he thought. Only, no. Nat had said he had never been south or southwest of the Trust, so perhaps he did not realize how near they were.

Later they were barely able to make out in the thick darkness an old shelter amid a tumble of foliage. It was only a roof of flat metal held up by a few rusty poles on each side, but they all clustered thankfully underneath. They fell asleep in their soaked clothes, but when they woke they were almost dry, the sun up and slanted in over them. A scratchy sound on top of the roof suggested something walking or stumbling along with an uneven gait. Kyle started crying right away, and that was a good excuse to push further along their way. But then a smell rose on the warm air, something dead and foul.

Eventually they reached the remains of a building, the upper floor fallen but the lower left standing. There was a huddle of large black birds on the top flopping in and out of what seemed to be an opening on top, and here the smell was so overpowering, no one thought of going inside to see what could be found.

Even when they had walked for half an hour or so along the road, the ghastly smell persisted, and another broken shelter along the way, with only a metal sheet for a roof, had something on top that they could hear hopping about. It was Brand who first summoned up the nerve to dart away and scramble up a pile of bricks to peer up at the roof, and he called to say it was a corbeau diving in and out to pick at something, but he could not see what. Shant caught up a stone and hurled it, but he missed and the ugly bird took off. Flap, flap, flap–flap, sail, wheel, flap–flap, sail.

The children hurried away from the stink, barely watching their path, and Indira squealed as her foot slipped into a crab hole and twisted violently. Then Myche had them tear off a bit of the precious cloth and bind that ankle tight before they could move on again, more slowly. By now even the older ones were crying from hunger, silently but openly. The tears washed down without any of them bothering to wipe them away.

They must have strayed west again after the turn inland that Myche had insisted on, because they stumbled onto a road leading north with glimpses of the sea opening up here and there on their left hand. Along their right ran a hill that had been cut away to leave a rocky wall with the grey stone split by black crevices and tufts of grass and sparse bush tumbling out of the sheer face. Then the wind swept something sweet and tangy to their nostrils, and even those who didn't recognize the smell rushed forward. The tree was laden, the underneath strewn with ripe fruit.

"Guava," Brand breathed, and in the scramble to collect as many as they could cram into their sacks while biting through the pale thin skins and spitting out what seeds they had managed to separate from the soft pink centre, even Telma neglected to shout, *Watch out fi worm!* It was as well that a mango tree turned up almost immediately afterwards and some scattered bushes with pigeon peas after that.

Only, as the hillside receded inland and the ground flattened and spread out by the sea, the bush and trees were black again, and piles of rubble and twisted metal rose up on either side. And now the wind swept in the smell they thought they had left behind, and it was worse than ever – so foul they had to cup their hands to their noses and take only what shallow breaths they must in order to breathe at all. They broke into a run, headlong, tripping and righting themselves, the bigger ones driving the smallest ahead of them and passing the remains of buildings they might otherwise have searched. The stench urged them away. There could be nothing from there that they could swallow. Besides, they were in terror of seeing whatever . . . whatever it was.

When the road forked, one arm headed west into other ruins that they could see stretching along the sea, while the eastern branch led away from the shore through high grass. They turned right without hesitating, inland. Then they slowed, rested, argued, walked again until they came to another road crossing that one, broad and flat, wider than any they could remember seeing before. When Nat glanced at the sun, he said that this road led straight north, and they must take it for a while.

A hazy mountain ridge rose far ahead, as their road cut through hills that scooped up and away from them on either hand. Recent experience of the coast road made it easier for Myche to convince them that they could afford to take their eyes off the sea for a while, so they trudged on, making only those frequent stops that naturally followed a feast of guavas and mangoes on empty stomachs.

At last the rolling hills opened out into a wide flat sea of lush green. The plants were fountains of long leaves and thick, mottled stalks, and Myche cried out in pleasure.

"What is it?" Wikki asked, but she simply dived off the road, shouting at him to bring the long knife.

It was what Celie had called the sweetlands, and looked just as Shine had once described it – miles of hard stalks they could peel and suck. He had brought a few pieces home for them only months before.

"Just cut one at a time, though," Myche insisted. "If we drag a set of heavy stalks along, it will mash down the weed and thing. Then anybody can see where it is we pass."

For Brand, it was vaguely worrying how orderly the plants grew, as if someone had set them carefully in rows, but perhaps these rows were from long ago, for now it was wild cane shooting up from old times, among high coarse grass and tangled bush. Weeds dragged at their feet, and Wikki said he was glad he had allowed Telma to wrap his legs against the mosquitoes. Little red-brown stems stroked them as they passed, but they seemed to be harmless, only spreading tiny half-circles of seed pods everywhere they touched.

A mound like brown sugar burst into frantic activity as they brushed near, and Wikki jumped away, almost but not quite in time.

"Ants," he howled, stamping and slapping his feet, and they all watched the ground more carefully as they went on. But the ants had crawled under the wrappings on Wikki's legs, and in no time his skin must have been burning like fire. Brand saw he was crying silently and nudged Myche.

She halted the group and shut Wikki up when he said he was all right. As she tore off the cloths, she shook her head. His feet and legs were red and swollen tight.

Telma brought out the cream. She had tried it out before, and it had worked well, except on Colin, who reacted badly to stings.

"Gi me um," Wikki said, reaching out.

"Move you hand," she said crossly, batting it away. "Nobady know what in the medicine. Next ting you put you finger in you mouth and you start choke."

"I don't suck finger," Wikki yelled.

But Marilyn insisted he wash his hands all the same, and she made him walk with her so she could watch him.

"Like she suddenly remember is her bredda," Telma remarked under her breath. "Better late."

After a while, when the burning subsided, they were able to distract him with little sticks of cane that Nat and Myche had managed to cut.

So at last they went along happily enough. They sucked cane as they walked, sharing the tales one or other could dredge up from memory about the sweetlands – of great machines, huge rats and enormous carts drawn by bulls. Some drew up vague pictures of sugar in little bowls or stirred into drinks, tales of the rum made from the same plant – so Thelma said – that had people getting on wild. "Must be that make them cruiters so dread," she concluded.

Wikki recalled a snatch of song from a story long fallen from mind and forgot the livid swellings on his legs enough to belt out a few lines. "*Yo ho ho,*" he shouted, till Myche reminded them that Pwessus or Tweetums might be anywhere. Listening. Wikki froze and stared around, but only a hawk wheeled overhead among gathering clouds.

Then something among the mottled stalks took shape and faded away again so swiftly that when Brand called out and pointed, there was nothing to see. Myche said he had imagined whatever it was, but an hour later Brand inclined his head towards the shifting stalks, and after that she grinned and called him *hawk-eyes*. A weight seemed to fall away from the two of them, because One Thousand Eyes was keeping track of them wherever they went.

It was easy to wander under the overcast sky, chewing cane and gathering the trash to tuck far down among the stalks so as to avoid leaving a trail. Nat kept an eye on the sun – so they would not circle out of their way again, he said. Then it rained, but only long enough for them to fill the gourds.

"Watch me. Leh we just stop here and live." Five Cent had been quiet for a long time, apparently planning it out. "Them plants tall so nobody wouldn' see us. Ent? We would see them first and just lie flat. We could . . ."

"We could shut up and walk," Wikki said, "and leave you alone to sleep in the cane with the ants."

"And the snakes," Telma added helpfully. "Or we could try get back to the shore and look for all-you stupid bridge."

"Shh!" Robber Boy said, and he was a fine one to tell anybody to be quiet, but he seemed so stunned that they turned in the direction of his finger.

And that was when they saw it swaying far above the cane, beside the only real tree they had glimpsed for a while – a long neck mottled like the cane stalks. No. Marked out definitely, in wide brown patches. A mouth tearing young leaves from a branch and savouring them with sloppy lips, and sleepy eyes under little knobbly horns. They froze, staring as the cane nearby parted, and they glimpsed long spotted legs splayed out and another neck, longer than the first, that had been stretched down for something deep out of sight in the sea of green and now raised up to gulp down whatever it was.

The older children broke into excited whispers about pictures some of them recalled, and Ananda squealed in delight, causing the two giraffes to take off, their strange gait complicated by the cane stalks. The children stood there watching as if waking from a shared dream.

"Africa," Myche protested. "I remember the books."

"But after this nah Africa," Telma objected.

"How you know?" Ananda objected.

"Nah."

After a while Josiahmarshall demanded, "So where this is?"

No one wanted to bother with Josiahmarshall – even Five Cent let it pass – but after a while Nat snapped, "WeLand," which kept the little pest quiet for a while. But it was just a name, not an answer.

They walked on in silence, pondering.

The cane fell behind them as they approached the river. It was a broad dark tumbling serpent of water that stopped them with such finality they would have lost heart and turned back. Only, Myche remembered Shine saying that Sonson had spoken of a crossing, so they followed the water for a while, more and more downhearted.

Then they came to the place and stopped to gaze at it in wonder – a solid paved way arched over the river, crumbling at the edges but wide enough for them to walk across four abreast, close to each other.

"See?" Ananda said. "It really have a bridge."

Marilyn steupsed.

Myche came to a halt and gave her a long hard look. "You are the one who bring up this landbridge in the first place, Miss Marilyn. You same one."

"But is you said we must leave the Trust," Marilyn returned, quick as a whip.

"No." Brand turned on her instantly. "Myche knew *she* had to leave. But we all talked about it, and everyone agreed to stay together." His voice rose as a rush of fury overtook him. "But you could always go back if you could find your way. Who need you?"

Nat said, "Done it," and Brand and Marilyn subsided grumpily.

"Just watch where you put you foot before you drop and land up in river-bottom," Telma ordered.

Myche's mind was clearly elsewhere already.

·········

The far side was unpaved and muddy, and it smelled of rot. Although they were past the river, the ground gave beneath them and sucked at their feet, each step raising a scourge of mosquitoes. There was no sitting anywhere there, so they kept walking while they pinched out the last of the pigeon peas they had found near the stink place and ate what mangoes they had left, even though they were overripe. They felt the pounding of hooves on the ground before the four huge beasts came into sight – water buffalo, their black hides crusted with grey mud. The children backed away as two more crashed forward, churning the soft ground with broad hooves, brutally long sharp horns sprawled wide and their heads swinging side to side as they thudded by.

"Bison," Five Cent whispered. Proudly, as if he owned the herd.

Then they were gone, uninterested in the bedraggled band of small humans.

As they moved on, they came upon wider pools with the areas between them so murky it was hard to tell whether they could walk through safely, and still mosquitoes billowed up. A picture of sheets blowing on a clothesline across a yard floated hazily back to Brand as he slogged on through the mud; but now these were mosquitoes sweeping up, clustering around the children's legs, arms and faces as they splashed along the edges of the pools. They tried to wave the pests off, but then Nat said they should hold hands in case some places were deeper than they thought. There was nothing to do but bear the pitching and jabbing and all the time that maddening whine.

The smallies tried to run, ducking in all directions, but the rest snatched them back. "It will be worse if you fall in some hole," Janice snapped. "I know we shoulda never leave the Trust." She had tied Tiffney onto her, and she crossed her hands in front, across the child strapped to her body, so as to hold Josiahmarshall's hand on one side and Ananda on the other.

"Here must be what Mitch used to call Little Wet," Nat said, scooping up Chunks and wearing her on his shoulder.

"Little? Nothing likkle bout this," Five Cent grumbled.

No one bothered to answer, but it was obvious to all of them that if this was Little, there had to be a Big. When Telma whispered it, Myche felt in her sack, slid out a paper and glanced over it.

"Shine leave a map?" Telma demanded, eyeing the paper sharply.

But Myche shook her head. "He mark it on the ground, and I kinda remember and draw it on the paper." She didn't mention his visits, although these seemed long ago now, and the last had been so short it hardly counted.

At first there was nothing to support the worry that had caused her to bring it out, but then she found an area to the east with the words *Great Wet* and groaned inwardly, tossing her head against another plague of mosquitoes. So much to look forward to.

"I bet it have snakes here," Five Cent moaned an hour or so later.

"Right," Telma said. "Or follow the river out to sea, and you might run into some eel instead. They have big eel can swallow all like you whole." She had been helping Janice to carry Tiffney, and was tired and more cross than usual.

Five Cent scowled for a while, but when that turned out to be useless, he shut up and pressed on as the ground grew firm under their feet. He was the first to see clumps of corn growing wild and shouted out to the rest.

When they had settled among the stalks, shelling and munching corn grains, Nat came over and eased himself down carefully between Myche and Brand. He was lean, and his limbs moved without quite the usual concord between them, yet not clumsily. He spoke with less ease; all the words were there but sometimes came haltingly.

"What Shine said?" He just threw it out, baldly.

They didn't want to lie to Nat or even refuse to answer, but no one was to know Shine had been in touch with them.

"I saw him," Nat insisted. "When I realized we left the two of you behind alone, I turned back. I see this man coming towards you and, well, then I saw was Shine." They were still silent, and he blurted, "You don't understand?" He paused and marshalled what he had to say. "Is me the cruiters coming for next. But they not going to want me to work on any ship. They won't think I'm worth keeping. Or selling. I have to know what it is I'm running from –" He broke off.

Brand nodded. The thought of Nat . . . thrown away . . . was unbearable.

Myche hesitated. "Shine said never to tell anyone, unless . . ."

". . . unless we had to," Brand concluded. And they had to, because the cruiters, as they called them, were what Shine termed pirates, and they were merciless.

But even that was a useless thing to say, because it made the cruiters sound as if mercy was something they withheld when actually it was something they had no notion of. There were all sorts of feelings the youngest and most untaught children had, Shine had told them, but those were not in the make-up of the pirates.

In fact, he had made Brand understand that the children shouldn't call them cruiters anymore, because real recruits had a choice. *Cruiters* was a word people had come up with when they were willing to work with the pirates and wanted to deny what they were. Others who lived under the threat of the pirates called them cruiters to hide the truth from themselves.

Brand and Myche told Nat how Shine had explained that the pirates had never experienced mercy and had none in them, but also, they had no fear. They lived in the knowledge that they had little time before them and must snatch what they could before their own end came. Brutally. Shine had flashed a grin at Myche and said that word looked both ways: their end came brutally and they would snatch what they could brutally. A steups from Brand made him get back to business. The point was, he said, the pirates knew death was upon them anyway, so they might as well share it out.

And no. He did none of those things. They needed him for an entirely different reason. He was their map man. He got together information like landmarks to keep a record of where they had been, so that they could always find their way back. Well. Not always. Brand remembered how Shine had winked at the two who watched him with dawning smiles. He could lead the pirates away if he had to, but he couldn't risk doing that often. Anyway, he drew their maps.

"Why nobody stops them?" Nat demanded, and Myche said, "That's exactly what I asked him."

Shine had explained that they had bigger and better ships than before, even though these were nothing compared to the size of the prey they went after – without a pause even to think it through. They had swarmed aboard a tanker with machetes, herded some of the crew into cabins and locked them in, tied up others and dumped the rest overboard – fast, fast. No stopping to sort them out, no reason behind who they chose to lock up, tie or dump. One man managed to send out a distress call before the sweep of a machete gutted him and he went over the rail. There was nothing to think about in that, as far as the pirates were concerned. What was important was plunder. They broke the safe, reboarded their ship and made off, leaving the tanker still ploughing forward at full speed. "Unmanned," Shine had said, as if he still couldn't believe it. Rocks, reefs, other vessels, whatever might lay ahead of the charging vessel never entered the pirates' minds.

"What happened to the tanker?" Nat asked.

They told him Shine had learnt that almost an hour had passed while a few of the tanker's crew got free and brought the ship under control. The pirates knew because the crew sent a further call. But no one answered. "Knowing the ship's location, who would?" Shine had said. "Anyone near enough to receive the call had more to gain from working with the pirates or turning a deaf ear to their victims." The wealth of nearby ports depended on a little deafness.

And now the ship Shine was on brought in more and more wealth to the port nearest of all to them. This freighter's original owner and crew were at the bottom of the sea. Not only was it what some people called a *phantom ship*, but the pirates had actually renamed it *Phantom*, bold and brassy as you please.

Neither Brand nor Myche shared Shine's account of how people who vanished in pirate attacks sometimes turned up again, cast up days later by the sea or stacked as burnt remains in a freezer, unrecognizable. Why make Nat feel hopeless about his chances if he were caught?

Besides, Brand thought Nat might escape notice and even – quietly there in the shadow of the bush – lead any number of smallies out of danger. And what if he could help Myche hide?

Brand thought of himself alone without Myche or Shine. Or Nat. It was not the first time that had occurred to him.

"I want us to come with you," he had said miserably, clinging to Shine when he stood up to go.

"Nah! You crazy?" Shine shook him a little as if to wake him up. "Watch. You have Myche. And I know you won't forget me, but from now on trust Nat. And take care of him when you can. I can't promise when you going to see me next. All I can – well, I try."

In no time at all, Shine had said, he'd be on another ship, because he did not *belong* anywhere. No one did. The next ship could be anything. The crew were already grumbling that they should never have let that tanker out of their hands.

8

BRUKSTONE

MYCHE

SUNSHINE SHOULD HAVE BROUGHT RELIEF AFTER the damp, but for Myche the heat and blinding light set off a headache. She gulped down extra water as Mitch would have commanded and was glad to lie about in the cornfield for another day as the rest ate and filled their gourds.

She could feel Nat's anxious gaze.

When he found a chance, he whispered, "Don't worry about all Brand told me. I would never let out one word about Shine."

"I know." She waved his words away. "Is just my head." Long spines like those on the prickly pear seemed to lance through and through it.

When they set off again, they came upon a broad road with thorn bushes jutting out on either side from an expanse of chickweed and burr-grass, with a little verven scattering small violet flowers in between. Here and there the bush on each side gave on shattered walls and heaps of rubble. The sun was going down at last, so they stopped and looked for somewhere to sleep.

Bush clustered round again, overgrowing the road, but they came to a covered way of rusted uprights with thin wavy metal sheets for a roof. It stood open all along on both sides and appeared to lead nowhere, from nowhere, but it was smooth stone beneath and protected above, so they squeezed close to each other beneath it. The stone was hard, though, even with their bundles under their heads, so they crept out again and spread what they could under a tree with thick soft grass around the trunk.

Myche struggled to sleep, but the night that had seemed blessedly quiet at first – then, too quiet – grew steadily busier, filled with troubling noises. First only the lightest of breezes sounded a faint flicking of leaf on leaf far above. Then a rustling of grass disturbingly near, a hurried swish of branches overhead that set her wandering what had disturbed them and whether whatever it was might startle something larger out of sleep and send it charging in. Then there was the moon.

She began to imagine, then feel sure she could hear the moon creaking apart the branches and straining pale fingers in between to reach down for her. An owl whooped maliciously, sending a shudder through her even before she heard the terrified squeal of some small soft thing in another corner of the dark. Not a far corner from where she huddled, curled tighter and tighter, contemplating what else prowled or huddled a matter of feet or inches from her own soft throat and belly.

Then it came to her that she had not seen or heard Brand for hours. How could she, in the thick darkness?

"Brand?" she whispered. But that only brought on a terrifyingly sudden and absolute silence. And if she called Brand and woke him, or got no answer, what good was that? If she got up quietly and tried to find him, she might wander away and lose herself. Then what use would she be to him?

She had been still for a while when the sounds of the night started up again. She wrapped her arms about her knees and listened to the whine of insects. Taunting, wailing, shrilling, drilling. She steupsed. Her thoughts were colliding, with a hollow echo that sounded like Robber Boy's rhymes. But she had brought him as well as Brand and the rest here, turned them from a group of abandoned children (well, even Robber Boy *was* sort of like a child) into . . . into what? The words tumbled in her head like rocks that might harbour slugs beneath them until these eased out into the night to chomp holes in leaves. Turned the children from the Trust into what? She sifted words. *Nomads, pilgrims, vagabonds.* To decide on the right one, how much did you have to know about where you were going? Or coming from? How many nights did you have to spend in one place?

Before dropping off to sleep at last, she thought vaguely that from then on she should take a stone from every place where she spent more than one night, a small one that would not weigh her down.

········

In the morning they ate whatever corn was left in their gourds and tramped on while it was cool, and by the time the sun rose higher, the sky was overcast anyway. Pushing on, they stumbled upon a pile of rubbish with a huge transparent bag filled with plastic bottles, and Nat said they must fetch out as many as they could carry until they found clean water to wash and fill them.

A few low-lying fields spread away, with white egrets stalking along with their odd dipping walk, necks bobbing, between furrows glistening in parallel streams of dark green slow water. Everything that sprouted on either side of the furrows tangled into bush now, whatever it had been before. In the midst of nowhere rose a small, oddly shaped building, somehow intact yet dingy, with a rounded roof on which some flaking gold surface remained and stone jars around, mostly upended and shattered. Overgrown grass with beige broom-like blooms waved all around it.

It was too small for them to shelter there as the rain started again, so they pressed on, wet and miserable, Kyle sobbing, and Colin and Bry grumbling about toting a set of empty bottles.

"Never mind," Telma said unfeelingly. "Soon as we find good water, you going tote full bottle instead." She wound a withe around the necks of four large containers and tied the cluster on her back.

What had been a faint shadow of hills now loomed ghostly through moisture, and as the children walked, these spectral hills materialized, darker against pale, ashen clouds. In between, two poincianas just ahead flared boldly in flame and gold. But apart from these trees it was a drab, damp day, and Myche shivered unaccountably, her thoughts blurring and a dull ache spreading along her limbs.

Her mind darted back to the green water and mosquitoes. That was behind them, but it still made no sense to rest here, where, all at once, roads seemed to diverge in every direction bordered by signs that told nothing – Bamboo 1 & 2, Coca-Cola, Revival Centre.

Robber Boy put on his hat with enough of a flourish for Telma to shout, "Nah!" Then she pointed two fingers on each hand like guns and belted out, "Sign say Maggi, sign say Flow – which is the best way to go? Even Rabba Bwoy don't know." And the rest howled in delight. Myche had to smile, but she could not keep it up.

A rest of a few hours made no difference. She got to her feet feeling worse than she had when she lay down, but the thought of falling behind kept her plodding on after them, taking in nothing along the way. The others stopped abruptly, gaping at the ruins all around.

Huge slabs, split and toppled. Towering piles of brick, and pulverized stone. Yawning cracks at the base of thick walls and radiating from blackened craters. Rows and rows of fallen concrete, mangled steel, asphalt, glass. The glass had rained down. Rows of buildings that must have been taller than any trees – what the older children now vaguely recalled as . . . a town. A city. "Must be here Shine and Mitch called Brukstone, then," Nat said. Staring at the pockmarked walls broken and strewn along the gouged roadways, Myche raised them up again in her head. High buildings, huddled close, and between them streets, blaring cars, trucks and buses. The scurry of people. Dressed.

"Cloth," said Myche. Sweeping back into her mind were the endless possibilities. "Remember jeans?"

"Towel, bedsheet, housedress," Telma added.

"Sari and cushion cover," Indira sang out. "And curtain."

Nat said, "Cassock, jacket and tie, camouflage shirt and coverall."

Brand of all people added, "Evening gown."

The dense ruin around them brought back the variety of buildings – houses, schools, offices and stores. Malls. A parallel universe where things that could have gone differently had not gone differently.

Myche shot a look sideways at Telma and saw it was the same for her. And Janice inhaled sharply, trying to covert a sob to a cough, but her eyes were streaming. Nat turned his face away.

They walked on, speechless. On and on. All was broken now and, on the seafront, walls and mangroves were blasted so the waves had eroded the shore, and a few concrete structures were tumbling into the water.

It was not like the Burnout they had left weeks ago. It may have been more like those ruins in the stink place, had they gone further there to look. Here, buildings were not just burnt and crumbling: they were blown apart, walls crumpled to shattered brick and splintered wood, offering little shelter, especially near the shore. After following the seafront for a while they met a wall of coarse thornbush that had grown up through the rubble and they turned inland, walking down the centre of a wide street. Wikki reminded them of the finds they had made in the burnt place to the south, and they went further along the street looking for somewhere less shattered, with perhaps a little left over from whatever life there had been before. But if anything had survived for a while, it had since been cleaned out by others.

Others? Not a sign of life but for the odd cat that crouched hissing, then leapt aside. More and more of those, strangely. So at least probably no rats, thought Myche.

. . . .

Nat turned them along a road past which they caught sight of the mountains again, and in an hour more they came to a wide space. A park in the middle of the city was overgrown with sedge, its rusting stands given to the birds. Beyond, trees blossoming with exquisite puffs of pink and curls of yellow and an expanse of low bush that was now a playground for squirrels, a flat space opened out inhabited by huge machines that Nat said reminded him of something he called an *amusement park*. Indira cried out, yes, she remembered something like this where she came from. All around her, where she had lived, everyone seemed as poor as herself. Then some discovery brought sudden wealth and new pastimes, and a place like this opened up for a while.

"What happened to it?" Marilyn asked.

Myche had wondered, but her tongue stuck dry to the roof of her mouth and her lips were sore.

"Don't know," Indira said. Someone had said that other people had taken over the wealth of the country, bought up property that should never have been sold. She stood, looking up. "Vish and I rode one like this t–together."

A great wheel, with seats. Beside it, a round stand supported its circle of smiling creatures with painted saddles, forever still. In Myche's head it turned in time to tinkling music that amplified in her mind with a metallic echo. Not far off lay a huge spiderlike thing with boats at the end of each arm. Rough grass waved tall all around it.

The sun had come out again in full force, beating down hard until it throbbed hotter, more brutally inside her head. She wished Five Cent would shut up, going on and on about how his father had talked while he rowed – to keep their minds busy, his father had said, so they kept quiet in the boat. Five Cent told them how his father said things used to be, near those very stands, and the children could glimpse through the story the people of Before – gyrating bodies, bouncing, jiggling, bending then throwing their heads back to bawl out a chorus, their faces contorted as if in pain (but it was a sort of crazy happiness), the smell of rum, sweat, corn soup, man peeing on the roadside, the choking smell of traffic gone solid, mixing with that of rain on hot asphalt, and fry chicken. Ent? Five Cent asked Robber Boy, who nodded – without a gesture, even without raising his face. Not a word.

"Traffic," Janice murmured.

Five Cent said his father had turned the boat and was taking them back to the island they had run from months (or was it years?) before, because it made no sense ketching you tail in someone else country – better you ketch it in you own. Then his father had begun to row faster and faster, like he was mad. "We land," he had said. "Best we go back and dead there." His father had chattered as he rowed, and rowed and rowed wildly till he collapsed, and after that they had drifted, until the bigger boat pulled up . . .

Here they were in the overgrown flat land, not an hour's walk from the vast jumble of scorched and tumbled stone. The children's voices rose, each clamouring above the others' in search of answers. What and how and why? Janice's and Wikki's voices pounded in Myche's head, and her thoughts bashed against each other, setting off shock waves of pain. When they found a dark hollow in another pile of burnt wood and concrete it was a relief, because the air seemed clean on a strong breeze gusting in. They shoved aside some of the rubble to let in more air, and the draft raised stuff from hidden places, strange feathers and glitter, then tiny round shining disks, thin like fish scales. And where the light came in and glinted on rolls of material stacked along the wall, they saw there was cloth covered in the little scales of gold, silver and metallic green, and the cloth was falling apart and letting its scales loose all over the ground.

"Sequins!" Only Nat recalled the word, but a few had seen them before.

By the time it occurred to them that they might find rolls of good material in such a place, the smell of rotting cloth rose up, choking, so they had to get out, back amid the litter of brick and fallen plaster.

We have to leave this place where everything has stopped, Myche thought. Somehow she could not bring the words out, but the need gathered weight and impelled her forward, although her legs felt like crumbling. We have to get to a place where things can still happen. But she was beyond forming the sounds to deliver the command she could still feel pressing up, and as the rest overtook her and trudged on and on, she tottered after.

"This is where the giraffes came from," Nat said suddenly. The sign at the entrance to the zoo was still there, and Nat read well. A notice explained that the authorities had freed the animals, except for the tigers and others for which "more extreme measures were required."

"So is not Africa in truth." Josiahmarshall's voice trembled in disappointment.

Janice explained. "He had a book, *Animals of the African Plains* – with the pictures."

After a while, Josiahmarshall asked, "Where this is, then?"

"WeLand." Five Cent raised his shoulders, puzzled. "Like you doesn't listen."

Myche felt vaguely thankful that the elephant she had glimpsed wandering the savannah forlornly might not, after all, have been brought on by the fever.

9

THE ROAD NORTH

DARATI

FOR DARATI, THE WORST OF IT was that the world had fallen apart so easily.

Suddenly little black rectangles with white spots dappled her mind. They had belonged to a man in her mother's house, and she and Telma were never to touch them. Only he was allowed to play with them, at night with his friends, slamming them on the wooden table her mother would have liked to keep polished. Loud rough friends who smelled of rum.

The girls hid when his friends were there. Their mother said, "Get out the house and hide till you see me come out fe you." She gathered up the little black and white tiles and put them in their box, where the man could find them at once without flying into a rage.

But in the morning when he slept, snoring heavily so they could keep track of him, Darati and Telma would get the box out and build towers or set them out standing one by one in line, the flat sides facing each other. When they were all in place, she or Telma would touch just one, gently, to watch them ripple down.

Now as she looked around, it was as if all that had held the world together had been wishful thinking, and the great cities of picture books in school (she had loved school; it was a refuge), even the city she had lived in a long time ago (unless that really was a dream), had been lightly balancing in place or keeping upright as if each part had been put to stand on its own with nothing to keep it up, and with a breath everything had toppled, flattening whatever had found its way beneath them and sending a shudder on and on through anything else left standing.

It had seemed over the last couple years that Telma, Shine and Myche would be the pieces to stay standing. Then Shine was gone.

When Myche fell down on the asphalt and lay still, Darati ran and turned her over, for she was a taller, more heavily built girl than Myche, though a year or so younger. Then she jerked back her hand in shock and leaned in to see her face. Myche's skin was burning hot and her lips cracked, parted so Darati could see the tongue looked odd. Dry, that was it. Tongues never looked like that.

Josiahmarshall piped up. "She dead?" And the rest stopped and crowded round in alarm.

Brand fell on his knees beside Myche and shook her, but Darati caught his shoulder and pulled him back. She put a hand under one arm, and Brand, Nat and Telma took the other arm and the two legs and got her into the shade. Then Darati found that Myche's water bottle was dry and pulled out hers to tip a little into her mouth. Myche gulped automatically, and her tongue looked better at once. Nat glanced up at the sun and said they had sort of circled through the ruined town and might be coming out of it again, further north.

In a while, Myche opened her eyes and sat up. After a little more water, she was able to stand again and walk on slowly between Darati and Brand.

·········

As the road curved northwest, Darati could see it was driving them towards hill and forest. What shore there was narrowed against rough rock, and they could only follow it by looking down from a track that led uphill. Myche cried out and pointed, then whispered that she had seen One Thousand Eyes dancing on the water's edge below, back and forth as the waves came and went. Her eyes were open, but it sounded more like some sort of dream.

Further on, they came to a crevice in the hillside where a roof had formed by branches falling across the top, and inside was cool and relatively clean but damp to one side. Myche had sat down at the entrance and would not answer anyone, even Brand. She turned her head this way and that. Looking for someone? Darati wondered. Then she thought, Myche must be trying to work out where she was, or even just to find a position for her head that she could bear. They picked her up again and followed the cleft that sloped further up into the hillside. When they had put her down and examined this new shelter, Indira cried out, "Water!" And true enough a narrow clear stream of water seeped in through the rocks on one side and then out again. Telma set the smallies to wash and fill the bottles, and Wikki said everyone must clean out their gourds and keep them only for food.

Nat collected all the cloth they could find to push under Myche, because she was twisting about on the ground and bruising herself. Then Darati realized that although Myche cried out sometimes and muttered a lot in between, she did not answer anything the others asked. Her lips were blistered, and her tongue looked dry again, so Brand poured water into her mouth. Of course she choked, and Darati had to push Brand away and roll her over so the water came back out.

Darati stayed then, putting a few drops at a time into Myche's mouth, and she began to swallow, bigger and bigger sips, so Brand understood and took over. But with his quick thoughtless movements he tripped and spilled it over her face – which was good, for she gave a groan of relief and smiled. After that he could be depended on to sop some on her every now and then, and eventually she stopped tossing and seemed to sleep.

For days Myche slept and tossed, and swallowed the water they dripped between her lips, and slept again.

. . . .

Three days later, she woke up properly when Darati had turned her over and was washing her back. Then Brand helped Darati move her across to a dry spot and cover her with a sheet, and they sopped her forehead with a few drops of the precious rum from the Burnout.

"You getting better?" Brand asked, and she nodded.

"Cool here," she whispered.

She seemed happy on the soft pad they had made for her on the flat stone, her form barely outlined under the cloth. She was thinner, Darati saw, though not thin enough where she needed to be.

She sniffed, and Darati realized that for the first time in days, Myche had caught the smell of food. Wikki was just outside churning the contents of his pot with a big spoon, and her face turned to him and then to the riot of green outside. Gradually life seemed to be seeping into her again, the world edging back layer by layer as her eyes searched it out. Darati felt it coming back to her too, in tinier amounts, raindrops flowing over the slippery tracks of snails, on fallen leaves, on moss, on thick roots, in soil, on clay, on bedrock.

Brand had hardly taken his eyes from Myche over the three days, and now he grinned at her and began a story the others had heard several times, how he had caught a chicken in the bush and stolen some of the salt Myche hoarded in her own bundle. He said how Darati had brought out the pigeon peas when they thought no one had any left, and Wikki threw in a pepper he had been carrying, drying up in his pocket. Five Cent still had a handful of the corn he had shelled off. Best of all, Thelma put in, she had found cassava growing on the hillside and an okra tree.

Only then there was an outcry, for how could cassava and okra be best of all where a chicken was involved?

"You clean it good, though?" Myche's voice came out with a little croak, but urgently.

She clearly suspected that Brand would have been slipshod where cleaning anything was concerned, once she was out of the picture. But he insisted righteously that he had cleaned it better that she could have.

Every time Telma said it smell fresh, Five Cent objected, "Nah, is not fresh."

Brand had washed it again, thoroughly confused between the two of them, until he discovered they both meant that the chicken smelled clean. And anyway, he added, nobody wasn' forcing her to eat none.

So Myche sat up hurriedly, shuffled forward on the pad of cloth and held out her gourd for Wikki to fill.

That night they lay about with the empty pot inside the entrance, the wood still glowing just outside, and, closer inside, the clean-sucked bones scattered on the ground between them. Wood gathered for the next meal stood stacked along the wall. The sheen of Telma's skin on the arm against Darati's gave back a soft gleam where the moon penetrated the velvet darkness of absolute night in that fissure in the rocks under the deep bush. An orchestra of frogs hit soft but echoing notes, *pling, plong*. Music with a tune one couldn't make out.

"I remember a music something like that," Myche whispered, and Darati listened more carefully to the notes echoing, high strident and soft tremulous, a mellow pulsing *plick pong-ong-ong plick plululul*. Her head filled up with the phantasmic tremor of note after note, Myche nodding beside her as if her head no longer ached.

Perhaps because she had slept so long with the fever, Myche drifted in and out of sleep. Then she woke Darati with a jolt. An unusual sound, a deep, breathy growl. They both sat up abruptly. Now another sound came from a different direction. Darati searched the darkness and picked up the cluster of shadows at the entrance, and pointed.

When Myche shouted, the other children sprang up instinctively, reaching for anything that came to hand, the stick for poking the fire, the heavy pot spoon and the long knife they had used to chop up the chicken. They yelled threats till the entrance cleared, and then huddled together once more, watching the dim opening. Soon Darati could make out the shadows gathering again noiselessly, then a head outlined against the faint light.

"Doggie," Josiahmarshall called out happily. "Come, boy. Let's give them the bones."

As he started forward, a rough growl and flash of bared teeth halted him. Dogs, yes. But not pets like those some of the group remembered.

"Wild." Nat barely breathed the word.

Their eyes glittered with hunger. One went down on its belly and began inching in through the narrow opening. Wikki hurled a bit of firewood, and it leapt back yelping. But the pack crouched and padded around just outside, ears cocked, eyes shining, a tongue slapping greedily around open jaws. Only the hot pile of wood glowing to one side of the entrance seemed to prevent them pushing in.

Brand drew a thin stick from the stack against the wall and told Marilyn to light it, but she reminded him it wouldn't catch just like that. They had had to get a heap of dry bush going before Wikki had got anywhere with his fire. What about the cloth? Wikki demanded – and when she protested, he said the cloth would be a fat lot of good to them if the dogs got in.

"But cloth going to burn up so fast it wouldn't make sense," Janice said.

Before anyone could stop him, one of the smallies – Bry it was – scooped up a set of bones and pitched it towards the entrance, where a few tumbled beyond the fire towards the dogs.

"No!" Myche snatched back his hand, but the damage was done.

The dogs had leapt at the offering, snarling and snapping at each other ferociously, and now they darted their necks in for more, eyeing the rest strewn between them and the children. The largest began slouching forward. Wikki grabbed up a small log and pelted it.

"Why I don't just throw you," he shouted at the quivering Bry, who started bawling, until Robber Boy gathered him into the folds of his oversize shirt and said, "Hush, you going get them more wild."

Darati registered vaguely that it was the only normal thing they had ever heard him say. But the folds of his shirt, the talk of cloth – something prodded her brain.

Cloth. Marilyn ripped off a strip from the ragged edge of a sheet and grabbed up Brand's stick, really a long hard stalk from some huge leaf or flower, and tied on a bit of the precious cloth, then she gouged a hole at the other end, fitting in a pointed end of another stalk and tying that on, then another, one long bit after the next. But it sagged, so Wikki hurried to splint it with a few hard straight branches before pushing the whole rod towards the entrance, till they got the front piece with its flag of cloth into the glowing pile.

Nothing happened. The glow was dying, and the pack at the entrance grew active again, paws dancing forward and back impatiently, eyes on the bones inside and the children beyond. Muzzles quivering at the scent of warm flesh beneath flimsy fabric, at the smell of fear.

Cloth. Almost without thinking it through, Darati tore off her dress and wrapped it around a short, heavy block of wood on the ground, and there was Myche staring at her with pity in her eyes, as if Darati's mind were coming completely apart at last. Shivering more with terror than the night chill, she felt her fingers stiff and awkward, but she managed to grab the bottle, unscrew the cover and splash rum on the ball of cloth with its hard wooden core, and with all her might she flung the rum-soaked package at the glowing pile. Her heart plummeted as it fell short, but it tumbled on. *Whoosh*, and the flames leapt up.

This time the dogs fell back yelping, and in an hour or so, the long sticks the children had pushed and wedged into the flame had caught. They could wave the rickety torches at any of the dogs that gained courage to creep forward again. And that was how the night went.

When it got light, the dogs drifted away, but not far. As soon as the children's terror subsided, there would be a scuffle, a pawing and scratching around the entrance, and greedy sniffing. Although Wikki and Nat kept the fire going, that did not solve the ultimate problem of getting out for food let alone making their way on. They had agreed the evening before that now Myche was well enough to walk, they would pick up the coast again, but that hope vanished in the urgency of pushing their dwindling stock of dry branches toward the fire.

Later, the rain swished down again, water flooded around the entrance, put out the fire and soaked the wood once and for all. When evening returned and the dark gathered, the lean forms pressed forward eagerly. The smallies began to cry, and the dogs grew visibly more excited and bolder. Not even Wikki's threat of picking up anyone who cried and tossing them to the dogs made a lasting difference, for eventually, one by one, the youngest succumbed, raising a wail of terror that heightened the dogs' frenzy and drew them on snarling and snapping.

What would Shine do? Wedged between Myche and Telma, Darati searched it out, seeing him painted with mud and ash for a raid on the ocelots; and strangely, as if the two girls were thinking along the same lines, Myche hissed. The others took it up, not sure why, but the collective hissing between the narrow walls confused the dogs, and those in front shied back, sending the ones behind in retreat beyond the entrance.

Then, another noise. Above the wailing of the smallies and hissing of the older ones, and the growls and yelps of the confused dogs, rose a deep grunting, almost a coughing that ran together into a roar, and outside the yelps thinned to sharp squeals drawn out to one prolonged scream, and then another. Suddenly they were all gone, the dogs bolting off into the night.

The children crushed close, clutching each other in a tangle of arms, dreading whatever might come through the entrance next.

But nothing did.

In the morning, Darati looked out to see two dead dogs, one so brutally slashed that when she pointed them out, Myche made the older ones gather branches and leaves to cover them from sight for the sake of the smallies. Telma got Shant and Marilyn to empty, shake out and refill the bottles from the stream in the shelter. Then they packed up Wikki's trolley and made to set off while it was still early.

Just outside, Darati, close and watchful at Myche's shoulder, stopped suddenly and squeezed her arm. In the mud from the night's rain was a muddle of dog prints and one other – a heavier, well-padded paw.

"But that couldn't have been no animal," Brand whispered.

Just as well he talked softly, Darati reflected – no point setting off the smallies again.

"Why?" Myche demanded. "You didn't see the print?"

"One of them dogs," he said, "when I was covering it up, I saw its head. It had a hole in its skull like, I don't know, like someone drove in that ice pick."

"What?"

"Remember the thing you called an ice pick in the stuff Wikki found? The other dog was just ripped up as if an ocelot had got a 'gouti or something. But this one had a hole in its head as well."

Myche quickened her pace, and they headed away up the rocky hillside, but she looked satisfied rather than afraid.

Nearer the crest of the hill, the ground got harder and drier. From there they caught sight of the shoreline and followed the edge as far as they could but with less and less hope of seeing anything leading away from it across the sea.

· · · · · · · · · ·

Over the next two days, the land turned them in towards the bush.

"I hate this," Shant muttered resentfully. "Tree trunk and vine going on forever."

"And we had all those choices, ent?" Janice was not enjoying it but knew it couldn't be helped. "Where you think we should be?"

"I don't know bout you," Shant said, "but I shouldn't have been allowed to leave home to holiday in a place that was smaller and more helpless than where I came from."

"And just where should Your Majesty have gone?" Janice demanded. Shant was getting on nerves that were oversensitive to begin with.

"Obviously the family should all have gone together – wherever," Shant responded grandly.

Brand was tired of him. "Homeland, right? And who there want you anyway, you goat?"

Robber Boy took over firmly. "But when some misfit outside takes a boat (can't even float), toting their spawn along (no pride), hitching a ride in some bus, towards *us*, then that's all. We throw up a wall. Next thing you know our towers 're blown up, waves of cowerers from sick-soul countries lapping on our shores. Nope. Not through our doors. *These* are the threat; fret about them. Forget truths twisted, facts resisted, women mauled, climate change so-called, denied. I decide, deride, bestride the earth I have it in me to destroy. Revoke the air and sea across the globe. That's *my* abode."

Brand grabbed Myche's arm and pressed forward to overtake them all and get out of earshot.

"No," she said reluctantly. "Next thing we get separated. You can't tell what next Josiahmarshall and them might do."

She signalled to make them swerve, forcing their way back for a sight of the shore. Then Myche asked where Kyle and Bry had got to, and Telma started calling, but neither answered. Five Cent ran back and forth shouting, and Nat sent Brand clambering up a tree, but neither could see anything through the thick bush. Wikki said the two smallies would come back for food, but Telma pointed out that they weren't children who liked to eat. Half the time Bry wouldn't swallow anything unless you stopped everything to play some game with him. Nat grew silent. Myche looked ill again, and Darati felt her forehead, which was clammy, but concluded all that was wrong with her was fear and grief. Myche whispered to her that she didn't feel able to go. Her feet . . . wouldn't.

For hours they searched the bush nearby, then made their way back along the cliff. Nat lay on his belly and peered over the edge but saw nothing. In the end they spent the night.

The next day they walked on, dispirited, shouting again and again for Bry and Kyle. Along the way, Nat, Janice and Indira gathered christophene from vines that ran wild over the hillside. Then they all stopped, wondering whether they should turn back in search of the two or if they would only miss them in the bush. In any case the shadows were lengthening and now the whole group was reluctant to head deeper in. So they spent the night again.

On the second morning after missing the children, Myche announced that they had to move on some time. From this point, the way that seemed least overgrown lay downhill and swung left, perhaps nearer to the shore. Whatever Myche and Brand said, the rest were scared of going forward in the dim forest and meeting whatever had killed the dogs. And how would they find Bry and Kyle in there anyway?

"What if your weird monster ocelot ate them?" Five Cent asked helpfully.

"No," Brand cried. "He wouldn't." He shoved Five Cent savagely.

"Shut up," Myche shouted, so loudly the others fell quiet. "We have to stay close together, so we don't lose anyone else. And don't chat stupidness that makes things worse."

To Darati's relief, she had taken charge again. Myche at least was a wall that had not fallen permanently.

They trudged along wretchedly with Nat dropping behind and then breaking into an unsteady jog to catch up.

Myche slowed down and said, "I don' know where we hurrying to. We could just as well be leaving the two little pests behind. Nothing makes sense."

"Unless a set of us go on as fast as we can and the rest wait behind," he said. "But then, we mustn' split up."

After a while, they convinced themselves that the children were safe and waiting somewhere ahead and, anxious to keep going, they hurried on.

From there on, they all bunched closer together as they moved forward, swerving into the bush for shelter from the sun. They made a new set of hats from smooth wavy-edged leaves they had found deeper in the woods, then, after a while, returned to look out from the high shelf of rock. On one detour into the trees, they found good clean water breaking out of the rocks, and Darati gave Myche a little push towards it.

While the rest filled their bottles, Myche drank all she could. It meant she had to stop to dive into the bush every so often as they went on, but nobody cared.

A feeling swelled over them all – Darati felt it and sensed it in the others – that they were caught in a sort of current carrying them on and on, with no harbour in sight. The bush whispered to them that it was all there was in the long run, and they began to feel it crowding forward, reaching for them, lurking above or throwing fitful patches of shadow that flitted about. The sunlight broke through erratically, in painfully bright jabs between the close, almost stifling dimness.

And then, One Thousand Eyes posing off on the tree. Just so. Where the trunks towered up thicker and taller than any the children had met before, a mossy limb curved out over the way, and there he was watching down. For days they hadn't glimpsed him. The way leaves moved against the sunlight that peeped among the branches, the shadows shifting elusively, there was no telling whether the other children had made him out, but Darati caught Myche flashing a furtive glance around, and Brand nodded. The cat stared straight into his eyes, then hers. He never looked at Darati. Then he dropped his head and appeared to sleep.

"Like he waiting there for us days now and he tired," Brand whispered to Myche with a snigger, and she nodded.

Not that the cat stayed. He left again, suddenly as he had come. Now that he had grown, he seemed to hunt differently. First he had caught agouti and manicou, but now Darati noticed him carrying off a funny little thing covered in hard plates and thought about the dog Brand had told Myche about – the one with the pierced skull.

Yawning before dropping his head to sleep, he had shown inches of fang, and Darati thought those teeth could rend just about anything. The lot of them walking with no idea of where they were going – it was easy to understand why Myche thought it safer to have those teeth close by. And the sense of big paws, sharp-clawed, padding a couple steps behind or ahead. *Nice.*

Meanwhile the sharp rock underfoot extended in from the coast to force them deeper into the trees and dense undergrowth. Nat insisted this was better anyway, because the forest was where they would find food.

"But the landbridge –" Marylin began.

"Landbridge stupidness," said Telma. "Dat is pure talk. One minute you preaching it, next ting you say smaddy make it up."

"Then we might as well have stayed in Little Wet," Five Cent wailed.

"We might as well have stayed in the Trust," Janice muttered.

Telma ignored her and turned on Five Cent. "Or what bout in the sea where all of unnu wash up – with pretty snake riding branch? You shoulda keep them smallies quiet, not set them off bawling again. You not worth two cent."

Darati felt a little sorry for him, but after that he stopped whining once and for all. He stayed away from Telma and took up with the littler ones, and soon, almost by chance, had them minding him. He shepherded them together in the middle of a path between bright green plantain trees gathered on either side.

Odd. All at once so many plantain trees.

It was about then that Brand started getting jittery, herding everyone together and shouting at whoever strayed away, even within sight.

"What's wrong with you?" Myche demanded at last. "You looking over your shoulder all day."

"Days," he responded, under his breath.

"Eh?" Myche was startled, and Darati leaned forward to hear him too.

"Pwessus and Tweetums have been following us for days."

Minutes later, when the shadows among the plantain trees took shape and form, it wasn't either of the twins; it was a woman.

Darati's skin crawled. This was an adult, thin, supple as a vine, the colour of tree bark and swathed in a mottled green cloth that had made her invisible against the leaves. She stood beside a flat rock with a huge leaf on it – plantain, banana or something else of the sort – and on the leaf was a small clay dish with a flame. Scattered around these were bits of sweet potato, small handfuls of peas, corn and green leaves that could have been shadon beni, and a number of bright feathers. But none of this was as strange as the woman.

·········

There had been adults Before. And faded pictures of Mumma, of Tourisslady or Gran Gran edged Darati's mind, remote and worn almost transparent. On the nearer side of Before were other adults, grabbing, hurling babies, old people, even strong men, into deep water, slashing and rending. The last big person Darati had seen was the man who had torn off Spat's skin, and when this woman materialized in front of them, Darati leapt back as if something monstrous had gathered form in front of her – not a straightforward threat like tumbling water or fierce dogs, but an eerie visitation from another life she had carefully forgotten. A haunting.

As if to confirm the intrusion of a strange power, the woman held Myche's eyes with hers and said, "The fever pass, but you need rest still." Her eyes swept from the fading rash over Myche's cheekbones and limbs. "You need to eat, and drink plenty water. Good water. Draw karaile bush in a warm bath for your skin."

"Who are you?" Brand's voice was rough with anxiety.

"Good afternoon," the woman replied sternly, and waited.

"Hello," he returned, his expression wary, mutinous. "Who you are?"

"A warden." As he tilted his head, confused, she added, "I watch the birds. I learn their calls and know when something interrupts their song, or their normal flight. I am a sort of . . . guardian. To keep us safe."

"Us?"

She turned away, waving them forward without a glance to check whether they were following. Darati would have held back, but as the woman's tone and gesture woke in most of the children some instinct (long dormant) about those older or bigger than themselves, about *women* especially, they trailed after her automatically, carrying Darati along. Even when they lost sight of her, they kept walking the path she had chosen for them.

PART 3

GROTTO

10

BRANCHING TALES

MYCHE

"**What you suppose dem want us** for?"

Myche started at Telma's voice just behind her. She didn't think for a moment that Telma was talking about the birdwoman. The strange adult disturbed but compelled them. To most she appeared more dream than threat – perhaps because she seemed part of the landscape and had melted back into it rather than pouncing on anyone. Cautious as Myche felt, the woman looked no more threatening than the immortelle trees or wild coffee along the way. But the others were even less worried about other things, things dangerous to forget. Like where Pwessus and Tweetums might be. With another jolt, Myche realized she too sometimes forgot they existed, although Brand had not. Indeed, some of the younger children hardly seemed to remember even the ultimate threat that occupied the older ones more and more – the cruiters. *Pirates*, Shine had corrected her.

There was no need to ask who Telma had in mind. "Same as anything else," Myche muttered, so long after Telma's question that the other girl looked puzzled. The pirates were greedy for everything, Shine had warned them: ocelot skins, turtles big as boats, tar from the black lake, iguanas for curry, mahogany, strong young bodies. "They go after whatever they can use or sell."

Telma absorbed that, then leaned close to Myche, breathing in her ear, "You mus' strap you chest tighter."

Telma herself was taller, but thin, "and flat like bammy," as she liked to say. Myche wasn't and knew that Brand had noticed. He had told her that she always seemed nervous, that he could feel her tensed up beside him. He had said it gently, for Brand. He didn't say he had seen her when Darati was bathing her down during the fever, despite the cloth drawn to keep her from sight, but he had helped Darati turn her, and Myche had seen his eyes widen and dart away.

He must have some inkling of why she needed to be afraid. And she was — frightened of her own body that was getting beyond control, curving lawlessly, sprouting dark hair under her arms, which was hard to hide or get off. They had always shared a shelter, and she had not hidden from him when she began to bind the cloth around her. By now he knew that she wound it as tight as she could, sometimes until she was short of breath.

"They'll come after us whatever we do. Only . . . if we could hide someplace," she said to Telma, peering along the path hopefully.

Was it a path? The birdwoman had disappeared, but there had been no definite trail to begin with; nor was there now some easy turn-off branching in any other direction. So they must be on track.

"Like we getting somewhere at last," Five Cent piped up.

Baby, baby, living on maybe, Myche muttered to herself, but she said nothing out loud, probably because he was trying at last. He was somehow keeping the smallies together, singing or playing quietly. But how long had he been listening?

And what had suddenly gone wrong with Indira, hopping from one bare patch of ground to the next and looking around frantically?

"What?" Myche demanded.

"She fraid tarantula," Nat replied, his voice tired.

"Where?"

"Wherever. She say forest must have tarantula."

Caught up by Indira's antics, Chunks tripped over a root and fell, howling. Someone would have to check her knees later, and she would howl over that too. So many children, dodging, following or reaching for Myche. Confused, she squeezed her eyes closed for a second to unclutter her head. Her mind could have been so clear if all these others weren't looking at her to tell them where to turn. How she felt about them was not straightforward. They were like that stand of coconut trees against a fine sky, shafts of light darting between each frond a-flutter, rippling along each bough waving yellow-green. Sway, flutter, ripple-ripple of scattered light. The view would have been clear without them, but blank. She did not wish the other children away. She could not imagine herself without them. But she had no idea what to do with them.

The vague route they followed after the birdwoman seemed to take them along a river valley shrugging off its early morning veil of mist and exposing shoulders of bare smooth rock rising out of the clear gurgling water. The trees rose taller than ever, with hefty branches interlacing above them and reaching over their heads. There was no sign of One Thousand Eyes. Presumably he was off hunting again. Somewhere. Anywhere. The idea that he could be far away made her uneasy. Then, Kyle and Bry. The thought that she had lost them pierced deep again, and her eyes blurred.

In that instant, Tweetums crashed down from a thick limb and sent Brand flying. The rest were too stunned to move, barely recognizing the broad hairy form of the boy who had grown with them in the Trust. It was Tweetums, though. He had always been a little heavier and slower than Pwessus. He grabbed Myche roughly, in a powerful grip there was no resisting, and dragged her off backways behind him into the trees, her arms flailing. She kicked her legs, trying to brake his progress. She yelled, bringing the rest charging forward – and Pwessus pounding after them from behind. While Nat, Telma and the rest turned to fight off the other one, Tweetums hauled Myche through the wall of dark green. As even Robber Boy and Shant swung back to face Pwessus, only Brand and Darati ignored him and pressed on to keep Myche in sight.

Myche flung herself down on the ground, so Tweetums had to tug her along over the small ferns, fallen leaves and twigs, soft earth, mossy stone and the points of broken branches. She felt the skin on her back tearing, a slice in her thigh, and she grabbed at anything to keep him back – tufts of grass and thick stems of bushes – until Darati grabbed up a rock and flung it directly between Tweetums's shoulder blades. Myche felt Tweetums lose his grip, and she rolled and leapt up as he turned to snatch back at her, lowered her head and swerved round to butt him full in the belly. He bent forward, winded, and she dropped again and tumbled out of reach.

But he did not dive after her, as they expected. He froze, stock-still, staring at something behind them: Wikki chasing Pwessus, holding up something that flashed in the sun, half covered by a bit of cloth. Pwessus, casting his eyes back as he ran, stumbled and fell flat.

"Crawl away." Wikki's voice was clear and hard, and the long shining metal glinted steady in his hand in the strip of thin cloth.

Tweetums shouted, "Is a knife he have, boy. Come fast."

Pwessus rolled out the way and shot off into the trees with Tweetums slouching more clumsily after him.

The children ran in the other direction as fast as they could, Brand keeping just behind Myche and urging her on until, breathless, they fell together in a heap. They lay in a clearing far inside the knot of trees. Most of them had dropped stuff they had been carrying for weeks, months. Only Nat and Telma had everything strapped to their backs and Myche still had the pouch tied to her waist. Wikki had left the pot in its trolley so far back they had no idea how to find it now.

"But at least you still have the big knife," Marilyn said.

Wikki gave a strange gaspy laugh. He drew the long shining metal he had run with from its light sheath of cloth, and it was just a handle broken off from the pot spoon he had flung at the dogs. Brand's shout of laughter, almost a squawk, repeated on like Qwa's *awk awk awk* as he winged away into the distance. Telma steupsed, but Brand bent double, too breathless now for the laughter to sound out, so he could only clap his hands and shake his head.

Marilyn regarded them in disgust. "We better keep going before them two turn back," she said. "Unless Robber Boy really have gun in place of finger. We lose the birdlady track long time though."

Telma didn't think so. The trail – if it was a trail – had followed a stream. "And this side damp. Must have water nearby." Her palm was pressed to the ground, and her face had a listening expression.

Nat nodded agreement, so they went along behind her.

Wet leaves trembled over greening stones along a narrow strip of ground with a light cover of grass and Ti Marie. It was overhung by some sort of fern Brand must have half remembered from the expression on his face. In Myche's mind too, a woman's hand pointed, her voice murmuring fondly, long ago.

"Maidenhair," Brand whispered.

Myche nodded, her chest feeling as if it might burst, and she looked off quickly. A few feet beyond was a printing fern like the one Shine had pressed on Brand's forehead a year or so ago and left the pattern he refused to wash off for days.

Nearer at hand but out of sight came the sound of rushing water, louder than the little stream they had followed earlier. When they pushed through the curtain of green, they came upon it. Now the rains had come, and a thunder of water from the spring plunged to a smoky blue-green pool that overflowed and burst between rocks that would normally contain the force. The water launched down into the valley past a huge tree blanketed by a vine trailing lilac-coloured flowers. Under the tree grew clump after clump of begonias. Bursts of colour from pink and yellow poui distracted them for a while, until they noticed the white begonia flowers again and fell upon them in delight. They ate the blossoms until the plants were stripped, but away under the fan palms nearby were more begonias between patches of dasheen bush, and beyond that, a hillside of sweet potato. They stopped.

This part was too clean, too orderly.

A bird fluted, and the birdwoman reappeared holding aside the veil of palest purple-studded vines and pointing among the trees along . . . not a path precisely, but an absence of bush. Then – a clearing, with big people. For the first time since meeting the birdwoman, Myche found it impossible to take another step forward.

The two groups, of persons large and small, held back from each other suspiciously for minutes, but their curiosity grew, and they sidled ever so slightly nearer. Warily.

When they all came face to face, the stories the children had heard and passed on to each other but never truly believed fell together. The men and women before them seemed abnormally tall, because few of the children had seen an adult for years until their encounter with the birdwoman earlier that day, and it turned out that she was relatively short.

"How many of you it have?" Nat asked, while the rest hung back again, studying the strangers.

For adults they seemed strangely nervous, almost alarmed by the ragged band of children edging out of the bush yet poised on the verge of retreat. But one of the tall ones leaned forward studying the upturned faces.

"How many of *you?*"

The clearing was like any other natural pause in the endless ranks of trees and undergrowth, a space where the forest thinned to leave a place of sunlight, still shady but not dim like the dense bush. A few flat rocks were scattered near together, perhaps more of them than one might have expected. As her eyes searched for however many more of the baanya might lurk behind that wall of greenery beyond the clearing, Myche made out a mesh of branches and sturdy vines that seemed to conceal a living space from which one group, perhaps a family, came and went. There must be others like it discreetly tucked into the forest nearby.

The effect of big people – not even singly but in groups that sepa-rated and merged fluidly – awed the children. The smallest huddled speechlessly around Five Cent and Darati. Marilyn, Wikki, Indira, Telma and Brand all stared, guarded, at every move the adults made in their direction. Only Robber Boy seemed merely interested rather than unnerved – perhaps planning his next performance, Myche thought fleetingly, crazy as usual.

She hovered with Nat and Shant, between the others and the baanya. It was unreal, big people coming and going with pots and baskets. As she nerved herself to interrupt, the birdwoman spoke directly to her.

"Nobody's going to hurt you or touch any of the rest. Watch. These belong to you, ent?"

To their amazement, she gestured to a pair of children running forward eagerly – Bry and Kyle looking clean and pampered. Bry was even wearing clothes. Five Cent darted to them, and they laughed and hugged, tumbling down and rolling over and over on the ground and chattering so excitedly there was no making out their story.

A tall stooping old man who had presided over the reunion with a smile waved the others to sit down. "You'll have plenty time to talk. Eat now." A sturdy middle-aged woman he called Cora pulled aside some greenery (which seemed woven together, now they looked). She shooed them gently onto the low bench she had swept bare beside the fallen tree. When the other children were sitting, Myche planted herself at the end of the bench. Then Cora leaned over and drew Myche's hand in hers, clasping firmly when the child tried to pull away, and ran her eye along the scratches on Myche's arms and legs and over her face.

Groups of the baanya, adults and children who seemed connected in some invisible way, began to sit too, but they waited for the new children to be served first.

Cora slid her hand off Myche's and stepped back, "Right. Didi here," she said.

An older woman with a basket handed out bread and something made with eggs and vegetables. Ananda's mouth hung open, her eyelids heavy as if mesmerized; and it was dreamlike for all of them, soothing and troubling at the same time, to sit at the bidding of adults and have food put in their hands. There were children among the strangers too. A couple came forward with cups of milk.

"You want to know who we are." Didi smiled indulgently. "Eat, and listen." As the others at the table helped themselves to food, Didi nodded respectfully towards another adult who was still standing, and said, "Come, Pawi."

A short, thick, sparsely bearded man in a tattered deep blue robe separated from the rest and took his seat on one of the flat rocks on the other side of the tree trunk that was their table. He eased himself down with the care and hesitation of one in pain, rubbing his knees and flexing his shoulders as if he would fly off if need be, however much it hurt. He studied them with an enigmatic smile, and then, turning his eyes up, seemed to forget them, searching his storehouse of words.

After that, it was hard to tell when his songs left off and his story began, or where his voice ended and the drifting light and shadow took over.

11

CHANTWELL

NAT

"**How many of us, they ask,**" Pawi began.

Nat noticed that the chantwell looked away from them and around at the other baanya.

"What is in their little heads about *us*? Children weave together scraps of stuff they do not understand so as to explain things in a way that makes them comfortable."

No, Nat thought. Nothing that came to them about the baanya had ever been comfortable. Pawi's gaze swept him and passed on.

"It went nothing like that," the chantwell said, "but what could they know?" As he turned to look over the newcomers again, he locked eyes with Myche. "It wasn't as if we got cast up on the same shore. More like each of us fluttered in from different worlds through some special doorway, to take up our perches. We roosted in the same place, but we didn't feel we all belonged together, and when the thing happened, we were hurled apart."

"What you mean?" Nat interrupted. "And . . . and what happened?"

Pawi held up his forbidding palm. "We'll come to that," and they all kept still, but his eyes were drawn back to Myche's. "The warden who found you had studied birds for many years, especially those that hover in the air. Really hover, not just ride air currents. We were working in a valley nearby when disaster fell. When we left the forest and went our different ways, I couldn't find my way home. Familiar buildings, signs, even trees – everything was down.

"And everywhere people were in shock, trying to work it out. Most believed whatever account they heard, so rumour blossomed into myth."

Myche inclined her head to Nat, who whispered, "He still hasn't told us."

Pawi must have heard. He glanced at Nat with an expression Nat had seen before long ago, then away. As if Nat wasn't good to look at or think about for long. The chantwell's bright fierce eyes fixed back on Myche. "Not everything good to talk straight out." Then he seemed to relax. "You're tired," he said. "What a long walk, and some of you so small. Tomorrow will be time enough for more story."

Myche realized she was exhausted and the youngest ones almost asleep where they sat. They were barely aware of the shelter where Cora led them and settled them, spreading covers about and making shushing noises, and none of them knew when she left.

Although Cora and Didi came and went the next day, the children spent the time mainly on their own, eating and sleeping again, bathing under a gentle fall of water from a stream minutes away. When it grew cool and shady, they gathered again for a meal with the rest, and Pawi took his seat so as to resume his tale.

"Could we ask something?" Myche said right away, but softly. The children had never heard her voice so quiet, yet everyone around, even the adults, fell silent. "You've been kind, so . . ." In the little pause, Marilyn sniffed. "So kind. But there are things we need to know. Most of us hardly remember what it was like Before. Even though you said it's better not to talk about it, we can't help thinking."

Pawi sighed. "We all understand that." He glanced at Babu. "Listen, before it all we had had our thinkers – artists and scientists. Now, here, the wisest among us decided not to keep going over and over matters that could only make us cry. Sometimes, though, one of us will feel something big float up in his mind and pause, just below the surface like a great fish in a lake, like you could just see it beneath the ripples. That is a fish we throw back. We don't reel it in for it to destroy us."

"Fish?" Brand scowled. He swung round to Myche impulsively. "What fish have to do with anything? He don't mean to tell us what happened or what?" He had never been a child to care who heard what he said, and the chantwell stopped, looked him up and down.

"Wait," Cora said. "These little children haven't had big people teaching them," she reminded Pawi. "Don't vex." Her voice took on the lilt for soothing babies as she turned back to the children. "How will it help you to know sad things?"

Pawi took over again. "This is just what I'm saying. There have been one or two who insisted on it and sang about pain in ways that brought that pain back. One man – Singerman, he called himself, as if there were no other singers besides himself. He liked to sing about the explosions, but a sudden noise could throw him down on the ground, trembling so hard his body jerked about violently – the sort of thing no one likes to see. And still he went on and on about these things, until some of us who had run to the forest for peace and quiet had to put him out."

"Out where?" Myche asked, more politely than Nat had ever heard her before. "Could you tell us where they went, and how?"

Pawi turned his face away but went on studying her from the corner of his eye as if she might be trouble, given a chance. And Nat thought, this man had no idea how much trouble she could be.

"The so-called singerman joined up with friends," Pawi said, "and they went their way in search of some other life. But there is none."

"What about a bridge?" Marylin asked shyly.

"Say what? Bridge? Nah! It have no way to leave the island – except by boat."

The finality of Pawi's words brought tears even to those like Five Cent who had always refused to believe in the bridge.

Pawi went on more gently. "Watch. You see this dream of trekking out? Perhaps when the world was young, some of the islands were connected, a mountain ridge, volcanoes – maybe in what scientists call geologic time. Not in our time. One or two in our chain of islands might boast a sometimeish volcano or a hot water spring or fuming pool like our own Healing Hole. And there are ridges here and there on land and undersea. But there was never any question of a bridge out for any of us."

Pawi ran his shining black eyes over the children kindly but pityingly. Poor stupid little things, his eyes seemed to say. He avoided looking at Nat altogether.

"Then what are we to do?" Janice asked first, then a barrage of questions broke out from the others.

"Where we must go?"

"How all–you manage?"

"So all a unnu couldn't go back whe' you come fram? What stap you?"

"Then you live just so in the bush?"

Pawi drew himself up proudly.

"Even if we aren't angry and on fire, we aren't like you little lost ones either, rootless and thrown away. We have a rich past. This was a wealthy country, small as it was, and even though we live simply in this wild place, we carry that old life still, inside us." Five Cent and Indira exchanged mystified glances. "We cut ties with all those who remember what will drag them down rather than what lives on in our hearts."

"These other people who left the forest are different?" Nat didn't care whether the chantwell wanted to talk to him or not. He required answers. "How? How they were different? What did it matter?"

Pawi got to his feet. He seemed ruffled, although Nat had shown no disrespect.

"We are nothing like anyone else," the chantwell declared. He paced a bit and then settled back on his seat as if to take up his story again. "We are the only real, belonging ones, because we were always here, and we are here to stay."

Myche broke in again, her voice urgent. "But can't you tell us what happened? We want that more than anything."

Pawi cocked his head and seemed to be sorting out a set of answers at his disposal. "Where to start? I think the disaster was waiting to happen, but others say it began with a few youngsters who left this island and travelled far away to war and somehow, when they came back, brought it home with them."

"A war? Ah." Brand leaned forward fascinated, and Pawi turned to appeal to the other big people gathered around.

"Where does one find words to explain to a child how thousands might pour their lives out willingly, spill their own blood?" He turned back to the children of the Trust, who were hanging on his every word, however bewildering. "I who have lived so long never felt anything like that. But you know what it's like to be caught up in a wave? It sweeps you up towards the light and air, so you don't flounder and choke, but it can just as easily crush you deep into the dark.

"Only, now, suppose you knew it was taking you to this shore of pure, soft sand, and beyond it, everything you could wish for. This wave I speak of was like that, a longing to fight for God, so they said: it swept you up and carried you away. Your own body, your children's lives, whatever was beautiful on this earth – all emptied of value before this surge of . . . of . . ."

"Of what?" Five Cent asked in a small voice.

"A desire to serve God, they said. So strong that nothing and no one else mattered, and giving one's life or taking other lives became easy. Who knew what these fighters were about? There weren't many from here anyway. One or two in the community said, 'The fellows must know what they're about.' Some sent money without worrying what it was for. And then one day, the handful of soldiers came back home."

When he paused, Brand asked, "And do what?"

"It was a time of trouble," Pawi said carefully, "and plenty talk – from people in charge and people who wanted to be in charge. In the end, I believe talk was what brought it all down."

"But how?" Telma was running out of patience. "After you still don't tell us what happen."

Pawi's answer, about money draining away and long lines of people who wanted documents to travel, snaking away along the dusty city streets, raised up memories Nat had mislaid for years.

"People panicked in airports and families sat there on the floor, stranded with their luggage," Pawi said.

"I was there, seeing off my brother," Cora put in. She was so excited she had dropped the singsong voice. "By the time he board a set of people rush the airport, so they close Departures. Then they start and wreck the place, and after we leave we hear how police storm in."

"And not only here," Pawi threw out to everyone around. "Same thing went on in other islands, ent?"

"Things like what?" Myche asked.

"Gangs and killings," Pawi responded. "I had a brother-in-law who used to say: 'Remember – what illegal for we to buy is legal for someone else to sell.' Gangs got more guns and bigger guns than the police. More people took fright and tried to leave the country. Then this handful of the soldiers who came back from the foreign war – they started to complain. But who have them to study? Only, Homeland had this vast, delicate system for listening, and all sorts of information about us got to the commander-in-chief."

Marilyn was nodding off now, and Ananda had fallen asleep with her face pillowed on a soft bread roll beside her plate. But the bigger ones, especially Shant and Robber Boy, were leaning forward. The chantwell went on, encouraged. "The commander-in-chief had strong opinions but no experience in government or any interest in advice."

Suddenly Pawi's attention shifted and fixed on one member of his audience in surprise. "You, young man, tall fellow with the orange hair. I see you nodding like you know what happen next. How you would know? . . . What? You're *who?* Eh? Who son? . . . Yeh, right. But of course, tell us, since you know so much."

Robber Boy didn't need to be asked twice. He rippled his fingers along an invisible flat line level at his chest and belted it out. "He tweeted: Cell? Hell, no. One or two grow, like cancer. Here's my answer. A cell or two is all I need. Little turd of an island boasts of harbouring every creed and race. Waste any place that sets up to breed terrorists. We don't let them in, get them over, pet them, fete them or forget them, while they immigrate, instigate, conflagrate.

"They're losers. I'd send bruisers, battle cruisers. We don't live beside them, lie, buy, abide with them, allow some period of grace, share airspace. That word rings bells: cells, sleeper or no. Know: I'm the Reaper."

Robber Boy's extravagant gestures concluded in a twirl of his fingers and sweep of the stupid hat that was fraying over his eyes. The others beside him on the bench drew away wearily and turned back to Pawi, who had sat in dignified and amused silence.

"So, okay. Strong words from the commander-in-chief, but here too people got restless. First they protested through a little harmless chanting, then by cursing. Bottle pelting, machete brandishing. Then gunfire. Hostages. Police stormed the wrong building. The owners of that building had rented out the backroom to a preschool. Children died."

"No one took charge?" Myche asked.

"Who? Over time a lot of know-how seeped away. It was the hardest thing to get anything fixed – computer, roof, car, toilet."

The children exchanged blank looks and whispered questions.

"Eh? What is a *toilet*? Nah! You joking, right?" Pawi cast his eyes around the gathering. "Like they not joking." He looked back at the children. "Watch. If you couldn't get simple things fixed, who could fix a country? When the money trickled away, so did the experts in just about everything – well, the young experts. Some stayed to take care of others who couldn't go – like Casey there. He was an engineer teaching at the university, and his wife was ill. As the country got to look bad in the news, other governments began warning their people not to visit us, and stopped allowing us to visit them. Business slowed, and life got hard."

"How?" Myche was not about to give up. But then, Nat had known that all along.

"Local bad boys got bolder, swaggering into stores, offices, hotels and police stations to hold up whom they pleased. Then they felt free to chop or shoot tourists or foreign businessmen. Between that and the bragging about sleeper cells, what happened afterwards was inevitable."

At last, Nat thought, and Myche and the rest sat forward again.

"Aah. Curious little ones. So full of questions. How did we survive, you want to know."

Nat saw Myche press her fingers to her temple, but Pawi couldn't or wouldn't read the signs.

"I'll tell you," he promised graciously. "We accepted the situation. The hills and forests are ours. We eat well, and we have wardens to study the habits of wild things and warn us when they're restless." Now he looked around at Cora and the rest as if he had forgotten the children. "We've re-learnt the art of healing in the old way, ent? Physic nut, chandelier, ringworm bush and wonder of the world. Each of us builds some little area of knowledge to help us live one day after the next. My work is to draw up and unfold our story – how we make the most of what we have left."

He turned his eyes back to Myche. "Stay with us, little people. We who live in the forest have made our peace with loss."

12

HIDING PLACES

MYCHE

Whatever hesitation Myche felt, there was no withstanding basket-fuls of warm bread or the bustle of confident adults intent on sheltering them. The baanya swept the children in with the soft shuffle of a mother hen spreading the fluff of her warm underside and swishing them close with her wings.

Still, it was awkward encountering other settled ways of doing things, and a vague threat persisted – these taller, older people looming above them. Particularly men. Tall, broad men.

"No. Don't frighten," Didi said to Myche, as if she could see her disquiet. And there was nothing scary about Didi personally. "You all together here, not so?"

Perhaps, Myche thought, it was just the strangeness of beings from far-fetched tales materializing – not as the odd stray encounter either, but in a group. A group larger than the children's. Men, women and children. And those children stared as if the newcomers might not be real after all and might vanish without warning. Or as if Myche and the others only looked like children and could really be demons.

It made Myche feel insubstantial, almost unreal. Yet what the baanya thought a simple thing, like tea, warm and sweet, was reassuring. In the night they stayed dry, although there was a light drizzle for a while, and when it turned cold, they drew the big piles of cloth Cora had brought and snuggled closer together. A few weeks would pass before they were content to break up sometimes into smaller groups and join one family or the other. Even then they didn't want to separate, but Kyle started it by wailing that he wanted them but couldn't leave Didi.

"And what if rain really come down?" Didi said. "This big shelter wouldn' keep you dry, with the side partly open and thing. The smaller ones thatch good."

So, little by little, the children found themselves pulled into subtle arrangements between scattered shelters that blended into thick foliage, a canopy of leafy branches over several levels of bush and tangles of ropey vines that together made up what the baanya called their homestead. There was still a creepiness to it, though. Myche couldn't put it into words.

The homestead was borderless. Nothing distinguished it from the rest of the forest around them, which teemed with life and colour.

"We'll show you all you need know," Cora assured them, and after that, she or a couple others would lead them around.

Thick stems leaned forward to prop up torchlike red flowers or dangle deep pink blooms edged with green-streaked yellow. Ants marched in smart formation in and out of the furled leaves. Little pools of water trapped by the rocks shimmered in between, reflecting a soft blue-grey head pecking forward, then the lift of brighter blue wings and the hop-hopping from one rock to the next around the water. A quick sideways twist of his head and swifter dip at the water, then a shrug of wings and a swivel of neck again. "Tanager," whispered the birdwoman.

All around, the bush was aquiver with birds and throbbing with their calls, and, when the children sat still long enough, offered glimpses of other presences, a long reddish furred arm or curl of tail above, or a scuttle of glossy brown hide back into the undergrowth. But never an ocelot, nor even the odour of one that had recently passed by, and never a glimpse of One Thousand Eyes.

The baanya were better at avoiding tracks than the children had ever been in and around the Trust. Myche searched for hints of how they remembered their way through the bush. She tried to sketch ways through the forest on the few precious bits of pencil and paper in her pouch, but it was no use, for the baanya left no actual tracks and rarely took exactly the same route twice.

Once, she saw Didi watching her with a secret smile playing around her mouth. But Didi said, "You'll see. We'll show you everything."

The next morning, when fine tendrils of mist were still curling up between the trees, she signalled them to fall in behind her as she took a turn leading them around, not crushing the groundcover so much as parting it with her feet. Didi was tall and thin with thick, straight grey hair that dropped down her back almost to her waist, after which it was black for about five inches at the end. Her skin was dry and rough but firm, and her posture erect, not like Babu's.

Every morning Didi took them to tell Babu good morning, and every night they stopped shyly before him to say good night after eating. Babu's back arched over so that his neck stuck forwards and his shoulders curved round to his caved-in chest. Knotty veins wound down his arms and over the backs of his hands. He breathed hard, especially in the early morning when it was cool and damp under the trees. His skin was soft and etched in odd patterns, like a turtle's. Everyone in his household, young and old, ran to help him over uneven ground or pick up the things that often slipped from his fingers. If he saw at all, what he saw must be blurry. His eyes had a strange milky film.

In his household, like the others, the members held tightly together the way Janice, Josiahmarshall and Tiffney did, or like Myche and Brand; but most households had eight to ten adults and children, including a number who looked nothing like the rest. When Myche asked how they came to be together, Didi said the people in each household were a family because they had been reborn from the fire together. Each group had been in the same office, house or store together when the explosions started. Or sitting in the same taxi. They were now so close that they did not allow children in one household to marry each other, even if they were from different parents. If they were not related by blood, they were by fire, Didi said.

Each morning after another tour, Didi led the children back to the clearing near to Babu's shelter, and there were clean broad leaves spread out for them with fruit and some sort of bread that was flat and soft and smelled of the fire. Didi spread it with the yellow thing that melted at once and made them feel they could never stop eating it. She handed round cups of milk, and for a while everything was quiet.

One day Babu groaned, trying to stretch his leg. "Rain," he said, and Myche nodded, remembering how, the night before, Telma had pointed out the halo around the moon.

After the children had eaten, and while two boys from Babu's household were clearing the leaves and cups away, Babu said these new children who had come to them had lived long enough in the temporary shelter or in short visits with one family or another. Soon they should move in permanently, one by one or in small groups – just as they liked – with different families and learn about whatever tasks those families normally performed.

By now Didi had introduced them to other households, especially those with children within the same age range as theirs. These baanya children peeped at the ones from the Trust with interest but gave Robber Boy a wide berth. It would be weeks before the baanya children began to move comfortably among the new arrivals.

Meanwhile Myche learnt that Didi's household specialized in minding deer, which the children were anxious to see, because there had been none around the Trust. Deer had to be especially shy if none of the children had ever glimpsed one before, even on the long walk to the place they had come to know as High Forest. Didi made them crouch on a slope well behind the edge of the bush without a movement or whisper – and there he was, reddish brown, a nervous twitch of the ears, a twist of light grey throat and head with short spiky horns. He had come crashing towards the bush, then froze – a flash of white under the tail and he was gone.

On the way uphill they met the birdwoman, Ena, whom Didi reintroduced as her sister. There had been three of them, Didi said. A third sister had died last year, and her daughter, Ferne, lived with Didi now.

Ena was scattering seeds for a flock of pigeons she seemed to be rearing. Or perhaps she helped them rear themselves. She showed the children how to let fall handfuls of what looked like peas or grain and pour water into small troughs of bamboo strategically placed to seem as if they had accidentally toppled among the tall leaves.

When Didi led them deeper in the bush, they met a man gathering fruit for agouti, although sometimes the animals paused on the way to the feeding places to nibble at flowers near the path or even fungi sprouting out along the way.

"Casey, I bring these young people to see how we live," Didi said.

And he showed them around, saying he would have tried minding tatou as well, but it was burdensome to catch enough bugs, spiders and even scorpions to attract them, so he contented himself with whatever tatou Bois managed to catch, and focused on setting food for agouti instead.

At the mention of tatou, Myche thought of One Thousand Eyes crunching the heavy armoured little beast, and a smile escaped her.

"You like tatou," Didi teased. "I see you laughing like you could taste it in you mind."

Myche shook her head. "I never eat that yet," she said, adding hastily, "but I wouldn't mind."

Five Cent asked, "The animals don't run away from all-you?"

"They don't have to," Didi answered. "We leave them wild. They just come where they find food easy to get. If we build a set of pen and cage, the animals wouldn' be happy and breed. Besides, people might see."

People. The children understood about hiding from people.

Like their animals, the baanyas' plants grew helter-skelter. Anything that might betray cultivation lay a good way from the shelters, with a couple young ones on watch to sound the alarm if they sighted a stranger. There was a special birdcall, but when Brand enquired, they would not tell him which it was.

One night Brand nudged Myche and asked in a mischievous whisper if she didn't think it funny how, all the time these people heaped soil around plants, milked goats and gathered their poop, the baanya spoke of themselves as this great and proud people with a glorious past and future. And how were they going to make the great comeback? What were they *doing*?

"Staying alive," came Didi's voice from somewhere beyond the entrance, and Brand looked away in embarrassment.

The baanya were ridiculously sharp-eared.

"Them doesn' miss nothing," Brand grumbled afterwards.

For now, the baanya were content, Didi explained. They had seen terrible times, but they were holding on until they could take up their old way of life again.

Nat broke away from the other children when he saw Myche walk off towards the goats and stand studying them.

"What?" he asked.

"Where they get all the manure they have in that set of bag?" she demanded. "And where they get them bag?"

"You don't see the old people weaving? Is bag and thing they weaving."

"Where they fill the bag?"

"So what you care bout manure?"

"Where?" she said fiercely.

He shrugged. Some things were mysteries, that was all. Then he reminded her. "The goat and thing."

She pointed at the little hail of pellets one of the goats was producing before it wiggled and bounded off. "That don't look like what I saw them spreading from the bag. And it don't smell anything like that."

Nat steupsed. "I ent have time to stand round sniffing goat crap." Still, she had caught his attention. He thought for a moment. "They have plenty, in truth. And they dragging this thing so far. I don't see why they have to travel up and down so far gathering it in the night and toting that around the forest. Or even how they live squeeze up in this set of little shelter. Who it have coming by sea who could find they way up in this bush anyway?"

It was true that the hillside where the frail shelters blended in among thick vines was remote and steep – inconvenient enough to put off the cruiters.

Five Cent asked Myche where the baanya kept their things, though.

"What things?"

"You know. Anything they not using every day. Them shelter have partly nothing inside, gyul."

Myche cracked her knuckles, then looked around guiltily. Didi had warned her about the habit – the sound could give one away. Myche turned back to Five Cent and regarded him thoughtfully. She had always felt he was not the eejit Telma called him.

"And they always look like they have everything they need," Five Cent added.

"Then what bout matches?" Brand demanded. "Where they getting match to cook food?"

No one had any solution to suggest.

The next morning, the children woke to great excitement, as one of the young men had surprised a quenk by stumbling near its burrow. He had barely time to catch the strong musky odour of surprise and a bark of alarm before he grabbed a low limb and hoisted himself out the way, for it charged at him and almost gored a leg with its two wicked tusks. The children clamoured around Didi for more of the story, because none of them had ever seen a quenk and few had even heard of one.

"Is a pig," Five Cent threw out importantly.

"Really like a wild hog," Didi said. "But is not pig self."

"Good thing he was by heself," said Bois, one of the hunters. "Normally, quenk does keep household, like we. And it take a good few of them boys to kill he one."

They waited on tenterhooks for the arrival of what they thought would be an enormous animal. But when the youngsters dragged it in, it seemed no more than a short bristly piglike thing, not two feet high if it had still been standing.

"That's all?" Brand said scornfully.

Babu smiled his watery smile and shook his head gently. "You don't know how quenk could fight, boy. Dangerous too bad." He paused for a fit of coughing. "When you taste that, though, you go change you tune."

That was true. After laborious cleaning and chopping, picking herbs and peppers and slicing them fine, mashing garlic, arguing over salt, sprinkling and rubbing all of it into the flesh, gathering wood and nursing that first precious glow, fanning and urging the fire, laying out the meat and covering it, peeping, turning, basting, sprinkling the fire to avoid scorching – after what seemed an endless preparation of meat and fire through the morning, the rest of the day seemed to pass in more fanning, sprinkling, basting and turning.

"But nobody wouldn't see the smoke?" Telma asked.

"Them boys still downhill watching out," Bois said. "If they sound the alarm, we douse that and gone."

"Gone where?" Myche piped up, and caught a quick exchange of glances between Didi and Babu before Casey stepped in by passing out little tastes of the meat.

That night they crowded round Pawi to pelt him with questions.

"What you worried about? You safe here. We all safe," the chantwell confirmed. "It should have had more of us, if the rest hadn't left," he added, "but they left of their own choice. No one dragged them away."

"Left?" For a moment wild hope blossomed in Myche and again she asked, "Left how?"

"Walked."

Brand leapt to his feet. "Walked where?"

Pawi regarded them thoughtfully, then smiled. "So many questions? So hasty for answers. The answer to every one of those questions is story, but I will give you a short answer this time: The ones who left walked to another part of the island. Gone down to find their own way, some of them."

Nat was hesitant to ask more, but Myche could see his eyes probing the chantwell's face, which had a faraway look.

"There were always a few yearning to fit in with whatever powers there might be, somewhere else," Pawi continued vaguely. "Then there were the angry ones; there were more of those. They took the road into the swamp and disappeared into the mud."

When they pestered him about that, he laughed and said this was the area that his people knew best, and he promised the children they would see more of the forest.

In fact, they had been walking with Didi or one of the others almost every day, until one evening when Nat was massaging an ankle and muttered, "Like they want to show us everywhere in truth."

Then Telma asked, "But what it is the rest doing when Didi and Bois and them showing us around? When we came back it have stuff that wasn't there when we wake up. And a set of ting we see there before we leave gone by the time we get back." There was a little silence while they turned that one over. "And you know what again?" Telma demanded. "When dem take us out all day, is what we really see beside bush and rockstone?"

Yes, they walked and walked along rock walls smooth, gritty, pitted, flaky, layered in different shades and textures. They walked among dark towering tree trunks with pods overhead that split and sent seeds whirling down, and they negotiated thick-stemmed broad leaves with curling edges and others that were velvety and so wide the smallies could hide under them. They walked past huge blooms – or what looked like flowers, only they were circles within circles of spiny hard leaves that were bright pink or deep purply red with clear water cupped at the base of each, and once, a tiny frog like gold jewellery climbed out. They walked along mossy banks with delicate sprays of ferns or other plants they did not know, fine like droplets of water, and looked down over steep drops onto bright or darker green tree-tops parted by flashes of flame trees in between. But all the while the baanya encouraged them to talk and ask questions only about what they saw along the way.

Myche, Telma – all of them – realized soon enough that no one else was going to give more information that the chantwell. Most of the baanya told the children to take their questions to the one who had woven all their knowledge into words and song.

"Except," Babu said, with the tone of one trying to be scrupulously truthful, "for the knowledge of healing." For that they sometimes needed to go outside.

"Outside where?" Myche asked.

Babu said that Cora, the healerwoman, sometimes worked down-hill of where they lived, gathering herbs, flowers, special bark and mosses beyond the nearest edge of forest where a deep valley opened up, and those who ventured beyond that would come to a waterfall. Following the river downstream, they would reach the Healing Hole. If the last of Myche's cuts and scrapes didn't dry up quickly, he said, Cora would take her there.

"What if we just keep walking downhill – we would come to the sea?" Nat asked. There was the usual little pause, as if the adults were deciding how much to say. "Is that where it have the place called Freedom Bay?"

Babu's head jerked back as if someone had swung a fist at his jaw, but he responded in a measured way.

"You will reach a place where the ground turns to mud and the river slows down, and after a while, you don't know where is river and where is sea. You wouldn't find your way through the Wet." Babu turned sorrowful eyes on them. "Poor little people. You would sink down in the mud."

"So it don't have no people there?" Nat demanded.

"No real people."

Of course it was Telma who demanded, "It have any other kinda people? Not-real one?"

Nat's questions dried up, as the baanyas' faces closed. Disapproval crept into Baba's gestures and stiffened his posture – a turning away of the head with a tilt up to the sky as if for enlightenment in the face of such discourtesy.

Even later, the chantwell had little to say about the Wet, except that after the fires, some baanya had gone directly in that direction. Well, they made their choice. Since then an occasional youth, too angry to bide time in the forest, had run off. No one had seen them since.

And on past the Wet? What lay beyond the mud? Was there something called a *port*?

Aah. The *enclave*? That they would not talk about at all. Babu's mouth twisted as if he had picked up a nasty smell.

Confused by the hard stare from anyone they asked about the east,

Myche and Nat consulted each other with their eyes and led the other children to shift their questions.

"What about a landbridge?" Marilyn was nothing if not persistent.

The baanya smiled tolerantly, and Pawi explained that was a fairy tale and not even an old established one. The only thing he would add was that the children were welcome to stay in the forest as long as they liked. It was best for everyone.

"What does that mean?" Nat pondered aloud, when the children gathered together where their long shelter had stood, chatting before breaking up to go their separate ways.

Wikki pointed out that the forest screened them from cruiters, from Pwessus and Tweetums, and from hot sun and gas pains. Even Ananda, who was still terrified of any substantial shelter, could be happy there, and when she chattered nonstop, none of the baanya seemed to mind. They just pinched her cheek and popped something into her mouth. There was plenty to eat, and Tiffney was getting so fat it was just as well she could walk now.

"I keeping the two of them right here," Janice said. "As long as these people let us stay."

At twelve, she was taller than Myche, but she too was filling out and more panicky than ever. Yet she overindulged Josiahmarshall, who was a year older than Brand but unreliable, so anxious for attention that he could easily betray the rest by his thoughtlessness. Worse, he was too much of a joker to take seriously some little sign of danger or subtle gesture of warning. Janice did not rein him in. Tiffney of course was just a smallie, plump and tumbling about, happy or whiny depending on whether she had her way.

"Janice don't teach them two anything," Marilyn complained. "How they will make it in the bush? Nah. They going put the whole of us in trouble. Tiffney don't even know to hush when you put finger to mouth."

Telma said Marilyn was a fine one to talk, and Myche said that was unfair. It was true Marilyn was jumpy, like Janice, and too overweight to skim up a tree or dive fast behind a bush, for she still ate nervously when she didn't need food and had been putting on flesh dangerously.

"But look how she manage Wikki," Myche argued. "Watch him. Can't be more than a year older than Josiahmarshall and he doing everything – hunt, fish, find food in bush. Much less cook."

"Is true," Telma's face softened. "Sweet hand fi true. Is like a magic."

Even now that they were all fed and cared for, Wikki hung over Didi and Bois when they seasoned meat or turned provision with garlic and onions in their huge round pots. Best of all he had learnt to spin the bread they called roti on the flat iron surface, so it swelled and gave out that maddening smell without scorching. The smallies worshipped him, and he was learning more every day.

"Right," Nat said. "So, staying here might look good for us. But what makes it good for everybody? *That* is what they say. How it helps them if we stay?"

"Why you worrying about that?" Wikki insisted. "The people say is good for them and we know is good for us. What's your problem?"

"If part of what they say ent true, how I know the rest true?" Nat returned.

Later Myche felt okay telling Nat that she sensed something lurking beyond the kindness. She could not put it into words, she admitted, for what could the baanya want of them? And Nat said these big people must see how weak and confused the smallies were, how talkative – which meant, how dangerous. Anyone could tell that the pirates would make mincemeat of whatever handful of young children they caught. Or even the older ones. Brand would probably hold out for a while, but in the end, Nat said, even he and Myche could be made to babble out whoever they had encountered on the way.

Then she saw: That was it exactly.

The baanya knew that the moment the children fell into the wrong hands, the forest would no longer hide anybody. So the children must never leave carrying in their heads the secrets of High Forest.

"But then," Brand put in, "why they show us all over the place?"

And Nat said, "Maybe they haven't."

13

UNWRAPPINGS

MYCHE

After that, Myche told Nat what Brand's sharp ears picked up, what some of the baanya whispered to each other. They said these new children were good, strong, joyful young folk, who brought fresh blood into the community. One day they could intermarry with the children born in the forest.

Myche set her mouth mulishly and said she wasn't going to live and die in no forest to please any of them. She and Brand had got to talking openly with Nat about what they should do next.

"For I not going to sit around so they could intermarried me," she said. "You ever see a book here? Anywhere here? What it have to *do*?"

Later that day Nat wandered over to the tree Myche was sitting against. He dropped down beside her.

"I've been meaning to tell you for a long time. I don't know why I haven't. I found something. Back there, in one of the mash-up buildings in Brukstone. But you weren't well enough at the time." He reached a long arm over his shoulder, back into his pack. His face was alight.

She felt something coming towards her and for no good reason was certain it was better than anything she could imagine. Her heart rose up to meet it.

"What?"

He held out something wrapped in banana leaves and tied with a withe. When she held it on her knee and gazed without opening it, he said, "Didi will soon come and herd us off."

She tugged off the withe and unwrapped the leaves, and there were two books. She ran her fingers over the titles. *The Hobbit*. And then, *Escape to Last Man's Peak*. Neither title meant anything to her, but they were *books*. She clutched them close and rocked back and forth, trying not to cry. She couldn't speak, and, when she stole a look at him, found she didn't have to. So she wrapped them back, and he helped her stuff the package into her pack. Then they went off together to find the others.

·········

More and more as time went by, the baanya enfolded the newcomers, fed them riverfish that Babu (who seemed to be everyone's uncle) had his nieces steam down with tomato and peppers. The chantwell set his palms flat on his thighs and seemed to look inwards so as to gather intricate strands of memory into stories, while his wife, Jasmine, prepared warm sweet puddings made with grated cassava and coconut milk. Bois pounded together seasoning from his little clusters of garlic and bhandania. And Casey curried duck.

"How you know what to put together like that?" Wikki asked reverently.

"I'm a engineer, ent?" Casey's smile was pleasant but sad.

But the day Babu's nephews brought up those two ducks from the river, Brand reported that as he lay on a high limb watching the line of adults filing away, he noticed the line fork in two: one group continued down in the direction of the river, while the other swung away and turned up another slope until they were out of sight in the dense bush. That was the group with Bois and Didi, because he could see Bois's deep rust-coloured headwrap and, well below it, Didi's swishing hair and straight slender form. And it was Bois who later produced an extra-wide and much heavier tawa, so when they lay the dough on it, they were able to make a different, more silky kind of bread, one with fat kneaded in. They hit it with a paddle, and it broke up hot and flaky.

Nat whispered to Myche, "I never see any paddle like that round here before now, much less a iron big like that."

So. There *was* somewhere else. A secret place.

The next day, out of the blue, Brand asked, "Can we see the caves?"

Didi was quiet for a while, then said, "What caves?"

"My brother said there were people who ran away and lived in caves." After a pause he went on. "Which people ran to the caves? It was all-you?"

Didi shrugged. "So how you didn't ask you brother all that?"

Well, if it was a secret, there was no point enquiring about it. The thing was to watch, without giving any further sign of what a few children from the Trust suspected. After all, everyone had secrets.

Myche sat on her heals under a plum tree and sifted through the puzzle that was her life. She kept her face composed and relaxed, so no one could tell that she was curled in the hiding place of her mind. And as her body changed, dangerously, she grew her mind as well to accommodate her shifting situation.

She grew it with those stories that had come to her and with those she developed through the little *what if* mechanism in her head that constantly fired off new stories, reassuring and scary ones beyond her control to choose between or to govern. As more and more of them overtook her, she collected fresh words to keep up. She even asked Robber Boy again where he had got his own gush of words, but although she grasped his tale about having been alone for a long time with nothing to do but acquire and practise them, she got lost in his talk of screens and something he called a *tablet*. She decided nonsense was all he could produce, because his endless flow of words told her nothing. Instead, she fed what she had to the other children to see how easily her own words could be used or played on, and she fed them stories too, so as to distract them from fear and pain or give them a reason to go on.

She in turn became a hiding place for them. But it would be a long time before she realized this.

· · · · · · · · ·

It was both a relief and an added anxiety that most of the children nestled in unquestioningly among the folk of High Forest, while Myche and Nat thought it all out, worked out any number of ways it might go, over the weeks. Over months.

Myche regained the weight she had lost during the fever and bound her chest tighter still. Cora told her there was no need for such discomfort here but couldn't rid her of that prowling unease. She rubbed cocoa butter on Myche's skin, on the scars from her fingernails raking the rash and bumps from mosquito stings and from the jagged branches or tree stumps that had torn her as Tweetums dragged her off. All faded over those months until her skin glowed silky.

More and more, the children felt themselves to be safe from outsiders. They slept in the shade without starting up to look about nervously. A sense of well-being spread from eating cooked food regularly, from having adults pay attention to their hair and teeth, from the sheer reassurance of much larger bodies than their own between them and the world. And yes, these things soothed Myche too, but most of all she felt revived through the reunion with Bry and Kyle. There they were, not broken at the bottom of a cliff, nor gouged by thorns, nor shaking with fever, but plump, with laughing, gleaming faces.

Relief swept over her again every time she relived her first glimpse of them in the clearing. She had steadied herself against the tree trunk and kept darting little glances at them to make sure they were real. They frolicked about with the baanya children, strong and frisky as ever. It immediately endeared the forest people to her, and that cord of gratitude tugged tight.

But once they accepted that there was no landbridge, a few of her group spoke of going back to the Trust. They studied the map Myche drew in the dirt for them from memory (still hiding her tattered paper sketch), although she knew her rough map was incomplete on the eastern side. If all they had to do was complete the circuit of the island, they would probably have set out and returned to the Trust. But they took note of the baanyas' warning that they could not pass the Wet and would have to turn around and go three quarters of the way back in the direction from which they had come. That gave them pause.

Then Babu reminded the children of the twins they had mentioned, of Pwessus and Tweetums. The children stayed still a little longer, thinking about that too.

Every day Didi taught them about new plants and even animals they could eat. "Yes. Iguana. You can't skin up you nose at that. Is a clean meat."

"Like mountain chicken," Wikki put in, and Marilyn covered her smile with her hand.

Baba had a couple boys show them how to trap agouti and clean the meat properly with lime juice. How to boil water so as to drink it safely. Cora pointed out leaves that killed or cured, and advised them to try noni, while even Cora's niece told them what to burn so as to keep off mosquitoes. When Ferne heard that Myche reacted badly to smoke, she pointed out the neem that seemed to grow by chance all around the homestead.

For a long time the chantwell told tales only about Before. How huge machines drilled down into the earth and even deep below the sea, and tanks filled up with precious oil, and towers fluttered flame that burnt away waste chemicals, and miles of pipelines conducted the wealth of the country to waiting tankers. But at last he sang about the fires and of what had brought the fires on.

"One morning, early-early when all was quiet on the oil fields, four men and three women set out in their different directions and it was all timed to a fraction of a second, so the first set of explosions went off at the same time. And all those seven people died – either because they had planned to die or because others shot them and disappeared in the confusion afterwards. Not enough was left of any of the seven to work anything out."

"So how they knew it had seven?" Brand demanded, and Pawi shook his head and smiled.

"People knew," was all he would say before moving on with the tale. "Some said they blew it all up to prepare for the coup that came after; some said the coup was just another stage in the destruction."

Brand knew nothing about coups, so he interrupted again. "But how people knew it was seven?"

Then the chantwell said that perhaps it wasn't. Perhaps it was six or eight. Perhaps that was enough story for tonight. Still, he told the children, they were right to ask questions. Old-time people used to discourage children from asking questions, he said, but that was wrong. It was best for the little ones to know all they could.

You mean all you are willing to tell, Myche reflected, and beside her, Nat nodded. He had begun to read her thoughts.

At first it had seemed to them that the baanya had an unlimited number of stories for around their fires. But gradually the children from the Trust realized these adults really had just the one story, the great all-encompassing tale made up of a thousand small anecdotes of their past and how it had slipped away.

Their own children, though, talked of other things. After Myche and the rest had been there for several months, Cora's niece whispered about the hidden place.

"For ent you staying here?" argued Ferne. "You going to live with us. For you can't go by the cave unless you staying," she went on. "But you have to stay, ent? All-you have nowhere else to go." It was probably okay to tell, she reasoned.

You had to walk three hours from the shelters along an old road that had all but disappeared after the last rains. Even this narrowed to a track practically lost among tree roots that met and interlaced. Once one of the coils suddenly unwound into a snake that darted away down a crevice.

You had to hike up ridge after ridge, and after a while you smelled it, and by the time you scrambled down the steep hill to the dry riverbed, the stink was stronger because you were near the entrance. You walked in for a while before it opened out in the first chamber, where there was light, quite a lot of light in the day. Yes, she had been there often, Ferne said. She loved it because it was safe. It meant so much to them all, they hardly smelled it anymore.

The children from the Trust thought of their ocelots and how the musk had long ago stopped bothering any of them.

No, not dark, Ferne insisted. Holes let the light steal through. In the next chamber the roof was high – her mother had said *like a cathedral*, but she did not know what that was. The chamber had pillars of rock made by drippings from the roof over millions of years.

Yes, Myche thought. She could see it. It came back to her, a place someone, a voice in her memory, had called a cathedral.

Ferne had never needed to be there at night, but her mother had told her it was not bad then either. You tried to get in or out well before nightfall, before the birds started turning out in search of food. The birdwoman, her Aunt Ena, had said the birds there fed by hovering before whatever fruit they found – like hummingbirds, only they were so much bigger. Ferne had never seen them in any number, because she had never gone in past the first chamber or even been near the entrance except in bright daylight. She had heard them, of course.

These birds in the cave – they called them oilbirds – were forever wailing, and anyone could hear them. Who would go into those chambers where they clustered with all those sad voices? But she had seen a few: they were big birds almost as long as her arm, and their wings spread twice as wide as their length.

"Why we didn't see any since we come?" Brand asked. "If it have so mucha dem and ting?"

Ferne said her Aunt Ena had explained they came out to feed at night. They could see in the light, but they moved about outside in the dark by making sounds that echoed off anything nearby. The few that lived in that outer chamber had built nests on a ledge far up the wall of the cave, so no one could see into them, but these big nests would each have a few eggs that hatched into young birds; and these became, for a while anyway, bigger than their parents, because they were just stuffed with oil.

Indira gasped. "Oil?"

"Oil." Ferne paused and asked if they wanted to hear a scary story.

They nodded enthusiastically and crowded near.

Well. Once when her mother and Aunt Ena were young, they ran with some others in the group far inside the cave to hide from two seamen who had lost their way and were approaching the shelters. The bigger, stronger men and women stayed near the entrance to keep watch and deal with the strangers if the alarm sounded that the shelters were discovered. Meanwhile the younger ones were to keep inside the cave.

Ferne's mother and aunt strayed too far and got themselves lost in the dark inner tunnels, slippery with bird mess. And the birds lining the upper walls of those inner tunnels were crowded together and got so flustered and desperate when the girls got in there with them that the noise was maddening. The passages led this way and that, and sometimes a shaft plunged almost at their feet.

When night came on, even the little glimmers of light through cracks in the roof of the cave were gone, and the two girls could not think how to move their feet in the pitch darkness, Ferne said. They would have fallen down a hole if they hadn't had some hard pieces of root they had broken off from a crack in the low roof, and they used these to feel their way. Only, they had to move gently with them, because these roots weren't that dry, and they didn't want them to bend up and be useless for tapping along the ground.

Now, they had two matches, just two, but they were afraid to light any, because when those went out there would be no light again – perhaps ever – for who knew whether the chamber they had wandered into in the night had cracks in the roof that might bring in light when day broke? Still, what could the light of two matches do anyway in a whole cave? Whatever sticks they could get at – the roots, you know – were too damp to burn. Then, feeling their way along a ledge in the dark, they happened to run their hands over a nest of young birds, and that was how they got out.

"How?" The children stared at her, Brand furious with impatience.

"They robbed the nest. They shoved two of the young birds onto the sticks – my mother said they were dead already, but I don't know, I hope so – and they struck one match to light the baby oilbirds and used them as torches to find the way. They saved the other match and carried two spare birds, but they didn't need them; and they said they couldn't have thought they'd be able to hurt a baby bird or a baby anything, but they had to get out. They felt they would go mad if they stayed in the dark with the birds wailing, and by then they were beginning to hate those birds anyway. But at last they got back to the outer cavern, so they put the two babies that were alive in a nest they could just reach and left them there."

....

A cave, Myche thought as she lay there, sleepless under the onslaught of disturbing images, of prowling seamen and torched birds. She was sorry about the birds, but she had lived in the wild so long, hiding and hunting, vying for survival, that the image of being hunted herself appalled her more.

That was exactly what they needed. A cave of their own. If only they could get to see what one was like.

"Cave? What cave you want to see?" asked Cora. "All right, all right. When you get bigger, we going to take you to a cave." Cora and Didi smiled comfortingly and ran their fingers through the hair the children were allowing to grow.

But eventually the fact that the baanya restrained them at every turn – gently, yes, but unyielding, "like rockstone," Telma said – began to unnerve the older children, and then to chafe them. When Pawi promised to tell them more about the fires but stalled, or Didi said she would take them to see their caves in the mountains and stalled again, some of the children whispered to each other about slipping away during the night and going south along the east coast. Only Janice insisted she would stay on; she wasn't going to take Tiffney or Josiahmarshall to fight up in any mud. But she told the baanya nothing of what the rest of the children were saying. Of that Myche and the others were sure.

By her own count Myche was now almost thirteen, not tall but sturdy, still less inclined to talk than most of the rest and a lot more determined to have her own way. She moved most of them like a current, without effort on her part or struggle on theirs. But not all followed unthinkingly.

"Robber Boy seems to go along just to see what would happen next," Nat observed. "Then Shant – like he have to keep moving, as if he searching for something."

"All like him can't travel by heself," Brand jeered.

"Who can?" Myche pointed out. She ran her eye over the rest trooping after Didi. Five Cent didn't care which way he went: he hadn't time to care, because he was not taking his eye off the smallies. And Darati? Darati operated on the principle that Myche was always right, while Telma would do exactly as she pleased. One would have to live with that, but at least she had sense.

Otherwise, Myche drew most of the group round to whatever plan she had, and left them to believe they had thought it all up. Brand was different. She had to force him when he disagreed. Nat could not be forced, but that did not matter because he generally came, by his own route, to the same conclusion she did.

By now Myche had learnt them all.

It was her way. She watched and listened and remembered. She laughed as much as the rest of them, but most often inside, secretly. She refused to let any of them push her, least of all Brand – although he was most likely to persuade her by pleading. She turned an especially receptive ear to Nat or Telma.

One day, thinking them through while plotting her way ahead, she decided she needn't depend on the chantwell or anyone else to deliver their version of life. She could very well work out her own, and her story would look forward, not back.

The forward story most difficult to track was Brand's, because there was never a clue in advance about where he was going. Brand was more unmanageable than ever, yet more dependable, so rash and so nimble she had to be constantly on the watch. He was determined to have his way, and there was no telling what he might do at any time, especially if he thought she was under threat of any sort. Then he could be positively dangerous. What was he, ten? Whatever. Already he was warrior material. Myche noticed Darati had attached herself firmly to him.

In her silent world, vague to most of them, Darati seemed to come alive only if one of them was hurt. Then her meticulous cleaning or binding transformed her into an entirely different girl from the one who normally trailed uninterestedly along.

It was Nat who was most to be depended on. Slightly older than Myche, lean, calm and clear-thinking. Recently he had befriended Brand. Myche suspected it was for her sake and that Brand saw through that but accepted it. Shant and Wikki liked to *trouble* Nat about Myche, as they put it. But not Brand. Brand had time for anyone who looked out for Myche. He had no time for people like Janice and her tribe, who were so wrapped up in each other that the rest of the children were little more than a cover for them.

One day Brand said, "The Josiahmarshall faas enough to bring down confusion on the whole of us," and Janice was furious. Brand turned on her savagely. "If he wasn' digging up in that hole Didi warn him to stay away from, he wouldn' be lying there now helpless like baby. Bry, Ananda, Chunks – not even Kyle woulda find himself in that sort of trouble. And Josiahmarshall much older than the whole of them. He'd a dead if this thing did happen when we was in the bush on our own."

"Exactly!" Janice almost screamed at Brand. "And you sister nagging us to go back into the bush. If we listen to her, we all going die, yes."

Brand went from blazing mad to icy. "Actually, he woulda die anyway if Myche self didn't grab him up and run with him to find the healerwoman. And if Five Cent didn't start off right away to run ahead of them and try bring the healerwoman to the stupid boy. He woulda die, because he can't listen when people tell him to leave snake-hole alone."

"Well, if we go back into bush it won't have no Aunt Cora for Five Cent to bring."

By now they were both yelling at each other. Myche signalled Brand to give Five Cent a hand sponging down Josiahmarshall and glanced witheringly at Janice. Five Cent wasn't noticing any of them.

His eyes were fixed on the younger boy, who was now giving signs that he might live.

Five Cent was no longer a smallie. He had arrived four years ago and was nine by now, still know-it-all and occasionally whiny, but kind-hearted and more responsible. The littler ones worshipped Wikki for his food, but they would do anything for Five Cent. They avoided Indira because they said she preached vegetables and they had no patience with her routines and ceremonies, but Five Cent didn't mind her. He would come and sit nearby for her pujas. He even shared his allocation of vegetables with her because he said Indira wasn't doing a soul any harm, and they should let her pray as loud as she liked if it made her strong. Telma said that was just because Indira had always listened to Five Cent's moanings and sympathized. But it was more than that. He was an unselfish boy, Myche decided.

"Not like Shant," she grumbled to Brand. "And he's years older than Five Cent. He just don't care for nobody." Least of all for the two boys thrown off the boat behind him. Right in front of him, the pirates had killed their parents, tourists who had been stuck on the island nearest by. But Shant said that didn't make their children his burden, and three years in the Trust and then on the road with them had not changed his view.

Five Cent hated him for being miserable to Colin and Zef, and now they were older, Five Cent demanded, "What it is why all-you try to friend up with Shant, when you know years now how he miserable?"

Like Bry and Kyle, Ananda and Chunks had settled in with the baanya and their animals. "They'll never leave," Nat said, "worse again, Casey bring Ananda this pup." Then Qwa and all arrived and took up his dwelling in a tree above the light shelter she was now willing to endure.

Myche agreed that Bry and Kyle, after enjoying the other children's celebration over finding them not only alive but happy with the baanya, had settled in permanently.

"Bry still won't keep on clothes," Brand said, "unless they bribe him with sweets. And you see his teeth?"

"Those will drop out," Myche reminded him, "and Didi will make him take care of the next set."

Myche never gave voice to one thought about them that bothered her. Neither Bry nor Kyle ever asked about Ash anymore. Perhaps they had forgotten he had ever been there. Which was a pity, she thought, although she couldn't actually say why – except she wondered whether there was some part of Ash they could not see, something that survived.

The day's chores over, she sat against her favourite tree sorting things through. Three pressing problems, really. One was Robber Boy, who was harmless despite his bragging of terrible exploits – more of a nuisance and an embarrassment than anything else, and now he had been with them so long there was no question of getting rid of him. The chantwell regarded him with amusement, invited him to talk sometimes and other times shut him up. Robber Boy couldn't be trusted to keep his mouth shut, though, and that was a hazard.

The other two problems, the serious ones, were Pwessus and Tweetums. They might still be somewhere around and, at fifteen or sixteen, would be tougher and more brutish than ever. Myche was guarded about what she revealed to the baanya, but she felt that she and the rest needed advice about staving off the twins' next attack. Later that evening she told their story and described the two in all the detail she could.

"They never going to get at you here," Didi said. Her righteous satisfaction got on Myche's nerves.

But as what she said was probably true, Myche held her peace, especially since Didi distributed small chunks of sweet, soft, brown candy. *Chocolate.* It melted on the tongue and had every one of them groaning in ecstasy.

That night, though, before parting for bed, Myche whispered with Brand, Nat and Telma. Some of them, especially the littlest, were better off with the baanya, but Myche had decided to take her chance in the bush.

How did the baanya get to know? Myche realized their ears were everywhere (which was why they had lived on), and Nat believed they thought the only way to prevent the more restless children from moving on and falling into the wrong hands was to get rid of them once and for all. He had never trusted them. Still, he agreed they were not the sort of people who wanted to kill anyone, let alone children. But those who left needed to be pointed in a direction from which they could never come back.

The baanya talked things out with them as pleasantly as you please. They permanently settled the youngest, Kyle and Bry, Chunks and Ananda, in two households. They would have kept Colin and Zef too, but that pair were reluctant to part with Shant, who insisted he was leaving. It was as if he were hunting for something or someone, Nat told Telma. For what did Shant want with Myche and the rest? He was lazy and self-serving and could live in greater ease with the baanya.

"Nah!" Telma objected. "Dem going make him work. You see any of them lying around under tree a cock-up foot? Janice different. She will work once she know her two pickney safe."

. . . .

The baanya prepared to part with those who were intent on leaving.

Didi had Casey construct a new trolley for Wikki, and she gave him one of their smaller pots. Then she had Bois pack as much food as the children could carry. The baanya had already given them not only clothes but shoes (which they hated but accepted out of politeness), but now Cora added a supply of medicines, from fever grass to something they called binding weed for belly troubles, as well as a cleaning moss for bites or wounds. Pawi's household bestowed a huge cassava pone, and his son oversaw the packing. Babu insisted on his nephews wedging the pone steady in Wikki's pot with a bottle of honey. At first Five Cent had decided to stay with the smallies, but he changed his mind at the last minute when he realized Colin and Zef were insisting on going forward with the older group.

Only, when it was finally time to go, Ena and Didi directed the children to turn back for a short way and find the gap to the north that would allow them a shortcut to the western coast. At that point, they said, the children could turn south to retrace their steps. Otherwise, the baanya said, they couldn't allow them to leave. It would be irresponsible. There was no landbridge – a foolish idea – and pressing south along or even close to the eastern shore meant certain death, or worse.

In fact, as a gesture of supreme sacrifice, Didi and Bois would go along some of the way to keep the youngsters on the right road.

The children ate everything they could before leaving, then turned back northwards with their guides and went around the hillside where they had first seen the sweet potatoes flourishing. They passed blooms like torches, red and orange, that flamed up along their way and others that dangled bright boats of scarlet, yellow-edged, which sheltered tiny white flowers. The sweet potatoes they had seen cultivated were gone, though, and the land had returned to bush. The baanya led them in what seemed to be circles for a while before they arrived at the next gap, which should lead west.

"They never mentioned any shortcut west when they talked earlier, before we said we were leaving," Myche muttered to Nat, and he nodded.

Still, however impossible living permanently in High Forest had seemed to them, the baanya had fed and cared for them, and Marilyn cried a little, and Indira and Five Cent clung to Didi for a while. Bois shook Brand's hand and told him he must go hunting with them when he came back their way. Nat watched without a change of expression, but in the end he thanked them for the food and shelter and for being so kind to the smallies.

Then the two adults stood watching the forlorn little group sadly, as the children headed down the rocky path. Didi and Bois waved until their charges were out of sight.

After napping in a cool cavern in the rocky side of the path, the children crept out. Myche peered about to make sure their guides were truly gone and felt a strange mix of anxiety and release. They stretched, bickered and elbowed each other, and made a few nervous jokes. Then they drank the passion fruit juice the baanya had prepared for them and set off back up the slope to the fork in the path. There they took the southeast road and walked until night, arguing all the way about what could have lain in store for them along the path the baanya had directed them to take. But truth to tell, they took the southeast road for no other reason than that they had been warned against it. Along the way, they ate half the pone.

In the morning, they finished the pone and kept going until they came to a riverbed and followed it. Eventually something came to them on the air, a whiff of rotten eggs. By the time they reached the springs, the smell caught in their throats and set them coughing. The fumes made their eyes water, and when Myche leaned on Brand, choking, he drew her away behind a thick bush where she could catch her breath.

She had barely begun to breathe normally when a man's voice said, "I've been waiting."

14

OF FOLLY AND FIRE

MYCHE

"I've been following you since you left High Forest," he said, and even in her terror Myche knew that voice, though it had become not only deeper but quite hoarse.

The rest of the group had wandered on, and Myche and Brand stared at Shine, taking in the beginnings of a beard, the curly hair tied back with bright cloth. She could hear the other children's voices float back from a little way ahead, as Shine crouched then hustled them further through the scraggy bush along the dry river until they reached larger trees.

"You sick?" Brand asked. "Your throat?"

"No, it's the shouting on the ship. All the time." Shine glanced around as if already anxious to be gone. "They have me here to help round up some of the others. Those are the orders. I'm to get one or two for the ship."

"No." Myche felt the shock like a punch to her belly. "How you could do that? Who you rounding up?" She backed away, searching his face. Suddenly he seemed a stranger.

"Well, that's the point. I'm to bring in some child that's big enough. They'll kill me if I don't deliver. I here trying to work out what to do."

"Pwessus," Brand returned instantly. "Well. Hard to tell apart when they aren't together. Except his teeth are worse. One of them, any-way. Been following us for hours." Myche threw him a look of shock and accusation. "No point telling you," he added sulkily. "You'd only have carried on. Like he picked up our trail when we left High Forest."

Shine interrupted impatiently. "And the other one?"

"Nah! He must be take off."

Shine shook his head. "Not a chance. Unless one is dead, they're together."

"Or one is lost," Myche said, "and the other is looking."

"How could one be lost?" Shine dismissed that notion. "They're never apart. Is some trick."

"He had a chance to catch me, but he wasn't interested," Brand told her. "He's been watching *you*."

Shine ran his eyes over her and seemed to reach a decision. He said the twins were the only solution he could think of. Or rather, one of the twins. Either. Whichever he took might hold back on some information so as to protect the other. Just possibly.

Myche tried to focus on the instructions he threw out to them hurriedly before vanishing again into the forest.

. . . .

When the two caught up with the rest, they had a few guavas to show for their detour into the bush and a couple fish Brand had rounded up in a slow stream. Wikki was prepared to cook, but in the end, they decided to eat fruit and more of the baanyas' food to avoid sending up smoke. They packed away Marilyn's store of cassava from the baanyas' scattered provision grounds in High Forest and regretfully dumped the fish. By the time they had eaten and cleared the signs away, the sun was going down.

They were straggling along, spread apart on a stony clearing, when Pwessus bore down on them, grinning viciously and swiping a machete back and forth. The children scattered as he swept up a bag of their food. Gripping Brand's hand, Myche sprinted for shelter behind an outcrop of rock.

"Pwessus," she got out as her throat tightened, "I can usually tell."

Tweetums landed heavily in front of her.

"Not so fast." As she dodged, his fingers locked on her arm. "You're our dessert."

Shine hit the back of his head with a thick stick, and he fell without a sound. Then Shine swung around to face Pwessus, but he was already pelting off into the bush. At a jerk of Shine's head, Myche and Brand pounded along between the trees, in the wake of the other children.

Then from behind them came Shine's whistle. Myche grabbed Brand, and they fell back again from the others, squatting behind rocks to watch. In no time four burly figures had joined Shine and taken charge of Tweetums. The men laughed, clapping Shine's shoulder with a force that would have felled Myche or Brand, and congratulating him on a good catch. Then off they went, dragging Tweetums roughly.

Hours later, she was still awake in the hurried shelter she and Brand had thrown up a little way from the other children, a sorry thing made of fallen branches and broad leaves that were too soft for the job and would crinkle up and fall through in no time, though perhaps they might last the night. Something had set her nose off, and she was too stuffy to lie flat in any case, so there was no likelihood of sleep. She jumped when she felt fingers on her lips. Shine could materialize without a sound and vanish as silently.

Knowing he might be gone in minutes, she told him quickly how the baanya had directed them.

"No. You can never go back to the Trust," he said. "Tweetums is on the ship by now. I already told the rest what a liar he is, but when he's done talking, the sailors will check the Trust for sure. And they'll be on the lookout. Especially for you."

"He'll have said we're your . . ."

"That'll look like an effort to spite me with his lies. I told them I came ashore with a sister and brother, that one died almost immediately and the other two years ago. But they'll look all the same. You've grown . . . so you've got to live in the bush."

"Forever?"

"Only if you are very lucky." Brand laughed, then shut up when she shot him a look.

Shine worked it out that he had made such an impression by turning in Tweetums no one would be watching him and he needn't hurry back to the ship. Still, he jumped when a shadow crossed the space in the bush beyond their shelter, but it was One Thousand Eyes who padded forward softly and sprawled on the ground between them. They hadn't seen him for months, but as usual – having never offered a glimpse of himself in High Forest – he had turned up when Myche was convinced he had lost them.

She told Shine how different he was from the ocelots they had known in the vicinity of the Trust, yet the other children had begun to accept his trailing them because sometimes when he dropped in openly he might bring an agouti or an armadillo.

"That *is* different." Shine threw him an interested glance.

But had Shine ever seen a cat that big? Brand demanded.

Shine had, he said, a female blacker than the tar. It lived on the ship with them and had come from the same litter as One Thousand Eyes. So, no, these were not ocelots. They were from another place, a vast land south of the island.

"He likes water a lot," Brand said. "He swims or just lies around in it."

"Not like house cats," Shine agreed.

"What's a house cat?" Brand asked, but Shine waved the question away so as to get on with what he came for.

He drew a new and bigger map on the ground and said they must afterwards rub it out with their feet in case any of the pirates passed that way. Otherwise, nowhere on the island might ever be safe for them again. When Myche told him how she had made a sketch from memory, he ordered her to bring it out, snatched it and ripped it to shreds.

That done, he confirmed what the baanya had said: There was no other shore the children could reach. It had begun long ago with planes being refused permission even to approach the mainland.

"Planes," Brand breathed.

"Right. And now that hardly any ports in the region are safe for tourists, cruise ships are more popular than ever. Cruise lines have started advertising: *Enjoy the tropical seas without ever going ashore.*"

"Like Telma's tourisslady," Brand reflected, "except she went ashore."

"Yeah," Shine said. "Only now, with droves of people desperate to board anything that might float, the cruise ships shy away from most island ports." Out at sea, along the usual routes, the pirates lay in wait. The grander cruise ships became, the more they enticed pirates. It maddened them, Shine said, like blood dumped in shark-infested waters. Now the pirates came prowling further and further inland for anything they could get.

"Should we have stayed with the baanya, then?" Myche demanded. "Do *you* think we were safer in the forest?"

Shine said he wasn't sure himself. And yes, the baanya of High Forest were a quiet peace-loving people, but not straightforward. Their ancestors had come from different places and hadn't always got along. It was the catastrophe that brought them together on their tight homestead. Shine supposed it was true enough to say they were survivors – which just showed they were tougher than they let on.

"After the fires died down," he said, "the baanya must have lived for a while by stealing from ruins – mashed-up malls, dried-up sugar estates and a set of industrial plants that had been shutting down one-one for a while. Those who lived in the cities were foraging about." He drew them pictures with words – silent panyards, plague-desiccated coconut groves, but, most of all, burnt-out towns and blasted villages.

"How they all ended up in the forest?" Brand asked.

"They didn't," Shine replied, and Myche had already worked it out.

One set comprised households strewn through camps in dense bush and caves that riddled the hills. Those who had broken away had learnt to manage a different terrain – wetlands that were impassable for anyone unaccustomed to them.

"But didn't they all drown?" Brand exclaimed. "Pawi told us they went down into the mud."

"Masters of double meaning, those forest people." Shine smiled bitterly. Those who made the swamp their home had no hesitation about picking off strangers who lost their way and wandered in, he added. It was *garrison*, a term Shine didn't pause to explain but that they understood, because Telma used it to describe how the ocelots kept the borders of the Trust.

The scattering of baanya that took place after what the world called the Liberation had driven the most rebellious towards the Wet. Myche recalled how the soft-spoken people of High Forest had lifted their shoulders in bewilderment at all that useless rage.

And yes. All right. There *was* a third group. Shine was surprised the forest baanya had acknowledged the Shoreliners even indirectly.

Myche said, "No one ever says what *happened*."

"Because they wanted to forget," Shine said. "Same as you."

"*You* told us to forget."

"The ship. I said forget the *ship*. I didn't need to tell you to forget the rest – although, at the time it seemed useless to keep crying over it."

"Well, I don't know the rest," Brand put in crossly.

Shine shut his eyes, clenched his jaw. Then, shaking his head, he opened his eyes and took up his tale.

"When things began to fall apart, and foreign help dried up, many of the people who could have made things work flew out to jobs in other countries. Places that were less crowded welcomed them."

"Like where?" Myche asked.

"Would it make a difference if I told you? Calgary was one place I heard about," Shine said. "It was so cold that not everyone wanted to go there, or so people said. Their government let you in if you were bound for areas like that, once you were highly skilled or relocating with a set of money. But I don't have no time to talk about Calgary. What? *Me?* Go Calgary? What ticket I look like I could buy? Must be rat-passage." He flashed a grin.

Natural disasters began to hit the islands harder, he went on. A volcano in one or the usual hurricane that blew in could bring down a whole country, because no aid came in from outside, and the islands nearby were caught up in their own emergencies. That meant more people with no shelter, no medicine and hardly any food in place after place. Those who had sent their money out had no way of entering the country they had sent it to, but they paid to get into whatever boat was available, carrying what valuables they could. All this encouraged a whole new industry – only, no it was an old, old one. And it didn't stop with piracy. When the boat people got where they were going and were turned away, the crooks who had collected fares in advance cleared their vessels for the next crossing. They got rid of passengers who had nowhere to go by forcing them overboard. Then the sea made its own adjustments. Sharks multiplied in the suddenly well-stocked feeding grounds.

"And here?" Myche pressed.

"You forget here is not the only place to worry about," Shine said. "You sounding like Five Cent." He tumbled his hand through her hair, which had never been so long. "But yes, we had troubles inside as well as out, lawlessness through and through." He reached for his sack and pulled out a box of food and divided it between them. Long white stuff, hollow like little pipes but soft and creamy with cheese.

"Weird," Myche said, but smiled. "It have more?"

He watched them wolf it down. "All-you like to eat out my food, yes," but his eyes lit up with amusement.

Myche said, "No one ever told us what started the fires," and Brand added, "Or who blew up what."

Shine shook his head. "Too many accounts. Some say a few fighters who came home from a foreign war grew disgusted with the government and joined up with a set of frustrated youth. But they probably had nothing to do with any of it. They were the obvious scapegoats for what came next."

Brand raised a finger.

"I mean people used them as the excuse for what happened," Shine said. He paused and watched Brand. "Well, what?"

"You don't have anything else?"

"To eat? Have mercy."

Shine drew a package from his sack and unwrapped a couple slices of sweetbread with raisins, and other things they did not recognize. Then he rummaged for something else.

"Almost forgot," he exclaimed, tossing a small bottle of Vicks to Myche. He waited as she dipped her forefinger to smear the inside of a nostril.

"Go on. Go on," Brand demanded, licking crumbs from his fingers.

"Well, suspicion and fear spread like fire," Shine said, "and when a rock smashed through the stained-glass window of a church, talk started about who might have a grudge against churches and what might happen next or could have happened already. Rumours tickled those who thrived on panic. But these versions also found their way into newspapers so they became harder to ignore. People in bars, offices, living rooms and taxis murmured knowingly that there was no smoke without fire."

Brand put in mutinously that he didn't know what those places were, and Shine said, "Doesn't matter. People were ready to believe any tale at all and arrived at a sort of crazed group position. A popular account that blamed soldiers funded from outside lit a match. There were calls for the army to take control, and some little local hate group no one had ever heard of before claimed responsibility in advance. For what, no one said."

When he paused this time, Brand and Myche stayed still. At last they would know. Shine would tell them.

"It did come. No one knows from where. In the south there were five attacks on oilfields and refineries that had been closed down without proper safeguards. Over weeks those fires ate up villages and countryside, and wiped out most of the city in the south."

"What about Brukstone?" Brand asked.

"In truth. Well. Everyone knew someone who had seen something," Shine said. "Just as no evidence came out to support news reports about suicide attacks in the south, claims about a coup organized up north got repeated loudly and often enough for the world to believe."

"Coup?"

Shine got to his feet and dusted off the crumbs that Brand had spread everywhere. "Whether people really overthrew the government on purpose or not, the whole confusion brought trade to a halt. For who would do business with us? But worse than all of that," Shine added, "was the effect of terms like *coup* and *suicide attack* on neighbouring countries — especially when the commander-in-chief of the most powerful of them was ruthless and scorned advice. And was bordering on dementia."

He leaned back for a look outside the shelter at those patches of night sky he seemed able to make out between the branches overhead and then scrambled to his feet.

"Got to go," he said abruptly. He stepped over One Thousand Eyes and waved once before vanishing into the night.

15

CELLS

BRAND

"**WHAT YOU THINK DEMENTIA IS?**" **BRAND** asked Myche when they woke up next morning and were pulling down the flimsy shelters and tossing the branches apart to leave no sign of them ever having slept there.

The only trace of Shine's visit was a host of ants that had come for the sweetbread crumbs. Regretfully, Brand watched one raisin that had escaped him being born away.

"There was an old man who had it, in a book Shine helped me read. Is some sort of madness, must be. Shine said tiny areas in the brain break down, and you can't think straight any more." Myche stood there trying to remember. "The old guy was a king who had a set of children he didn't like again."

"They liked him?"

"One of them liked him whatever he did. I didn't always understand what they were saying, though."

Brand grinned. "One must be Robber Boy then."

By now they had joined the rest of the group, and they were walking once more.

Myche said, "I going to ask Robber Boy self what it was he said about some cell or the other."

Telma overheard, stopped and stared at her. "You going make him start talk? After nobody but Pawi could ever stop him."

"Nah!" Brand agreed.

"But I want to understand this business about cells," Myche argued. "Or how will we ever know what happened?"

Robber Boy had heard his name and hurried to her side. He swept his hat back on his head, and Myche groaned but let him talk.

"Well, if they can't run their own turf, tough. Other stuff makes me get rough. Coup? Let em stew – depends what crew takes over, shakes up, breaks down. Stakes are high. That's why we gotta pry, keep track, watch our back. Why we hack into their mail. Harvest every tale of disarray, watch every sign. But bottom line is time and time again another sick-soul hole in need. They plead and try to bleed us. Another yelp for help.

"We gotta sort em out. One cell can unleash hell. That word sounds gongs and sets off bombs. When I look back and count my wrongs, I've had enough. No one's as tough. 'Not this side of the world,' I shout. I tell the aircraft carriers and other gizmos, come about. You bet. Who's going to let a clear and present threat (one plagued, besides, by debt) grow at our side? That's not an error I'll be making, having terror breaking out. I shout: Suicide pact? Hacked. Release peacekeeping forces for attack."

"Oh Gaad." Telma groaned. "Don't me tell you say this boy mad as a shad? You going listen to eejit raving and call it history?"

16

MONSTER WAKE

MYCHE

IN TRYING TO WORK OUT THE sequence, Myche ran through her head everything she remembered the older children saying. Mitch had said, "If we're to make it on our own, we need what other people have who live together. Build shelters, gather food, watch the animals and the weather, find plants for fever and girl pains."

For Myche, the question was whether this flat easy terrain they had come to now was the right place to make their own. Marilyn, Indira and Shant insisted they would be better off with some group of adults, and that might be true. What did Myche know about how best to provide for the rest of them?

She went back to that exchange between Mitch and Shine.

Shine had added, "Teach the smallies everything we know."

"How?"

"Don't know. Make up songs. Tell stories."

Stories. There had been stories about ships that belched flame, about dragons, about soucouyants. Now Myche had seen hair growing under her arms and some sprouting on Nat's chest, she knew either of them could be snatched away at any time, so she gathered the fragments of information she had and pieced them together for the other children.

But a couple of them were still so little, and even one or two who were older had known only life in the Trust for almost as long as they could remember. How could she tell it to draw them all in? Besides, what she wanted to say wasn't only about what may have happened, but how it might have felt and what they should do about it.

She worked it through and through, thinking of Zef, Colin, even Indira, and later that evening when she began to talk, the rest fastened their eyes on her as if they could never tear them away, not for a second.

·········

"Once there was a necklace with a jewel so bright and rich there was no other like it in the whole world. It was so big it floated sparkling in the sea, and people lived on it.

"One evening a girl of about ten, and her brother, who was six, were walking away from their home on the jewel when they heard a roaring overhead. They looked up and saw huge bright bodies streaking across the sky with wings sloped back and smoke trailing behind. The creatures had no faces, only sharp, sharp beaks. And they spat fire."

"Dragons?" Colin guessed hopefully.

"Aah. Only their hearts were of steel."

The others leaned forward as Myche told them how the two children whirled around to head home, but their house flashed open in front of them and flames gushed out, so the brother and sister tore off to see if they could find help. All about them buildings blazed and crashed, and there was no big person to tell them what to do. As they ran they met other children – one whose father had been dragged away because everyone blamed him for the explosions, another crying that he had got separated from his parents in a crowd storming a gate to board the last plane.

The trees that were not burnt bore magic fruit that kept the children strong, and they shared them with two others they found lying on the road recovering from a terrible fever that had taken their parents. For when the mangroves got burnt out, so did the creatures who lived there to feast on mosquitos, and now some people who had escaped the fire lay roasting with fever. But a greater menace was in store. Four little girls strayed in, soaked down with seawater and blistered on their feet from hot sand. There were murderous rogues at sea throwing children away and then gathering them up again for sale.

"The last child who joined them said that a powerful country nearby was boasting about having freed the island of terrible danger from groups that hid in the dark and struck out unexpectedly. *Cells* they called them." Robber Boy scrambled to his feet, and Myche held up her palm firmly. "No, thank you." When he bowed good-naturedly and settled down again, Myche resumed her tale.

"Nothing was the same again. The children couldn't find anyone they knew. But they were not alone, for they had each other. They talked about leaving, but none of them knew how. Bandits had looted and terrorized towns and villages until folk cleared out and searched for hideouts in the wild. The wilderness grew and grew until it devoured most of the country, but it was kind to the children. They felt safe there, once they dodged the pirates – who brought wealth pouring into towns on one coast after the other while keeping off all the wanderers nobody wanted ashore. Which was why no one stopped them."

"Who you think it have could stand up to pirate?" Shant burst out. "You make it sound so easy."

Brand fired up right away. "Then you wouldn't fight people who ready to hunt you like quenk?"

"Forget the Shant him," said Telma with a contemptuous flip of her hand. "What bout dem big place with plane and warship? What dem do?"

Myche raised her shoulders. "They say they did all they could for us by breathing fire from the sky. And they left behind their peace-keepers, who do nothing about the pirates either."

Darati passed Myche a cup of water, and she squeezed the younger girl's hand thankfully before draining it. Now she had to finish, and this was the hardest part.

"The children found no big people they could stay with as happily and safely as they could live with each other. The adults who had been left shared little in common with each other besides having been born here, in better days. That was not enough to keep them together. So they came undone, fraying into three strands that just dangled there. Only the children wound themselves together and made each other strong.

"Meanwhile, this island had got unstrung from the original necklace, and it quivered there on its own. No one abroad thought it was a gem anymore. From the outside it must have looked more like a bead of sweat. Or a teardrop.

"Only the children knew it was the same jewel it had always been, and it was theirs."

When she stopped, everything was quiet for a while. Indira looked confused and Marilyn pouted. Perhaps they had wanted a happier story, one that solved everything, but Myche didn't have any of those.

Zef said, "We just gotta make another Trust for ourselves. Somewhere. That's what." And Darati started clapping until the others took it up. Nat nodded without a word.

"At last smaddy try make sense of this ting," Telma said, rumpling Colin's hair. "Don't it?"

"Yeah," he said.

All the same, Myche knew in her own heart that the past remained a vast mystery, and she would never get to the bottom of it.

The next morning, Myche crouched behind a guava tree at the furthest edge of the little cluster of sleepers. She drew up her knees and rocked back and forth, waiting for the cramps to pass. Her body was behaving in the scariest ways, and she would have been more frightened if Shine hadn't warned her about what he called *the signs*. At the same time, he had made her understand *why* he was warning her – and that was more petrifying than anything else.

She sipped the cerasee tea Telma had drawn for her. This mysterious wonder-brew had turned out to be no more than karaile bush, but it helped. She glanced over her shoulder and felt afraid to turn her eyes front again. She was beginning to jump at shadows – and this, just when she should have felt older, stronger, more certain of what to do, more in charge of herself and Brand. Still, now she knew more about the island. To make the story, she had had to assemble all sorts of oddments from her memory. The fact that she had gathered that much of it told her the island was a small place, and if Shine could find her easily in this part of it, so could anyone else.

Feeling naked suddenly, she scrambled to her feet to find Brand, so they could rejoin the others and tell them she was ready to leave, for all their sakes. They could go on together, or split up, just as they liked, but she would have to move on from this last tenuous stopping place they had contrived. Again.

Telma and Nat understood at once and were as anxious as she was to find somewhere more sheltered and secure to settle down. Marilyn, they said, should come along, because she was only a year or so younger. Shant didn't count, but then, there was no question of deserting Brand, Darati, Five Cent, Wicki, Indira, or Colin and Zef. Even that fool Robber Boy, big as he was.

In the end, after bickering into the afternoon, everyone agreed to move together.

"Is where, though," Telma said later, when the older ones were talking quietly. "You have somewhere in mind?"

"Well, if we leave north and we don't find anywhere west and we musn't go east, we only have south," Myche reasoned. "Remember when we reached the sea and turned towards the black lake?"

"We couldn't have passed if we turned east then," Nat said.

"Right. But now we coming from north," Myche said. "If we don't go too far east and we can turn south, we might get to this place with no roads left and no shore."

"Eehi." Telma breathed a sigh of relief. "So nobady can't get to we. We better tell them we think of a place before the Marilyn and them start whining."

The hint of a destination soothed the rest of the group. That night they told tales again, but mostly about the Trust and the ocelots.

. . . .

At sunrise they slipped off once more among the scattering of trees. They passed old gnarled coffee bushes interrupted by the occasional huge silk cotton, catching sight of a few pigs that shied away, and soon Myche felt the ground more rocky beneath her feet. They came upon broken houses, glass crunching underfoot. They tugged on the worrisome footwear the baanya had insisted on, and it protected them, but when the ground softened again to fallen leaves on grass, they shuffled the shoes off in disgust. They turned east, then south, in the direction of another range of mountains. One Thousand Eyes showed up from behind a silk cotton and followed for a while from one ancient coffee bush to the next; then a scuttle of small hard feet under a bush caught his interest, and he lunged out of sight.

A plain with wild sugarcane raised their spirits enough to make them talk about catching one of the goats that had suddenly appeared, running everywhere.

"Or some pork," Wikki offered.

"Them big ting like what you see this morning? Them pig so wild they more likely to eat us," Telma said, puncturing that.

When the bush thinned, the coffee disappeared and there were more ruins, and behind these stretched a wide area covered with stinking litter and huge black birds with bald heads stumbling and flapping over it. Myche hurried them away, because it was just the sort of place to have rats, she said.

On they went, and ended up in an area where there was only thornbush, the ground thick with dry leaves.

When Colin screamed, Telma didn't even look back. She just snapped, "Shant, leave the little boy alone. After he not doing you nothing."

But it was not that kind of scream, and it skewered Myche, twisting her around in search of whatever had befallen. Even Shant was startled and ran to sweep Colin up from the ground. He boxed off the scorpion that was still on the child's leg and yelled for Darati. But

it was no use. The healing leaves they had were for ordinary stings —
ants, mosquitoes, even wasps. Myche remembered how ill Colin had
been once when a bee stung him, how long it took the swelling to go
down, how he had almost stopped breathing. This time the struggle
was much worse.

Zef squatted beside him, swaying from side to side, his pink palms
upturned for help, his wrists marked by blue veins under the translu-
cent skin and his eyes wide grey pools. Indira prayed, Darati ran back
and forth snatching one water bottle after another so as to cool Colin's
forehead, and Telma laid soft cactus flesh on the swollen foot. The
cream had been no use, and Myche let it drop, pressing her hand over
her mouth as she swayed on her feet looking down at him. When the
boy lost consciousness, it was almost a relief.

Shant held him and rocked him back and forth, and Zef clung
to them both, but it was useless, and no one was surprised when he
grew still, just as Ash had a few years before. But Shant had not been
with Ash while he died; he had only found out afterwards. He did
not know what the stillness was, and for a long time he shook Colin
and howled at Darati and Myche to do something, anything. To wake
him up. Myche shook her head, unable to word the fact that nothing
could wake him.

This time there was no sea or river nearby, no Place of Return,
and she had no idea what to tell them they should do. It was Nat who
whispered that they could use some branches and sweep the dry leaves
together as high as they could. They heaped the leaves over Colin,
and Indira chanted something they did not understand. She wanted
to light the leaves, but Shant would not have that, and Telma pointed
out that the whole area was dry and the fire would take them all.

Eventually they led Shant away, looking for a different kind of
place now, somewhere with a clear hard path, some higher, damper
ground. He didn't care; he just followed, tears flowing down his face.

But Zef had stopped crying. When Shant tried to put an arm
around his shoulders, the child boxed it away. "Don't touch me," he
said. "Don't ever touch me or talk to me again."

Shant was alone in his own morass of guilt and regret.

For the others, the only relief was that most of the smallies had stayed behind in High Forest.

"I start to think we shoulda stay north with the baanya too," Telma said, and Marilyn nodded.

"I never wanted to leave," Marilyn confirmed. "All-you say we had to."

"No," said Telma sharply. "Whoever did want to stay coulda stay. Don't Janice stay? I did ready to leave: If I make a mistake is fi me fault. But nobody didn' *make* me leave, or you. In fact, is you dream up the landbridge foolishness to begin with, so shut you mout'."

Myche walked with her lips clamped tight together, and the shock of losing Colin reverberating so violently that she heard only snatches of what they said. No place to settle, nowhere to step with any certainty. Dry leaves in the wind and underfoot. Forever looking over their shoulders. Backing away from the protection of High Forest, they had all followed her here. Barefoot.

But as the clean mountain paths and the healthy life with the baanya came back to them, the group as a whole, without consulting one another, turned their way more determinedly uphill. They soon found themselves at the foot of another range. The thought passed unspoken among them: *Perhaps we could just live here.*

"Only, we don't know whether we are near a shore, whether there is some trail nearby that the pirates use," Myche said, searching in her brain for the map Shine had drawn in the dirt when they saw him last.

"Watch!" Nat pointed up the slope to a high flat patch of green, and behind it they could make out fissures here and there.

"Yes," Myche said. "If we get up and find a cave, we could use that, the way the baanya did. We could fix a couple shelters for everyday and have the cave to hide in."

"Or even stay dry in the rains." Telma reached out and snapped off a straight branch to help her up the slope.

An hour later, they came to the entrance of a cave. A strong wind had pushed a mat of leaves in through the entrance, but they could always sweep those out later. Though they wrinkled their noses at the smell, it was nothing compared to that of ocelot spray that had built up over time. While it was still bright, they put on their shoes so as to get their few possessions stored just within the entrance, and then they set off to build a light shelter in the thin cluster of bushes not far from the cave, one they could take down easily and hide. There was a trickle of clean water nearby but such a thin supply that they knew they must find more before the dry set in properly. They decided to sleep in the shelter, because no one felt up to braving the darkness of a cave as yet, and there was no need because it was a warm dry evening.

"And you don't notice it have no mosquito?" Five Cent sounded pleased, as if he had personally arranged matters so.

Wikki had got the last of the sweet potatoes boiling, and said salt was done but if they didn't like the food they could sit and watch it. Marilyn giggled and blurted out that was what their mother used to say. *Mother*, she had said. Just like that. In the shocked silence that followed, all they had lost crushed down on them, and it was the weight of sheer emptiness.

"So nothing cyan't stop the cruiters and them?" Indira whispered minutes later.

Not really. Myche tried to gather the energy to explain. It was a huge industry now. The pirates had captured bigger and bigger vessels, yachts, freighters, cruise ships, small naval vessels that came already armed. She had learnt from Shine that a tanker was their latest acquisition, but she did not say that, because she would not have been able to explain how she knew. Right now, it was best to hide, she concluded. Her voice sank low, almost to a whisper, she was so tired. Just hide. Somewhere remote, like this. It would be good not to have to walk all the way south to somewhere they hadn't even seen.

She supposed she would become accustomed to this place, even though night had transformed it into something strange and uncanny. All around, tall trees bearded with trailing shroud-like mosses barely let the moon shine through, a ghostly web of pale filaments that no wind stirred. An eerie silence rendered the landscape more ghastly, but she had travelled far enough to know most places looked better in the morning. Perhaps they need only wait.

They had woven their shelter well, as the baanya had taught them, and after a brief light rain in the night, they woke dry and comfort-able, though ravenous with hunger. They tumbled out from the mesh of leaves and branches to see that the nearby trickle had swelled to a regular little stream, and Five Cent discovered a few crayfish between the rocks. They were swift, though, impossible to snatch from the narrow crevices, and in any case, Five Cent's attention was mainly on Zef. There was still a bag with some rice and small parcels of dried peas, corn and other seeds, but Telma said if they ate all the seeds and didn't plant any, one day there would be nothing to eat. Marilyn said there would be nothing to eat in just two days, and what made Telma think they could hold out for food until some seeds grew?

They argued about the place with the ruins and quarrelled with Myche for rushing them away when they should have stopped to search for food, or even just salt. And Myche said yes, and whatever food they had found there with a little rat pee on it would have served them right.

But by afternoon she had decided there was no point any longer in hiding the saltfish she had got from the baanya, wrapped tight in leaves to keep in the smell. She had carried it the whole way, even though Telma had grumbled about people who were not cleaning themselves properly and smelled like fish. And all the time Myche had been planning to keep it as long as she could and bring it out when there was nothing left; and now there was nothing left but plain rice, and she could bring out a little piece of saltfish for flavour and horde the rest on the ledge in the cave where she had stashed it.

·········

That was why, that evening before sunset, Myche ran back into the cave, only to be met this time with an onrush of vague, flittering shapes, a dark cloud billowing towards her. Leaves blowing? Her first thought, instantly dismissed, dissolved into panic as a thrum of soft flapping gathered to a rumble. She twisted away, screaming, "What?" and flailing with her hands as small winged bodies fluttered around her face, her arms and belly and legs, the air suddenly thick with mouselike things coming at her from every direction, mouthing silent shrieks, yet here and there piercing the dusk with shrill needles of sound. The multitude of vicious little rat faces sent her heart into palpitations, her chest tightening as if they filled her very throat, smothering her. She froze in horror as thousands upon thousands swept past, and her own flesh, writhing then shrinking aside, faded into this havoc of beating shadows. And it was like a murky river parting before and rushing past her, out of the cave.

Then silence.

At the core of the stillness, she drew in, shut off, shut down.

Someone spoke, as if far away.

"We won't have to worry about mosquitoes inside the cave, then," Brand said helpfully, his back to her as he stood just outside, face calmly upturned. Then he looked back, swung around to grab her hand and peered into her face. "You okay, or what?"

Her knees were crumpling, her feet sliding. Her body would have folded up right there on the stone of the cave floor if it were not, as she made out now, thick with droppings and writhing with roaches, a stink rising from the disturbed mess around her feet. Her hand reached out and gripped Brand's shoulder.

"They still around," she rasped, "everywhere."

"Looking for food."

"Blood?"

"Mostly fruit and insects, I think. Maybe some want blood."

"We can't stay. Not anywhere near."

"Bats are all about. You can't find a place without *any* bats."

"But not, not all at once. Not this . . ." No words came to her for that surreal onslaught. Her voice tightened in its narrow thread of air. "Get me out. All I want . . . out . . . out."

Brand's shouting seemed to come to her from a distance, and then there were others milling around as he held her up. Her hands clutched Brand, shaking, while their voices came and went, but nothing made sense. There were only broken phrases, a few words dangling – *What? How?* – as she felt herself gathered up and lifted.

Then Nat's voice: "Get her as far from the cave as we can."

As they laid her down, the occasional screech still escaped her. Someone's hands – her own? – batted around her head, away from her face, fingers clawing at her hair.

"Give her space," Nat said, and most of the rest must have drawn back, because then only Nat, Brand and Darati were nearby. "They gone for what we left in the cave."

She was quieter by the time the others returned, though she found herself crying softly, and now and then she heard her own voice whimpering, "Get me out." Again and again, "Out, out."

Then she felt herself walking downhill, supported by an arm on each side, heard arguing over whether the path led southeast. Some grumbled along the way, but half-heartedly.

Telma said it was one thing perching their things on a rock ledge that was relatively clear, but what if they had had to hide there for a few days? For that was the whole idea of the cave, wasn't it? "Who going sleep in bat doo-doo and cackroach? Must be unnu."

Their argument came and went and faded out. Darkness fell. The ground beneath bruised her legs and bottom, but it didn't matter. Her head sank between her knees, and her arms wrapped around her legs. With the light, their voices rose again, and it must have been Brand occasionally prising her chin up to put water or fruit into her mouth. "She won't chew," he complained. Small soft chunks of mango or banana slid into her mouth and down her throat. All around, the children sounded nervous, irritable, and some part of her realized they needed her – that none could conceive of her not being in charge.

"Even when she had that fever, she was bossy – once she woke up," Marilyn said.

But for Myche it was all disconnected – the children, the trees, the rocks, her own unresponsive, quivering knot of limbs.

"Well, is either you get up and walk, or we have to leave you here pon ground," came Telma's voice.

A hand under her arm was Nat's, and there was Brand throwing

a look of pure venom at Telma. Marilyn and Five Cent shouldered
Telma aside to press forward in case they could do anything.

Someone said, "Where Darati?" and Darati hurried over, breathing
hard and holding up Myche's gourd and backpack, retrieved from the
ledge in the cave.

They propped Myche up and got her walking again between Nat
and Brand, and that way they trudged a good distance downhill until
they were in the forest again.

"Put out your foot." It was Brand trying to get Myche's shoes on
her feet – the ones the baanya had made for them.

When they started walking again, she saw Telma going ahead with
a light branch, brushing fallen leaves and dry bush out the way.

Then Myche lost track of time until they stopped again.

"Watch." It was Five Cent, pointing at Shant in amazement.

Shant was clearing a place for Myche to sit, and when she sank
down, he rolled up a bit of thick woven coverlet he had been carrying since he left High Forest and tucked it under her head. Her body
stayed limp and still as if asleep, though she knew her eyes were open.

"Myche?" It was Brand, but in a small scared voice. When her eyes
blinked, he seemed to take heart enough to continue. "Watch. You
have to try get better, you know. Shine gone; we don't know when
they coming for Nat or Telma. Or you self. You can't just quail up
there so."

A snort just behind them made him jump and startled her out of
the fog she had felt around her for hours, or days – she was not sure.
It was One Thousand Eyes, stalking forward without a glance at the
rest of the children, carrying some grey-brown animal in his mouth.
He padded over, dropped it in front of Myche and licked his tongue
around his jaws. Then he strolled away unhurriedly, stopping at the
edge of the clearing to turn and stare at her for a few moments before
disappearing again into the bush.

Myche lay with her eyes focused on the offering, a little animal,
and Brand tugged at her to sit up.

"Is a tatou," Five Cent whispered reverently.

Supporting herself with one hand, she jerked her chin at the armadillo curled up in its tight hard armour, and felt around for her voice.

"Give Wikki," she said.

. . . .

Three days later, she was back in full force.

They had now passed into damper, lusher surroundings. Five Cent insisted that a place like that would have snakes even if it had no scorpions, and for once no one argued with him. An iguana waggled by as if to confirm that this was a fine habitat for reptiles.

But as the forest gave way to dense mangroves, the group quickly lost all sense of direction. The ground softened to mud that sucked off the light shoes and squished between their toes. The greenery above them was busy with darting lizards and raucous with yellow-headed parrots and other birds similar to parrots but bigger, with red bellies and sweeping tails, hopping, flapping, and skimming in and out. When Five Cent pointed wordlessly and lost his hold on the mangrove root, it was Myche who grabbed him and shouted for help as he slid down into a dark pool. By the time they got him up, the huge boa that had uncoiled to watch them advance had disappeared.

"He gone longtime," Brand said encouragingly, but Myche thought the boa may as easily have just gone still against the dappled leaves and bark and be right there in front of them. And what else might there be, close but invisible simply by lying motionless.

"Watch out for caiman, eh?" As she called out, she unfolded a stained and cracking paper from a plastic bottle she had wedged among the other treasures in her pillowcase sack. She had drawn another map from memory of what Shine traced out in the dirt. She smoothed it out to see what lay to the southeast, then folded back the top so as to hold it with one hand and trace with her finger the only way she could imagine them going.

Nat bent over it with Brand craning to see over his shoulder. They had to go on in the hope of finding some way to cross the river.

"You don't draw no river," Brand complained. But Nat said, "How could she? It's all over the place anyway."

WeLand

Her sketch of Shine's map couldn't show them where to cross the river, or how to avoid the morass around it. Yet he must have crossed it to describe any part of this area well enough for Myche to guess where they were, Nat said. But he didn't sound sure.

"If Janice and the rest change their minds," Brand whispered, "how will they find their way after us without any map?"

"They won't," Nat dismissed the idea once and for all. Janice had been wrong, he said. For the baanya might be good to her and the younger ones, but they would never allow them to leave once they showed them the cave and anything else they had kept secret.

Myche was thinking more about the stories they had heard regarding the wetlanders, tales to frighten children from wandering, or perhaps to lure children who left High Forest to some other place they could never leave. What if the High Forest baanya really had passed on to the wetlanders the problem of catching and either keeping or dispensing with these wandering children?

When Myche unfolded that theory, Brand objected. "They warned us away from the swamp. They turned us in the other direction."

"Aah." Nat smiled ruefully. "I didn't see it before. They were depending on us doing whatever they warned us against. Not so? They don't want us straying around and getting caught, then telling the way to their homestead."

After a while Myche folded the map, slid it back in its clear tough wrapping and then into her pack. The sun was climbing overhead, but even Robber Boy, who was the tallest, could not look over the lower shrubs to guide their way. Or perhaps he could not see the point of looking, for he just went along twirling his fingers and trying out one stupid rhyme after the next. Still, when Zef tumbled over a root and lay there refusing to get up, Robber Boy fished him out of the muddy puddle and jacked him up on his shoulders.

Deep in the bush, with the trees reaching higher and thicker above them, the children lost all track of direction among the channels of water whose depth they dared not test. They floundered in the trap of this endlessly encircling shore and consuming bush. In the confusion, they were aware of life rustling, honking, squawking all around, ducks with glossy brown backs and red bills, toucans with fiery chests and blue faces ending in huge curved beaks, and other nameless creatures hopping along thin bobbing branches, scurrying through dry leaves, padding along musk-marked paths invisible to the eye. Then, where the children stumbled on a clearing, there came the erratic swoop and hover of wings beating too fast to detect as anything other than a shimmer of light. But there was no avoiding the thick greenery all around, and once under the foliage, they could not be sure of going in any particular direction.

Still, Myche and Nat made them press on in search of a track at least, even as the ground grew damp between wider pools. There should be some road along the shore if they could reach it, Nat said. Meanwhile the plants grew creepy, arching in and out of the water, and here again there was no telling branches from stems, or where stems began and roots ended.

Then they came upon an expanse of shadowed water, spreading ahead and on either side, with small patches of land. Or mud. Who could say?

"This have animals that eat mosquitos," Indira said, as if pleased to be there after all.

"We could hold the hard stems or branches and feel our way to see whether it's deep," Nat said, peering anxiously at the muddy tangle.

"I'm staying on the dry." Myche set her mouth mulishly. "So is Brand."

"We won't find the shore by staying on the dry."

"We won't find it by sinking down into that mess either."

"Then we have to follow the river, for it will come out in the sea."

"So will we, if this is the river and we get into it."

Brand stared, considering. "What if the rest of WeLand is mud, all the way to the sea?" He paused, his eyes closed. He seemed to be dreaming.

"Then there wouldn't be no shore, right?" Myche steupsed. "So maybe we never got here." She was in no mind to be fanciful.

But under Nat's patient prompting, they broke a few stiff branches to feel their way along till they came upon solid ground again.

Water that was obviously deeper slid slowly by them, jungle green, lit in places by white-ringed necks of birds with sharp beaks jabbing at whatever lurked below. The mud beneath Myche's feet oozed grey-green and slippery. Ahead, patches of clearer water were slimy at the edges. A mudbank heaved briefly, and the ooze gleamed slick behind the downward slither of a caiman. A long, narrow beak came up with a fish, tossed and snapped shut above a bulge rippling down a serpentine neck.

The children exchanged glances at the thought of food among the roots. But how to get anything from the depths, or know whether it was safe to swallow? They knew never to eat anything raw, much less from a swamp. The thick green water mesmerized them, and it was when a powerful flapping noise broke out over their heads that they looked up and the unruly root system arching about them splayed above too like the frame of a vast shelter no one had bothered to complete.

Or . . . or what? There drifted back to Myche's mind a huge place, a church – *cathedral*, whispered a voice from the past. *Where God lives.* It was when Brand was very small. They had taken the baby (brand-new baby brother) to be baptized, but afterwards they went on calling him Brand. Shine had held him till the man in the black robe lifted the baby up and marked him with water. She couldn't remember the name he spoke, but beneath these arches and sky deepening to rose with nothing, not even glass, between, a hush fell and spread among them, and in Myche a recollection welled back, a sense of something vast and reassuring.

It was cooler now, and a gathering flock of long-legged, long-necked, long-beaked birds flapped in and up, lazily, to roost above them in the trees. Birds the colour of the setting sun. It was the same on each mud-crusted island with its clump of mangrove that reached out and interlaced with the next. The dark green mantle lit up as the red birds sailed in before dusk to set the swamp alight, briefly, with blooms of flame.

So now the quiet was broken up, and the children too shuffled about pushing and nudging for space. Indira, who was growing into a tall, thin streak of anxiety, relaxed unexpectedly into play, stalking with exaggeratedly long, languid strides.

"Watch me. I'm red bird," she cried, placing each stiff leg gently before her and rocking forward and back while shifting weight from one leg to the other.

Five Cent, and then Brand and Marilyn took up some alternative self to fit into this impossible place, trembling hummingbird wings, whining insect-like, skittering, darting, droning, till the shadows rounded them up closer and closer together.

As the light went, the children settled underneath the arches of mangrove wherever the ground was firm but especially where leafy branches spread between them and the birds ("because they *will* poop on us," Brand grumbled, as if that was the general intent of the flock in roosting there). By the time darkness crept over and through the leaves, they were twisting restlessly from hunger, while mosquitoes billowed around at every turn they made.

As she drifted off into an uneasy sleep, Myche heard Marilyn declare, "If we had a good few of Myche bat now, mosquito wouldn' be driving us mad so."

In the morning, after a beastly night, they pressed on without any idea of whether they were still moving southeast. The mangroves opened out on a plain of grass and sedge, ending, in the distance, in an expanse of water with islands here and there. Only those might not be solid islands but clumps of vegetation. As the children prepared to let go of the mangrove roots and set out for the plain, they saw it was not a plain at all, but floating grass and other tougher stuff. When they poked at some nearby, they glimpsed long tangled roots reaching deep beneath them, but other plants seemed just to drift on the surface.

The little drenched band fell back, clutching the mangrove roots and feeling for whatever purchase their feet could find in the muddy shallows. And as they hesitated, clinging to the roots, they became aware that the water was higher on their legs than when they had reached this place. That it was *rising*. But when they glanced behind to see how best to retreat, it was no longer possible to tell how they had got to where they were. The little mounds of more solid ground were now lost below a level sheet of water reaching back among the trees as far as they could see.

Glancing at each other, their terror mounting, they pulled themselves higher on the arching roots as the green water inched up.

PART 4

WATER DREAD

17

THE GREAT WET

MYCHE

AFTERWARDS BRAND AND MARILYN ARGUED ABOUT who had been the first to see the figure standing in the water so close they could have touched him, but Myche knew it was Brand's quick eyes that had picked up the thin man with the fountain of hair tied at the top of his head and falling down his back.

As the man moved in the shadow of the mangroves, he disappeared and appeared again almost before their eyes, like a mist that condensed, thinned and came together of its own will. Then he vanished once more, but when they could not see him, they heard him. He hummed a tune that seemed at first to have no rhythm. Eventually they caught onto it, but now it came on the other side, from the lake of floating plants.

In a while he drew up on a raft of bamboo laced firmly together. Another raft followed from behind a clump of sedge, and he talked them calmly off the mangrove arches in the water and onto the dry bamboo. The man on the other raft had nothing to say, just offered them a gnarled hand to settle them so the rafts remained steady. Then that second raft headed off with Marilyn, Wikki, Five Cent, Zef and Robber Boy, while Brand, Myche and Nat clambered into the singerman's vessel, where Indira, Shant and Telma were already sitting. Darati hung back until she saw both Telma and Myche board it. She was more afraid of men than of rising water. The man who had found them watched her carefully alight, without stretching out his hand to her as he had to the others.

He regarded them silently as he pushed off, wielding the pole expertly before he began chanting again.

"Who are you, likkle yout'?" The singerman paused, then answered himself in song. "I say all-you the drifting people, lash by the sea, toss up by currents. Drown people, float up again through cracks."

Drown. It sent a shock through the children, the forbidden word falling carelessly from the lips of an adult. Myche tightened her arms against her body to quiet the shivering. Some of his phrases she blotted out without even meaning to, but others slipped through. *Washed up,* she heard him say. As the water slapped the side of the raft, a wave of anguish heavier than any water swelled over her, and when she tried to gulp it down, it was a flood she choked on, fighting for air. Her stomach churned now, yet she was not sick. She knew she was not. It was the fear of being hunted and found. Or of sliding through some fissure and never being found, ever again.

The singerman poled along among the nearby clumps of floating grass, then on beyond another set, chanting softly all the time. "Mangrove and floating grass that connect forest and sea are ours, but so is the water that parts the forest from the sea. The river is our road. We do not lurk and hide forever behind trees. We only lie in wait among the arches of roots for those who would enslave us if they could; so make no one cross that line of palm trees." Then he glanced back at them kindly. "Nah. Not to fear. Let the little lost ones come unto us. They will eat what we eat: fish, vegetables, all meat except pork. And quenk, for that is wild, not unclean, not pork. Our souls are clean, wash in this water that have a little salt but not enough to corrupt."

"Who you are please, sir?" Indira asked. "What sort of song that?"

"Hear me – our songs are of Jah, and we also sing our brothers' songs of battle, of loyalty to the gunarch, because they are our brothers in the Wet. Our music is not of war like theirs, but is not dance music neither, nor the noise of Babylon the wicked. Our singers are wailers and warners. We are the legacy of Jah, speared from the thunder of the downpressor – not just stories to frighten children into staying home. Our music pound out on taut-drawn hide and fired through flesh. We are legend."

"So you sing songs and you are a story too?" Indira seemed pleased to have figured it out, but the others were surprised about her speaking up.

Myche could tell the singerman was pleased.

"You get it right," he answered. "We the ones they couldn burn, couldn drench. So we tell the world, *keep out*. The people of the Wet done make their peace with death."

Eventually he drew up beside what seemed to be yet another floating pad of grasses but turned out to be a wide platform with groups of adults and children, the children leaping off into the water then clambering back up again. Even the babies rolled off and darted under the surface like the little fish Telma called tiki-tiki; then they held up their arms to be lifted out. There was a ladderlike step at one end of the platform, though no one seemed to use it. Here the raft bobbed gently in place for Myche and the rest to climb off.

"Listen," said singerman when they had all sat down. "You like to hear story sing? Or you only looking for what you know already? Can't go so. Is not one story it have. Song is a thing we don't *make*: it find its way out, and we help it if we could. Story unfold, and we feel after it to see which way it would take us. So many of us it have here – and as many stories. And you self bring a new way the song could go."

He turned and called for someone to bring juice for the children. When he was passing it around, he paused as Robber Boy lifted down the child he had been carrying and settled him on the ground.

"What a sad little face," Singerman said. "What *you* name? Zef? You sure? All right. That is all right. I name Isaiah. Zef, as how I see you face looking tragic, I feel you hear scary story about all-we in the Wet, and I say dem ting make up to keep you from wandering away from home. Where you now coming from? North? Aah. The mountains. Well, they don't send you here, *although* we are savages. They send you *because* their story say we are savages."

He sat down nearby and shook his head, his locks tumbling. "Nah, nah! We just people trying to live like people anywhere. We don't want to hurt no likkle yout', and we don't send you out for other people to hurt neither. And now you see we here: flesh and blood. We not no jumbie or jinn or any make-up something." He studied them a while again – kindly, Myche thought.

"So, is north you say you pass? Perhaps you now getting to see that the last story you hear about us make up to keep you from leaving a set of people in the forest who want you to walk their path and think their thoughts. People who feel they have the true story, the one song."

"So it's you who have the true story?" Myche asked, laughing because she felt easy with him right away. "Yours is the one song?"

"Never. Song is a thing that branch in and out and curve back like the path through the mud or the roots of a tree growing out of water, because – hear what I tell you – different ones of us see different things, in different ways. And the song and them come to me through different mouths. Only, first, before all these words choke us . . ."

He handed out small crunchy fried fish with some dumplings. It had only a little fish, but they could share it, he said. There was always plenty dumpling.

Across a few more corridors of water and floating grass lay solid ground walled and shaded by gru-gru and royal palm. Parrots flapped and squawked overhead, arguing over delicacies clustered between the palm boughs, and Singerman chanted as if they had come all that way just for his songs. The man who had brought the other raft, who said his name was Bunji, gave them tastes of a rich stew made from something the two of them had caught way off in the forest the children had come from. Singerman and Bunji had just cleaned and prepared it, they said, when they noticed the children headed for the water.

Both men were taking it back to the others, because this thing Bunji and his brother Isaiah had hunted was not large but dangerous and hard to procure. It was precious, and each person could get only a couple pieces, soft and juicy with bones they could have sucked forever and a thick chewy skin.

The children clapped their hands, and Wikki shouted out, "Quenk!"

"Yes," the singerman laughed. "You know this thing, man."

"Vicious and delicious," Robber Boy began – but Telma and Nat stopped him right there, and the children waited politely for the singerman to resume.

Isaiah recounted how the people of the forest had told and retold their story to their own children, but there were a few who couldn't sit still and listen so as to chorus a familiar punchline. Some of the youth had no interest in reverently repeating the wording of their parents or grandparents. Nor did they care to pass on a moral. Restless ones like Bunji drew their own hasty conclusions, filled in explanations they regarded as common sense and rendered back their own verses in songs that flaunted different skills to their elders. They swapped words to fit or bend meter or just to shock and annoy the older heads. They flouted whatever was expected; they sang out about things the forest people meant to leave unspoken.

"What it was you weren't to talk about?" Nat asked curiously.

"Well, the youth sang out about the threat in some note a woman had left before driving onto the oilfield and blowing it all up. The oilfield and herself with it. They put in a chorus about whooshing flame and body parts thumping down. Some of them wailed out the bawling of the mourners and mimicked the looters laughing and the commander-in-chief from the next place ranting and raving. And they drummed, doom-doom, how his bombs fell, and they roared out his rain of fire. When the elders tried to shut them up, they yowled the forest burning all around and chased about like a set of maddened animals in full flight from it."

"So wha wrong wid dat?" Telma demanded.

Robber Boy nodded sagely. "I agree. Free speech and song is key, or we must live in jail . . ."

"You better shut you tail," Brand sang out, and when the children and the adults nearby had stopped shouting with laughter, he bowed to the singerman and said, "Please finish you story – just don't notice – some of them don't have no manners."

"Thank you kindly. So where I was? Yes." The old forest baanya had warned their youngsters that the ocelot with one thousand eyes would return, outraged by their disrespect, and swallow them all. But instead of being filled with terror, the disobedient lot said, "Leh he come!" They would hunt he down and see who would eat who. And the youth went right on singing their own stories from their own pain.

Some left the forest on their own – here the singerman paused – and others were driven out. He, Isaiah, was one of the unwanted, and Bunji had followed him because they were brothers from the fire.

"Why they didn't want you?" Indira whispered.

The singerman said he did not fit in with the forest people, because he had an affliction that reminded them of all they were desperate to forget. The world was full to overflowing of things to be forgotten.

"What's an affliction?" Telma's voice was suddenly gentle and respectful.

Singerman only shook his head and then turned their attention away from one man's suffering so as to rivet them with tales of earthquakes and tidal waves and exploding mountains, or of lakes or islands that took form in days or months, then vanished.

After dinner the next night, they begged him to tell another, and instead he began to chant. He wailed laments for Deo, a stolen one, sold to swell a workforce about which there were only rumours, and for families who had been seized and carried from a sister island not far off and their children dumped offshore somewhere to the south. Then there was his brother, Sharo, who was so frightened by the looters who had stripped his home that he and his family set out in a boat that was hopelessly rickety, and already overfull of ragged people running from hunger or torture in some other place whose name no one could pronounce. But patrols from the mainland turned them away, into the path of the pirates, who came on them when they were almost home.

When he saw his family was lost, Sharo had jumped overboard and hid among the bodies rising and sinking on the waves around the big ship, and when the ship moved away he had got hold of the same empty old boat that had brought him there and somehow coaxed it to get him home. Indira's eyes filled up as they did so easily, but Isaiah did not stop the story, merely passed his hand gently over her head.

After the evening meal, the songs and stories, the children talked and played with Bunji's son and Isaiah's daughter. Bunji's wife brought them over and told Telma, "See? It have children here too. Lu Marie, these children have new-new stories. Adventures and thing. See if they will tell you."

And Lu Marie smiled awkwardly but seemed friendly. "Is true you walk partly all round the island? But where you really come from?"

And that was the problem, right there. For who would reveal anything that might betray the Trust?

Still, Lu Marie and the others were good company, and the children relaxed and began to feel less traumatized by the encircling water. But this floating life remained strange and troubling to many of them, and to Myche, ghastly in ways she could not word. She could not bring herself to work it out even in her mind. She asked shyly, not wanting to offend Isaiah or his friends, whether there was no solid ground that was safe to live on anymore. Or if not in WeLand, where then?

He took their questions not with that gently mocking air of the forest people but with deep consideration. According to hearsay, he told them, quiet organized places were still to be found abroad. But there was no telling whether they might fall into anarchy too. Boat people who gambled their lives on a rotten vessel to pass the rolling mountains of water prayed to survive a passage under a blazing sun without food, drink or medicine. After all this, many of them found themselves in countries whose own people were struggling to escape.

It was not hopeful. The singerman's songs were mostly mournful, though full of dangerous exploits and courage the children loved. Some were about struggle right here in the Wet, not a mile away. Bunji and some other brothers patrolled their area to keep it clean of intruders. A smaller more warlike group lived relatively nearby, but these two main communities of the swamp did not interfere with each other. The other brotherhood organized themselves around a gunarch who traded in things Isaiah refused to speak of. Still, these rougher folk permitted the rest of the people of the Wet, Isaiah's brethren, to live in peace.

Myche pondered these two groups. Why were they two, and how were they different?

It was Indira, as usual awake before everyone else so as to say her prayers, sitting on a dry stretch under a stand of palms, who caught sight of a cluster of strangers on an approaching barge. Their guide turned out to be a man Isaiah later called Ouija, who came and went on his own and did not seem to be much liked.

When Indira cried out, men and women she had never seen before appeared from nowhere, as if they had surfaced from the water beneath rafts or tumbled out from the cascadou grass.

Bunji and his brother-in-law Suraj ran out with cutlasses, then slowed, lowering the machetes but still looking as if they wanted to kill these strangers. Then came a series of sharp, shrill whistles, and Bunji and Suraj trudged forward again. It was a halting, unwilling gait with the hint of a rebellious swagger, Bunji's jaw jutting with resentment, Suraj's mouth curled in repulsion. But they went forward nevertheless.

After a brief exchange, the barge drew up, and both of the wetlanders helped the strangers fix it in place so as to unload. Then the three heftiest strangers staggered forward under the weight of a big box thing made with planks of raw wood.

"Ent it have more crate?" Bunji demanded.

After a sullen pause, a couple more huge boxes lowered heavily, one by one, onto the rough grass.

Then the newcomers left, with a don't-care roll to their walk but also a few careful glances over their shoulders. Bunji told Suraj to take two men on his raft and go along behind them, just to make sure they passed where they had said they would.

"Ent Ouiji taking them out?" Suraj protested.

"Exacly," Bunji returned.

Later, Nat said he had found out the cruiters were paying what he called a tax (only they paid in goods, not money) to have some wetlander pilot them across the swamp, so they could move freely through areas on the other side. That way the seamen could seize and sell whatever they wanted.

"Like what?" Wikki demanded, though Myche and Telma turned aside, not wanting to hear.

Darati stared at Nat, hypnotized.

"Whatever. Ocelot pelts, yes, but also peppers, morocoy. Isaiah and them say they have to trade with somebody to keep alive, and the cruiters and others (I don't know who) don't let any other traders onto the island."

"But what it have here to sell?" Five Cent voiced the question in all their minds.

Isaiah's daughter, Lu Marie, answered from a flat rock where she had perched to view the whole event and lingered to hear the chatter among these new children. "Pa and them sell the passage. Or, sometimes, ferry one or two 'cross the water. Guide the way through the mangrove. And we does sell 'gouti too, and turtle egg. Iguana . . ."

Brand's mind snapped on it in an instant. "Turtle egg from where?"

"Boy, it have water all round. What wrong with you at all?" Indira steupsed, and Telma muttered, "Eejit."

"Big turtle you can eat is *sea* turtle," Five Cent put in. "Mitch tell me about some leather turtle or something. They come up on the beach to lay egg. But that is in the north."

"I think forest people from the north does bring egg down," Lu Marie said. "If you go through them mountain, is sea you reach."

"But what else the cruiters get here to sell?" Wikki was not letting it go. "They come through all this mud to get 'gouti and lizard they could find easy if they just walk through bush?"

Lu Marie's face blanked as she looked down to smooth her bright new top with its blonde princess on the front.

"Then unnu could do business with pirate?" Telma sounded disgusted.

But Lu Marie shrugged a little wearily. She couldn't make out what it was these strange, dense children didn't understand. People had to live. They needed stuff they couldn't get in the Wet.

Then a gathering of adults around the crates seized the children's attention. Two of the huge boxes were open already, but Bunji and a few others had dragged over a long metal tool with a cleft at the end like the quenk's hoof, to split another. Once it was open, they began to pass out, hand to hand, cooking oil, matches, rolls of cloth and plastic, medicine, salt, round pots with long handles and covers – the sort of stuff Shine, Daughts, Mitch and, later, Nat had foraged for over years.

That evening, the smell of hot bake and butter was so maddening it was impossible to think where the butter had come from or in exchange for what. The saltfish was prepared right there. Suraj's wife had salted fish that he brought in, and now she cooked it down with onions and peppers that a few of the others grew on firmer ground some way off. But the butter was the thing that brought tears to Myche's eyes, as if in eating the bake with the butter melting in between she was selling something too precious to part with but couldn't bring herself to stop.

In a small and humble voice, she asked Isaiah, "Who were those men?"

"Some were seamen, but I make sure none of them was any peace-keeper."

Isaiah said that during the bad times, twenty thousand troops had been sent to sort things out. He had been in the local coastguard – that was how he had learnt to handle boats – but the peacekeepers had jostled him aside as if he had no business protecting his own shore. As he spoke, his face took on a stern hawk-like look it never had even when he spoke of the pirates.

"Nobody never want no soldiers from outside. When they came first, people drove them out of stores and eating places, cursed and threatened them. 'Go home. Haul you tail outta we place.' One angry youth fired two shots behind them. Not to say he kill them – well, one dead a week or so after – but he did only mean to drive them 'way.

"It was after that it start for true," Isaiah added, "the drone attacks." Then a loudspeaker had ordered that people must evacuate certain areas. "Say what? People – like they run mad. 'Is we city,' they say. 'If you drive we out, we burning everything behind us. We leaving nothing for you to tief.' But it was when bomb go off in they embassy that Homeland send ship. And people didn give up easy," Isaiah assured them. "They fight back using some of them same gun from Homeland own gun trade, but of course, in the end, the city flatten."

The wetlanders hated the peacekeepers even more than the pirates. Eventually Nat and Myche worked out that the only other group with whom the wetlanders had no dealings whatsoever were the Shoreline baanya in the east, whom the peacekeepers protected and whom Isaiah referred to as *children of Babylon*.

"So it have a whole town of just children?" Marilyn demanded in a hushed tone.

"Nah!" Bunji put in. "Children? Dem is beast."

"But you do business with the pirates." Brand was nothing if not direct.

There was no choice, Isaiah pointed out patiently in response to the circle of bewildered or accusing stares from the children of the Trust. "It have nowhere else for the people of the Wet to go." It was about keeping control of the little footholds one had on the solid places in the Wet, giving in to some things so as to get goods through the seamen, feeding one's own children, wiping out would-be intruders.

The small group around him pulled back instinctively.

"Children different," Isaiah added gently. "Nobody here go do all-you nothing. Yout' must cherish."

The wetlanders fed them, sang to them, encouraged them to stay. But all the time Isaiah and Bunji kept watch to make sure these children never learnt the paths through the swamp, and Myche thought that must be so as to leave them the choice to move on if they wished.

It was Myche, as usual, who insisted they had to set off.

In the outcry that followed, Marilyn pointed out that Myche found fault with everywhere that offered shelter and a safe life.

"Safe?" Myche said. "On water? Green water? Water so dark green we can't even guess how deep?"

But still Marilyn, Wikki and Indira cried out against her, and Telma scowled more than ever. Who knew what this place down south was like? she demanded. Nat said Myche was right, and Shant and Wikki sniggered. The final crushing opposition came from Brand, who announced that he didn't want to wander around all his life. Nat said that people who would make deals with the pirates might accept money for anything, but some of the others shouted him down.

Brand began to insist on staying with the wetlanders. He was a fighter and belonged here more than anywhere else, and perhaps he should find the other community of wetlanders and swear loyalty to the gunarch.

But Myche refused. They traded with the pirates, she insisted, and they might trade her, Telma, Marilyn – all of them – as they grew older, fattened up for sale. Like a set of tame quenk.

"You can't tame quenk," Five Cent objected. "They too savage."

Brand nodded. "Nobody not taming me," he announced, casting a fierce eye around at the rest.

"Well, they done tame you already if they make you feel safe while they exchange goods with pirates," Myche answered coolly.

"The brotherhood on the other side of the Wet are fighters," Brand argued hotly.

She stared at him, willing him to remember all Shine had reeled out about weapons the pirates had, as well as swift skiffs for overtaking other vessels.

He had said private freighters were fitting themselves out with water cannons now, and larger commercial vessels used long-range devices that blasted high-pitched sounds they could turn up to be piercing.

Brand stared back mutinously for a while, then dropped his eyes. Even if the wetlanders were prepared to defend the children from the Trust, they couldn't fit any device to their rafts that could compete with arms the pirates would muster.

In the end, inexorably, Myche brought them round, and most agreed to leave.

·········

Isaiah and the rest were saddened, because it had nowhere else, he lamented. But when the children insisted on going on their way, he and Bunji loaded them on the rafts and poled them along by way of a passage among small islands studded with palms. Now and then the singerman let Telma try steering with the pole, and he called across to Bunji to give Shant a chance too. So the sadness of impending parting was lightened by excitement and squeals of laughter, and they paid little attention to each other.

But after a while the men pulled to the side to stop and blindfolded the children, and they travelled the rest of the way in darkness, and now the mood was changed. They floated along anxiously while Isaiah instructed them in his most serious voice to avoid the ways of the sycos, who would want to draw them east on the path to Babylon.

When the men finally helped the children off the rafts nearer to the edge of the swamp, Isaiah gave careful directions for them to wait until he and Bunji were out of earshot before taking off the blindfolds, then to follow the river until they reached a road to the south. Finally Isaiah warned them, sadly, never to come near the Wet again.

"Because," chanted the singerman, "you cannot fool Death twice."

After a while, the soft plash of the poles and even the men's voices faded, leaving only the sporadic shrieks of parrots overhead.

· · · · · · · · ·

It wasn't until the children got the blindfolds off and dropped them on the ground in the mud, not thick but still everywhere underfoot, and looked around and could not work out which direction the men had vanished into, that they realized Wikki and Marilyn were missing. The rafts had been in sight of each other and shouting distance, but far enough apart that each group had assumed the other raft carried everyone else. Marilyn had insisted the night before that they would be staying with Lu Marie and the rest, but no one had believed her.

Now it was real. Five Cent pointed out huskily that Zef was nowhere to be seen either.

"At least we know where they are," Myche said, heaving a sigh.

"How we'll make it if the group keeps getting smaller and smaller?" Brand demanded.

"It will be smaller still if we stand around here until the pirates come kill a few of us and march the rest off to sea," Myche replied crisply.

Yet there were few options left – nowhere to trek but south if they were to pick up a road so as to avoid the eastern shore that the baanya of both the forest and the swamp had refused to talk about. Even Shine had not been persuaded to drop more than scattered references to ill-gained luxury on the eastern shore, to the echo of pounding fists on thick doors in a mudstone fortress, and to blood washing in through sargassum seaweed.

"How we going follow the river through this mess without going in the river self?" Telma demanded.

Then Shant pointed with an exclamation of surprise. "Watch," he said. And there was the larger raft, the one the singerman had used, beached on a scattering of bamboo poles strewn along the riverbank. "They must be leave together on Bunji raft so we could use this one." He studied it, obviously puzzled that anyone would give up something so valuable to a ragged bunch who couldn't even be trusted to steer it safely.

"Nah," Telma said. "After we don't know what we doing. Next thing we overturn."

"And mash up the man raft," Nat added.

"And ourselves." But Myche studied it with a rush of affection. "He good though, eh?"

They pulled it up further on the bank, so it would be safe if Isaiah came back that way, and they set out on foot.

After a time, Telma worded the idea that had begun edging up on most of them. "Later we could build raft for ourself if we want. Don't it? Nuff bamboo all over the place."

And for peace sake Myche said, "Why not?" They were walking away from the river anyway.

Except they weren't. It wasn't long before they realized they had not really left the Wet behind, because whichever way they turned, they seemed to be working their way along the river.

Nat groaned. "May as well follow it."

Myche did not have it on any map either in her pack or in her head, and there was no sign of there being anywhere to cross. Surely it would take them east, though, keeping them on the northern bank when what they needed was to be on the other side, heading south. And even then, what?

When it got too dark to go on safely, they drew together under the usual arches of root and branch on a rise of ground as dry as they could find. Myche lay awake most of the night wondering whether she had been wrong to drag them all this way from the wetlanders, whether she had brought Brand and the rest out here into the wild again only to die. As she finally felt herself drifting off to sleep, she thought she caught the wail and sigh of Singerman's voice searching them out, rising, falling, then rising again, and she picked up snatches about Zion, the eternal city to be sought for deep within each heart. But in deeper, warning tones, Isaiah denounced some other, monstrous fabrication, Babylon, an edifice of evil, a denial of Zion.

·········

When she opened her eyes, Myche looked into two large liquid ones in a brown face rimmed with pale fur, and she thought suddenly of an old uncle from the country. But in what place? An island in the necklace, but which? She gasped, and whatever it was started back in a scramble of long creamy beige arms and legs negotiating the branches with four sure-fingered hands.

Brand came, dragging vines from the taller trees to where Darati sat plaiting them together, and there were Telma and Nat returning after retracing their steps to a bamboo patch they had passed the evening before. Shant, Five Cent and Robber Boy tugged the greenest poles they could find and move to the side of the water.

"How you could sleep with all them mosquito?" Telma demanded crossly.

Myche did not bother to tell her she had only fallen asleep as it was getting light. And her legs were puffy and red, welted again from scratching savagely at new bites through the night. She got up and threw herself into lugging bamboo and arguing about how they would get a whole raft into the water when a single pole weighed so much. Then Shant remembered Bunji dragging his in and out along especially thick, long poles that stayed right there on the bank, and they laid in place two that were particularly long and put together the rest of the bamboo on top of those. By nightfall they had eaten off all the bread and butter that Bunji's wife had packed for them, and the following morning they unwrapped the supply of dumpling from singerman before starting work again.

That afternoon, pleased with the result, they pushed their raft out while carefully holding the plaited withes for keeping it in reach. It sank instantly.

They stood watching bubbles and ripples left where their bark should have been bobbing on the water, and Telma produced a word none of them had ever heard before or wanted to question her about, then slapped her hand over her mouth and said, "Me sorry, you hear?"

They turned around dumbly to retrace their steps and find Isaiah's raft.

"He well know why he leave that," Telma said.

. . . .

The next day, tentatively at first, then more recklessly, they rafted along the river, poling closer to the side where the mangroves drew back, because there were too many of them on the one raft and it was low in the water.

They picked up speed again as the river broadened, but Myche said, "Watch, water up to my ankle. Push nearer to the edge before this thing sink with us. Other side, other side."

Once they were following the southern bank, they looked out for a sign of the road the singerman had mentioned, but they couldn't make out anything through the bush. In a while, though, they picked up a treble note of swift water over churning shallows and brief flashes of clean stones. Water was splashing up around their calves, and Myche shouted, "To the side. We going down." Then a brown pelican sailed overhead, folded its wings and crashed downwards, and they knew they were nearing the sea, so they clung closer than ever to the riverside, although it meant bumping between roots and jutting logs, and avoiding shoals on which they might hitch and be grounded.

Something old and rotten moved in Myche, swirling inside her stomach.

It was like that first boat, bumping the pier . . .

She must have woken up just as they were getting in, for her eyes opened at the jolt when whoever was holding her stumbled and clutched her closer. Her mother's hands pressing her close. It was her mother holding her, for Shine had Brand. Her mother had shapely strong hands that sewed and kneaded and scrubbed. And lifted. And sometimes she passed the palms of both her hands down the sides of her dress to wipe them, before crooking the finger of her left hand to raise a chin and stroking tears from the corner of an eye with the big thumb of her right hand. After that she would use the plump part of her palm under the thumb to wipe the cheek dry.

Yet only a short while before that, her mother's hands had rippled over a piano, a ring flashing green fire in the night. Her mother's back bare and smooth under the lights over the piano – all you could see of her on the stage from the audience.

The boat with her mother and brothers rose and fell, rocking wildly from side to side and crashing violently against other boats. It was very dark and the man who was trying to turn the boat and steer it out rammed into another. And so it went on – the jolting, lurching, slamming, cursing. A scream came from another vessel that a baby had slipped off and was bobbing in the water among the colliding boats. They could see the baby, afloat in a tangle of cloth, and the heavy wooden prow riding forward. "Oh God!" her mother screamed, and held her hand over Myche's eyes, while another woman who must have been the baby's mother shrieked on and on, then suddenly stopped. And the hand dropped from Myche's face as if in an instant it had gone lifeless.

"What happened?" Myche had studied her mother's face, now blank. Her mother's eyes turned to her slowly. Wide, gentle brown eyes with one eyebrow uneven, parted by a small scar where the hair would never grow again.

"The lady went to find her baby," she said. "Don't worry. She knows what to do."

That boat they were in had jostled its way from among the rest and was riding high on the waves, then plummeting down between them. Shine pressed close by, gripping Brand so hard that their mother said, "Not so tight." And she tilted her head sideways to touch his. Her mother forced out a crooked little smile and said to them, "Remember that roller coaster? We didn't like it very much then either." Myche must have closed her eyes as strong fingers tracked through her hair and smoothed between her eyebrows. "Hush, Popo."

Myche must have drifted off to sleep, because those were the last words she heard her mother say.

And now she was here with Brand in a sinking raft somewhere near the edge of the Great Wet where it met the sea. But Shant and Telma had poled to the very edge of the river, and they ditched the raft. The children started to trek away in the shallows, and Five Cent whined about the sharp woody stems and broken shafts sticking out of the mud.

"We could have gone further on the raft. Why we didn't keep on the raft till the last minute?"

"Because we didn't know when the last minute would come, or what it had round the next bend," Brand replied savagely. "What if we got swept out to sea on the bleeding rafts? Tell you what. You go back and get a raft and ride it out to sea —"

His words dried up as a band of men swept round a stand of palms, some dressed as Shine had been, in brightly coloured clothes and bandanas, though these were smeared and the tall boots caked with mud. The rest were dressed in soft grey or beige pants with crisp white shirts and wide-brimmed hats. They were trimmer than the others but for their boots, which were just as muddy.

Overwhelmed, the little band of children huddled tight together, speechless, as the two groups surrounded them on the soggy bank of the river. The men shuffled them in line and then prodded them into a march, turning east.

At least, if the map in Myche's head was right, she felt pretty sure it was east.

18

OFF THE MAP

ROBBER BOY

MAP, CRAP.

I've been everywhere that matters, gone with anyone who flatters. I'm the hand that scatters aid, the fist that shatters. Seen the cities, the resorts, got my logo on my cap. Who gives a rap for places off the map, little sick-soul places no one graces with investment, couldn't find em on a globe to save our lives, cure our hives, hone our knives. Hey, Sonny. You're dressed up all funny, and you're not one of our sons — stay away. I twirl my guns.

Get serious here. I'm the one to fear. Mine's the voice you'll hear, the face that will appear when all the votes are in. *Time* Man of the Year.

And, hey, dude — calling anything I say a lie is rude . . .

Robber Boy abruptly went silent, limbs slack, crumpling on the ground. The seaman who had clubbed him from behind swept him up and slung him over his shoulder like some sack he had dropped by accident, then trudged on.

19

THE ENCLAVE

MYCHE

MYCHE WATCHED ROBBER BOY'S ARMS DANGLE loosely against the back of one of the ruffians in baggy pants and shirts that smelt of stale seawater. As she walked she kept her eyes fixed on him, waiting for the limp head over the pirate's shoulder to stir. The flat path widened and turned firmer underfoot. Robber Boy's hand swung lifelessly, bumping against the back of the man who carried him, striding along as if his burden weighed nothing at all. His mouth hung open, silenced.

Dead? Myche tried not to ask herself, but then the answer came. He had to be alive, or why would they carry him? Then the path crossed a road paved with smooth asphalt, and the pirates broke away, with Robber Boy draped senseless over a shoulder. Without so much as a word, they headed on along the rough track that might easily turn down to the port or back inland. For now they were gone, while the rest branched off onto the road. Whatever had been said about the Shoreliners, it was a relief to see the thick-set, hard-faced seamen tramp away, especially as she had worked out that Robber Boy must be alive. (Only, it had been a few minutes now, and if he didn't wake soon, what would that mean? Shine had said something once about brain damage when people didn't wake up quickly. Although if he did wake up and start talking, they *might* kill him.)

She tried to distract herself by going over what little she knew about the port.

As far as she recalled, Shine had said he'd never met any of the baanya who lived on the seafront, but he had heard they traded in a friendly enough way with the forest people at first. Both wanted a peaceful life without fighting seamen or foreign soldiers.

Then a handful of Shoreliners did something unforgivable: they met with the cruiters and negotiated a more comfortable existence. As if that were not enough, they worked out an agreement with the peacekeepers stationed at Freedom Bay.

"That kept the cruiters quiet for a while then?" Brand had asked.

"At all." Shine dismissed that idea. "Look. There were these guys who swarmed aboard a luxury liner at King's Wharf, flourishing machine guns while taking over the ship, yelling at passengers on board to keep to their cabins or be shot. And they shot a few to make the point and then demanded ransom from the Bermuda government.

"But the government refused to pay. The pirates demanded the passengers' travel documents, chose twenty with useful passports and hauled out five at random to throw overboard. One was an elderly woman in a wheelchair, another an autistic child."

Myche had tried to stop him to explain *autistic*, but he said, "Later," and hurried on.

The pirates tied other passengers to rails around the deck so they could feel the first effects of any attack made on the boat. Ransom was delivered by helicopter, lifeboats lowered and hostages disgorged into them and sent off. Then the new pirate vessel steered off safely. So that had gone well as far as the pirates were concerned, and on they went to levy a tax on whatever islands suited them, and to demand supplies. No way were Shoreliners or peacekeepers going to keep that lot in order.

More had been coming back to Myche as she plodded along searching her memory. And yes, there was something else. Shine had told them the Shoreliners actually offered use of their port, and the seamen paid generously. Which was why the baanya of the forest called the Shoreliners collaborators, while the wetlanders, even angrier, called them sycos. When Shine paused and Myche got him to explain *autistic,* he also told them about sycophants. But in the end the only further information Myche and Brand wrung from him about the enclave was that life at Shoreline looked snug enough from far away but had turned into something twisted and foul. On no account were the children to wander in that direction.

Now, here were five men, clean shaven and dressed in smooth, light-coloured, well-fitting clothes as if they lived comfortably on shore, driving the remaining eight children from the Trust.

With the pirates gone, though, all the children had brightened at once. Now Five Cent looked shyly at the two men on either side of him and asked where they were headed. But the Shoreliners made no answer; they never even glanced at him. And so the walk went. "Get along there" was the most they would say – not roughly, but as if they had some routine task to complete. Like herding goats.

Relief frittered out. Myche looked around and saw Nat eyeing every landmark he could take in, Indira's lips moving soundlessly, Brand and Five Cent signalling each other (Myche could not tell what about, but communication between them was rare enough to draw her attention). Shant seemed agitated. Zef had stayed with Isaiah's family in the Wet, and perhaps that disturbed Shant, but Myche didn't think that accounted for it. Shant was strangely wound up

She continued her tense survey. Telma. Darati? No Darati. Telma was grim but determined rather than worried. So Darati had slipped away. But how would she make it by herself?

When the Wet fell well behind them and the ground was hard beneath their feet, the trees grew more spaced out. Now the land spread away mostly in thorny shrubs and high grass. As the light dimmed, it became clear they would sleep in the bush that night, and twilight found them in a clearing with bundles strewn haphazardly about. Here the men halted and gestured at the children to sit. They unrolled the bundles to set up cloth shelters with patches of fine mesh at the sides, airy without letting in mosquitoes. Tents for the men.

They might sleep soundly, Myche speculated.

But through the night, one sat up to keep watch. Myche snatched naps between fluttering images of what might lie ahead, mosquitoes circling and pitching, and the pressure building in her nose, gnawing and throbbing. She heard one of the men crawl out of his shelter, pee near a bush at the edge of the clearing and then relieve the one who had been keeping guard.

She had barely dropped off to sleep when a boot prodded her. She scrambled up, and it was another dismal day, grey and cool. A fire crackled with a pot on it, and one of the men poured a warm drink into a single mug and handed it to one child after the next, topping it up when necessary. Same mug, mouth after mouth. Myche had known better even as a smallie; Shine had taught her. Besides, she was still annoyed about the boot. When it came her turn, she shook her head sullenly.

They held her – not angrily, but as if this were normal practice. One pinched her nose tight till she opened her mouth, and they poured the drink in. At first she spat it up, then realized it was easier to swallow. If they were trying to kill her, there were quicker ways. When they let go of her, they turned to Indira, who drank it without protest, then vomited and wailed. They slapped her and handed her another cup of the liquid, and this time she kept it down. After the cup had been passed around, it was line up again and quick-step through the bush.

She had lost track of how long they had marched, when Brand caught up to her.

"Run," Myche said under her breath. Seeing his lips tighten stubbornly, she added, "Or you won't be any use."

The man nearest to them said, "Quiet," shoving Brand back behind her.

What if he failed to get away? The men had guns, she thought, feeling her stomach plummet. And what if he succeeded, running alone in the bush? Where was there to go? So, run? Don't run?

Run, she urged him again, mind to mind, but she kept her face straight ahead.

·········

Almost four hours later, the path ended at a fence with a gate that was a crisscross of metal bars like the one in the museum. It swung in silently over bright gleaming squares.

Tiles. That's what those were. Tiled walkways led from the edge of a road, which was a bit like the asphalt paths and roads they had followed, only those had been lumpy and broken by tufts of grass and weed. This was blacker and rolled flat with a smooth sheen but for faint flow marks. Shant's quick intake of breath startled her. "But this —" He broke off and pushed forward, only one of the men shoved him back in place.

The buildings recalled those in the Burnout – only not burnt out. Square windows behind fine grey net. The neatness unsettled her – straight lines and right angles. Past the houses stretched land that was clear of bush and fenced to keep in animals. And such animals! Fat pigs that were clean and pink, glossy brown chickens, shaggy goats. Further back, open land sloped upwards, dotted with cows, some shiny black, others smooth creamy white with black or brown patches. Around other houses there were no animals to be seen, only orderly rows of green, or vines draped over lattice with long beans hanging, or christophene, and then some other thing she did not recognize, like a big dark purple teardrop.

On higher ground, clear and rocky, stood a couple of boxlike buildings overlooking the sea. There the group paused while the men consulted each other at a turn-off to another road. This was wider, with tall narrow buildings crowding close to the edge and drawing her eyes immediately up to the sky, a narrow strip above. Then she looked down again at the street itself and started, with a quick step back, squeezing her elbows tight against her body and darting a look at the children beside her. Big people hurried along the street, this way and that, in and out of doorways. Thelma grabbed her hand, shocked, but Shant craned his neck to peer down the road, as if searching faces.

Telma noticed it at once and said, "Is who you looking for? What happen? You know this place?"

He glanced around with a wild, pleading look, but shook his head. "N–not sure. It looked like . . . somewhere."

"Quiet." A man's voice, irritated.

A few passersby near the corner stopped to stare at them. There were adults in clothes that seemed moulded to them, set flawlessly against their bodies, hair slicked away from their faces. Women with jewellery dangling around their necks, bobbing from their ears. They leaned a little forward to see the children better then swung hastily away, and Myche was suddenly aware of their own tattered clothes patched with leaves, and of the gourds hanging around their necks by withes. Five Cent's T-shirt (dug up in the Burnout) was on inside out, Myche noticed, and perhaps that was what had brought bad luck. At the sight of the band from the Trust, a few of the women drew their own children closer, and one caught up her little girl and covered her eyes. Some of them seemed to be whispering to each other, but it was hard to tell against the noise and the distraction of sudden movement all around. Beyond them cars sped by and trucks roared along. Men and women strutted and sauntered carelessly on their way, shouting across open spaces as if they had never needed silence to save their lives. Or had never had to tiptoe.

The men who had brought the children there set them moving again, driving them further along the road that followed the rocky overhang along the seafront, and although the strangeness of all that caught Myche's eyes unnerved her, the worst of it was the maddening noise. Hammering, jabbering, blaring, impossible to think against, until the men brought the whole group to a halt in front of a high stone wall. The one in front seized a rope that hung down with a knot at the bottom, and he pulled. A bell clanged somewhere inside, and a slat opened up, eyes peering out from it.

"What you have?"

The man who pulled the bell shouted, "Douen!"

The children jumped, and Myche glanced around nervously.

Huge doors groaned open, high and pointed at the top, like the place they had taken Brand to as a baby. *Brand.* She looked all around, and no sign of him. Gone. It echoed in her like a spasm of pain and a shout of triumph at the same time. She summoned up a picture of him darting through the bush, with One Thousand Eyes bounding along beside him, and she breathed a little easier. The men shoved her forward with the other children, and the doors slammed behind them. As the clamour of the street was locked out, the wide, cool space inside went dim.

Near the doorway stood some sort of table surrounded by three or four men. There was so much hurrying back and forth that it was difficult to count any group at a time, but at the table they huddled over stacks of papers. A huge book lay open, a pen on it chained to a thick table leg. And then drawers. It was a . . . *desk*. At the desk sat a heavy man with a fine pointed stick in his mouth, bobbing on his lips as he spoke. He stopped to dig between his teeth with it, then put it back. After some conversation, he bent to write something in large letters at the top of a fresh page and beckoned the children forward. Myche craned her neck to see. It said, *Douens*.

It rippled over her with a chill, sending little prickles through her hair. But when she glanced around she picked up the weirdness of them, of herself and the other children, reflected in the men's eyes. She caught a glimpse of the group from the Trust as she never could have before, from their hard bare feet with the splayed toes, bruised and spattered legs disappearing into tattered pants rough-hewn from bits of old and mismatched cloth held together with thread of any colour or thin withes, hung with packages of leaves and vine, dangling gourds, scraped elbows and calloused hands, lean, almost wraithlike bodies topped with close cut, almost shorn heads, some covered by floppy hats made from broad leaves, their voices suppressed by caution into little more than whispers and their eyes darting with suspicion. Retreating faces. Faces that said, *Lef we alone and we go back-back into the bush. We going disappear.*

The men stared back, hushed for a moment, for a few seconds made uncertain by this intrusion of the uncanny, as if writing down the unthinkable – let alone the unspeakable – was what made it real; but they recovered swiftly.

The one at the desk raised his pen with a growl of disgust and flagged his other hand at the children. "Sort them."

Guards separated them: boys and girls, then over or under twelve years old. They did the last grouping by eye, perhaps because it was beneath them to ask. But asking would have made no sense anyway, for how would most of the children know their exact ages?

"Storage," said a man who seemed to be in charge, with a last scribble in the book before slamming it shut.

Two others led Myche and the rest out through another, narrower door, into a brief blaze of sunlight with the smell of the sea and another onslaught of noise – workmen yelling to each other and equipment grating. They had crossed to a towering stone edifice, with dark slots at regular intervals on each level and guns pointing away on one side, like in the pictures Shine had drawn of old ships. Another rope to tug, another clang from inside. The entrance yawned – not doors swinging apart this time, but one solid metal slab lifting from the bottom upwards with a screech. Then they waited in a cavernous space lined with huge crates and barrels. It smelt of spice, mould, sweat, rum, salted meat, rotting wood and somewhere perhaps a long dead rat. All the while the Shoreliners argued with and about people they called merchants.

Dressed much like the cruiters but in more sober colours, the merchants had the same rolling walk. One was shouting that he made this trip to the archipelago twice a year. Further up the chain he had taken up allspice and nutmeg and got through promptly. He didn't expect to be kept waiting just because his business was legal. Just because he was collecting scorpion pepper and shadon beni instead of flesh didn't mean he must give up his place in the queue.

The Shoreliner at the desk eyed him coldly till he simmered down, and then reminded him that when merchant ships sailed from Shoreline they crossed a lot of sea before they docked again. Everyone knew it made little difference whether one was in a convoy or not. What mattered was the logo. He slapped his hand on an emblem carved into the front of the desk: *SL*. The officer allowed a minute to let his words sink in while the merchant fumed silently. An attendant came for the children to lead them upstairs.

Nat shot Myche a bright look before they were separated, the sharp angles of his face softened by the curl of his lips. For the first time she saw that the corners of his mouth were not quite in sync, but that twitch at one side enlivened his whole face. It reminded her that they had come this far with most of them alive.

Once he was out of sight and the cold grip of terror closed on her again, Myche still expected glimpses of him or the others, still assumed the bustle and racket of the fortress would go on assaulting her senses unbearably. Some of the upstairs holding rooms did overlook the ground floor, and she had hoped to see others from the Trust who might be taken in or out. But Myche passed the first few days within four thick walls, with a woman who neither spoke to her nor looked directly at her or anything else but only sat staring at the stone floor; and now the onslaught of silence and inactivity was worse than the hubbub outside. The noise broke through only when the cell door opened for a few moments before slamming and cutting it off again.

Myche craned her neck to see through the thick glass pane near the top of the door, so as to catch sight of anyone below or going up or down the steps. But it was too high. Then the guards shifted her to another room, where she was alone with nothing in view, not even a silent woman, and the walls began to crush forward until she wanted to batter her head on them. Only, she forced herself to hold back. *Wait!* her mind screamed.

The days unspooled shapelessly one after the next. Food and water were pushed in, a metal plate with bread or rice and mushy beans, pumpkin or cabbage, and every other meal came with a mug of tepid tea. She worked out that the tea marked morning and evening but couldn't bother to count them. After a while, a sort of haze enveloped her, and she almost couldn't be bothered to swallow anything, but again she took hold of herself sternly and forced down whatever the guards brought in.

Every afternoon they brought a fresh bucket of water. Tiny events brought relief, and washing herself came to be the high point of the day. Afterwards she felt lighter and more alert. It was at one such point that Myche discovered she could hear things once she lay flat across the door with her face to the crevice underneath. Voices floating up, and occasionally an order would be barked nearby, feet tramping in shoes or shuffling almost noiselessly without them. Children whimpered as they were dragged away or shoved back into their cells, but Myche did not recognize those voices. At the thought that they may not have caught Brand, a sense of release surged in her. Still, she agonized over Nat. Somehow she convinced herself the others might be all right, but Nat. *Nat.*

·········'

In time the guards moved her to a cell across the corridor against the outer wall. This one was like a cage with one side of it looking off over the sea.

Waves and sky. A vista of swelling and churning water. She squeezed her eyes tight, but the noise of it went on. And the smell. She had to open her eyes again to assure herself that the sea was not in the cell with her.

A wide platform of smooth wooden planks jutted out into deep water with a boat docked at the end. Between the pier and the larger vessels farther out, brightly painted launches tooled back and forth. Boats rose and fell in different rhythms, dizzying in relation to the still wharf, until the stillness of the wharf became hard to maintain in her mind, and it too seemed to rise and sink and rise again. Then her stomach heaved, and the morning's bread and tea landed splat on the floor.

·········'

It must have been weeks later, though it felt like years of trying to look away from the sea while blanking out the unchanging walls, that a guard threw between the bars of her cell a roll of cloth that turned out to be a sack-shaped garment with underpants.

"Wash and dress," he ordered.

When he brought her downstairs, he turned her over to a burly man who wrote in the massive, mottled green and brown book with ruled pages under a column that said *Property Manager.* Shant was standing only a few feet away, his shoulders shaking and his face as anguished as it had been when Colin died.

"What?" she cried. "Shant! What is it?"

But he did not answer or even look at her. It was as if he didn't have the will to raise his head.

"Sure you don't want this one?" Now there was a woman at the desk, and she gestured at Shant as the property manager shook his head firmly.

So the guard grabbed his arm roughly and said, "Where?"

"Upstairs," the woman answered, "while they decide."

Myche hardly had time to reflect how few women she had seen in Shoreline, or to grieve over Shant's stifled sob, before the property manager hustled her out and off down the street.

A long walk while the sun climbed in the sky brought them to a high stone wall. At least the surface of the wall looked like stones cut smooth and flat, but perhaps they were not real, she thought, for they were all the same shape. Rain misted down with the sun behind it, a glitter wafting around her. The wall hugged the path until the monotonous stone surface ended at a metal gate in an oval frame. The gate had thin metal bars radiating out like a spiderweb, and it swung open when the man with her raised a small black gadget and pressed a button. Inside, at the end of a walkway, they stopped before an enormous door and pressed a switch at the side. The door swung inward, and the bulky man pushed her in wordlessly and closed it behind them.

So far no one in Shoreline had addressed more than two or three words to her at a time or even seemed to see her. She felt herself fading from sight and sound.

Inside the door was another man, wearing dark clothes with shining buttons like a uniform she had once seen in a picture, and he glanced past her to the property manager, who handed over a sheet of paper and said, "Delivery for Madame St Juste."

He pointed to an open doorway to the right. "Wait in there."

· · · · · · · · · ·

Casting her mind back to some of Shine's warnings, it came home to Myche with some relief that at least there were women here. That made her less edgy, and she could take in the room she was entering. Cautiously, wishing she were still outside in the bush, she crossed to a wide-open window where the light shafted in through overhanging trees.

Light gleamed between the branches onto the polished surface on which she walked with her feet no longer mud-stained but still hardened by corns and her spread toes – unlike the feet of the other children she had seen on the street, feet gracefully encased in shiny leather and improbably shaped. Shoes pointed at the toes.

Light moved, too, on the sea far beyond. The water reflected it like a shattered mirror.

On the other side of the room where she waited, a door slid open and a large woman swept forward. She was dressed in white trimmed with blue and had something on her head shaped like a small boat.

"And your name now?" the woman asked.

The surprise of a door sliding and not opening back on hinges was enough to silence Myche. In any case she had not used her own voice for so long that she came out with a little croak and had to repeat herself twice before the woman could make sense of her.

"What sort of name that? Well. We go see what Madame have to say. Come. Let me fix you up a little before she call for you." Over her shoulder she added, "You could call me Nurse Flo. Or just Nurse."

In no time she had Myche scrubbed all over again and dressed in a stiff scratchy material.

"Why's it so hard?" Myche asked. She pulled at the garment, so like a big dried leaf that she thought it might snap.

"Is starch," Nurse said.

"Starch?"

But along the corridor people did not stare now as they had when the children first arrived at Shoreline. It was the change of clothes, she knew. But also, her hair had grown since she had last sawed off what she could with whatever came to hand, and she had slicked it down so it did not stick out. Then Nurse had given her a strip of cloth to tie it back from her face.

They stopped at a door, and all at once Myche knew she did not want the door to swing open, slide open or up – whatever else doors did here. She knew that whatever was beyond it was something that owned her now without having the slightest use for her life. She stared at the door with narrowed eyes and gathered her skirt tight around her legs, clenching both sides in her hands.

When Nurse Flo opened the door, the figure sitting at the desk continued writing without raising her head, and when she did, she looked directly through Myche. She was unusually tall, taller than Myche even while sitting, thin but for her belly, which was full and rounded and set on her lap as if it were not hers.

Her eyes travelled over Myche up and down, taking in the hard feet that inched back almost imperceptibly under her gaze, flicking over bruises, scars from insect bites and rashes scratched raw and healed, callused fingers and wear-darkened elbows and knees, butchered hair. The woman's lips twisted in disgust, and her eyes flickered, searching on. She reached for a fan and swept it back and forth slowly, swishing the air away from her face as if the fan was not for cooling but protection from whatever plague this creature from outside might have brought in with it. Her nostrils pinched as if they picked up something foul.

That was not so disturbing, though, because Myche knew herself to be clean and strong, her mind quick, clear, bold. What terrified her was the hardness of this face, its chiselled brow and jawline. It was the dismissive turn of body and above all the emptiness of the eyes that saw nothing human, nothing of worth before them. Those eyes that looked past Myche reflected that she was no one, that she was briefly useful perhaps but, ultimately, pointless. She was to serve and be discarded.

As Madame St Juste completed her inspection from a careful distance, Myche's first shocked response to her face gave way in a rush to another, milder yet still more troubling sensation – a sense of the familiar, which made no sense at all.

Speaking to Nurse, over Myche's head, Madame warned that there must be no contact with her children for a time – while they observed the creature, Myche concluded – but instructions would be sent, Madame added. For the time being, Nurse must have charge of the douen girl.

And suddenly Myche realized. *This woman was afraid.* Myche was utterly in her power, yet the woman was afraid. And there was nothing reassuring about that because it meant when she was done with Myche she would get rid of her absolutely. Myche would be gone without a trace.

As Nurse Flo pressed her hand against Myche's back to propel her from the room a handwritten word caught the child's eye, sprawled as it was across the top of the page in front of Madame St Juste: *SureLine*, written in red. And Myche barely contained a snicker of ridicule. The woman couldn't even spell.

· · · · · · · · ·

But contempt would be a hard thing to maintain in the face of luxury flaunted for all to see and gasp over. The St Juste spread overlooked the coast across a lawn of flawless bright green that seemed unusual for grass near the seaside, and soon enough Myche discovered that it was not rooted in the stony ground beneath. Nurse Flo explained that it came years before in huge rolls that the gardener cut to the required size and set on a padded base so that the St Juste children would not hurt themselves if they stumbled. But there were real plants too, Nurse said as she trimmed Myche's hair in front of a window that opened on the garden, and she advised Myche to learn their names in case anyone sent her out to pick flowers or shrubbery for a vase.

Over the next few days, as she scrubbed and ran errands, Myche's thoughts kept turning to the others.

Brand and Nat occupied her mind almost to the exclusion of the others, even of Darati. She had a vague sense that Telma could take care of herself, felt unaccustomed pangs for Shant and Robber Boy, wondered anxiously about Five Cent and Indira. But Brand and Nat . . . Even Brand, she thought, would survive on his own for quite a while. But what might become of Nat in their hands?

All along the way Nat had kept hope alive, and even when there seemed none he had buoyed them with the recollection of what they had found possible so far and might manage again. "I can see the Trust in my mind," Nat had said. Birds flew to it in one season and away from it in another. He said he was sure he could find it too when the rest were ready. The direction of sunset, the drift of coconuts on a current they could glimpse from the shore even where all the palms left standing were burnt or blighted – there were signs they could follow.

But what value was Nat to anyone else? And where were the rest? Still in the place that crouched like a fort on the cliffside with its guns turned to the sea?

Meanwhile, there was so much here that was new to her. Then, no. Not new – and that was what jarred most. Here inside the house at every turn she encountered something known before but so well forgotten as to rise before her with the eerie quality of an apparition. So the sight of a rocking chair, a reading lamp, a pair of spectacles sent her stomach turning over with the shock of recognition. One rending followed the next, like the parting of some thick, dark blanket, years deep, that had concealed familiar objects from her mind's eye, and something in her awakened with the uncovering of another clue to what she had lost. Happening on a piano in a corner – no one used it; it was one of the St Justes' *pieces*, an antique for show – she shrank back. That it should materialize there stopped her breath, and the image of a phantasmal hand rippling over a scale set off wave after wave of memory, and sent chills down her back.

Outside, now, and differently disturbing came an onslaught of strange unnatural shapes. The gardener had sliced the privet hedges to exact rectangles that marked out the borders of the property. The dark blocks of privet contrasted with pots that constrained thorny bougainvillea with lavish untidy blooms in yellow and lavender, and ficus that should have taken over was manicured to smooth cones.

And everywhere was a gadget or machine that interrupted the natural order of things. The main gate at the back slid open or closed at the touch of a button, revealing a street parallel to the one from which she had entered, and that was where the car drove in and out.

Until Shoreline, Myche had forgotten about cars. For years.

Now she thought back to piles of twisted or scorched metal, broken glass and melted rubber they had encountered here and there in the Burnout and later in Brukstone, and along one or other of the overgrown or potholed roads. The children had thought no more about them than they did about piles of stones.

Cars. There came back to her the feel of smooth padding underneath her legs, which had stuck straight out in front as she strained up to watch trees whiz by the window.

From the gate to the St Juste house, a procession of crotons lined the drive in a way plants never would do naturally. At the back too, a small shelter Madame called the gazebo, supported by white painted swirls of metalwork, offered sheltered seats that overlooked the pool – as if anyone would want to sit looking at that. No pond or lake was ever like it. Another *rectangle*. Ha. Shine had taught her that word for those hard shapes of things people built, like this deep, still trap of water. To Myche's shock, the young St Justes, Cerise and Roget, jumped in and out of it with their friends as if water were a plaything. Even from a distance, the sight melted her knees.

Though, there was that man they called the lifeguard. Nurse Flo said Francisco would pull them out if they got in trouble. But that would only be if he were as strong as he usually looked, Myche reflected. He seemed strong most of the time, when he thought anyone might see, but she had heard him breathing heavily after lifting a wrought-iron table. After setting the table down, he sat hunched over on a garden bench, his hand to his chest, his face grey, probably thinking no one could see him. Of course she *was* no one.

Like all the guards, he had a wide range of other duties, which was why he had been with the Shoreliners who rounded the children up with the help of the cruiters. Myche recognized him, although he showed not a sign of having seen her before or of seeing her now.

Perhaps douens were invisible to him. *Movement of douens strictly pro-hibited*, the woman at the fort had read out aloud as she turned back to her desk without another glance at Shant or the burly guard who hauled him back to his cell. Perhaps Francisco saw only *real* children. If Myche were sinking into the pool he might not see her . . .

What if the real children got in trouble in the pool when Francisco was out in the forest rounding up the not-real children? Just as well, Myche concluded, that there were no errands they could send her on near that pool. Of course it was not dark green like the still water they had learnt to avoid. It was always being cleaned. These people were obsessed with cleaning and always looked at her as if she smelt, although she washed herself every day as she always had, except when lost in the swamp. Only now she used the taps they had that let water rain down from a pipe. Who were *they* to turn aside their noses when they kept what they called chamber pots right under where they slept – or at least Celeste had one under her bed, so presumably they all did. And *that* was clean?

Anyway, a far more urgent problem had presented itself, a riddle really. A week after arriving at the house, Myche had first come face to face with Roget St Juste, and felt her mouth go dry, her hands cold. She was suddenly disoriented, like when she'd had that first glimpse of the bats rushing towards her. Roget was Shant – Shant as he had been years ago when she first saw him. Of course Roget was not years younger than Shant now; he might even be older. Shoreline children always did look younger than Myche expected. Sheltered and pampered as they were, their skin was softer, their arms and bellies rounder, their cheeks and foreheads baby smooth. It was only the set of their mouths, the shape of their eyes . . .

Roget. No. She had never seen eyes like his – a similar almond shape but a lighter brown than Shant's, and like hard bright glass. They had that unseeing gleam of the fake eyes on the stuffed caiman in the museum.

She recalled Shant's eyes searching the perimeter of the town, and his shoulders shaking as the guard led him back upstairs.

There was nothing anguished about Roget. He was contemptuous and self-satisfied. Like his mother. He looked like her. Then she remembered that elusive familiarity that had troubled her on first seeing Madame St Juste. *Shant.*

Myche had learnt to hold her tongue and arrange her face. Look compliant, she reminded herself. She remembered how, on the long march to Shoreline, she had occupied herself by turning over the words Shine had taught her again and again, and one of those words was *compliant*. But what if while she was practising *compliant*, Shant got shipped off somewhere else, and his family (for they could only be his family) never knew he was alive and close by? If she asked to see Madame, she was sure to be refused. Everything must pass through Nurse.

When she approached Nurse hesitantly about speaking to Madame, she learnt that Madame St Juste was tied up with business affairs. She had jurisdiction over the fort and was making a site visit in a day or two to review its holdings. So Myche relaxed. Soon enough, Nurse came back to warn her not to talk to anyone about this boy, Shant. But that was all right. Myche waited eagerly. Shant would come back with Madame, be embraced by his family. Wait. It occurred to her that he could have the children from the Trust set free. The Shoreliners would take them in the way the forest baanya had, and the wetlanders.

Unless Shant was already assigned to some other family . . . This popped into her head at night when the evening sounds were all gone and the early morning ones not yet begun. But then, she argued to herself, then she would be sure to glimpse him when she went out with the St Justes. The St Justes must surely glimpse him. She might glimpse them glimpsing him.

She sharpened her watch.

· · · · · · · · · ·

Meanwhile, from what she saw when she accompanied the family on visits, the homes in Shoreline were much alike. Myche gathered from Nurse Flo's prattling that the Council had organized the town so as to recapture all they had lost – or claimed to have lost – for that old life the Shoreliners kept bright in their minds seemed to have little to do with the WeLand that Shine had pieced together for Myche and Brand.

The upper level of society on this eastern shore had memories that reached for some ancestral place back in their deep past and skipped lightly over their more recent years. Perhaps that was why they didn't worry about the WeLand of other people, about what had happened to it or might happen to anyone else who lived there. For the St Justes, and other families like them, such as the Ramnarines, there were no cities like the ones where Nurse Flo's brother had worked and died in the fire, or where his house had tumbled down and buried Flo's mother when the nearby buildings blew apart.

Nurse Flo moaned and covered her ears again at the thought of the explosions. She had a slow, faltering way of talking, and you had to ask your questions a couple times before she responded. Not so smart, Myche decided, but kind, foolishly so. Nurse Flo actually liked the St Juste children – who were little demons as far as Myche could see. Well, Cerise was not that bad. But Roget was a jinn.

They made her long for Tiffney and Josiahmarshall – whom she had once thought spoilt – and even more for Five Cent. She dared not think of Brand; yet she couldn't *not* think of him. Whenever she did, there he was, slipping back and forth through the trees with One Thousand Eyes. Then she wondered whether Shine might find him, and she began to hold that up in her mind, Shine finding Brand and keeping him safe.

For now, Nurse Flo was the only one who spoke to her, and Nurse was not supposed to talk as much as she did. Little vestiges of the past lodged somewhere in Nurse's head and brought her to tears if she mentioned them, but the St Justes cried over no one. Perhaps their past was further back than Nurse Flo's past.

"No, none of them does cry . . ." Nurse Flo had been chattering in her low mournful voice that sent Myche's mind straying. Flo's eyes squinched up as she tried to work out how it might be to have blank years just behind one, no one to mourn over and nothing left in pieces, just a gulf between Shoreline and the golden deep-past that its citizens were so proud of. Flo didn't know about those earliest days, but they clearly helped the family and their friends look forward to continued luxury and wealth as a future that was their ancient right.

As for what had overtaken the rest of WeLand, Myche overheard St Juste and his friend, shifty-eyed Sir Hector Ramnarine, refer to it over drinks. They spoke about all those fools who had run away while ranting about foreign interference, refusing every overture for cooperation, scorning aid. All those so-called patriots and fiery intellectuals, where were they now? Founding fathers of Shoreline could congratulate themselves on having taken charge of their own lives and those put in their trust.

Trust? The word startled Myche as if it were one she had not expected their mouths to form. It brought back Shine, under the spreading samaan that dropped silky puffs of pink, the promising cluck of wild chickens, the security of prowling ocelots circling the borders between the children and the Don't Trust. In those days she had no idea that the Don't Trust harboured the likes of Sir Hector.

Sir Hector recalled how some of the old lot had looked down on him and his circle, scoffed at them and called them *mediocrities*. Apparently displeased by this recollection, St Juste nudged the conversation along a different track. But soon enough Sir Hector waved it all aside. For it was men like themselves who had made Shoreline into the haven it was now, by hammering out agreements with the peacekeepers and the Association of Merchant Seamen regarding acquisition and recruitment. St Juste had developed policies to protect maritime businessmen who could afford to pay for them.

That was the first clue Myche had that SureLine was no misspelling; it was a stroke of genius through which St Juste flung the mantle of his insurance firm over the whole town and identified the firm and the town as somehow one and the same.

The more reckless servants whispered stuff Myche barely understood, smatterings that hardly held together. She eventually gathered that the prominent citizens who governed Shoreline might not have been into History or Science, nor could they care less about Art. Some had made their way up what Francisco called the financial ladder twenty to thirty years before. "I know," he said one night. "I was a banker in my own country all those years. But I had to run when it collapsed, so what papers could I produce to prove I was fit for anything but physical labour?"

Myche realized she liked to hear him talk. He pronounced *fit* like *feet*, as Nat did.

Whenever she could, Myche liked to sit on the stool in the corner taking in every word, as Francisco poured a bit more in his mug from the bottle that was going around.

That was how she learnt more about the word *SureLine*, which she had seen on the paper in front of Madame St Juste. It was the name of the family business. The St Justes had made their fortune through insurance that offered indemnity, some sort of protection, against piracy. Myche shivered but leaned forward. However, Francisco was talking broadly about all kinds of ways of getting rich, and he moved on without expanding on the ways of the St Justes.

"The big people in the town got rich through what some call the dog-eat-dog world of business," he said, "some not so legitimately." A few inherited wealth their fathers had amassed by passing bad money through successful restaurant, furniture or hardware chains.

Cook put in that another man – whose name she would not call, for she had children to feed – had come into the property this man's mother had got hold of as a lawyer manoeuvring her clients' affairs. "So now dem people could tot up points."

"For property, sí," Francisco agreed, "but for connections too, although some of these connections they should be afraid of."

Yet there were also rich and well-connected families without such secrets. Nurse Flo reminded them how young Jacob Linsey's parents had disappeared while on a cruise, in one of the early pirate attacks. "They leave he home with who to take he to school and keep he happy. Anything he want he get. So when the parents gone and dead Jacob get everything. One chain of supermarket," she recalled.

Yes, Francisco said. He remembered hearing that the boys' parents had long shifted most of their funds into US currency in a Canadian bank, so the Linsey fortune had survived the long train of devaluations that made rubbish of local money. They had also thoughtfully put his name on every account and property title (including those for townhouses they rented out in university towns in the United States), and so, automatically, it had all become his.

Except that Jacob Linsey had neither instinct nor training to invest any of it. In fact, he had no thought in his head but to live comfortably on the proceeds. Fortunately there were lots of proceeds, so his points added up, and he ranked high in the community without the slightest inclination to do anyone any harm, or any good either.

Gradually Myche gathered that the stronger minded leaders in Shoreline held to their own beliefs and brought up their children (as they liked to say) to know how the world worked and who was who. All this talk, this mesh of whisper and riddle and story, gripped her even more than the television Nurse had told her she could watch at night. The television had stunned her when she saw it first, this strange flat rectangle on the wall like a window for spying into other lives, other places and sometimes even other times. At first she had no recollection of anything like it. Then she thought back to a box on a table long ago that had shown fuzzy pictures before breaking down altogether. The TV here was terrifying to begin with and remained unsettling, although she saw it could be addictive. Cerise would sit in front of it for as long as Nurse allowed.

Yet the TV was nothing to the chatter of the other servants for unlocking the mysteries that concerned her most.

Shant? Madame's visit to the fort had had to be postponed for a week. Nothing would be done there without her permission.

Meanwhile, one day in the Affirm Manse, Dean Ivan Blake's message on what he called a *text*, "render to Caesar," hammered out the duty to respect the law, parents and social authority. Madame St Juste laced her fingers through her husband's and smiled at him mistily. Myche passed her a tissue, thinking how different she looked at the moment to the slab of stone that was her normal businesslike self, before Myche turned to retie Cerise's bow that was coming undone at the back of her waist. Then everyone joined hands for the passing of the peace. Well. Everyone who was anyone. Not for the first time, Myche's mind reached back to Brand's christening and the cool quiet and play of colours through the stained glass, when something had lifted her. Something, she thought, but not anything like this.

If Nat were here, they would have talked about it afterwards. Where was Nat?

Myche went out only if the family might need help with Cerise, who was Brand's age but thoroughly incompetent. Roget was big enough to manage himself and more than mean enough. There was little to occupy Myche's mind however hard she worked, and time enough to study everything around her. *SureLine*: bold letters on a billboard they had passed on the way to the manse. *SureLine for Protection at Sea.*

Myche was turning it over in her mind at Affirm Manse even as she noticed again how many more men there were than women. Then she recalled asking Shine why he spoke as if the Shoreliners were ·mainly men. He had said he believed that fewer women than men had cut themselves off from the forest baanya, and that some of those women who did had died in childbirth or before – *miscarried* was the word he used. And women died of all sorts of illnesses no one knew how to treat.

Myche noticed that when Cerise showed a touch of fever, it was she – the douen girl – they sent to attend her, watched over by Nurse Flo, and Nurse reported to Madame St Juste. The children's father enquired dutifully from his wife over breakfast, for men went nowhere near sick children. Nastasia St Juste was expecting and took her own precautions, especially against fever: long white leggings under her skirts, long-sleeved and high-necked tops. She screamed at anyone who left a screen door open.

But of course, Nurse said. If Madame came down with fever, the baby could die or come out deformed. And not to say it was the first she would lose. "Was three of them," Nurse whispered. "One of the boys lost when he did go on holiday with he mother family. Nobody hear bout he since then."

The chill ran down Myche's back again. "What was his name?" she asked.

"They doesn' call he name again. Is like he never exist. They wouldn't want all-we to talk bout that."

"Why that's a secret? It's sad, but why we can't talk?"

"Shh! Nobody want to remember them bad time. Now is the new order."

And what exactly was this new order? Myche probed. Flo couldn't explain. Something to do with points.

So Cerise and Roget had points?

Nah. Children didn' have no points of their own. Of that Flo was sure. They had what people called potential points, which she didn't understand. She only knew that those depended on the parents. Myche didn't pursue it, because her suspense over Shant's fate pressed aside day to day operations at Shoreline.

That was the afternoon Madame St Juste completed her report on the site visit to the fort and made recommendations for what the keepers must do with everything acquired and held there. She had returned alarmingly pale and retired early to bed, with Myche standing close on call. But a little faintness was not unheard of during pregnancy, Dr Chesterfield remarked, as he prescribed a tonic to build her up. No, her husband answered the doctor's polite enquiries, nothing out of the way had occurred to distress her. Just her delicate condition, he was sure. She had been well enough to put in her report.

Her face was like the grey marble faces cut into the pillars of the Affirm Manse, blank and hard.

Myche's thoughts whirled, her mind chaotic. Was the woman ill because she had done something unbearable? Because, if so, she was bound to question herself. Myche knew how compulsively one questioned oneself about people one hurt, let alone lost. She kept her eyes glued to Nastasia St Juste's face for a flicker of doubt. She *must* rethink, and Myche would pick it up because she could stare at Madame all she liked. No one saw: douens were invisible.

St Juste exchanged a glance with his wife after the doctor was shown out. "You did the only thing you could," he said, pressing her hand.

But she turned to him with an expression of bewilderment. There was nothing like grief in it, Myche saw. Horror but no regret. The woman was shattered because she had come face to face with something long gone but . . . undead. Unnatural. She had nothing to rethink.

When Dean Blake dropped in, it seemed it was only so as to share a drink once they had got past the brief prayer of assurance. Myche wondered idly what they believed and whom they prayed to, but only briefly: she had no use for it. Not – she admitted to herself fair-mindedly – not that that blocked out other possibilities. Just because you don't believe what one smaddy say, Telma had argued, don't mean everybady a lie. You have fe believe someting sometime.

But not the St Justes or anything they held up. The piety they smeared over their doings repelled Myche.

·········

Over the next couple days, she watched and listened, feeling she would burst if no news trickled in about Shant. She would have prayed if she knew how to form her thoughts. Telma and Darati had known how, she remembered. And – it came to her blindingly – so had Shine. Then she got to wondering why he hadn't taught her that, and she realized that he must have thought she knew. That it was so obvious. So now she felt more helpless than ever about Shant and listened even more avidly.

What she heard was that, as usual, the better behaved of those currently held at the fort were for work in the community, the more stubborn for shipment. But an odd provision did find its way into the servants' gossip: One child was for immediate conduct by barge to the wetlanders, who would be paid for his safekeeping.

·········

"Compliance?" Dean Blake would begin, leaning forward while the youngsters of his congregation intoned. "Compliance is the cardinal virtue of children." The adults had little pet phrases like that. They would begin them and the children would chorus the rest.

But there were compensations. Myche had to admit that to herself. There was comfort. Doors that slid open in front of you. (Creepy, though.)

After the long walk and hardships of the trail, it could trap her, this ease – food coming out of cupboards unhunted, juice cold from the fridge, warm rice, tender meat, water from taps. Beds under soft covers, just waiting there. She had walked into this painted, tiled, embossed and cushioned trap. And they could all have walked into it. She realized now, after weeks of studying the position of the sun and the moon and stars, that she really had made almost a complete circuit of the island with the rest of the children. If only they had turned east instead of west after witnessing the rise of Jumbie Island, and if they had made their way beyond the place with no roads or shore, they would have arrived at Shoreline without any of them being wooed away elsewhere. Colin would be alive. They could all have remained together.

But no, they would have been sorted, distributed. Only a few would have been chosen for Shoreline, to serve in smothering comfort. If they resisted, they would be shipped; if they allowed themselves to fit in, they would become like Roget.

Once she grew accustomed, she'd be finished – a prisoner to ease. Food and shelter. Unlimited Vicks. Though, she had thought there might be books. Books and books. But no, what she'd seen were mostly thin sermonish pamphlets that bored on and on about obedience. The television brought its barrage of incredible scenes, confusing because she could not distinguish what was real and what was fantasy. She was never in front of a screen long enough to work it out. There was so much, too – stories unfolding at different speeds and in different voices. Some channels had a wide range and others narrowed in on topics and personalities.

One obsession was with a man whose jowls drooped, and whose eyes sagged with the weight of the bags that hung heavy beneath them. Even his hair flopped. He too seemed obsessed with compliance, but there was no one to explain to her what he had to do with anything, this wide-set man, flushed and dispirited. He seemed tired of everything and everyone. Portraits showed him sitting at a desk or standing behind something like a desk but higher, wearing a look of petulant boredom, as if he had a right to be entertained and people around him were too stupid or bad-minded. He seemed fed up with everyone talking instead of listening when they had nothing to say that he didn't know already and mostly knew to be wrong.

Why the stories of this man should occupy everyone remained a mystery to Myche, but she watched him closely when he appeared on the screen, because she felt something about him – his hand movements, the shade of his hair, the bragging – something irritating and familiar. There was no putting her finger on it.

20

SYCO SPAWN

ROGET

EVEN THE LIMITED VIEW OF SHORELINE from the office window upstairs pleased Roget. Tall stone buildings, smooth roads, a meticulously raked beach – the St Justes tallied it often to remind themselves how far they'd come. Roget's father had been at the core of the group who built the life they enjoyed and the point system for ranking had been his mother's idea.

"No, no." Nastasia St Juste waved aside her husband's boasting about her and insisted that it was his own brilliant operation of the family firm that had secured their fortunes. SureLine – the logo leapt out from signs along the way, embellished buildings even as it endowed ocean vessels with safe passage in what had become the most dangerous maritime area in the world.

"And it will all be yours," Roget's father liked to remind him.

The single hurdle that had surfaced from nowhere had been dispensed with, and outside the family only one person knew about it – if it could be called a person.

Fortunately, the St Justes were unassailable. Roget gazed down on the tables Francisco Marquez had set out around the pool under his mother's exacting eye. It was one thing to be successful. A certain level of entertaining drove the point home: one's fingers played with the stem of a crystal wine glass, one's lips hovered at the thin edge of a bone-china cup of chocolate. A couple of servants in starched uniform circulated with trays; a hanging pot of orchids turned gently in the breeze; citronella torches beyond the veranda marked the border within which guests might be expected to wander. His eyes sought the edges of that border. His mother had missed something. It was not like her, but he was sure of it. And there was no room for error.

Normally his mother was meticulous. Her social events only supplemented those official duties that lay at the heart of the town's operations. "I know what I'm doing," she had assured him curtly. "You forget I oversee the accounts and I direct the fort's acquisitions and its shipments." How could he forget? Yes, he had dismissed memories of some earlier times, but not of those recent years during which he had seen her scrutinizing the books, noting details in long columns and checking that it was accurately totted up: the value of items in storage, the tax that merchants paid for safe passage of goods past the people of the Wet, the fee rendered to seamen for leaving Shoreline undisturbed, the degree to which these costs were amply offset by earnings from the trade.

Roget knew all about it. He knew what used to be whispered and was now ruthlessly silenced. Yes, people said there were songs chanted about it in the bush, but he had learnt early that only those who had failed to take control of their lives suffered through the regular business practices among civilized folk. "Backward people are brought down by their own failings," his mother said. SureLine thrived and was to flourish even more. For there was to be this canal.

The canal to be blasted east–west, between the Great Wet nearby and the Little Wet on the other side of the island, would let medium-sized vessels into the interior. "Look," his father had said, rolling out the map on his desk, tracing the route with his finger. "We'll get access to those old oilfields *and* make it possible to move asphalt across to the port. And we'll use the asphalt ourselves."

Even one well-repaired highway would break the hold of those ragamuffins over the Wet and rout the cult in the mountains. So the canal would open up other types of traffic as well as ridding the

Shoreline society of troublemakers who holed up in their little pockets of forest or swamp. Eventually it would snuff out the fiery resentment that smouldered on in ignorant chants and savage tales. Best of all, the profits from the canal project would find their way into safe and capable hands that already managed more than half the wealth in Shoreline.

"You may as well learn all you can now," his father had said. "You know who'll have to run it someday." Nothing and no one would be getting in the way of that.

But recently he had seen his father speaking to two of the wetlanders – who as usual resembled nothing so much as half-drowned rats. One of them was the man they called Ouija, come as a guide for the guard St Juste had selected to deliver that upstart – the boy who had claimed some relationship to the family. As if a family like theirs could misplace a relative long enough for him to deteriorate into a vagrant. *And* live like an animal in the bush for years. The tramp had got better than he deserved, this vagabond who had the impertinence to come after all that should rightly be Roget's. The wretched boy ought to be shipped – and was going to be if the wetlanders should lose track of him and let him turn up again around Shoreline. And then there was this interfering little savage who had opened up the whole matter with her boldface request for a meeting with his mother. That creature ought to be permanently shut up.

The utter deceitfulness of the douens rose up anew and infuriated Roget all over again. His mind ran back to his earlier years and a lesson about local fauna: *Douens are not human; they have no skins, only fragile hides that break easily. They have no souls – has anyone ever heard one of them speak of God? So they leave nothing behind even in the spiritual world if wiped out.* And the sooner the better. Imagine one trying to insert itself into the family!

It was not just a matter of points. The gaps between ranks were clear and important. Ranking members of the community had the money and points to control the rest, and it was natural for them to command obedience. Persons with property had greater right to property. But no, it was more than that: Douens were irredeemably worthless. They were not poor people; they were subhuman.

In fact, that type was not only well served but better off as cargo. All that old hysteria about shipments had died down long ago. Procedures had become routine for harvesting the wealth of the island, and Roget's father had pointed out how this shipping of lost souls actually benefited the cargo. "What the recruiters are doing is to redirect them to organized and fruitful lives elsewhere, lives they could never have had otherwise," he said.

So their sea captains were received in the best society. There was one right now, on the veranda with Roget's father, accepting a glass from a silver tray. In any case, the recruiters boosted business ventures inland as well. SureLine had been able to raise its premiums for pirate attacks on vessels in the area. And profits had soared.

A breathy wail from along the corridor brought a tolerant smile to Roget's face. A healthy baby sister was further cause for celebration. Another girl too, so much the better. Roget wanted to hear nothing further about brothers.

The laughter downstairs floated up, the music, a little louder, muting the actual words and the chime of glassware. A breeze wafted in the smell of meat turning on a spit, of fresh rolls and sliced pineapples. The chatter and aroma distracted, soothed – relief for those who held together this delicately balanced way of life – and fragments floated up to him: *will probably take the sailboat to the cay . . . picked it up in the most unlikely store – eighteenth-century Venice, I understand . . . for a holiday abroad next year.* All of it reinforced the family stature, and Roget felt content to survey the scene.

The sight of the douen girl, moving calmly around outside, galled him. She collected the trash Francisco had carted to the edge of the gathering, and stoked a citronella torch before slipping out of sight.

He was another one, this Francisco. The word had got back that he claimed to have been a professional in his own country before their troubles. Yet what documents did he have? *Dr* Marquez. Should have stayed in his own country. But at least he worked as if grateful for the job. Roget's eyes shifted back to the douen girl, who *never* looked grateful.

Charity, his mother termed it, but her unspoken reason was that it was one way of garnering news about what lurked or bred in the bush. To Roget's way of thinking, work offered a chance for some outsider to get in; though wardens policed the inland borders, outsiders posed a threat. There was a sentimental dimension he had not expected in his mother – this trying to turn douens to good use rather than treating them as the vermin they were. Then, what about the perversion about it all – children growing untaught, roaming in bands without adults? What could be in their heads?

The douen stood now just beyond the torches, their light flickering between smoke and shadows so her upturned face was there, then not there. Then there again, her eyes directly on him.

A faint chill raised the hair on the back of his head. The douens may have been lurking relatively close by, unseen, for months, years – who could say? Intruders, whether they meant to be or not. And if they were not hostile to people who belonged, what made them look over their shoulders at every other step, or back away as if retreating from sight? What had they come east for anyway? To lure away decent children into their ranks or to supplant them, that was what.

"What is it?" His father had come up behind him and dropped a hand on his shoulder. "You look troubled."

"That." Roget inclined his head in the direction of the douen, but she had disappeared. "Those filthy parasites from the back of beyond."

"No threat to you. You know that," his father said heartily. "Come enjoy the party."

Roget went along – the people were his guests too – but the more he thought about it, the more convinced he grew that it was madness to tolerate wanderers from outside. Spat out by the sea, they had taken shallow root in the bush, among the rocks, no doubt enticing others with their show of freedom. They could only have banded together that way so as to practise some devilry. Just another dimension of the threat all outsiders posed, sneaking, whispering, chanting vicious lies about the people of Shoreline – that they had made their peace with corruption. When Roget thought of how his father and mother conducted themselves and what they had achieved, he had the urge to take out his father's gun and shoot the savages himself.

. . . .

A few hours later, when the last guests had straggled away, Roget strolled in across the living room, running his eyes caressingly over the silken surfaces of tables and cabinets, and at the quaint items they displayed – cashmere tea cosies, a monkey jar with a gilt cover, damask fingertip towels, ivory-handled cheese knives, a pair of silver inkwells, a marble and mahogany plant stand from one of the northernmost islands, pickle forks and tortoiseshell combs, and any number of paper-thin china cups, gold rimmed. He could have done without the Fire Island yabba and the silvered coal-pot, but perhaps his mother was right in thinking that a nod to ancient folk culture showed some flexibility of outlook. He paused at the trolley outside the kitchen to pull out a soft roll from one of the Irish linen contrivances (each pocket secured by its tiny pearled button) and smeared on butter. The St Justes knew how to comport themselves.

Perhaps not all. By the morning after the party, to Roget's disgust, everyone's attention was focused on his uncle's wife, whom he knew well because his mother had considered her a protégée and had taken some care with her. St Juste's younger brother had married Elizabeth Yap Lee a few years before, and only last evening, Roget's mother had said, "Pity you have no little cousins yet," which he at once understood as a lament about the girl's general incompetence.

This aunt was young, though, barely a year or so older than Roget. Her father, who had been ailing for years, had been pleased with the engagement and had the marriage ceremony conducted when she was twelve. Then, only shortly afterwards, the news came that the old man had died. Now she was fifteen, and things had taken a grim turn. Roget's young uncle had come down with fever, headache and swollen joints.

Elizabeth was one of that age group whose education had been cut short. "Things were such" – his father's closest ever reference to circumstances the family had overcome and need never dwell on again. A child with lost school years like Elizabeth needed her life arranged for her, and marriage was the smoothest way forward. Ignorant as she was, Elizabeth had had no clue how to act on her own and her husband's collapse terrified her. She called Dr Chesterfield at once, but by the time he arrived a rash had flared together with bellyache and all that went with that. The young man tossed restlessly, hot then cold, until he started bleeding through the nose and purple bruises showed up on his skin. By the time he began to vomit blood, Chesterfield could do nothing for him. At eleven thirty that night, only three days after the first sign of flushing on his face, the news came that he was dead.

The stupid girl had folded up screaming.

Who had time for her? She had no value outside of the marriage. She had nothing to contribute or earn. The Honourable St Juste had lost his *brother,* and now had the worthless wife left on his hands. Roget and Celeste were no longer to refer to her as their aunt. She was neither qualified, a person in her own right, nor anyone's daughter, wife or sister. Widowhood had delivered her into the ranks of the pointless.

"Only one thing to be done," Roget's father said in disgust, "if the little fool isn't to end up in Xanadu and disgrace us all."

(Xanadu? Roget pretended all he knew was that *that* was a question for when he was older.)

"What do you intend?" his mother asked.

"Well, I'm having her brought here. I know, I know," he said as a flicker of surprise passed across her face. "But who can tell what she'll do? Or say?" He turned to his children. "So no wrapping up with her now. Those days are done. The mess she's found herself in doesn't put her in a good light." For the St Juste children there was no need to spell out the stigma attached to anyone without property or expectations. Roget, certainly, knew better than to demean himself.

Four days later, when Ramnarine dropped in, Roget shook his hand and strolled out, leaving the adults to their rum and coconut water. He knew as well as his parents why Sir Hector had come, and later his father confirmed it after gesturing Celeste away, up to the nursery.

"Approached me about Elizabeth," he announced. "Best thing for all concerned."

Roget knew that under other circumstances Ramnarine might

do better, but whispers had circulated about the death of Sir Hector's wife three years before. "He was taken with Elizabeth to begin with," remarked Roget's mother, "but she was already married when the wife died." She added, "Never a shred of evidence regarding anything amiss in his household, whatever people said about her having become a domestic and even financial burden. But of course people talked."

"People always talk," Roget's father said shortly, "and they blow up stories like that out of their own idle craving for drama."

Now that both Elizabeth's husband and old Madame Ramnarine were gone, the matter was straightforward. No one could have expected what came next.

When Nkomi St Juste formally announced the plan to the family, Elizabeth shouted, "No. No, you can't make me. Please, oh God, don't do me that," and collapsed sobbing and pleading on the floor, holding Roget's ankle and making such a spectacle of herself that St Juste shouted at her to shut up.

She screamed at him that he was a monster, they were all monsters, and no one could make her shut up. Roget lost patience and kicked her in the diaphragm, cutting off her cries. While she tried to get back her breath, St Juste called his property manager to put her under lock and key until she regained her senses.

For Roget the problem was compounded when his mother appointed the douen girl to carry Elizabeth food and drink. She was also to let Nurse know the moment the stupid young woman calmed down. "Counselling," Nastasia reminded her husband, squeezing his hand and glancing at him significantly. He met her eyes with a look of appreciation for always remembering what was correct and due to their position.

From his mother, Roget learnt later that it was not the little freak – Myche, she called herself – who discovered the tattoo, but the girl who had sponged down Elizabeth when she had stopped bawling. The fat girl from the settlement along the forest fence laughed about it with Nurse Flo, and old Flo was too shocked not to mention it to her mistress. Roget's mother went to the servants' quarters herself, to confirm with her own eyes the outlandish story that Elizabeth had a cobra tattoo on her spine. Nastasia wasted no time over enquiring into how a girl of Lap Yee's family could possibly have accessed the sort of savage skill required for a tattoo, let alone escaped the guidance and protection of her father long enough to get it done. Enquiries of that sort would only drive whispers in the servants' quarters further abroad.

Madame St Juste at once packed the fool of a maid off for shipping, but when Roget told her she should get rid of the douen too, she refused. "We need someone taking care of her who can easily be shut up, and we can't keep opening the thing up to one servant after the next."

She told him she had been thinking the problem out. Needless to say, Nurse Flo had reasoned it out in her own way — a woman with a mark like that on her skin must have bitten and poisoned her husband, subtly enough for it to seem he had died of natural causes. Well, Nastasia had no patience with such nonsense, but she did mention to Roget that Elizabeth had conducted herself beneath the standards of Shoreline, and some sort of cleansing would need to be on record if it got out.

"But, Mamam, any sort of ceremony will have the story all over the place," he objected.

They went to Roget's father to be on the safe side, and Nastasia reluctantly raised the question about a visit from the Order of Light. She was still pale from her recent setback and looked positively ill now. And with good cause. Roget thought of the attention that the Order of Light would draw — men in grey robes singing, praying and waving thick books over their heads. The devotees set themselves apart from regular life, and their business was to keep regular life regular. They alone were authorized to evaluate the world outside Shoreline in accordance with the teachings of their books, and they ruled on the proper attitudes to the poor, to pointless women and to outsiders from other nations or the wild interior.

As usual Nkomi set their minds at rest. He would not be calling to his home just any insignificant member of the college; he would require no less a person than their Dean, and the Dean would come alone.

· · · · · · · · ·

When Myche reported that Lady Elizabeth was eating again, St Juste invited Dean Blake to counsel her. She stood before him, head down and shoulders drooping. Then, abruptly in the middle of the interview, she fainted. They dragged her to a sofa, where she came around quickly but bled copiously over the champagne-coloured upholstery. It came out that she had indeed been expecting a child and was now losing it. Habitually inept, Nastasia murmured, throwing up her hands.

This was nothing to pester Dr Chesterfield about, so they called in the woman, Naomi Ali – she actually called herself a doctor – and made the douen girl get in there and be of what assistance she could. Wiping up blood and such. Dean Blake had withdrawn in good order.

Like St Juste, Ramnarine and Blake, Roget had no doubt how the matter would end. There would be no child from Elizabeth's first marriage to complicate negotiations for the next. Not that they couldn't have sorted that out, for he knew there were systems to address problems of orphaned children.

Celeste, of course, was young enough to be protected from such details. So much so that she expended a lot of concern over Elizabeth, who, she heard, was terribly unhappy and quite ill. Tiresome little girl, Roget reflected.

If only it had ended there.

Celeste wandered down to Elizabeth's room to enquire how she was, and Myche said the lady was ill because someone kicked her in the chest and she lost a baby. And so much blood.

Then there was Celeste screaming in front of the servants.

"The douen," Roget hissed, white-hot, when he confronted his mother. "If you don't drown that little rat, I will poison it."

PART 5

VISITATION

21

BRAIN CHILD

NAOMI

So many voices. Babel? Babylon. Naomi had opened her door when
she heard the pounding and found Myche outside shivering in the rain.

"What are you doing here?" She pulled the child inside, dragging
a towel from a small heap of cloth she had been stuffing into a bag
and she mopped the wet face and hair.

"I can't stand them. I couldn't sleep. It was like scorpions crawling
over me, and I kept waking up. Francisco said Roget wants me dead.
I climbed out the window. Don't send me back. Don't. Just let me
get back out into the bush." She babbled on, batting her hands away
from her face as if to ward it all off. "And why it is no one must help
Elizabeth?"

"Listen, child: Naomi won't lie to you." She held Myche's chin
gently and turned it so they looked into each other's eyes. "Shoreliners
excel at putting themselves in the right and everyone else dead in the
wrong, while they negotiate with thieves and murderers and suck up
to tyrants for their own protection. No one's too low or vicious for
people like St Juste – no one here, no one abroad."

"Who *are* these people?" Myche's voice was husky with grief and
exhaustion. "How do they do horrible things and . . . everyone seems

to" – she searched among her treasury of Shine's words, which seemed suddenly all she had left – "to emulate. . ."

"Business people, they call themselves," Naomi said, "but do you know what they sell? First there's this insurance firm, SureLine, for selling safe passage by sea. They split a fee with the pirates to leave ships with the SureLine logo alone, and shipping companies pay millions of dollars for that assurance."

"But why they pay?"

"Because it costs more to lose ship after ship with its cargo, or to equip ships with radar, tracking devices, guns and rockets, and robot patrols. It costs millions to reroute ships through safe waters. A few shipping companies have tried to make up for losses by scuttling their own ships – blowing them up or sending them to the bottom – and claiming insurance. But they've been no match for SureLine. The firm's lawyers seem to just rename things so the company never pays."

Words. Myche felt she could grapple with those. "What you mean, rename?"

Naomi explained they would look at hull damage and reclassify it as machinery peril – not covered. They'd argue that some sea passage where pirates lurked in ambush was a war zone, so the ship should never have ventured into the area. Not covered. They'd cancel protection in waters they suddenly declared to come under no jurisdiction of any country in particular. Or, just as abruptly, they'd stop coverage of a vessel because its crew took up arms in self-defence, saying it was the crew who brought down the violent attack on themselves.

"So nothing can stop them?" Myche swung away from the damp towel Naomi was rubbing over her body.

"What is there to stop the St Justes and their kind? The Shoreliners have forgotten history, and some of the governments they befriend know little history either. They make it up to suit themselves."

"You can't make up history," Myche said.

"'Course you can. People do it all the time. And this lot have never stretched their minds over fiction or poetry so as to practise viewing things from other angles. The world is what they've fabricated to suit themselves, and they're untouchable." Naomi pulled a dry T-shirt of her own over Myche's head before continuing. *"Truth be damned* – that's the unspoken motto that drives them. They've forgotten (if they ever knew) how long ago the West cast off a way of valuing people that was based on breeding and money, for a new way based on character and education. Now, their new order bases itself on money – without breeding or education, let alone character." She stopped to reach for a loaf of bread and some cheese.

"But what has that to do with anything, with how they get on now? And how they get away with it?" Once she got the question out, Myche sank her teeth into the bread thankfully.

"Will they get away? You know, most ranking members of Shoreline Council are clueless. Dishonest, yes, but without the skill to compete with hardened criminals. They don't realize they've placed themselves at the mercy of cutthroats." Naomi put her head to one side and studied the girl. "What you said your name was? Myche? Unusual. Nice, though. Myche, don't trust *one* of them. What children? Least of all their children, for *they* have never known anything else. That Roget is a mapepire."

Myche went pale, breathing as if someone had a hand on her throat.

"What did he do you?" Naomi demanded. She reached for a paper bag and put it to Myche's face. "Don't talk for a minute. Just try to breathe normally."

Myche did so, and after a few moments, Naomi said, "Okay. Tell me."

"Francisco – a man who works there – he came with a white powder and said Roget told him to put it on my food. Francisco said if I ate it I would scream with pain and I would die, but he had to put it. 'So don't eat,' he said. 'Just leave the food.' He needed to keep the job."

Naomi had to close her eyes for a few seconds, and when she opened them she couldn't speak.

"What's he hate me for?" Myche burst out. "What I did him?"

"You've seen through them and you might talk. It's like that for me too. This young woman – Elizabeth, is it? This one they called me in to patch up for the old murderer Ramnarine – oh yes. He did it. I *saw* his wife; he brought her to me before she died, and no one else knows the condition she was in. Ramnarine. He had worked with St

Juste and Blake on committees like the Justice Brigade – that same unscrupulous gang that subsidized some of the violence that brought down the government – even before the so-called *Liberation*.

"Listen. The Shoreline Council cooperates with anyone who has money, so we are a crossroads now for transhipping drugs and . . . and people. Children. *Children*, Myche."

"How can that work?"

"Well, they turn the money around to look like earnings from asphalt, shadon beni and the rest. Rum, they say. Who hoeing canefield? Oil? How? Like they know anything about drilling? They wouldn't know how to extract oil let alone find it in the first place. They buy from outside. Refineries here shut down years ago." Naomi paused and regarded Myche, her heart full of regret. "I don't know how to help you, child. St Juste is at the core of so much evil. This young girl, this Elizabeth, was for sale. To Ramnarine, to the pirates. Whoever. St Juste and the other councillors have one policy for the rest of us: comply or die. They will ship me out and cast you away to prevent any talk about Elizabeth. That scandal has to stop circulating among the St Juste servants. That's why they placed you with me to begin with, to nurse Elizabeth. They put you where you couldn't speak to anyone likely to listen to you. You could talk only to me and tell me what I already knew. And now – well. I have no time left."

Naomi began talking faster so as to pass on as much information as she could to the girl, because that was all she had to give.

"All these years I've taken care to stay close-lipped about my clients' affairs. The council called it my *grandiose term of observing patients' privacy.* Calling myself a doctor, no less – I've heard St Juste repeating that in disgust. It was Shoreline's worthless women that the council officially put in my care, but never mind that: in an emergency, the great families smuggled me into their homes secretly.

"When I protested, when I showed my certificate, they justified their treatment of me by citing statistics – the death toll among my patients. But my patients were mostly the poor: persons without property have shorter lives, fewer live births than the rich. They are the pointless, and they die of it."

"But Elizabeth wasn't poor," Myche protested.

"Sure she was, once her husband was gone. Elizabeth? Poor girl. Aidan St Juste was as decent a lad as that family could produce, and he'd stood between her and the in-laws. But Nkomi St Juste isn't only domineering – he's grasping. Ravenous. From the first he grabbed the lion's share of the dowry, insisting *he* had made the match, and he threatened to withdraw all support from the couple if Aidan resisted. When Aidan died, everything became Nkomi St Juste's by law and – naive as Elizabeth is – she knew she'd spend the rest of her years working, morning till night, for her sister-in-law Nastasia. What Elizabeth had never foreseen was that she'd be sold off to a diseased old man who had poisoned his previous wife.

"When she refused, they had her beaten and kept for yardwork. That might have lasted but for some encounter with St Juste she hasn't dared repeat even to me – except she said she was no better off than if she had married Ramnarine. By next morning he had her put out on the street. That's why you haven't seen her since. I caught sight of her this morning as they marched her to the wharf."

Myche had finished eating, and it was just as well because she had gone pale and looked as if she might be sick.

"I'm sorry, Myche, I have to tell you this, unpleasant as it is. Girls in Elizabeth's situation have few choices. When St Juste put her out, she made her way to the poorhouse and tried to live decently, begging when possible, as discreetly as she could. But at last the police arrested her as an unnecessary charge on the state. They bound her over to appear before Mr Justice Gerard Cuffee, and he upheld charges of vagrancy and insolvency. On his ruling, the fort authorities sold her to the so-called recruiters, so the government could recover what she had cost it. I know this because they called me in to assess her health. They needed to set a value on her. Fix a price, I mean."

"And she can't get away? At all? There isn't any way?"

"Their officers hunt down whoever slips away," said Naomi, "for what decent, law-abiding person would run from such an ideal way of life? Our law enforcers convict and hang anyone who seeks to undermine the security of Shoreline – if they have to. More often, they turn their eyes away and leave it to the seamen to proceed in their own way with anyone who presents a threat. And now I am a threat."

When Myche shook her head and tried to protest, Naomi gripped her hand.

"No," she insisted, "I'm *telling* you as it is. In attending to women of every level, I hear more than is good for me. I overheard the plan for the canal and for the flushing out of the wetlanders, and I sent word to the people of the swamp. But the messenger I paid came back and sold this information about me. So by morning I'll be gone. Aboard as cargo."

"Nooo."

Myche's drawn-out wail wrenched Naomi's heart almost as much as the thought of what lay ahead.

"You have to get away," Myche said. "We'll go together. Isaiah and them will take us."

"You don't understand, or you won't." Naomi shook Myche roughly. "They're coming. They'll have me by morning. You *must* leave here before then. Get back to the St Juste house, and tell them I put you out for refusing to run away with me. Tell them I begged you to lead me back into the swamp to the rabble who infest it, and that you refused." She softened, squeezing Myche's hands more gently and then drawing the girl's head to her shoulder. "I hope you'll carry with you what little I could teach you over those days when we nursed Elizabeth. For I *am* a doctor – whatever they say.

"I'd finished my degree and begun work in the hospital before things fell apart. I tried to get out like everyone else, and the hospital wasn't far from the airport, so I set off without stopping to line up for gas. The airport was crowded. There was nowhere to park, nowhere. You just left the car anywhere, for you were never coming back for it. There was nothing to sell anything for or buy anything with, although there were piles of worthless money in home after home. There was nothing to stay for. People had been eating dead bison, dead horse, some already foul; some people were poisoned by rotting meat. I know because they crowded into the clinics and died in waiting rooms.

"The only thought was to get out. You drove as far as you could in the direction of Departures and left the car without even bothering to lock it. Then you walked the rest of the way until you were inside this glass-topped airless dome that only gathered the heat. Sweating officials were taking foreign money for passages that were already overbooked, cancelled, not arrived, grounded. When you couldn't board, they returned none of it. 'Try by boat,' they said." She tightened her arms around Myche. "I think now, at last, I am bound for a boat."

22

SYNDICATE

MYCHE

TRY BY BOAT. NAOMI'S WORDS ECHOED in Myche's brain because she had heard them before.

That was when Myche knew that every word Naomi said was true – when she started to talk about the boats. Ports, wharves, yacht clubs – the waterfront everywhere, Naomi had said, piers and even private jetties were jammed.

The recollection of boats rising and falling on the swell made Myche dizzy, and she squeezed her eyes closed, then forced them open again so the image would disappear. She must have fallen asleep on Naomi's bed, but not for longer than half an hour.

When she opened her eyes, Naomi was gone.

Myche tried to follow her advice, although her head ached and the sun made it throb more as she made her way towards the St Juste property. Every prompting in her urged her to run in the other direction. But where to? And she trusted Naomi.

She felt hot and cold with terror. After a while the pain was blinding, and she could hardly distinguish one person in front of her from another. In the haze of fear she hardly knew when she reached the house or whom she spoke to. Eventually Madame St Juste's voice said the douen girl no longer had anything to do there and belonged to no one, and St Juste (who overlooked no detail) sent his property manager to march her all the way back to the old fort that served as a holding place and market.

Perhaps she would see the others there. But how? Where were they? The questions fired through her temple and lodged in her brain. After the comfort of the big house, and despite the coldness of Madame and the vicious glances from Roget, she was afraid now of the stone cell over the sea.

She could not have expected mercy from the St Justes. Not after the way they had dealt with Shant. Now, despite all the helpless rage Shant had called up in her from time to time, there rose a surge of pity for what had overtaken him – first for the torment of guilt that followed on Colin's death and then his own family throwing him away. And when she looked back over his small gestures of rejection over years he could never undo, the uselessness of his tears to Zef, the silliness of Colin's bare feet in dry leaves – was it all his fault? For why hadn't *she* screamed at Colin to put on the shoes, however they bruised? It was only because she too felt the sheer joy of casting them off after months of cosseting and scolding in the forest, and the sense of being invincible – for what did dry ground have that could hurt them when nothing ever had?

Ash had been different, wounded beyond anyone's skills before he came to them, but Colin should never have slipped through her fingers. Shant was no more to blame than she had been. She had had Shine, but what did Shant know? He did not deserve his family. And now he had slipped from her too. Like all the rest.

Inattention – that was the enemy. Keep your eyes open, Shine had said. Time after time she had gathered the other children and kept watch over them, but now every one of them was out of sight.

By the time the guard pushed her into a cell and she crumpled in the corner furthest from the light, she could hardly see anything nor distinguish any sound but a whooshing inside her head, as if the blood were backing up then breaking free to surge forward then retreat again. No one interfered with her. She knew to keep her eyes down and her tone obedient so as to be all but invisible, and now the truth was that she had backed away somewhere else behind the curtain of pain, ignoring it as the fine pinpoints of light flashed inside her head.

Pictures from another time flashed on and off as well. Her mother read to her, little stories and rhymes. Not like Shine, who was going to school and studying stuff. Why the pain brought back her mother she could not imagine, but, looking back, she recalled her mother's stories about the little mermaid, about the Vikings, about Jesus in the boat. And she could see Shine listening when their mother read something they called poetry. He seemed to look out into a different world Myche could not see. During his time at the Trust when he searched out books on his foraging expeditions, there was so much else to carry that he would sometimes bring in only a page or two. One scrap had Moses in the bulrushes and another, a huge page he had folded small, was about boys trapped in a cave and people swimming in to get them out. Then there were writers who had produced books right there in the region, he said. Some even wrote poetry.

She couldn't see why that mattered, but after all that had happened, she felt it had to be important if Shine thought it so. He gave her a page to keep because he said what was written there was the thing that had jolted him awake. She did not know what that meant, but she had kept it and reread it until she knew it by heart, lines that meant nothing to her but everything to Shine. She folded what remained of that small page into a plastic envelope tied round her waist, even when only a few words were legible, and although she could not understand them. *Death rides at anchor in the deep.* There it stayed, the paper frayed to scraps with a few scattered dots, what had once been poetry.

Her brothers, her mother. Nothing connected with her father, though. Nothing summoned him up. As her mind backed away, it flashed unaccountably to Robber Boy, who had said his father was the Man. A bragger, a swaggerer. He said his mother was a soucou-yant. She'd flown in, met *him*, flown out and could not get back *in*. His father said they did not exist and set up some sort of wall to keep them out. They called it – but she could not remember. It was a line they could not cross; he was the Boss. Restraining order, was it? At any rate, they couldn't cross the border.

Robber Boy had appeared outside the Trust and then disappeared with the seamen along a track into nowhere.

Tiny bits of things had been left by the fire. Some people were fragments like that. Nurse Flo whose brother, whose mother . . . what was it? Fire in the sky, the buildings, everywhere. Leaving Flo too confused to explain. A shattering. Scarlet feathers strewn on swamp water. Even Isaiah with his odd walk when he got stressed out – as if his limbs had disconnected and not been properly realigned or couldn't manage to operate in sync, and the way a sudden noise, the crack of a tree limb in the quiet night, could throw him into a frantic trembling and twitching. He would toss his head or arm or leg back without seeming to know that was happening to him, and when he did that, Bunji would run out and grip him tight by the shoulders and say, "Is all right, man. It go pass. The thing finish and done longtime."

Didi had said the fire had nothing human behind it. Pure evil, she said.

Why you say that? How you know? Nat had asked.

I was there, Didi said. She was there the night of the soucouyant. Hurtling through the sky – a ball of fire with a woman's shriek and hair of flame flaring behind. It set the night aglow, lit houses ablaze, whooshed up dry trees, raged through churches and shops, crackled along hedges and dried lawns with fallen leaves, roared over shingled roofs. Coconut trees were torches: their boughs flamed, then dropped, blazing, on pedestrians and traffic beneath. A car exploded, bits rained down, metal fragments and burning rubber, blood and glass and flesh. Didi had been there.

And now there they were, all of them, inside of Myche's head. Sometimes they all came fluttering and shrieking soundlessly at her like the bats.

She held her head very tight to see if it would shut down, and it came to her that her mother used to have bad headaches she called migraines. Just before she dropped off to sleep, she caught the sound of Zef and Colin weeping for each other across a gulf where the ocean scoured between towering rock walls. A treble of small boys wailing inconsolably.

She may have slept for a while, for when she opened her eyes it was better. Only the whooshing. Then she realized that was outside of her head. Outside of the cell. She edged to the other side to look through the bars.

The fort stood near the edge of a rocky shelf pounded by the sea, and one long narrow row of cells with Myche and others – she did not know who – those few cells hung over the waves that swept in. Myche could neither bear to look at the water nor to look away. Every glance brought her back to the long fall from the ship into the heaving blue. If she shut her eyes, she heard Shine's urgent whisper: *When you hit the water, kick your way up, to the light. Keep your eyes open. When you reach the surface, kick in the direction of the land. Keep your eyes open.*

The surge pounded beneath them and sprayed up. You could hear and smell it. *Keep your eyes open.*

·········

One day there was talk of a hurricane, and her face must have shown that she had little idea what that was. "Wind and water," said a guard, grinning. He liked to push his hand through the bars and reach for her with his fingers. "Even if the sea don't come up or the rain pour in and drown you, the wind going come screaming round and prise off the roof and tear you out. Then it will pelt you down for the sea to swallow you up. You going be glad to hold onto me then." He shoved his arm in again, clutching with his fingers, but she stayed out of reach, flattening herself against the bars and squeezing her eyes shut to pretend the bars were not all there was between her and the sea.

Keep your eyes open. Shine's voice was so near, so definite in her head that she opened her eyes at once and looked around wildly for him. The guard was pushing in a stick with a thick hook, and she grabbed the end, twisting it away, but he was too strong for her, and she knew he would get it into her clothes, under her arm and through her skin if need be, and drag her to him. Suddenly, the jingling of the warden's keys, and the guard ducked away. Boots pounded along the passage.

"What's this?" The warden eyed the hook in Myche hands and the long rod protruding back through the bars of the door. He drew it out and cast a glance over his shoulder. "Who was on duty here?" Myche couldn't catch the name shouted back. "Get him in my office." He turned back to her. "Now, girl."

The warden had brought one of the cruiters who was looking over girls the Shoreliners needed to dispense with. When the warden tramped off, the seaman pressed his face close to the bars.

"I gotta know which of you is Shine sister?"

He was scarred, mean-looking. Myche was afraid of missing a chance to escape, but more afraid of doing anything that could hurt Shine. She shut up.

"I gotta to see them properly," the man shouted, and another guard came along. "Make them strip down."

When she had nothing left on but the thin underwear she had from the St Justes, he stared at the cord and the plastic sheath strapped around her. He nodded as if they were somehow in agreement. But she knew it had to be some trick, and she made no response.

Later Myche would learn he had chosen her with four others for immediate delivery, but she was the only one from the Trust.

········

Guards marched them from the fort along the edge of the forest, a man she had never seen before tramping ahead, swinging his machete. The one who had selected her followed with his gun slung over his shoulder, and she was at the back of the short line. As the path swung around a bend, he shoved her roughly off it into the thick foliage and kept walking. She ran fast as she could, hearing the cries of "one of them gone", and of feet beating behind her. Then Brand tumbled out of a tree and pushed her further from the track into deeper bush, where they lay still, listening.

"Over here, you say!" A man's voice, and he was hacking the bush beside the track with his machete. But he was going the other way.

She flung her arms around Brand and squeezed with all her might.

"Okay, okay." He patted her awkwardly. "Glad to see you too."

"How you come to be here by the path?"

"Shine sent word. He paid some guy."

· · · · · · · · · ·

Hours later they were trudging through wet leaves around a pool shadowed by dense forest. Brand. It was beyond everything: He was alive and in command of himself. In touch with Shine, in communication with all the others from the Trust that he could find. Relief filled her like warm bread.

Brand gripped her arm and pulled her away from a limb that forked low over the way, and it was not a fork in the limb but something coiling up from it, then round again, gliding along. The anaconda slid away even as something disturbed the water, breaking up the smooth sheen that had extended to its edge under the overhanging leaves. Now it was Myche who grabbed Brand's arm to pull him back into the bush, but he stretched out his hand, and a shadow among the water hyacinths sent the blue flowers bobbing aside as a huge cat rose out of the forest pool and padded towards them on silent paws, streaming water from bronze fur. He walked past without acknowledging them, and they followed until they reached Brand's shelter, a rough lean-to indistinguishable from the bush around it. Inside, One Thousand Eyes turned around a few times, then slumped down and regarded them sleepily. He filled up most of the walking space.

"Soaking wet," Myche protested.

Brand shrugged. "Wet half the time. He goes all in the sea."

She stared at the cat. He had not only transformed from the oversize kitten Shine had brought in nearly three years before but had grown bigger since she had spotted him last, five times larger and heavier than any ocelot she had seen, with strangely short, rounded ears on a broad head. No face stripes had ever come in. If he stood on his hind legs, he would have been Shine's height, perhaps six feet tall, but he was short-limbed, stockier, in fact much heavier – at least twice Brand's weight. Her time in and out the fortress, being weighed and measured, made her think the cat must weigh around two hundred pounds. His thick fur, amber as it began to dry out, was marked with black rosettes, and on the wide face, the great gold eyes were intent, almost smouldering, above powerful jaws with three-inch fangs.

He regarded her through half-closed eyes and gave a low snort that drew out into a snore, then flung himself on his side, tilting, almost on his back. His belly was mostly white blotted with irregular dark patches. He waggled a bit, playfully, eyeing her sidelong. The temptation to give in and rub his chest with her foot was strong, but she had seen ocelots playing together, more violent than anything she could bear, and she knew this cat had the power to kill her quicker than thought, even if by accident. He rolled over and eyed her reproachfully.

"Don't *ever* play with it." Shine had said. "It can tear you apart without meaning to. It's accepted you, perhaps loves you in its way – but it will always be wild." That was months ago.

"Good cat," she murmured in her most soothing voice, and he snorted affably and was gone again, soundless on the dry leaves. Perhaps it would have been all right to scratch his chest. Or not.

Every now and then a near-miss crossed her mind – just a detached awareness that sent a cold shudder over her – of a tree root she hadn't stumbled over or the edge of a ravine her feet had skidded towards, or a rock fall that had happened just before she passed that way and left only this pile of boulders in her path with a fine spume of dust still smoking upwards. It could all have gone differently, it would occur to her. But now, that evening, she sat down on the floor of Brand's shelter and said to herself, it could all have gone differently every time, every step of the way. And perhaps once would have been enough.

Then, just as she was about to get up, she thought – perhaps it did. Perhaps it did go differently, and that was why she was here. Only she could not work out where else she would have been. And different from what?

What if there had never been a ship to draw alongside their boat? What if there had not been a boat or need for a boat? What if. What if the soucouyant or dragons or planes from the fire-hair man had not screamed in to rain death on WeLand.

·········

Shine arrived the next night. He was obviously accustomed to Brand's shelter and at home though never familiar with One Thousand Eyes.

He asked Myche to describe the workings of the enclave to him but first she demanded whether he had seen Naomi. Yes, he said, the woman they called the doctor was being loaded onto a cargo ship. She didn't look good. He knew nothing about any Elizabeth, but she would probably end up on that same ship. A girl such as Myche described might be well treated so as to fetch a good price. Naomi, though, might be almost worthless.

"But she's a doctor," Myche argued. "Wouldn't they want a doctor on board?"

He thought about it and admitted it was possible.

"Couldn't you get her on board your ship as a doctor?" Myche persevered.

"My ship, as you call it, is not a good place to be," he said, adding that he had no connection with the vessel Naomi would be on.

Since he could do nothing about that, he insisted, what he wanted to talk about was the enclave. Piracy provided most of the wealth that underpinned its operations. What seemed to be other sources of income depended on the pirates in one way or another. The St Justes sold insurance policies that covered what they called *war risk*. Calling ransom, kidnapping and damage to cargo and hull *war risk* was possible once the region was classified as dangerous, like a war zone. The SureLine logo marked ships whose owners had already paid the pirates a sort of ransom in advance, called *indemnity*.

For always, always, everything came back to money.

"Does your ship hold others for ransom?" Myche demanded.

"Of course. Not long ago, the men captured an oil tanker and held it for ransom. Under the threat of environmental destruction, governments agreed to pay. Now there's another tanker they've got. They're taking it around with them."

But Shine said things at Shoreline were "coming to a head", then he added, "I think this is the chance we've been waiting for, coming up."

"What you mean?" Myche jumped up from where she had sat and came close to him.

"The ship I'm on used to be a luxury liner," he said, "but the pirates armed it and set it up as their lead vessel. Now they're scrubbing and repainting. It's for a meeting they're calling a *summit*. It's to bring together Shoreline authorities, captains of major pirate vessels, even a few representatives from one or two neighbouring governments. Top officials of the peacekeeping force are coming too, from Freedom Bay."

He paused but saw Brand watching him breathlessly, so he continued.

"It shouldn't take long. The liner's easy to clean, because it wasn't ever a freight vessel – only one that chased and acquired merchandise. They were quick about transferring any human cargo it picked up to a proper freighter. So the sailors won't need more than a day or two to scrub away the smell." He rubbed his hands together as if the important part of what he had to say was coming next.

"Now, before the summit, Shoreline means to celebrate the launch of its canal project. Afterwards we'll send off a small smart vessel to collect the dignitaries and bring them aboard together. That's when they'll sit down to work out how to share control of the island. What the pirates want is to legitimize their business internationally. They're looking for acceptance from other nations. They're going to propose that the group form what they call a syndicate."

"Legitimize?" Myche's voice shook with rage.

"Make it legal . . ."

"I know the word." She barked it out, but he didn't react, just moved on.

"Where were you planning to be on Friday evening?" Shine asked, offhand but watching them intently while he spoke, as if their every thought and gesture mattered as much as their words. But also, strangely, as if he could never look at them enough, as if he needed to capture their faces and carry them with him.

"Storming the enclave, with Isaiah and them," Brand responded, as if it were how anyone might spend an evening.

Shine stared.

"I've been in touch with them most of the time Myche was at Shore-line," Brand continued. "It was me holding them back till she could get out. You see this whole canal thing? The wetlanders just want to burn the town down. But I wasn't sure where she was at first, and since I've been in and out for months finding out what I could, they waited for me to get all the information we needed. About the safest ways, the peacekeepers' routines – all that. And then, too, the High Forest people won't want to have anything to do with setting fires."

"High Forest?" Shine broke in. "You don't mean the two set of them working together?"

"Oh yes. Darati was willing to go to High Forest on behalf of the wetlanders." Brand turned to Myche. "Remember she turned back to stay with Isaiah and them? The two of us joined up and made our way back to the swamp together, until Suraj found us and picked us up. Then when they were talking about finding the forest people, Bunji said he would go along with anyone who might know the way. And Darati offered to trek back to the forest and make a try."

"But how that could help – Darati going, I mean." Myche spread her hands in bewilderment. "Darati doesn't talk. What do you mean *offered*?"

"When we were all arguing about who should go, she stepped up. The wetlanders refused to let me out their sight, because I was the one who knew the town. And none of them wanted to make that first move to speak to the forest people. Then Darati said she'd go. We know she made it there okay, because Ena turned up a few days after with this pigeon she sends back and forth, and we got word yesterday that Casey, Didi, Bois and the rest were already on their way southeast. Well, obviously not Babu. Not Ferne and them either – the way them forest people baby their children."

"But Darati doesn't *talk*!" Myche said again. "She hasn't for years."

Brand just shrugged. "She does now."

"Right." Shine stared at Brand as if seeing him for the first time. "Now we have to put together what we know about Shoreline. How it's laid out. Where everything is." He picked up a pointed stick and began to draw on the ground, connecting what he knew with what Myche could add. Brand shoved in an occasional correction.

Beyond the bush and the fence, and after a few small farms, lay the town – mostly in from the bay. Wide curve of shoreline: scoop down, then up again between two horns, thick and stumpy like the head of an old bison, the southern horn longer, the northern one more crumpled. A jagged cliff scoured away underneath made up the northern horn, and at its base, a strip of rocky land ran along the sea with an old jetty sticking out into the water. On the top, after the cliff flattened somewhat towards the bay, stood a small lookout for the peacekeepers, for just a few bored guards, lightly gunned. Then, past the first turn-off to the commercial area, the road from that station ran on towards the fort.

Then Shine tapped the other, southern horn of the bay that he had drawn with his stick. "That's the main station." It was built far above the waves that broke and sprayed around the rocks under the cliff. That, together with the sheer rock wall that ran well inland from the bay, secured Shoreline from an approach from the south. Brand said houses of really poor people were scattered underneath that end of the southern cliff. Myche had not known of the settlement, because it was nowhere the St Justes would visit, and it was out of sight from their land.

"Oh yes," Shine said thoughtfully. "Out of sight. I almost forgot." He drew a spyglass from the light but bulky jacket he had on and showed her how to use it. Then he picked up his stick and began drawing again.

"Here on the clifftop, behind the large south station and some other buildings at the back of it, rocky ground reaches far inland before it gives way to bush and then deep forest."

"The forest there and behind the other end of the town is fenced off," Brand said. "And they patrol it."

"Although," Shine reflected, "most attention will be on the bay that night of the attack."

Myche's mind had stayed on the spyglass, but now she snapped to attention. "Attack?"

"Just listen, for I'm going back to sea. The children who've come all this way with you, and those who haven't washed up as yet – we're their last defence."

Before she could absorb that, he was sketching again with his stick. In the depression between the horns where the shore curved in spread the commercial waterfront north of the beach, and from the shoreline the land swept up and back to the business centre on the northern side, and residences more to the south. The fort, just south of the northern cliff and built into it, might present a problem, Shine said. The big question was when, or even whether, to fire on it.

"No." Myche sprang up, her eyes fiery. "All sorts of prisoners there. I don't know where Nat is. Telma. Shant . . ."

"Shant's with the wetlanders, Isaiah and them," Brand said. "Nat and the rest are out already or will be by tonight. Our problem was you – way off in that area with the fancy houses. Anyone left in the fort by Friday will be far to the end of the back wing. Now shut up and listen."

"I won't shut up. Nurse Flo – a woman at the St Juste house – she said there were explosives stored in the fort. So the whole thing . . ."

"Because we've been moving those for weeks," Brand put in smugly.

"We?"

Shine rapped his stick on the ground impatiently. "*Will* you both shut up?" He tapped the X marking the main peacekeepers' station to the south. "This lookout over the bay is much better equipped than the nearer one – more guns, and, moored below, more patrol boats. Behind this big south station lie their stores and munitions."

Shine said the armed liner he would be on was going to be anchored offshore, north of the big station, but south of the fort. The delegates for the summit would board it by way of a motor yacht that was already prepared and would be waiting by the jetty. The pirates needed to keep the cargo vessel downwind, closer to the south station. Further out to sea on the northern side of the bay, other ships would cluster around the tanker they had captured for ransom and, meanwhile, for protection.

While Myche was trying to work out how a tanker could protect other ships that were probably armed, Shine and Brand talked about the fort. It was of rock and built on rock; yet there were ways in and out, and he and Brand had each been in touch with Isaiah and his people. A wide drain ran under the fort where Bunji and Suraj had spirited out explosives and ammunition over the past few weeks.

A group of them had come from the Wet together, Isaiah leading a small flotilla of rafts on the brackish water, and now he and his brother Sharo had transported the crates of explosive and other stuff through the maze of waterways in the Wet. One last set was left loaded on a little skiff that was supposed to be broken down and awaiting repair. Brand said Bunji had tied it to a disused jetty at the foot of the cliff where the peacekeepers had their small northern station – in plain sight. Was just a backup, Bunji had said obscurely.

Shine explained that on Friday night, he meant to target a handful of pirates and collaborators, and he would take down at least one ship if he could.

"Why not more?" Brand protested hotly. They might never have as many ships together in one place again. Ever.

Shine shook his head. The truth was that the whole fleet couldn't be attacked. No. For they would surround the tanker as closely as possible.

"Even a navy vessel doesn't fire in those circumstances – in case of ecological disaster." He paused to sketch reasons why the prospect of a tanker explosion might render a government almost helpless. "It's another version of ransom," he concluded.

"So the fish and birds and stuff are more important than us?" Myche demanded. She was seething.

"It's not that simple," he said shortly. Then he softened and held out a hand, the old Shine. "I forget sometimes how much you can't possibly know."

"And you've no idea how much we do," Myche rapped in return. But she came over awkwardly at first to where he sat, and then, all in a rush, she put her arms round him with her cheek against his hair. "If they catch us . . ."

Pressed against the soft curve of her flesh, his shoulder went rigid. "I know," he began.

". . . the fish, the birds, the seaweed . . ."

". . . and the whole sea and earth and sky won't make up for it," he broke in. "That does make it seem simple. But for now we can only plan on bringing down one ship and its rats. Get together all the others from the Trust that you can find."

Brand came across to them too and rested his arm on Shine's. "I'm in touch with most," he said. "But some of dem hard to hold back and others frighten to come forward. Now Myche is here, though – well. She . . . she's like . . ."

". . . their fortress," Shine said. "Make sure none of them gets in the line of fire. And now I get back to the boat and try what I can."

23

HELLBOAT

MYCHE

Try by boat. In her sleep, his voice mixed with Naomi's.

So it rose up in Myche again – what it was to be six years old on that waterfront with the air heavy-laden, pungent with the stink of untreated burn victims and overflowing diapers, making her eyes water and her stomach heave. She remembered the staggering man. A man tottered forward who had lost an arm and been roughly sewn up at home with no more than a little alcohol to pour over the wound, which was why he had lasted so long, and now the supply of alcohol had run out, and that was why he was pleading for rum – he said that was the reason.

Small boats choked the bay, rising and falling on the disturbed mass of water that swelled and sank again, bumping dangerously. A man screamed, drawing up a hand that had caught and smashed between colliding bows. There, blood darkened the water, while just here, a swirl of pink foam fizzed and vanished. An inflatable raft bobbed by. Dogs, cats, a rabbit were snatched away and pitched unceremoniously overboard, paddling frantically. A puppy struggling past children who wailed and stretched their hands wildly as their parents grabbed at their arms and pulled them back, adults sobbing, cursing, commanding, pleading. (That was most terrifying of all, adults helpless, every one of them.)

A bamboo raft pushed off and sank promptly but incompletely, its pieces jostled apart by colliding craft. Another, heavier raft burst apart, and the trunks let loose, ramming boats and bludgeoning those trying to swim for safety. Seamen cuffed unruly passengers out of the way in the struggle to turn crafts outward, some vessels rocking, tipping, one foundering. Faces bobbed in the water and hands reached for the side of the boat. Someone slapped one hand away, and someone else stamped on fingers that stayed clenched on the wooden side of the boat. A passenger leaned over and accepted a baby, and its mother gasped her gratitude just as the boat swirled. It knocked her face empty of expression before she sank from sight.

And the pictures flashed back between impressions, bits and pieces from the other children of the Trust. Phrases, mouths, stories, gesturing hands, questions, trudging feet, whimperings, arguments, recollections – all these jumbled back into her head between the bumping and heaving of the boats, after her mother had spirited her out of the house that was a shapeless blur in her memory, and before the men on the ship grabbed her up and hurled her overboard, before she washed up with her throat full of water and her eyes gritty with sand. That was before Five Cent's father – talking and talking, rowing and rowing. That was after Celie wandered off and came back with wild whisperings about jinns in the bush, and about people who lived on deep water and killed any strangers who floated in.

In the tossing and whispering of Before, Myche dropped off into an uneasy sleep, but the hands and the water pressed her, struggling, deep into the pad of fresh green stuff Brand had gathered for her, her nose clogging from the smell of torn grass. Something lurked just out of focus, and without seeing it, she knew it was foul and savage, bending to envelope her, its breath rank behind jagged teeth. Fear tightened her chest, paralysed her, throbbed in her throat, and forced its way out in a ragged wail.

The next night was the same – a different terror but the same smothering and rending. And the night after that, she did not sleep at all.

She dozed off in the heat of Friday afternoon and may have slept a couple hours before the silence woke her. At least, that was what she thought at first, because it seemed that the birds and frogs had hushed and even the mosquitoes quit their whining, and the stillness alarmed her. Then she knew it was not that. It was the cold certainty of Shine's state of mind that had come belatedly to her and blotted out all else.

He had been slipping out from their shelter when she said, "The sycos say they are founded on a rock."

And he had replied, "We will shatter their rock under their feet." Only, then he turned back to them and, after that, for the first time, he had not just disappeared. He had parted with them. He had walked back in from the entrance and flicked her cheek and touched Brand's head, and now that she recaptured his face in her mind, his eyes had had a blazing but faraway look, as if he were setting out for a war from which there was no return.

She sprang up screaming for Brand, except that the scream could not get out – it was trapped in her throat like in the dream. "Shine," she gasped. "We have to get to Shine."

"He's back on the ship. Days now."

"Then we have to find a boat and get to him."

Brand's eyes widened in shock. "You mad," he whispered.

She grabbed his arm, propelling him outside of the shelter. There was a small crowd there she did not take in. "You don't understand? Shine means . . . he expects . . ."

". . . to die in the attempt." That was Isaiah, suddenly before them in the bush, drenched to the skin, along with Bunji and Darati.

"Nobody wants you to do that," Brand snapped irritably. Then he waved at Isaiah apologetically and turned on Darati. "I thought you were with Didi and them. Why you leave them? So how you know the rest coming?"

"Them done reach long time." Darati's voice. "Casey down by the shore already."

Darati speaking – the wonder of it. For a moment the exhilaration of her having found words again distracted Myche from Shine's state of mind.

Brand swung back to her before she could boil over once more. "Shine knows what he's doing."

Right. He always did. She simmered down and turned back to Brand, confused.

"What it has to do with Casey? What's Casey doing by the shore?" she demanded.

Brand leaned towards her to whisper. "Something . . . I can't talk." She stared at him so unrelentingly that she forced a bit more out. "Casey setting up something real . . . dread," he said. "But if we get through, we going live safer than if we don't try."

Myche nodded, dumbly disoriented by fear for Shine, by finding herself not in charge nor inclined to take control, crippled by a sense of helplessness she had not felt since she was six. The others bore her forward in the direction of the shore as in a current, the children first, with Isaiah and Bunji trailing after them. Shant seemed to appear from nowhere. Then the bush on the side of the track parted.

"Anybody see that fool, Robber Boy?"

It was Telma's voice, but when they turned, Nat was with her grinning lopsidedly with a light in him that knocked the words out of Myche's mouth. On Nat's face even a forlorn hope brightened and warmed his eyes and curved his lips, so it was impossible not to feel lifted, buoyed by whatever it was he had glimpsed beyond anyone else's ability to detect.

"But how you came out?" Myche said eventually, staring at them through the tears that were spilling over.

"When Casey move the last set of explosive through the drain, him come back with Shant," Telma responded, matter-of-factly wiping Myche's face with the heal of her hand. "And dem get through a set of rotten door and rusty iron grille and leave a hole at the back of each of the two cell, block up with so-so rubbish. But if the guard-dem did see we cell empty, they woulda raise the alarm and find out about the drain and see the explosive tief out, and so we stay quiet-quiet in fi-we two cell. When we hear the whole bay ready for the ceremony, and the guard lock up the place tight and gone out in front to drink rum and watch firework, I roll up my sheet around a few loose brick on the bed and crawl down through the space in the cell wall and stuff it up with rubbish again. And I keep going till I meet up with Nat. Is when we get down to the space under the fort and think seh we well lost, cyan't get out, we see Shant come back for us."

"Then, Telma, you don't know me?" It was Darati, thinner and taller, but Darati, and Telma grabbed hold of her and squeezed as if she would never let go.

"We don't have no time for all the soppy stuff," Brand said.

Shant grumbled, "You know?"

"We have to reach the bay now for now," said Brand, and he hurried them east to the thin strip of shore that curved at the base of the northern cliff.

....

They arrived, nearing sunset, at a strip of sand with a tiny scattering of flat rocks beneath the cliff. Brand, of all people, had soothed Myche, insisting that Shine had everything planned. And now, whatever was coming, there was a space of a few moments for a deep breath of the salt breeze. Freedom Bay spread with barely a ripple in the cool evening, not merely peaceful but calming. Cleansing. It whistled through Myche's nostrils, and her face relaxed to a grin as a door in her nose that she had not been aware of slid open.

There was enough light, gold but softening to rose, to bring out the delicate scoop of shoreline, the slant and sway of palms and the darkening rugged wall of rock behind them marching inland, as well as the cliff on the other side of the bay. In the town and its suburbs that stretched inland and uphill, the lampposts and occasional household lights began to come on. The extra beam of security lights, triggered by dusk, flashed on in the commercial centre.

On the shore, it was dim but for a wide bright circle around the festooned marquee, which was not only sparkling white but twinkling with fine strands of ornamental lights lightly wrapped in transparent fabric for a fashionably muted effect.

"Weaste of claat!" Anger intensified Telma's accent as it always had, but that made her so reassuringly familiar that Myche flung an arm around her shoulders and squeezed tight.

The entrance to the marquee was out of sight, facing inland, but the exit was to the jetty, marked by a path of scarlet cloth that led up the shallow steps onto the wooden planks stretching to the yacht. The yacht bobbed gently, up and down, on the light swell that made no effect on the vast cruise ship waiting for it further out to sea. The sun had set, but the children and the wetlanders could see it all clearly, because moonlight flooded the night.

By now Brand had filled in Telma and Nat.

"The rest of the forest people too?" Nat asked incredulously. "I see Casey, but where the others?"

Brand signalled vaguely towards the northern horn of rock. "Behind that station somewhere. Well. They supposed to done they business and gone by now."

"Done what?" Telma demanded.

Brand just pointed back to the marquee.

"Watch," he said.

By now the canal project would have been officially opened except for the ceremonial lighting of the fuse that would blast a few trees and rocks some distance northwest from the shore – and miles away from the site where the work would begin. This small explosion that the Shoreliners had proposed bore no real connection to the physical opening of the canal; it was only a symbolic gesture of their intentions. It was merely to mark the occasion. "None of them going tramp through mud or thorn bush," Isaiah pointed out, and Casey added, "Especially when no one going be around to take pictures."

"Pictures?" Brand repeated absently but didn't pursue it. He couldn't spare attention from the group in and around the marquee.

Assorted sea captains assembled with Shoreline councillors, peace-keeper officers and visiting delegates. Together they made up a group of about twenty-five who would complete the ceremony on the way to the ship for the summit. So the canal launch would also mark the opening of discussions to set up the syndicate. The liner was just as illuminated and festooned as the marquee and no doubt as laden with food and drink. The children's eyes flicked hungrily from ship to tent and back.

Myche raised the spyglass Shine had given her and focused on the exit side of the tent to see who might come out. The sky was clouding up, but she picked out several, naming them off – Ramnarine, Blake, and others. There were the St Justes, the parents with Roget. Other faces she recognized but could not connect with names, and there were a number she had never seen before.

As they filtered out of the tent, pausing to place champagne glasses on the long white-skirted table beside the walkway to the yacht, Brand took the spyglass.

He whispered, "You notice it have nobody bowing and scraping this side of the tent."

Darati sniggered.

"Why?" Myche reached for the spyglass, and he handed it back without a word.

As the dignitaries made their way onto the jetty, a band struck up what should have been an inspiring march – only, there was no real band, just a box and microphone, because no one in Shoreline knew how to beat drums, strum strings or blow a horn or trombone. The music was trapped in this little metal cell and released inexpertly, frittering away thinly in the oncoming night.

"Nah!" Brand flung one hand forward, pointing at the figure on the yacht who was handing the dignitaries on board. Brand's face lit up as if some twist in the plan had suddenly made everything better.

Myche and Telma and the rest squinted into the failing light, but there was no missing the thick profile and shaggy head against the glow of ornamental lights swathing the launch. Shant snatched the spyglass for a few seconds before Myche reached for it again.

"Is Tweetums. One of them, anyway." Shant shrugged. "What's so great about that?"

A prolonged suck-teet from Telma summed up everyone's reaction to Tweetums. Then it was too dark to make out anything but the yacht pulling out into the night.

When it stopped, Shant asked, "What now?"

Brand replied, "They going trigger the fuse to launch the blasting of the canal."

"How?" Shant demanded. "The boat in the middle of the water."

"Electronic," Casey put in proudly.

Myche caught Brand's quick warning glance at Casey, but Casey was too proud of his work not to brag a little. "They don't know what I fix to they boat."

"Oh God no!" Shant screamed out. "Is . . ." But his voice was lost in the clap and thunder of the yacht splitting in a sheet of light and in the rain and hiss of debris into the sea. Shant plunged away, running madly along the fence, and Myche shouted that they had to go after him, because he couldn't know what he was doing.

Only, then another explosion rocked the bay, echoed by yet another, and Brand screamed at them all to stop. Shine had warned them to stay deep in the bush, or at any rate, no nearer to the town than that tiny ledge under the cliff. But now they ignored that, and Brand raced after them.

Shant was out of sight by the time they came up against the fence between the forest and Shoreline. The gate swung on its hinges, open and unguarded in the pandemonium that had broken out. A surge of bodies squeezed through and made off helter-skelter towards the bush, and Nurse Flo floundered out and crashed straight into them. Myche tried to question her, but Flo made no sense, only gasping that she couldn' go trough de ting again – nah, nah, nah. She chattered wildly, but there was no making out what else she said. She pushed them out of her way before stumbling away, into the trees.

But there were others too afraid of the bush to run far, cowering near the fence. From these stragglers, Brand and Myche learnt that buildings behind the peacekeepers' main station south of Freedom Bay had gone up in smoke, setting off a store of munitions. Then the fire took other inflammatory stuff, so that repeated explosions rocked the bay, warehouse after warehouse flashing apart. The peacekeepers posted in areas around the town were in disarray, but most ran north for the second station.

"Why them so fool?" Telma wondered. "The fort nearer, with the big guns."

"Them guns don't shoot," Bunji said. "Shant tell me them is just decoration."

"What he would know?" Telma demanded.

Bunji said nothing, but Myche came out with it. "Shoreline he come from. His father's St Juste – *was* one of the councillors on the launch."

That silenced even Telma.

"But where Isaiah?" Bunji demanded suddenly, turning from them and retracing his steps. He had very little way to go.

They came upon Isaiah not more than a few yards away, lying on the stone path shaking, his limbs thrashing.

"Why all-you bring him here when you know what going to happen?" Darati crouched beside him, then leapt back to avoid his fists, lashing about erratically. Only Bunji could get close, and he held him, talking softly all the time.

"Bunji and Isaiah and them didn't know all what would happen," Brand explained. "Nobody could know everything, in case one got caught . . . you know."

Myche nodded, her eyes fixed on Isaiah, who was still shaking but not flailing so violently.

"And he woulda come anyway," Brand added.

They got him back, further away from the perimeter of the town, and when he calmed, he retreated with them to their little lookout beneath the cliff.

"Bois said they would get around to the back of the town," Brand said, taking up his explanation again. "He made it through the forest and up over the rocks on the far side. Casey had packed . . ."

His lips moved soundlessly against a new thunder of fire. Shine's ship, the luxury liner the pirates had weaponized, had fired on the southern peacekeepers' station and hit it glancingly. Then the ship went dark; it could only have been planned – all the regular lights as well as the decorative strings vanishing at once. Under the thick cloud cover, Myche strained in vain to make it out against the tumble of black water.

Perhaps that was why the first volley of return fire from the south lookout missed entirely, but above, the cloud cover thinned and parted, so the second, crippling volley ripped into the ship. The vast liner still hung with party garlands took the hit directly. At once it discharged another volley on the southern station, but the peacekeepers returned fire, striking the hull again and opening it up even as fire ripped through their main guns and silenced them.

Myche let out a howl of dismay and plunged forward towards the narrow path that circled the cliff towards the bay, but Brand and Telma grabbed her and held her back.

"Shine will jump off and swim for it," Brand shouted in her ear over the uproar.

There was no point pretending the ship hadn't been mortally hit.

Nat extended a hand finely proportioned and strong-boned, its slight waver only a hitch in communication between brain and limb, and nothing whatever to do with uncertainty or force of mind – an open, eager hand gesturing at the liner.

"Watch," he said. The moon was easing out beyond the smoke, and the outline of the ship sharpened against the sky.

"You see?" Brand shouted.

For it might come true. One by one, dark forms barely visible against the sky leapt off, as smoke poured out of a hole low on the side of the vessel, barely above the water, and the ship listed. Myche calmed as the sailors struck off, swimming for safety, till they drew nearer to the shore. She strained her eyes for Shine, but there was no distinguishing one from the other.

Then a clap of gunfire from the waterfront. The peacekeepers who had found their way to the top of the fort levelled their weapons and began to pick off the swimmers, the vague forms making for shore jerking in the water, then going slack and sinking without trace or just floating face down.

Brand sank to his knees, his arms wrapped about himself, rocking in agony. Myche and the rest screamed around him, the wind tearing their voices away.

After a while, in a desultory fashion, as if shooting assorted swimmers indiscriminately had become boring, the peacekeepers took aim at the cargo vessel. But it was too far off.

Then they seemed to abandon the fort, making their way along the road towards the small north station, and in a while, the children could hear them on the cliff above, shooting at the swimmers again, Myche's yelling lost in the clatter of gunfire. Then a lone shot from the almost obliterated south station rocked the cargo vessel, before the damaged liner they had thought of as Shine's ship hammered the station again, leaving it flattened.

On the north cliff, above the children, the guns fell silent, as if (suddenly as they had started to fire) the peacekeepers had left off in disgust, and after a while, the children could see them wandering away and downhill, then along the waterfront and the moonlit beach beyond, till they turned inland to the town.

In the unreal hush, the children stared at each other before a babble of questions broke out.

"Like they tired shoot," Bunji whispered, still gripping Isaiah's shoulders, for the singerman had cast his body down on the ground and wrapped his arms around his head.

The peacekeepers weaving their way away from the beach were waving their hands at each other as if arguing about what to do next, or half-heartedly working out some other game.

Against the tumble of speculation, Myche's thoughts thrashed wildly for something real to grasp at.

Frozen there, she suddenly became aware that Isaiah had scrambled up and that he, Bunji, Brand and Telma had raced off, pounding along the shore beneath the nearer station, where they untied two of the longer patrol boats. They cast off, the boat with Isaiah and Brand heading towards the liner, and the one with Bunji and Telma towards the cargo vessel. Her heart in her throat, Myche strained to make out Brand and Isaiah, as they slowed to scrutinize the odd swimmer clinging to floating bits and pieces, too weary or injured to swim to shore. Bunji and Telma pressed on to collect anyone they could from the cargo ship. More and more wetlanders came forward to push out the other boats or to take turns when the first two got back in, but

Brand would not give up his place, because only he would know Shine.

"I'm staying on the shore," Myche shouted to him, when he and Isaiah offloaded the first group, "in case he gets in some other way. Hurt."

He nodded, and she set off across the sand.

By now the forest folk were making their way along, one or two in each boat, not that they could steer, but at least helping to haul on board those who climbed down from the cargo vessel or clung to debris around the liner, pleading that they were not pirates, just decent folk pressed into service. And how was Brand to refuse them? But after a while, there were fewer swimmers to pick up. Still, the baanya went on plying back and forth to the cargo vessel, bringing in those who had been stored for transhipment.

By that time, Myche had meandered among whoever had made it to land, searching the faces of the living and the dead. When she slumped onto the sand in exhaustion, still scouring the seascape with her eyes, she felt it pierce her – an unmistakable shaft through the heart – that Shine was dead. That he had gone this time for good. She had staved it off while the dark forms still plunged overboard, scrambling for boats or swimming for shore and washing up among the floating bodies the peacekeepers had taken down.

The end of the explosions and shooting had left behind an eerie stillness by the time she walked up to the edge of the sea to see what must be the last of the living stumble out. So she knew it was true that he had gone, as he had expected. Had accepted, she thought, closing her eyes.

Brand and Isaiah and the rest had come back in at last and thrown themselves down on the sand. They watched the stricken groups who wound their way among the living and dead on the beach to search for those they knew – sons or daughters the pirates had seized, or other able-bodied captors the councillors had packed off for shipping.

"There were sharks," Brand whispered, the horror of it still in his eyes. "The water was, like, churning with sharks and . . . blood, and bits of . . ."

When his voice broke off, Myche became aware of the crowd

gathering closer and closer on the shore. After the first explosions, the town had emptied. Men, women and children had fled out into the bush, but now bolder ones ventured to the waterfront even as the chaos unfolded. Regardless of what was washing up, Shoreline was still dressed up for celebration. The wharf buntings fluttered among the lights along with the pier, and the pier with its red carpet to take the celebrities out to the yacht remained intact.

Myche raised the spyglass to scan the water yet again under a clear sky. Then she froze.

Out at sea beyond the sinking liner and crippled cargo vessel, the cluster of other pirate ships was changing formation. Sleeker vessels were drawing ahead of the more awkward profile of the tanker and turning out to sea. Leaving it all behind. As if none of it had happened.

Myche sprang forward, breaking into a run, and screamed at Casey to get to the skiff. Nat darted after them but stumbled and ran instead for the sea, plunging in while Brand and the rest pelted across the sand after Myche. She glanced behind fearfully for Nat, who had dived out of sight and reappeared now, striking for the jetty. Before he reached it, something thrashed forward, and the thought of not only Shine extinguished but Nat swallowed up in the night almost felled Myche. But Brand grabbed her arm and urged her on, and when they were almost there, she saw Nat hauling himself onto the planks. Safe.

They reached the disused jetty at the base of the northern cliff almost together, and she shouted for Casey.

"And you have to do this." She was gasping, but found breath to scream, "Somebody you know dead or going to dead because of dem people."

Nat ordered the others to stand back and give Casey space.

Myche clambered into the boat. "I'll get it there. I know I can steer it, I tell you."

"No," Nat shouted at her, as she argued furiously.

Casey worked all the while, silent and intent as if alone there.

Singerman and Bunji cut in.

"Nah! You ain goin on no boat. Is to fix the steering," Isaiah said, returning a look as stubborn as her own.

Bunji added, "The two o' we need space to work."

At that she climbed out, and the two wetlanders crouched at the front of the boat, consulting each other as they tugged and tied what they had to, ignoring whatever Casey was about behind them.

By the time the three men jumped out, Myche had backed away with Nat and Brand, along the jetty to the shore. And the skiff was off with its store of explosives, on course – soon a small dim object indistinguishable against the dark water and with no human on board to steer it – directly for the tanker.

24

STRONGHOLD

FROM THE CORNER OF HER EYE Myche picked up the tightening of Brand's lips before she caught the word the wind was tearing away: "Run." He howled it as he shoved to whirl her around then slammed his hand between her shoulder blades and propelled her inland.

They were tearing in across the beach when she heard the roar from the tanker and the thump of the blast slammed her forward onto a bank of sand. When she pushed herself to her knees and faced the bay, roiling flame and smoke mounted upwards. Oil must have poured from the damaged hull for the blaze swept out on the water where wind and current sent it racing away to the other ships. By now there was barely a glimpse of the tanker itself, for it was swathed in flame from end to end before it disappeared in the cloud of smoke that towered up for two or three thousand feet against a clear night sky.

And all the while the oil slick spread rapidly on and on beyond the tanker and around its pirate convoy.

The tanker's swirling column of black smoke thickened and darkened, parting occasionally here and there to flash glimpses of the inferno. Another explosion blasted massive bars bigger than the thickest trees in High Forest, and a hatch-cover the size of the museum, hurling them up – pitch black shadows launched out beyond the smoke – to come crashing down again on the ships alongside. Then, there was still another explosion, and more hefty parts flung up and smashed down. A vast arc, like a bit of the bridge beyond Little Wet hurtled up through the smoke then slammed onto a smaller ship, but that one was on fire already, tilting, sliding down. And Myche too, even though she was lying on the sand bank felt herself keeling, sinking from sight as she had from sound into silence, and an embracing darkness.

When she came to herself on the sand, men and women from the town meandered about as if they could not make out where they were going, although the beach was perfectly clear of smoke. One or two staggered, holding their ears, and one remained crumpled almost beside her. She put a finger to her own ear, stopping the hole to pop open the airway that felt blocked and painful.

But right there on the sand the beach soon came alive with all sorts of people, some still dressed for the celebrations, some in rags as if escaped from wherever they had been penned up. There were even a few drenched survivors who had managed to swim to shore or scramble onto one of the boats people had taken out after the first explosion so they had got almost back to land before the sea caught fire. And, then, there were people from the poorer parts of town who had had little or nothing to begin with anyway and had nothing to lose by enjoying the spectacle – the pointless, as the St Justes had called them.

These people had crowded out of their dingy houses to watch the launch of the great canal project – hoping for fireworks, as they recalled excitedly, going over the evening's events. There had been this rumour of fireworks. Well, they'd got more than they could ever have dreamt up, they said. They stood there staring out at pirate ships burning and blowing up and going down; and they cheered.

Beyond them, in from the beach, the peacekeepers hustled back towards the north station, and a few paused and raised their weapons to take aim, one pointing his gun directly at Myche. But another figure, just getting to his feet beside her, dragged himself upright and lurched in between her and the peacekeepers waving urgently at them. He was tattered in contrast to their smart uniforms but his wild gesturing with an oversize hat – collapsed as it was – drew their attention. He shouted something that sounded like, "Cease and desist," but her ears were not working properly and she could not be sure.

He hurried towards them as they lost interest. Then they went on their way, drawing as little further attention to themselves as possible. When they reached the ruined station, they must have stayed there as quiet as they could for their wait took hours before the helicopters came clattering in for them.

Meanwhile Brand insisted on a last turn by boat and he went with Nat, Bunji and a couple others. They climbed in the two boats, a forlorn hope for survivors, and paddled off for they were out of fuel now and all they had were oars.

Myche watched for them more and more hopelessly as the night wore out. She waited until the black sky turned grey before backing away from the water's edge with its view of blazing ships – only to be startled by the sight of a seaman pelting over the sand towards her. For a moment hope flared that it was Shine against all odds and she flung open her arms. But this was a thicker set man who grabbed her shoulders and slammed her back against the pole of the marquee. She struggled, bringing up her knee as sharply as she could, lowering her head to butt him. But he was so much bigger that she could not get her knee high enough and her head bumped uselessly against his chest. He grunted, more in grim amusement than pain, and crushed her on the stones near to the wet edge of the shore where the waves were breaking and sliding back to the sea.

A whiff of stinking breath and she glimpsed through the beard a grin filled with rotten teeth. Pwessus clenched her throat in an iron grip, crushing her against the sand with one hand as he flicked a blade open with the other. But One Thousand Eyes erupted out of the water drenching them in a deluge of spray as he lunged at the man in the baggy pants and orange bandana, smashing him to the ground. Myche rolled away, dragging painfully at the last thread of air in her throat before she could scramble to her feet. She stared, stunned for a while, before turning her face away in horror and clutching the pole of the marquee for support.

When she became aware that the screaming had cut off, she found she was surrounded at some distance by a crowd, a hushed circle of strangers. She caught one signalling wildly at something behind her and looked back, and it was One Thousand Eyes stalking towards her unhurriedly from a still form on the ground. Her knees gave way and she crumpled onto the sand, legs sprawled at the edge of the water, but when the big cat lay down beside her a little buzz of relief or amazement broke out and died away again.

She must have been in shock to lie there for minutes more before she could prop herself up almost to a sitting position, and she stayed there watching the sea, for she expected nothing else to emerge from it alive. Shine gone, and now Brand and Nat. She felt too drained even for tears. But then, a boat bobbed in upside down, no one bothering about it because the fire and the sharks must have taken everything that was left. Then, the outline of the boat changed, the shadows moving barely distinct against the smoky grey behind. So Myche watched with disbelief as one form then another pulled upright and it was Brand and Nat, riding in towards her on the little upturned hull that had threaded its way between burning wreckage, the last desperate swimmers and no doubt a couple maddened sharks. They dumped their makeshift paddles and sprang down into the oily shallows.

"Popo," she whispered as Brand slumped exhausted at her feet.

Somewhere in the distance Isaiah's voice wafted up, something about livity and courage when time come to bring down fire pon Babylon even though it swallow up the brave. Gone up inna sweet smoke to Zion, he chanted. If it had been anyone but Isaiah this would have infuriated Myche, for whom there was nothing sweet about smoke nor cleansing about sacrifice of the good and brave. Neither had she picked up the slightest sign of a promised land anywhere near Shoreline. Unless perhaps it lay somewhere inside those who had survived and had yet to be hewn out.

Still, with Brand and Nat only a few feet away and so many of the others alive somewhere, the sea no longer seemed to lock her in, crush her down or rip all she had away. For an instant the grey pink sky and sea bent all around her like a domed shell in which she fitted and belonged. But there was nothing cushioning or cradling about that water either. This sea, wild and unstoried, could shape-shift in an instant to a fierce guardian that ate iron, swept away the soucouyant and quenched the fire breath of dragons, and, suddenly, its refusal to be pinned down elated her. Which meant she had changed too, from a child in terror of the waves. She could sit with her feet in the water and wait to see if anything else might come out. The idea that hope could stir in the midst of flame and wreckage all around seemed almost more mind-bending than the rest. It made her wonder what she had become. But she wondered that with a fierce yet calm curiosity.

It would be a long time before she realized she had become unbound.

········

One Thousand Eyes stirred first. He licked a paw, then stretched – a long, sinuous ripple of gold – before getting to his feet. He began to walk away, paused and stalked back. He butted Myche's shoulder briefly and quite gently with his huge head. Then he was gone.

She sat on until the sun was high in the sky.

Afterwards, those who had stayed there with her referred to that new day as the douen dawn.

GLIMMER

KISKIDEE

I AM HER NAMESAKE. NOT MYCHELLE, no. They named me Myche, just Myche, after my grandmother. I like it best when they call me MycheToo. But she only, always, called me Kiskidee.

I hung on her every word, but her words were never about that night.

I was still a child when I began to note down the answer to every question I asked about it and every tiny fact I could trace through the little that was written down. About the explosions, our history teachers told us that some other country might have had salvage tugs or helicopters to help what injured vessel they could. But this was Shoreline, in the dark time. Many people, like my grandmother, felt the blast like a punch that threw them down, and some could hear little or nothing for a while afterwards. It was my great-uncle, the commissioner – the one we all called Brand – who told me most of what I know, and he said it was days before Myche heard anything properly after that. I know her hearing was never quite the same again.

Brand told me too that they lived for a while in Shoreline with a boy called Shant, whose parents and brother had died and left him and his sisters (one a baby) with a house big enough to hold all the children from the Trust. But of course, Brand said, they eventually split up and found places for themselves. Decades later Myche and a couple others moved on from Shoreline. Again.

The town rebuilt what it had to. More important, it helped rebuild the country. From every corner people flocked forward to the task and some aid came later from other countries, especially from Homeland when one commander-in-chief had given way to the next. Whether or not it was true that the previous one lived on for a while in some institution I wouldn't know. News of other governments remains as contradictory as I suppose it ever was. Nowhere in any document did I find it spelled out how a such a vital little country as ours plunged from its bearings and slid into a pothole in time.

My grandparents, Myche and Nat, returned to the Trust when their daughter – my mother – was grown and married. Her godmother, the Reverend Dorothy Horton, conducted the ceremony, and only a couple years ago, Rev's sister, Dr Thelma Horton, flew in and stayed a while. She regaled us with news of Robber Boy. According to his own exaggerated accounts on stage, he was still running, stumbling along after the peacekeepers and barely catching up when the helicopters arrived. Whatever outlandish tale he had told them as he flourished the remains of his hat, they allowed him to board with them and took him along back to Homeland. And now performances abroad had made him a millionaire.

"Imagine," she said. "An eejit like that."

"Any word of Five Cent?" Nat asked.

Thelma raised her shoulders helplessly. "Don't know who to look for. We never caught his name." Then she smiled. "You've seen our own gourmet chef on the food channel though."

And the others chorused, "Quenk char-broil!"

Back in the Trust, my grandparents added an apartment when they finished rebuilding the museum. They had been back and forth to it over the decades – at first with clippers and machete, then with a little cement at a time, then with planks, nails and the rest - fixing small areas at a time. Then there they stayed for the rest of their lives while Myche wrote and Nat, well, he did not precisely farm the place – just kept it safe and comfortable for the wild things that came and went. In between, he fished and reaped what they needed. He became a sort of guardian.

When Nat died, the rest of us, and Rev Dorothy, went to the Trust so as to take the walk up to the cliff with his ashes, for the Return.

Afterwards, Brand stayed on with Myche. While I was there, he filled some gaps in what I knew about the aftermath of the explosions, and the notes I made on this added to the rest of my research.

An e-book I found in the Shine Digital Library said that the force of the blast blew out windows in buildings nearest to the bay and shattered glass some distance into town. But Uncle Brand said it also shocked and weakened vessels in advance of the fire that blazed on the water and eventually engulfed them. The tanker and its fleet burnt on for weeks. Homeland news reports, which came to Shoreline later when communication lines were restored, spoke of *the enormity of the sabotage.*

I found little about permanent damage onshore. The books my grandmother wrote and won so many awards for were not about that, and I had to enquire from really old people who had been there. A few Shoreliners ended up with minor injuries: cuts from glass, or bruises from being thrown against walls. Just one death onshore, they said: a man named Francisco Marquez lost balance and tumbled off the roof of the St Justes' house where he had been sitting to watch the opening of the canal. He had stayed right there after the launch blew up, riveted by the drama, until the tanker went up and the force threw him off. (Or perhaps he had a heart attack; they say he hadn't been well.)

It was weeks before most people grasped what the aftermath might be, and it outstripped anything Myche or the others could have imagined. Or wanted.

First, a few signs. Washed-up broken ships and boats. Little left of the pirates, for the sharks had seen to that. Remains of the sharks themselves and other flotsam from the water, and more and more of that would come in as the days and weeks passed. The wild things from the sea – the smallest of them, oil-clogged. Then those that fed on them: fish gasping, gulls limping, stumbling around, a couple mammals, not glued with oil themselves but poisoned by whatever they had eaten. An older woman my grandmother loved – Naomi was her name, I think – said day by day and wave by wave, the sea gave up its dead.

I didn't understand. When I pestered my grandmother, she told me the sea vomited dead things, and pieces of dead things, and I stopped asking. Still I wished I could have talked more with Naomi before she died. They named the hospital she headed the Naomi Ali Shoreline Hospital and set up an off-campus research wing there when the university reopened.

But Brand and Nat used to say that what it all meant fluttered in bit by bit and sort of gathered there in Myche's head – the months and years it would take to undo what she had done. Not undo: nothing could undo it. Months and years to bring the sea and the shore back anywhere near to what it had been before.

It was not just the lingering mess of oil and metal. The coast road and the long sandbar between the swamp and the beach lay open to wind and water. Rocks were gnawed away and soil sucked out so groves of palm trees lay flattened. Quite a way up north on that eastern side, the ruin spread through the swamp mangroves and unlocked the way for flood and storm surge. And then the pelicans, the egrets and ibis. People fell ill from eating toxic oysters. A whale shark floundering by with oil-clogged gills beached and stank.

But at the time – for they traced it to that very night – it began swirling in Myche's thoughts. Once she was sure she had lost Shine, that emptiness filled back up with rage and it had been easy to send the hellboat off. But she said afterwards that he wouldn't have agreed to being saved at such a cost, and he wasn't saved anyway. And that was why she refused to have Freedom Bay renamed after her. "For what did I ever *do*?" she said.

Yet, there were those she saved. My uncle liked to tick them off on his fingers – the pirates' once and future cargo, he said; Isaiah and his brethren whose last refuge in the Wet was to have been blown open for the canal; Didi, Casey and the rest who no longer needed to cower in the shadows of forest and caves. All the pointless of Shoreline. And the children from the Trust – their own small group would never have to retreat before the recruiters again, shaving, and binding their bodies. "And you," Brand told me, stroking my face with his quick, restless fingers, "you would never have been born."

Brand said it was some weeks before Myche could talk about that night at all, and she seemed calmer walking with him along the beach that the Shoreliners had cleaned up as much as they could. Only, then, her eyes flicked to a small silver fish with incredibly beautiful blue and indigo markings flipping hopelessly around her feet, and when she reached down to throw it back in, it shuddered and lay still on the sand.

"What would I have been returning it to anyway?" she whispered. And then, "What have I done?"

. . . .

So her story came to me through everyone except herself. I never heard her speak of it, for she was too full of the other tales whose strands she gripped relentlessly. Her story filtered through a maze of other people's recollections in the same way that her fierce watchfulness gathered the children of the Trust into her mind, piecing their pasts together and refusing to let slip the futures that scattered before them down the trackless years. Even I who came so long afterwards was a possibility not to be overlooked, any more than one among the living who travelled with her, or the dead she grudgingly gave back, or the rest of the unborn she had brought so far unknowingly.

I had no inkling of this when I was six years old, visiting the Trust to follow Nat around all day, pelting him with questions. But when night fell, I would sit on the broad step of the museum he had repaired, fitting my hand into that imprint in the concrete of a massive paw. And I would lay my head on Myche's lap, my eyes fixed on her face, her fingers moving through my hair while she unfolded some other tale, as the stars watched down.